The
Empress

Also by Meg Clothier

The Girl King

The
Empress

MEG CLOTHIER

CENTURY

Published by Century 2013

2 4 6 8 10 9 7 5 3 1

Copyright © Meg Clothier, 2013

Meg Clothier has asserted her right under the Copyright, Designs
and Patents Act 1988 to be identified as the author of this work.

This book is a work of fiction. Names and characters are the product of the author's
imagination and any resemblance to actual persons, living or dead, is entirely coincidental.

First published in Great Britain in 2013 by
Century
Random House, 20 Vauxhall Bridge Road,
London SW1V 2SA

www.randomhouse.co.uk

Addresses for companies within The Random House Group Limited can be found at:
www.randomhouse.co.uk/offices.htm

The Random House Group Limited Reg. No. 954009

A CIP catalogue record for this book
is available from the British Library

ISBN 9781846058219

The Random House Group Limited supports the Forest Stewardship Council® (FSC®),
the leading international forest-certification organisation. Our books carrying the FSC
label are printed on FSC®-certified paper. FSC is the only forest-certification
scheme supported by the leading environmental organisations, including Greenpeace. Our
paper procurement policy can be found at http://www.randomhouse.co.uk/environment

MIX
Paper from
responsible sources
FSC® C016897

Typeset by Palimpsest Book Production Ltd, Falkirk, Stirlingshire

Printed and bound in Great Britain by Clays, Ltd, St Ives plc

For my parents

FAMILY TREE

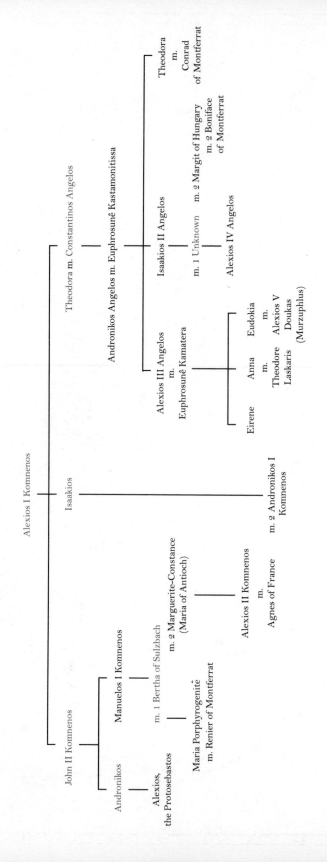

This is a *highly* selective diagram showing the Komnenos and Angelos families only insofar as they relate to *The Empress*. Many siblings and spouses are missing, especially from older generations. The people in fainter type do not appear in the book.

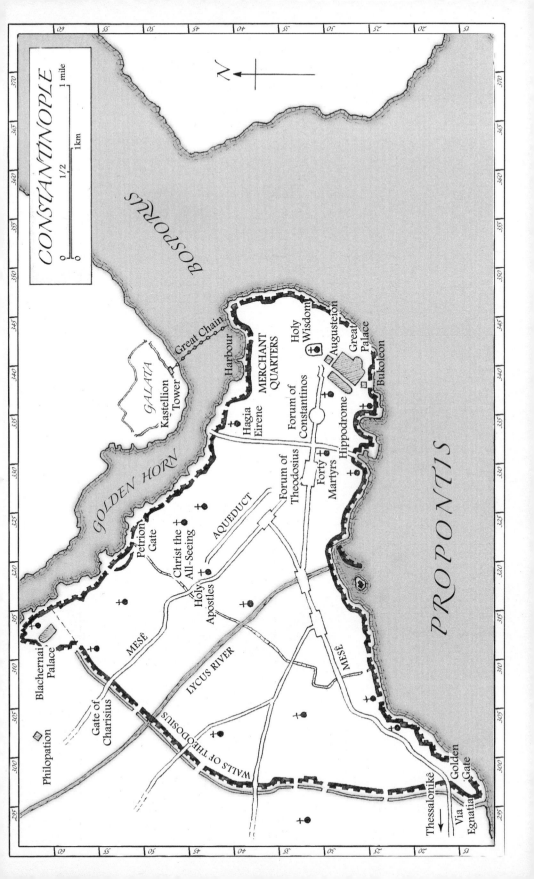

CONSTANTINOPLE

1 mile

1 km

BOSPORUS

GALATA

Great Chain

Kastellion Tower

Harbour

GOLDEN HORN

MERCHANT QUARTERS

Holy Wisdom

Augusteion

Great Palace

Bukoléon

Hagia Eirene

Forum of Constantinos

Hippodrome

Petrion Gate

Christ the All-Seeing

Forum of Theodosius

AQUEDUCT

Forty Martyrs

Holy Apostles

PROPONTIS

MESÊ

Blachernai Palace

Gate of Charisius

LYCUS RIVER

MESÊ

Philopation

WALLS OF THEODOSIUS

Thessalonikē

Golden Gate

Via Egnatia

The First Emperor

It is 6,650 years – give or take a few – since God made the world.

Two men, both squarely in their prime, both more than a little drunk, are sitting side by side in the Blachernai Palace in the Queen of Cities.

It is dead night.

Outside, marble columns glimmer, ghosts in the moonlight, but inside, thousands of candles and the best Thracian wine have turned everything dazzling bright. Golden mosaics dance about the walls, flame-haired girls whirl and bob, swords flash and disappear down throats and big cats roar as they leap through rings of fire.

The host of this great feast is Manuelos Komnenos, the most powerful man in the world. His guest's name is Louis, and he rules a little kingdom far away in the west.

Louis wants grain and guides, so that he and his soldiers of the Cross, camped in their thousands beyond the City's walls, can journey east and south to wage holy war. Manuelos wants them gone. They are wild, uncivilised; they are trouble. But they are fellow Christians – of a sort – and must be treated with care.

Servants refill their glasses.

'I thought you'd be a lumbering barbarian,' says Manuelos.

'And I thought you'd be a snake-tongued snob,' replies Louis.

The men laugh and talk of their troubles and their triumphs, of the men they have fought, the women they have loved. They talk of friendship and the future. Manuelos leans forward and grasps Louis's arm.

'When I am blessed with a son, I want no wife for him but a daughter of yours. What do you say?'

'I say you do me great honour,' answers Louis.

'Swear to it?'

'I swear.'

Hands clasp. And together they toast their unborn children's happiness.

The night ends, and the next day Louis straps on his sword and travels onwards to fulfil the promise he made to God.

Many years pass.

Manuelos's wife bears him two daughters – one lives, one dies. He marries again. Again he waits. And when he has all but given up hope, when he is all but an old man, a son is born, a son who survives the fevers of childhood and reaches his fifteenth year.

That is when the emperor in Constantinople sends word to the king of France and asks for a daughter.

The spring of 1179

'I'm going to be queen of the world,' Agnes sang to herself.

She stopped.

'No, not a stupid queen. Much, much better than a queen. Empress. Empress of the whole wide world.'

She skipped a little further.

'Empress of the City. *Basilissa tou . . . tou . . .*' The Greek her father had always insisted she learn, without ever quite explaining why, stuck in her mouth. She stamped her foot to make the words come.

'*. . . tou Poleôs.*'

She started to chant the phrase, the s's sizzling on her tongue. She swung her arms out, whirling in circles until the gardens around her blurred, green grass, grey stones, green, grey, green-grey. Then a flash of red and gold. She fell over.

Henri and Little Louis were standing there. Laughing. She stood up, brushed the dust from her dress and stuck her nose into the air.

'You won't be laughing when you hear what I've got to tell you.'

'You always say that and then it's always nothing,' said Louis.

'No, I don't.'

'Yes, you do.'

'No, I . . . Shut up. Don't argue. Show a little respect to your elders.'

It was a sore point. The three of them were almost exactly the same age – thirteen, twelve and eleven, on the brink of

5

adulthood – but she was the king's youngest daughter and they were his oldest grandsons, and that made her their aunt.

'That's what I say to respect,' said Louis with a vigorous hand gesture that made Henri snigger.

Agnes had no idea what it meant, but she guessed he'd learnt it in the stables, so she clapped her hands to her mouth and shrieked.

'Don't be disgusting, Louis! I'll tell my father, I shall, I swear I shall.'

She turned and started to run back to the palace – although not quite as fast as she could. She didn't want to look unladylike, not today of all days, and she certainly didn't want to see her father again. He was grumpy and had hair coming out of his ears. But he was the king, and the boys would be whipped raw if he found out they'd been teasing her, his treasure.

'Don't, Ness, please don't. Come on. Please.' They each had hold of one of her hands and were trying to drag her away from the garden gate. She tilted her head back so she could look down on them, and decided they were pleasingly penitent.

'Please who?'

'Please, Agnes. Please, Aunt.'

She smiled a little cat smile, gracious in victory.

'All right. I won't. Just this once. Little boys,' she tutted, knowing it would enrage them – and knowing they were powerless to do anything about it. 'Now, aren't you going to ask me what I've got to tell you?'

An emphatic *no* was forming on Louis's lips, but Henri thumped him. 'Go on then, tell us.'

'I'm going to be empress in the east,' she said, the words coming out less sedately than she might have liked.

'What? No you're not,' gasped Louis.

'Yes I am.'

'No you're not.'

'I am, I am. Father just told me. It's all arranged.'

Henri gawped. 'You're going to marry the Greek emperor? The actual real one?'

'No, ignoramus. He's already married. And he's older than Father. No, I'm going to marry his son. His only son, Alexios,' she said, caressing every syllable of his name as lovingly as one of her pet doves. 'Young, handsome, brave Alexios. It'll be the most perfect wedding the world has ever seen. And then, when his father dies, which won't be that long, Alexios will be emperor and I shall rule by his side.'

An image, as lovely as it was fuzzy, wafted through her mind. A pair of silver thrones surrounded by blue sea and white marble. Thousands upon thousands of people gazing up at her, all whispering the same thing. *What a beautiful couple.* She turned to her husband. Chestnut curls lapped about his golden crown. He took her hand, his blue eyes – no, she corrected herself, his *brown* eyes melting . . .

'Pah,' said Louis. 'The Greeks. They're tricksters and sh-sh—' the word fought its way out '—charlatans.'

'That's right,' Henri weighed in. 'They know everything about the price of gold and nothing about the weight of iron. They couldn't even fight the Saracens without our help. They're—'

'Shut up, Hee-haw,' she said, using his mother's pet name for him that made him mad as a wasp. 'Just because you're jealous—'

'Jealous? I'm not jealous.'

'Not jealous that I'm going to be grander and richer than your father – than *my* father – and every prince and comte and duc put together? Not jealous that I'm going to live in the greatest city there'll ever be? I'll live in a golden palace and eat off golden plates . . .' she wasn't sure about that, but as she spoke, it became true in her mind, 'and I'll have hundreds of servants just to sing me songs while I bathe and a pet nightingale and a pet leopard and . . .'

But before she could decide what else she needed in her menagerie, she clamped her mouth shut. It was too late.

7

'Pride is a grievous sin, sister.'

Her brother, Philip, had crept up behind them. He had florid cheeks and a thrusting chest and was duller than he had any right to be. But whatever she thought of him, he was their father's long-awaited son, the first child of his third marriage, the heir, the golden youth, and she knew better than to argue with him.

'Forgive me, brother,' she said, bobbing her head. 'I am so honoured to be able to serve our father with this match that I forgot myself.'

The two boys struggled to compose their faces. Philip became more pompous and preachy by the day – that was something they could all agree on.

'It *is* a very great honour, Agnes. A daughter's first duty to her family is to marry early and to marry well.'

'Yes, brother. We are so grateful that you are here to remind us that duty must always be at the forefront of our minds.'

She rolled her eyes at Louis and Henri from under her downcast lashes, making the laughter explode from them. Her brother's gloved hand lashed out and cuffed them both over the head.

'Don't snigger like kitchen boys. What are you doing here anyway? You're too old to be playing with girls. Where's your tutor? Go on, away with you.'

They darted off over the stones, leaving brother and sister alone. Philip began to pace before her, slow and measured, rubbing his face – probably to remind her that he now had to shave every morning. A lecture was clearly on its way.

'You should not encourage those boys to follow you about.'

'I don't encourage them, brother. Is it my fault they love to plague me?'

'You know what I mean.'

'I'm sure I don't.'

But she did, of course she did. Boys always wanted to be

near her, however cruel she was to them. She'd always known that. Men were the same – except she was never cruel to them.

Philip grew sterner, his voice more pulpit-like. 'Your face, sister, is not a face I would wish a sister of mine to have.'

'This is the face God gave me, brother. Surely you do not think his plan was at fault?'

'I would not have you proud.'

'So you said, brother.'

She had not lifted her eyes from the ground all the while he spoke, and it was clearly starting to annoy him. He took her by the shoulders.

'I wish they had not asked for you. I wish my father had said no . . .'

She wondered, briefly, why they had asked for her. Had they heard how beautiful she was? She was beautiful. Everyone said so. One of her uncles said she was probably nearly as beautiful as Helen of Troy. Lucky woman. Combing her hair while the swords of thousands of men crashed outside the city walls. It would have been better, of course, if Alexios had sailed west and stolen her away. But, she thought, you can't have everything.

'Sister, sister, are you listening to me?'

'Of course, brother.'

'The Greeks' city is a dangerous place. It is bloated with sin. Rank with luxury. Their ways are not our ways. Constantinople is not Paris. It is full of half-men and fallen women.'

'Have we no such women here?'

'No, none.' He looked sharply at her. 'None. Not one.'

He was shaking his head and so she shook hers as well. But all she could think was that she liked the sound of the City very, very much indeed. What was Blois, what was Champagne, what was Paris itself? Nothing. What was Constantinople? Everything.

* * *

Theo pulled up his breeches, relieved that it was over. Only then did he brave a proper look at the woman on the bed. She was smiling up at him – rather affectionately, he thought. That didn't seem quite right. She ought to look ravaged or ravished, sated or satisfied – at least a little bit tired. But she was already getting up, smoothing down her dress and pulling up her leg coverings. There was nothing else she needed to do. Even her hair was still more or less tidy.

What was she saying? He understood Latin all right. He'd spent enough time with his father in the frontier lands to the west to mean he'd grown up speaking it as well as the Greek of the empire, but she spoke a funny quacking dialect and had rolled her eyes when he'd tried a few basic words of proper Latin on her.

She ran a finger down his cheek and then – embarrassingly – patted his behind. *Run along.* She was telling him it was time to go. She twitched her fingers. *Where's my money?* He paid up and left.

At least the rate of exchange for his City coins was good here. He could never have bought a youngish woman with all her teeth for that little money within sight of the Hagia Sophia, the Church of Holy Wisdom. That was one advantage of Paris, which otherwise was the filthiest, most godforsaken, scrappiest little outpost that had ever misguidedly considered itself civilised.

He hadn't expected much, but as the imperial embassy journeyed through the outlying woods, he was surprised they could be so close to a city and yet find themselves in land so wild. Slowly, little houses climbed out of the mud, but it was hard to work out where pigpens ended and human living began. He thought of the neat fields that ringed the City and the lines of carefully pruned fruit trees that grew in the shadow of the great water road from the north.

The Frankish king's halls crouched on a stub of island in the middle of the river that mouldered through the town. That made good enough sense from a defensive point of view, but the river was so narrow that imperial sappers would be able to bridge it in a day – if the emperor ordered it. But why would he ever do that? He lived in splendour amidst the light and glory of the City. Who in their right mind would waste time trying to conquer Paris?

Theo sniffed as he crossed the river, a sluggish ditch compared to the Bosporus, so vast and alive, and cursed the day his father had sent him on this expedition. Not that he had anyone but himself to blame. Himself and drink.

Mikhail, his father's aide who was meant to keep an eye on him at camp, had got him tipsy – well, more like blind drunk, if he was honest – and promised to pay for his first legover. By the time they'd reeled to the fringes of the camp where the cheapest women congregated, probably half the garrison was on their tail, fighting over who would get to watch the great general's only boy *pop*.

His memory of the night was hazy, but he definitely remembered a huge pair of bosoms, an extraordinary sweet, meaty smell and cheering and clapping coming from all sides – and from inside his head. He had buried his face in the woman in front of him and started to fight open his clothes – but then he'd choked and gasped as somebody grabbed his collar and hauled him off. His father had got wind of it.

Alexios Branas was much too experienced a general to say anything to any of the soldiers involved. Their fear, lingering for days afterwards, would have been plenty bad enough. But with his son, it was a different matter.

Badly done, Theo.

Yes, sir.

Can't have the men laughing because they've seen my son trying – and, let's be frank, failing – to stuff his prick into the camp's favourite whore, can we?

Theo had opened his mouth.

Silence!

11

Yes, sir.

Partly my fault, though, isn't it?

Sir?

His father said he'd been neglecting him, said it was time to make amends, which sounded ominous.

You're my son, not a camp rat. Let's have a look at you. When did I last see you? No, don't answer. That was a rhetorical question. You don't know what that is? That's the problem. You, boy, need a little polish.

Theo had tried to tell him he was fine as he was, that he was just going to be a soldier, but his father had cut him short.

Just a soldier? There's no such thing. Generals have to be politicians. Politicians have to be generals.

He'd started to say that politicians were shit sacks, but his father held up his hand for silence.

You're arguing with me, and that won't do. When a boy tries to argue with his father, it's time for him to go elsewhere fast.

His father wrote some letters, sounded out some friends, and a few months later Theo found himself the youngest, lowliest member of the embassy that was bound west to collect the Frankish girl for Manuelos's boy.

What's wrong with a girl from the City, Father?

The west's power is waxing, son. A little honour, like this marriage, will go a long way.

Theo quickened his pace through the streets – he was late for the big introduction, the unveiling, the presentation, whatever they were calling it – and decided his father would be a lot less worried about the west if he'd actually seen Paris.

Agnes clutched her father's arm as the Greek delegation sauntered into the back of the hall. She knew he liked to feel strong when she was around, but for once she was glad to cling on to something. She was nervous – not the veneer of sweet timidity she had decided would be appropriate, but actually agonisingly nervous, like her stomach was a pond of jumping frogs.

She'd been fine getting ready, keeping her maids in order, considering her hair, selecting her clothes. She'd been fine, too, when her mother appeared in the looking glass behind her, tweaked a curl that did not need tweaking, told her not to be scared and dropped a white veil over her face. And she'd still been fine as she waited with her father in the little antechamber at the side of the hall. She'd even remembered to order her chair to be moved a little further from the fire. She wanted to make a good impression – better, she wanted them to be awestruck – and that wouldn't happen if she had a bright red face.

A footman stuck his head round the door and bowed to the king.

'They're all here, majesty.'

Her father nodded, and together they walked into the hall. That was when she saw them. And that was when the frogs came alive in her stomach.

If this is how the men dress, what, pray, do their women look like?

Her relatives dressed in leathers that smelt of dogs and horses. Their spurs clanked and their breeches creaked and they never, ever seemed to wash unless they were covered head to toe in mud. But the robes of the men in front of her swooped to the floor like waterfalls. What wasn't trimmed with fur was patterned with silk, what wasn't stitched in gold was spun in silver. It wasn't just the stuff their clothes were made from, it was the way they wore them, the way they stood, easy as angels on a cloud, and watched her approach.

Her father stood behind her, his hands on her shoulders, protective and possessive.

'My lords,' he began, speaking the high Latin of God and government, 'I introduce my beloved daughter, Agnes.'

He reached forward and lifted her veil. She chanced one

look, soft, fleeting, a hind darting into hiding, before her father replaced it. Through the gauze she saw a few of the men exchange the briefest of glances.

She'd hoped for rather more than that.

'Murzuphlus, Murzuphlus – did you see her?'

Theo had arrived too late and was now chasing after the delegation, who were doubtless on their way to some draughty hall to eat another revolting meal of boiled tripe and overripe wine. The young man he was shouting at turned round and waited for him in the corridor.

'Stop calling me that.'

Murzuphlus gripped him by the scruff of the neck, but Theo knew he wasn't really angry and wriggled away.

'It's a great name – makes you stand out. Go on, tell me, did you see her?'

Murzuphlus raised one of the preposterously bushy eyebrows that had earned him his nickname and wagged a finger at Theo.

'And where were you?'

'Oh, you know, seeing the sights. Come on. You got a peek, right? So go on, tell me, warts and all. Does she have warts? Or was she all dew-on-roses?'

In truth, he didn't really care, but he liked making Murzuphlus laugh. Also, he was probably still a little bit tipsy.

'Theodore Branas, is that a speech fitting to an envoy of the emperor? You insult our charming hosts.'

'Not one in a hundred of them can speak a civilised language. They'll think I'm conversing with you on matters of divinity.'

He put his hands together, furrowed his brows earnestly and spoke not the street tongue real people used, but his very best old Greek.

'Tell me, sirrah, the question is to me most vexatious. Doth she ripen?'

And he made two cupping gestures with his hands in front of his chest – unmistakable in any language. Unfortunately, his audience had expanded to include a party of Frankish boys come to bid them to supper, and Theo was neither quick nor subtle enough not to look extremely caught.

The boys squared up to him. Theo was glad he had Murzuphlus – a few years older than him and well built – by his side. None of the Franks looked older than eighteen, but he didn't want to take them on by himself. Four to two would be fine. But then he turned and saw that it was actually four to one. Murzuphlus was backing away, grinning and mouthing something.

You're on your own, mate.

Theo stood his ground – not that he had much choice. He was surrounded, his back against a stone wall. His father would have a thing or two to say to him about being caught outnumbered in a narrow, unlit corridor.

'What were you saying?' demanded one of the Franks.

'Me no understand,' Theo replied.

'Yes he bloody does. I've seen him talk well enough to haggle with whores,' said another.

'A joker. Come on. What were you saying?'

There was no need to confess that he'd been insulting their princess.

'My lords – my friends, I should say – my companion and I were discussing the differing and contrasting architectural merits of the spire—' he pointed his hands '—and the dome,' he said, repeating his lascivious gesture as learnedly as he could. 'Do you perhaps have any views?'

They hesitated. They couldn't possibly believe him, but they'd lost the momentum needed to pick a fight in their king's halls. Theo might have been able to turn his back and walk away, but he couldn't resist a final sally.

'For myself, I favour the more generous proportions of the dome . . .'

They charged.

* * *

Agnes had worked out long ago that a plea to feed the doves – *they are the holiest of birds, Mama* – was the only way to make sure she had time to think things through. Her maids only ever accompanied her as far as the herb garden, scared of the scratching claws, the sudden wings and the dark, sticky smell.

She stood scattering small handfuls of grain about her feet while the sky darkened overhead. Soon she would have to go to bed. She would say her prayers, lie still while they tucked her blankets around her, watch them blow out her candle. Then she would curl up and listen to the sounds of the feasting below. A feast in her honour, and she couldn't go.

The birds took flight with a great whoosh.

A boy – a Greek boy – had tumbled over the hedge and was staring about him. He caught sight of her and grinned, then threw himself into the seed bin and closed the lid over his head.

'What are you doing? Get out right now.'

She wrenched the lid open and a cheerful face appeared.

'Greetings, fair one. My enemies are close behind me. I beg you, keep me hidden. A kiss shall be your reward.' He winked, and pulled the lid back down.

She was about to tell him exactly what his reward would be when a hullabaloo of running and shouts swept towards her and a gang of court boys careered into the enclosure, puffing, panting, overexcited, with Little Louis and Henri cantering in their wake.

'Where is he?'

'Which way'd he go?'

'Which way did who go?' she asked.

'Some Greek who needs to be taught a lesson.'

'A lesson in what?'

'Manners.'

Her birds cawed down crossly from their perches in the dovecote. Agnes smiled and pointed.

'In there.'

But before they could move, the lid burst open and the boy was out and running. He dodged behind her and grabbed her shoulders, using her as a shield against the others.

'Get off me, all of you,' she shrieked.

The court boys, better used to her temper, retreated. The Greek boy edged backwards, dragging her with him.

'Definitely no kiss for you, traitor,' he hissed in her ear.

He pinched her cheek, quite hard, scrabbled up the wall of the dovecote and disappeared. Agnes rubbed at her face in disgust. *Boys.* Greek, French, they were all the same. *Idiots.* She stalked back to the palace counting the days until she'd be on her way.

Alexios, she was sure, would be different.

The summer of 1179

It was the third day at sea, and Agnes was sick — very, very sick.

She wanted to go up on deck and at least be sick in the bright air, but then everyone would see her, and she would rather feel like this every day for the rest of her life than have a single one of the Greeks see how hideous she was. She hadn't looked in a glass, but she could feel her hair clinging lank to her temples and taste the stench in her mouth.

The boat lurched once more and her insides followed. But there was nothing left to come — certainly not food, not even the watery green fluid that had appeared when everything else had gone. She retched hopelessly, again and again, until her throat burned.

Finally, in the middle of offering up passionate promises to God, her stomach so cramped and shrunken that she could only lie curled up in a ball, she tumbled into a deep sleep. The thwack of the boat falling off the back of the storm waves, the shouts of the crewmen, the thump of feet overhead might have found their way into her dreams, but they did not disturb her.

When she woke, either a few minutes or many hours later, the yawing no longer tore her body to pieces. Instead it cocooned her, caressed her, as if she too were a little boat bobbing on the waves.

She opened her eyes cautiously. A gouging pain tore at her belly and she tensed, waiting to be sick again. Then she realised that it was monstrous, overwhelming hunger.

18

Somebody had strung a slab of netting across her bunk to stop her being bucked on to the floor while she slept, but her hands were too cold and stupid to unpick the knots that kept it in place. She worried at them, cursing under her breath, then gave up and wormed through the minuscule gap at the head end. Groping about, she found a dress to pull over her – she sniffed – rather rank undergarments, and looked about for her cloak. It was draped over her maid, a bundle of misery lying at her feet. She whisked it off her and wrapped it round her own shoulders. The body did not move, but at the creak of the door it stirred and groaned up at her.

'Wait, my lady, I must attend you . . .'

'Don't be ridiculous, Blanche,' said Agnes. 'You can't even stand up.'

She shut the door behind her. It was dim below decks, but her nose detected the smell of bread baking and fat rendering. Her tongue tingled. Bracing herself against jutting bits of wood, clinging to stray bits of rope, she stumbled down a passageway until she saw a shape, burlier than any blacksmith, huddled over a spitting pot in a little cubbyhole that must serve as the ship's kitchen.

The man grunted when she asked for food, grunted again when he handed her a sloppy bowl of stew and dumplings, and grunted a third time when she asked how to get out of this miserable underworld and up into the light of day.

'Do you not speak a civilised tongue?' she snapped.

He shook his head, grinned and leered all at once and opened his mouth to reveal – nothing. Where his tongue should have been, there was only a darkening stump and a graveyard of teeth.

'Oh,' she said, backing away. 'Well at least you could point. You've got hands, haven't you?'

He grinned again and jabbed towards a ladder with his ladle. Now that she looked, she could see half a dozen stripes of light where the planks met overhead. It was hard negotiating each rung with the food in one hand and her skirts tussling with her feet, harder still to push the hatch up with her head – but it was worth it. It opened like a window on to heaven, a blessed blast of pure light and strong-scented sea air.

She placed her bowl on deck so she could climb out, but it immediately slid away towards the side of the boat, crashed into the side and tipped over. A wave broke over the bow and washed what was left into the gunnels and overboard.

She gave a howl of frustration, then the boat seemed to trip and lose its footing and she might have followed her breakfast into the Middle Sea had two hands not clamped hold of the hem of her cloak.

'Let me go!'

The hands, obligingly, removed themselves, but immediately the boat butted a wave and she had to save herself by grabbing the nearest thing, which turned out to be a heavy sea coat. She looked up and saw the traces of two black eyes and an unmistakably broken nose in the middle of a familiar face. It was the boy from the dovecote.

'They got you, then?'

'They got me,' he nodded.

A shout came from the raised deck at the back of the boat where four crewmen were braced against the steering oars. Another man, the captain, was stomping towards them, gesticulating and bawling in what sounded like Greek, but ragged and rotten.

'Get that *something something* princess off my *something something* deck or I'll *something* her *something* neck.'

The boy's eyes widened and he looked at her more closely.

'So you're our precious cargo.'

He might have been about to say more, but the captain was now leaning over them, wanting to know why the boy wasn't doing what he was *something something* well told.

'Instantly, good sir,' said the boy, unruffled. 'The noble captain, gracious lady, although rightly delighted to see you up and about, begs leave to warn you—'

'Don't think I can't understand what you all say, because I can,' she said – admittedly in Latin. She wasn't ready to risk her dignity speaking Greek, not yet.

She realised she was still clinging on to the boy's coat and lunged for one of the banks of ropes holding up the mast. He followed her.

'I hope you can't understand. Not the way he talks. Come on – I'd better get you down below.'

'I shan't go.'

'You must. He's not joking. It really is dangerous up here,' and as if to underline what he was saying, the wind whipped his hat from his head and sent it spinning into the froth and spume behind them. His hair was a deep, rich red, almost luminescent against the grey sea and sky.

'I can see that for myself,' she told him, 'but I'm not setting foot in that vile pit until it's been scrubbed clean.'

'Then you'll have to do it yourself. Everybody's sick in their bunks or sailing the boat.'

'Fine. I'll stay up here.'

'All right. But somewhere the captain can't see you. Tell you what, we'll go and sit in the lee of the chicken coop. It's sort of dry there.'

'We?'

'Yes, *we*. You've nearly drowned twice already.'

'I can't sit alone with you.'

'Course you can.'

'But protocol . . .'

'Even protocol gets overlooked sometimes. Specially in storms – not that this really counts as a storm, just a bit of a gale. Come on. I promise I won't tell your husband.'

She gaped. 'You? You know my husband?'

'You're surprised?'

'But he is the emperor's son, and you, you are . . .'

'What am I?'

'You're just a boy.'

21

'And you're just a girl.'

And with that he set off towards the front end of the boat, not even holding on to anything, sort of swaying in time to the sea. She tried to copy him, but then she nearly drowned a third time and shuffled prudently after him. He ducked in behind the chickens and settled himself on a pile of sacks. He was right. It was dry and they were out of the wind. She sat down beside him.

'I'm not *just a girl*. I have never been *just a girl*. I am the daughter of a king.'

'The ruler of a truly noble kingdom.'

'Exactly,' she began, then realised he was being sarcastic. 'It's true what they say about you Greeks. You're arrogant, you're . . . What? What's the matter?'

It was the first time she'd seen him look even remotely ruffled.

'I'm not Greek. I'm a Rôman.'

'What a ridiculous thing to say. You're from Constantinople, not Rome.'

'What is Rome? A pile of ruins overrun by barbarians. We're the Rômans now. *Greeks*. You've got a lot to learn.'

'You're wrong,' she told him. 'Oh, thank you,' she added as he passed her a piece of bread and cheese from his pocket. 'You're wrong,' she repeated. 'I've learnt a great deal about the City and,' she added decorously, 'my husband Alexios will be sure to teach me whatever else I need to know.'

The boy threw back his head and laughed.

'What's so funny about that?'

'Nothing. Everything,' he said as his mirth slowly subsided. 'No, nothing. Don't worry, I just like to laugh, that's all. Come on, look. The weather's clearing. It'll be a brilliant sunset.'

But Agnes wasn't interested in sunsets. She was interested in finding out everything she could about Alexios.

'Do you really know him?'

'I do. I've known him since we were boys.'

'You're still a boy.'

'Do you want to know about him or not?'

'Yes. Tell me everything.'

'Everything is hard. What do you want to know?'

'What does he look like?'

'Like the son of a great emperor.'

'I mean – is he handsome?'

'I can't judge whether a man is handsome or not.'

'Stop it. Do the ladies think him handsome?'

'The ladies are frequently to be heard extolling the rare beauty of his features.'

'I knew it,' Agnes said, profoundly satisfied. 'Why are you smiling?'

'Am I smiling? Oh, only because I see a beautiful rainbow. Look,' he said, pointing over her shoulder.

She poked her head out from behind the coop and a wave caught her slap in the face, soaking her hair, her dress, filling her eyes and nose with stinging, freezing water.

'You did that on purpose,' she gasped.

'Did I?'

'You did, you know you did. I shan't forget . . .' She stopped. There was one problem. His name. 'Who are you? Don't lie.'

'I would never lie. I am Theodore Branas, the son of Alexios Branas, the greatest general of the empire.'

'I've never heard of him.'

He looked insulted. Good. She'd meant to insult him. But then he laughed. It was true. He did laugh easily.

'That's because you're a girl. Name one general you've ever heard of.'

'Julius Caesar.'

'He doesn't count. He's dead. Name another one. One that's alive. I bet you can't.'

He was right. She couldn't.

'I can name dozens,' she said. 'Hundreds. But . . . but I find I tire of your company. Farewell.'

She stood up and stumbled back below decks. She'd kick Blanche awake and make her clear up. It was only when she was halfway down the ladder that she realised that for the first time, a boy didn't seem to have noticed what she looked like.

Many miles and a few weeks later

Blanche wanted to put her in a white, floating, frilly robe – *as befits your youth, my lady* – but Agnes wasn't having any of it.

'I'm thirteen, not three. I'm here to be married, aren't I?'

'But . . .'

'Don't *but* me. Come on. There must be something else.'

She didn't want Alexios to think his bride was all girlish innocence. She knew that men who married young girls took mistresses, visited courtesans, and although she wasn't sure exactly what that entailed, she knew it meant competition, and competition was not something she would tolerate.

Her maid tried to stand her ground until Agnes, wearing only her underthings, swore she'd force her way out of their cabin and turn the hold upside down until she found something bearable.

'No, my lady, please, my lady. Let's look in here.' And she dragged a little box out from under the bunks.

'What's all this stuff?' Agnes asked as she rifled through a jumble of oddments, ornaments – and clothes, good grown-up clothes.

'She wanted me to give you this when we arrived,' Blanche said. '*So she'll always have a little of me with her.* That's what she said. Your poor mother.'

But Agnes wasn't listening. She was gazing at something red and gold, stiff with jewels. 'Well done, Blanche. This is perfect.'

'My lady, truly, you'd much better—'

But she pulled it over her head herself. 'There. That's more like it.'

When she made her way up on deck, leaving Blanche behind to finish packing, she immediately detected a new interest on the sailors' faces and her mood improved further. They had grown too used to seeing her practically in rags.

One of the young Greek – no, one of the young *Rôman* men clustered about the other side of the deck saw she was unchaperoned and edged towards her, talking most civilly down a long, aristocratic nose, its impact only slightly ruined by his funny eyebrows.

'Your last morning at sea, ma'am.' She liked being treated as an adult, but maybe *ma'am* was going a bit far. 'We have traversed the Hellespont and are now navigating the Propontis. With the blessing of God we shall disembark at the Bukoleon before the sun reaches its zenith. The City awaits! I promise you a sight you never shall forget.'

You never forget your first sight of the City.

She'd heard that old saw repeated hundreds upon thousands of times by travellers returning to her father's court, but she wasn't going to be flabbergasted and dumbstruck like everyone else. She was going to be an empress, and empresses were not impressed by anything. She gave the young man an absent nod and examined the stitching on the cuff of her dress, stifling a yawn.

'Is Murzuphlus boring you? Or were you too nervous to sleep last night? Don't blame you. Big day for you.'

She looked up. Theodore, no longer kitted out in grubby deck gear, but smart and starched in a long embroidered tunic, was high in the rigging with the ships' boys, lounging on one of the spars.

'No, I wasn't . . .' She stopped. She couldn't believe she'd been about to argue with him in public.

'It's all right. You can admit it. You—'

'Shut up, Theo,' said the man at her side, adding a few more phrases in Greek whose meaning she could only guess. 'Accept my apologies, Princess Agnes,' he said, switching back to his rather stilted Latin. 'Young Theodore Branas is a most improper fellow and it is wholly meet that you ignore him.'

This Murzuphlus definitely deserved one of her warmer smiles.

'Is that the City there?' She pointed.

He smiled in a way that made her like him a lot less.

'No, ma'am, those are but a string of minor monasteries that lie beyond the walls. Look ahead, a little to port of the ship's bow. You can discern in the distance the Church of Holy Wisdom – the heart of the City.'

Agnes screwed up her eyes against the early-morning sun. Slowly, what she had taken for a small hill turned into the dome of a mighty cathedral. Her mind rebelled. The great churches of Paris, the pride of the kingdom, would scurry around its feet like mice. Men did not build such things. God created them at the beginning of the world and left them for men to marvel at.

Blanche appeared at her elbow and shooed Murzuphlus away. 'It is something, isn't it, my lady?'

Agnes forgot to be unimpressed. 'It is,' she whispered back. 'It really is.'

The boat bumped against the dockside.

At first all Agnes could see was blinding marble, glinting hot and hard, very still, very strong after the shifting sea. Broad white steps marched towards her, but she couldn't look at them. They hurt her eyes. No trace of a breeze remained and she was, she realised, horribly warm.

Above her, hidden deep within the shade of giant poled panoplies, her new family was waiting. It was hard to make them out. They were like the painted figurines she'd kept in a toy house when she was a girl, or like the archbishops attending to God's work at the far end of the church, small and perfect.

Half a dozen men formed ranks around her and ushered her down the gangplank. The ground lurched under her feet and she looked up in involuntary surprise.

'It is the land after weeks at sea,' one of the men told her, adding a condescending smile. He swept a hand forwards. 'Go on now, they're waiting. Don't be frightened.'

I'm not frightened, idiot.

A barrage of music – pipes, drums, cymbals, she couldn't tell which – struck up, drowning out the screams of the gulls spinning overhead. She started up the steps, walking slowly enough to look regal, but not so slowly that the sun would melt her before she reached the top. Three more, two more, one more – and then a plump man with a tremendous beard strode out in front of her. He had tiny feet and a tiny mouth and a barrel chest, which he expanded to produce a gargantuan voice.

At first she was delighted. A poem, composed in her honour, dedicated to her youth, her beauty, her nobility. That at any rate was the gist of it, but there was a great deal more, all definitely highly complimentary, but buried in mounds of convoluted Greek.

As it went on and on, her concentration began to slip, but the men and women in front of her were listening, calm and appreciative, apparently engrossed. Well, they could listen all they liked, but there was no reason why she shouldn't look at them.

It was obvious which one Emperor Manuelos was. He had the biggest beard, oiled and curled, ornate as a carving. He looked like he could hurl down plagues and split oceans. But she wasn't marrying him; she was marrying his son. Which one was he? She scanned the faces before her.

There, that had to be him. A young man with golden skin, thick bronze hair and the noblest bearing. He hardly had any beard – only the sweetest soft down on his cheeks – and he was every bit as beautiful as she'd liked to imagine him. *Maybe even better.*

The poet had, at last, stopped talking, although the climactic stanza still reverberated in her ears. Both his arms were raised high as if he were about to dive into a pond, and he held them there for such a long time that it was hard to believe nobody laughed. Finally, when she began to wonder whether his arms were stuck, he let them fall to his sides and bowed low – lower than low. He actually pressed his forehead to the ground while everyone applauded.

And then the emperor stepped forward.

He's just a king, the same as Father. There's no need to be frightened, idiot. But her father was such an everyday man, not like Manuelos, not like this walking god.

'Daughter of the west, I bid you fair welcome to the City of the Rômans. Your father was a much-beloved guest. We shall endeavour to honour the trust he shows us when he commends the brightest star of his family to our care. I say again, you are welcome.'

He had spoken in old Greek, the language of the dark years before the Son of God came to earth, as similar to the daily speech of the City as the slabs of marble under her feet were to rocks in the wilderness.

Then Manuelos smiled and the god vanished, leaving a kindly old man standing before her.

'And now, the moment we have all so longed for. Allow me to present my son.'

Her eyes flicked to the handsome young man, but he looked away and did not move. She looked back at Manuelos, saw him beckoning to a very different boy, and the sweet trill of her nerves gave way to a throb of disappointment.

He's not much taller than me.

That was her first impression, and it went downhill from there. His pale brown hair was thin and soft as weed and his pale brown eyes swam as if he had but to blink for tears to fall. As a little boy, he might have been pretty enough, but now, with manhood waiting, he looked ridiculous.

Before he came to greet her, she saw him reach down and clasp the fingers of a woman beside him. At first Agnes feared a rival, then she saw the woman was more than twice his age, although still far from old, and alarmingly beautiful. *His mother?* If her mother had been there, she would have jumped into the sea rather than look at her, let alone hold her hand. And yet here was this boy taking comfort like a baby sucking a bit of blanket.

'I h-hope we may be very happy together,' he began. She was surprised he did not lisp. 'I have been so excited about your coming. Here, I chose this for you from our best merchants. I chose it myself.' He reached inside his robes and pulled out what had to be a string of sapphires. 'They told me your eyes were b-blue. I thought they might suit you – and now I see that they do.'

'Oh, Alexios, well done.' Another woman came forward, laughing and clapping, a cascade of pearls jangling on her headdress. 'He's been practising that little speech for days,' she continued in a stagey sort of whisper, 'muttering it in the corridors. He asked me whether he might perhaps say it in Latin, but he couldn't seem to make the words stick in his head.'

It was cruel – but all too easy to imagine. She glanced at Manuelos; wouldn't he be angry? But he was chuckling.

'Do not tease your brother, Maria. As I recall, you were every bit as nervous when your Renier landed.'

Maria snorted, an emphatic and – to Agnes's mind – extraordinarily unladylike sound.

'I was not, Papa.' And now that Agnes looked closer, she saw that they could only be father and daughter. They shared a firm brow, a square jaw – which looked rather better on Manuelos than it did on her – and an unapologetic gaze. In fact, Maria looked more like the emperor's son than Alexios did. 'But I'd wager Renier was terrified, weren't you, my darling?'

And she reached out a hand and pulled the handsome young man over to her.

'Come, let me introduce us. I am Maria, your sister. And

here's my beau, the dashing Renier – all the way from Montferrat.'

He blushed and nodded, colour storming up his cheeks. He was much younger than Maria – who had to be at least thirty – affable and nonplussed.

'We are to be wed a month before you. A warm-up act—'

'Peace, Maria,' a chill voice interrupted. 'You will bewilder the child if you insist on talking like that.' It was Alexios's mother who now stepped forward. 'Time and again you forget yourself.'

Maria looked mutinous, but Manuelos patted her hand and stilled her.

'That is my daughter's way, is it not? Agnes, my dear, let me introduce you to my wife, Marguerite-Constance.'

Agnes knew that mothers-in-law were always a difficult prospect, so she mustered her most winning smile, a study in sweet docility. She received nothing in return.

'She does speak our language, does she not?' Marguerite-Constance asked her husband. 'She does understand what's said to her? She has said not one word.'

'Of course she understands.' Manuelos paused. 'Don't you, Agnes?'

Agnes nodded. 'I understand, basileus,' she said, pleased to remember the correct title for him. 'And speak also. A little.'

Manuelos smiled, encouraging, but Marguerite-Constance winced and turned her head aside to murmur something to him. Agnes only caught his reply.

'Certainly she will improve. Your Greek was not perfect when you came to us, was it, my love?' And turning to Agnes, he added, 'My wife is your countrywoman, did you know that? She grew up in the holy lands captured by the soldiers of the Cross, but her kinsmen hail from the west. You will be able to talk to each other in your own tongue.'

His wife's look was withering. 'She left all that behind when you betrothed her to our son.'

But then her expression changed – in another woman you

might have said softened. Watched by Manuelos and Alexios, Marguerite-Constance came over to Agnes and touched her cheek with one finger.

Close up, Agnes realised the flaw in this woman's astonishing face. Her milk-and-honey skin, her sugar-spun features were ruined by her eyes, the eyes of a bird, metallic, lightless, uninviting.

Those eyes were on her now, domineering, demanding submission, but Agnes would not look down. Marguerite-Constance raised one eyebrow in mock surprise, then placed her hand softly on the back of Agnes's neck, a caress, a vice, and spoke to her in the language they shared.

'My son, little one, remember that. *My son.*'

She twisted one of Agnes's curls absent-mindedly in her fingers and switched back to Greek.

'Welcome to Constantinople.'

'Bitch,' Agnes told the empty room with satisfaction. She didn't often swear, but when she did, she liked the way it tasted on her tongue. 'Stuck-up, uptight, tight-arsed, arse-faced . . . bitch.'

It had been a long day and a longer evening, and throughout it Marguerite-Constance – a ludicrous name if ever she'd heard one – had done everything in her power to undermine her. But she'd done it so discreetly that only another woman, who knew the rules of women's games, would have realised what was going on.

Manuelos and Alexios probably thought the little Frankish girl was getting on famously with her new mother, but Agnes knew that every conversation, every tiny glance and grimace, had been the opening skirmishes in what promised to be a grim war of attrition.

And her mother-in-law wasn't the only one who'd been at it. The other women might like to think she was too green, too awed, too *Latin* to notice, but Agnes had caught every veiled shudder, every delicately disguised wince. And the worst thing was that she had no idea what she was doing that was so wrong. Actually, no, the truly worst thing was that when she'd hosted her country cousins in Paris, with their fussy dresses and sun-brown faces, she'd shuddered and winced in exactly the same way.

At dinner in the Blachernai Palace, the men and women seated apart, she'd found herself trapped between Marguerite-Constance and a frumpier woman called something unpronounceable – *Yoofrozyoo*-something – and she knew they were both laughing at her.

The woman – who Agnes guessed had only been placed so close to the empress because she was as plain as Marguerite-Constance was perfect – offered her the vessel of oil that was by her place. Agnes had placed her hands together and whispered a little prayer – she thought it some sort of offering to God, a way of thanking Him for the food. But then she'd seen that everyone else was eating theirs. Eating olive oil as if it were as worthless as the bread itself.

Fine, she thought. She dipped a finger in the oil, tasted it, and found it was delicious. Rich and heady and so very different from home. For a moment, everything was right. She was, after all, in the seat of honour at a vast table in a vast room lit by rack upon rack of candles dancing on contraptions suspended from the ceiling by what could only be gold ropes, so that it seemed as if the stars themselves had crept closer to earth, and she had drunk more golden wine since sitting down than she had done in the rest of her days put together, and the hundreds of faces before her were dancing as bright and inchoate as the lights above.

My people. My future.

But then Marguerite-Constance whispered something over her head and the other woman smirked and whispered something back in a strange sing-song voice in the old Greek which Agnes couldn't understand, and they both laughed. She guessed they were quoting old poets – Homer or Hesiod or some other dead heathen – to each other to prove how clever they were and how stupid she was, and there was nothing she could do about it, apart from refuse, absolutely refuse to blush or look cowed or let them think they were winning.

But now, alone, Agnes burst into tears and flung herself, sobbing, on to the nearest pile of cushions.

'Come on, cheer up. Are you homesick?'

Agnes sprang back to her feet. Maria was eyeing her from a half-open door that she'd have sworn wasn't there before.

'How did you . . .'

Maria held up a bunch of keys. 'I go where I like.' She came closer and peered down at Agnes – she was surprisingly tall – squinting her eyes as if she did not see well. 'No, you're not homesick, are you? I know homesick tears – weak and watery. You're angry, aren't you?'

Agnes did her best to stop thinking angry thoughts. 'No, you're right. I am sad. I do so miss my—'

'It's all right. You don't need to pretend in front of me. It's *her*, isn't it? She's horrible. And you've only had one day of her. Just think – I've had to put up with her half my life. But, you know, I'd rather have her as a stepmother than as a mother-in-law. She loves her little Alexios more than she loves my father. Worse luck for you. But you didn't look like you were scared of her. Good for you.'

'How did you . . . ?' Agnes stopped herself.

'Oh don't worry, it wasn't obvious. Well, not that obvious. But I could see what she was up to. She's been practising on me long enough. By the way, aren't you hungry? I'm ravenous. I can't eat at those dinners – *she* always has something to say if I eat more than two bites of anything. It ruins my appetite.'

Maria rang a bell, and a servant appeared from behind a curtain that hid another door.

'Melon. Melon and cheese. And some bread – not this

morning's, either. Fresh. Off you go.' She turned back to Agnes. 'Don't let them palm you off with old bread. They'll try that because you're new – and because you're Latin. I say, do you have cheese in Paris?'

Agnes nodded and opened her mouth to speak, but Maria was already forging ahead.

'You do? I wasn't sure about that. I wasn't sure about anything, actually. I was worried you'd be like *her*. In fact I'd made up my mind to hate you. And I did hate you at first when I saw you tottering up those steps like a doll, a silly sparrow. But then I saw the way you looked at *her*, and I liked that. We'll be friends, won't we? Friends against *her*.'

Maria held out her hand.

'Come on, shake on it.'

Then she went still.

'Who's there?'

Agnes had heard nothing.

'Come out, Constantinos. It is you, isn't it?'

A low laugh. 'Your ears are one of the marvels of the City, Maria.'

A young man appeared from behind the curtain. *No, not a man, not quite.* Agnes tried to stop herself staring, but before she could rearrange her features to her satisfaction, the man's eyes were on her and – to her mortification – he was wagging one finger very slowly.

'Latins. You're all the same. Always inexplicably overexcited when you catch sight of one of us.'

'I am not—'

'Yes you are. You were thinking—' and he switched to immaculate Latin '—My stars, there's one of those eunuchs my naughty little playmates whispered to me about. I wonder, does he really have no—'

'I was not!'

'Yes, you were.'

'No, I—'

'Stop, stop!' shouted Maria. 'I forbid you to argue in a language I cannot understand. You could be saying anything.'

'Whatever I was saying, esteemed Maria, I can at least promise I was not trying to poison this poor girl's mind before she's even slept one night in the City. You couldn't have waited a day or two?'

Maria did look a little abashed. 'Don't tell Father.'

'We'll see. Now, kaisarissa, if you don't mind, I'd like a word with our new arrival. In private. And I'd better not find you within a hundred paces of this door when I'm done.'

'All right, all right. Goodbye for now, Agnes. Don't believe everything Constantinos tells you either. Sorry, sorry, all right, I'm going. Bye, Agnes. You're sweet. I'm glad you're here.'

She was gone and Agnes was alone with this Constantinos.

He looked her up and down. It occurred to her that she'd never been alone in a room with any kind of man before – apart from her father or brother. She pulled her shawl a little tighter about her as he wandered round the room, talking to himself – except he obviously wasn't really talking to himself, because he was talking in Latin.

'Not bad to look at, not bad at all. This time the envoys had no need to fabricate. A pretty child. So gold, so pink. The shape of the mouth is most interesting – a little bow. I see temper there. And the eyes are intriguing. Not true blue, no. Not the clear sky of spring. I see a hint of grey. A hint of storms. The weather on the turn.'

'Are you done?'

He raised one eyebrow.

'Normally little girls who find themselves alone in strange cities are more polite to those who can help them.'

'I'm not a little—'

'Yes you are. You're a little girl with a lot to learn.'

'And I suppose you're going to teach me?'

Constantinos smiled. 'I might.'

'Why?'

'Orders, orders. Why else? I help Manuelos with various matters. Matters such as his son's need for a fitting wife.'

'I *am*—'

'Not if today is anything to go by, you're not. I could hardly bear to watch you when you stepped off the boat. Like a milkmaid needing the privy, you were, hopping from foot to foot. You yawned, for the love of God, and I would be willing to swear you itched your behind. And your table manners . . . ! It won't do. You're a pretty girl, but the wife of Alexios needs to be more than that – much, much more.'

'For young men like Alexios, prettiness is what counts. Not that you'd know anything about that, would you?' she said, stung into rudeness because she was afraid that every word he said might be horribly true. But instead of being insulted, the eunuch doubled over, chuckling with delight.

'Is that my payback for calling you a milkmaid?'

Before she could answer, Blanche bustled into the room, followed by a servant carrying the food Maria had ordered. Her maid goggled at Constantinos – who bowed low to Agnes, mouthed *sweet dreams* and left.

After Blanche had unpinned her hair and helped her into her favourite nightgown, the one her big sister Alys had embroidered with lilies twining up the sleeves, Agnes suggested she sleep at the foot of her bed that night.

'I expect you'll feel nervous alone, Blanche, and if I need you in the night, you're bound to be slow to find me.'

Blanche nodded, her face correct.

'Of course, my lady. I'm grateful for your consideration, my lady.'

As she listened to Blanche's breathing deepen, Agnes found herself thinking hard, probably harder than she had ever done in her life.

He isn't weaned, that's all. He's never known any different, so of course he loves her. I'll show him there's more to life than her. I'll show him. I'll . . .

She stopped listening to her thoughts and began to listen to the palace. Whispered conversations and slippered footsteps sounded long into the night. Or maybe she was imagining it. Maybe it was nothing but the scuttling of night creatures and the swash of the sea.

Early in the year 1180

Muffled in furs, Agnes walked beside Alexios down a path dotted with patches of ice that the Great Palace groundsmen had missed. It was a cold, dull day, a week after the feast of Christ's nativity. She had only ever imagined the City bathed in sunlight, but it turned out the winters here were every bit as grey and chill as those in Paris.

She feigned a small slip and clutched his arm, smiling up at him as he steadied her. Soon they would pass the wild animal enclosures where lions and tigers huddled for warmth like so many cows and sheep. If Marguerite-Constance and Maria remained up ahead with the emperor, Agnes calculated they could snatch a few moments alone.

She glanced over at Alexios.

He was walking very carefully, poised and dignified, the way he did everything – so long as his sister wasn't about. It was eerie how *imperial* he was, especially compared with the boys she'd grown up with, boys like Louis and Henri who ran in packs, scrapped and blacked each other's eyes. What was frustrating, though, was that he treated *her* the same way everyone treated *him*, as something perfect and inviolable. In other words, he never laid a finger on her.

Not that he lacked encouragement.

She might leave a hand on the arm of his chair and all he would do was stare at it, mesmerised, as if the air around it shimmered. If she dropped a bracelet, a shawl, he'd hand it back as fast as if it scorched his fingers.

Maria found it hilarious. Manuelos seemed to be oblivious. And Marguerite-Constance? Her displeasure was impossible to miss and Alexios shied away from Agnes whenever his mother approached.

Just as they drew level with the cages, the keeper appeared carrying a dripping bucket of off-cuts. One of the lions, hungry, hopeful, opened its mouth and roared. It was no worse than a big dog barking, really, but she gripped Alexios's hand and trembled.

'There's n-nothing to fear,' he said, smiling across at her.

'You really don't mind them?' she said, realising with a flicker of triumph that he hadn't removed his hand. Out of the corner of her eye she saw that the imperial family had continued towards the game fields, dozens of courtiers in their wake.

'The lions can't harm us. They're locked up. Even if one of them escaped, *they'd* kill it.'

He pointed at his Varangian guards, three massive warriors with bushy red beards. At first she'd been wary of them and their two-headed axes. After all, they *were* northmen – Danes or Norwegians, or maybe even Englishmen whose forebears had fled when the Normans seized their lands – and no Frankish girl could fail to know how dangerous *they* were. Now she appreciated their fearsomeness, since it was her life, too, they were sworn to protect.

'But what if they weren't here?' she said.

He looked confused. She'd have to feed him his lines.

'Wouldn't *you* kill it? But of course you would. I feel sure you'd do anything to keep me safe.'

She took a step towards him and waited. *Come on.* She closed her eyes and gave a little sigh. *Idiot.* She felt his hand in hers start to shake. *Come on, come on.* She parted her lips.

'Agnes . . . I . . . w-we shouldn't . . .'

Suddenly tired of the whole stupid game, she dropped his hand and turned to go.

'Come on, Alexios, the others will be—'

And then she found herself seized, embraced.

'Why, Alexios . . .' she murmured, but before she could make the necessary protests, his lips were crushed against hers.

'Alexios! Your father is waiting for you.'

At the sound of his mother's voice, he let her go. Marguerite-Constance looked them both over, but said nothing other than,

'The dzoustra is about to begin.'

Theo brought his horse to a standstill after an easy win in his first bout. He wished his father had seen. A clean stroke, neat and tidy. No fancy flourishes. And that plump boy rolling on the ground, whining about his shoulder. His father's armourer's bill would be huge.

'There, what d'you make of that, Murzuphlus?' he called with some satisfaction to his friend, who was sprawled on a bench, talking to a gang of aristos on the row behind him.

'What do I make of what?'

He got to his feet, sauntered over and gave Theo's horse an absent-minded pat.

'You don't mean you missed it?'

'I should say everyone missed it, Theo.'

'They can't have—'

'Theo, Theo, how many times do I have to tell you? Nobody gives a damn about stupid bloody tournaments. It's a barbaric way to spend an afternoon. God only knows why the emperor enjoys watching them so much.'

Murzuphlus stopped and frowned.

'What are you looking at?' asked Theo.

'Up there, do you see?' His friend made a very small gesture. 'Now that's something everyone *is* going to give a damn about. The Protosebastos is back from Paphlagonia.'

'The who is back from where?'

'Get lost, did you, sister?' Maria grinned through lips covered with crumbs after Marguerite-Constance deposited Agnes in

41

between her and Renier and bore Alexios away to sit with his father. 'Well, you've only missed the first pass. Still, my money's already on Branas's boy. He's zipping about like a hornet.'

'He's not bad,' Renier agreed, leaning across Agnes to grab one of the cakes by Maria's feet. 'But I could show him a thing or two.'

'Why don't you?' asked Agnes, shaking her head as he offered her one.

'It's beneath his dignity, sweetie,' Maria answered for him. 'The husband-to-be of the emperor's daughter play-fighting? No, no, no. Terribly bad form.'

'That's funny,' said Agnes. 'Back home it would be terribly bad form for him *not* to.'

'Really?'

But Maria's attention, which flitted at the best of times, had shifted to a tall, thin man who was approaching the jousting ground from the direction of the palace buildings. Agnes watched him lean over Manuelos's chair and place a daringly informal hand on his shoulder. The emperor turned, smiled and patted the hand, gesturing to the men trotting to their marks down in the lists. The newcomer's face – hollow-cheeked, with deep-set eyes – was all attention, but Agnes could tell from the way one of his feet tapped that he couldn't care less about the sport.

'Who's that?' she asked, nudging Maria.

'Alexios Komnenos.'

'But that's—'

'Your beloved's name, yes, but it's his too. He's my cousin, the son of Papa's elder brother. Some fever did for his father, otherwise he might be emperor. Not that you'd know it from the way he behaves. The Protosebastos is *devoted* to Papa.'

'The who?'

42

'Oh, he goes by his rank. Seeing as my little brother has rights to his real name.'

The bout finished, the emperor motioned to the Protosebastos to sit beside him, and Agnes saw him pass Manuelos a letter. Marguerite-Constance got up from her seat to read it over her husband's shoulder.

'So he got it,' murmured Maria. 'He's sworn, has he?' she called across to her father. Her voice carried – Maria's voice always carried – but her father didn't look up. 'Papa?' Louder. 'Has he sworn?'

It was the Protosebastos who answered her.

'Yes, kaisarissa, he has pledged his loyalty.'

'Oh good.' Maria jumped to her feet and crossed to where her father was sitting. 'Does that mean he can come to the weddings now?'

'That man has no place at the wedding of my son,' said Marguerite-Constance before the emperor could answer. 'I am astonished – *appalled* – that you should suggest it. We can only assume this is one of your little jests. There can be no other excuse. *He tried to kill your father.*' The last words were mouthed.

'But he didn't manage it, did he?' Maria countered. 'Papa's still here. I say an invitation would be the very thing to let bygones be—'

'And I say you are a strange, callous creature.'

Agnes was watching so intently that for a moment she failed to notice the hand that had come to rest tentatively on her knee. Alexios was at her side.

'While they're all talking,' he whispered, 'I wanted to say h-how much . . .'

She looked away – shyness itself. She didn't want to miss the argument. Maria was now kneeling next to her father, an odd sort of supplicant.

'What do you say, Papa? Mayn't I invite Cousin Andronikos?'

Agnes saw Manuelos look down at her, then glance up and seek his wife's eye. Whatever he found there made him say,

'No, daughter, I think we can do without Cousin Andronikos.'

A tug on her dress forced her to turn back to Alexios.

'Agnes? Agnes? Have I alarmed you?'

What had he been saying? But she was saved from answering by Maria, who was stalking back towards them.

'Popular, is it, where you come from, Agnes?' Maria said, elbowing Renier out of his chair now that Alexios had hers.

'What? Oh, the dzoustra? Yes, unbelievably popular.'

'And it is true that it's judged a great test of a man's valour?'

'Yes . . .'

'And it is true that the bravest men tilt in honour of the loveliest women?'

'Yes. It's how a man shows his devotion to the woman he most admires . . .'

She stopped herself. She'd seen the glint in Maria's eye and knew, too late, what she was up to.

'D'you hear that, brother? We should have remembered how westerners love a touch of derring-do. Poor Agnes. She must be terribly disappointed.'

'W-would it please you, Agnes?' he said, a flush rising up his cheeks. 'I mean, to see me joust?'

Agnes looked at the boy by her side.

'Oh, no, Alexios, really. It's such a silly crude custom. I care very little for it.'

'Pay her no heed, little brother. I've been watching her. She's hardly been able to tear her eyes—'

'Honestly, Alexios, there's no—'

'But of course, if you're *nervous* . . .'

Alexios jerked to his feet.

'Agnes,' he said, with a funny formal bow, 'I-I do this for you.'

And off he went, walking with great state, his guards exchanging extremely worried glances in his wake. Agnes could do nothing but watch a slow, greedy smile spread across Maria's face.

'Attaboy,' she said.

Theo was limbering up for his next bout when he turned and saw Murzuphlus practically sprinting towards him.

'What's got into you, pal?'

'You're to fight the boy. Alexios.'

'What? Since when does he——?'

'Since he got hooked by our pretty Frankish princess, I suppose.'

'That's hilarious.'

'It is, but you don't have time to laugh. You've got to decide how you're going to do it.'

'Do what?'

'Fall off without looking like you did it on purpose, of course.'

'What the——?'

'Or maybe you can drop your lance and pray that he hits you.'

'I'm not bloody going to——'

'Theo, you're not seriously going to try to beat him, are you?'

'I'm not even going to have to try. He'll fall off as soon as he sees me coming.'

'Don't be an idiot.'

'I'd rather be an idiot than lose.'

And he wheeled his horse round and spurred it towards the lists, where half a dozen attendants had just finished kitting out the boy. He glanced towards the benches. The aristos were watching him now, all right. He looked back at Alexios. He was sitting very upright, but Theo could see from the way the tip of his lance quivered that he was holding it way too tight. The adjudicator strode to his block, raised his baton to give the signal and—

A scream pierced the air.

* * *

Agnes lay on the ground, her eyes shut, limp. Had it worked?

She'd watched Alexios slapping on some armour, everyone flapping about, nobody knowing how to stop him. She'd seen Marguerite-Constance notice what was happening, start after him, stop herself, lean down and whisper something to Manuelos – but the emperor had only shrugged. The tension had climbed up her throat, and all at once the answer came out in a scream.

'Poor girl fainted.'

That was Renier. She felt him hoist her on to a bench and prop cushions around her. She let her eyes flutter open. There was Alexios running towards her.

'Oh, I'm so sorry,' she said, hiding her face in her hands. 'I'm dreadfully embarrassed. It was just all too—'

'Don't say another word,' he said, kneeling at her side. 'You tried to put me off. I should have been more sensitive. Forgive me. Forgive me.'

He was holding her hands. Gazing into her eyes. She had time to register that she had finally made him fall hopelessly in love with her when his mother loomed behind him.

'What's all this fuss about?'

For a moment, nobody spoke. The day was failing. The sun had disappeared behind a bank of low cloud and it was suddenly very cold.

'My little brother was about to tilt when Agnes was overcome by nerves. A shame. We missed our chance to watch him dispatch—'

'I see,' said Marguerite-Constance, cutting Maria off and turning to her son. 'Now . . .'

Alexios squirmed.

'Mother, I'm sorry.'

'No, no. You young men must have your sport, but it is we women who suffer for it. Come, dear Agnes, I shall take you home.'

Varangians lined the route back to Blachernai through the City. They had their backs to the road, facing the crowds, weapons in their right hands, torches in their left, brightening the winter night.

Marguerite-Constance was silent until they'd left the smart houses by the Great Palace behind them, then she turned and began to stroke Agnes's face with slender fingers as cold as silk. Shadows cast by the guards' torches fell across the chair's screens, black shapes looming and vanishing, as if giants danced in the streets outside.

'Forgive me for speaking of intimate matters. You bleed.'

Agnes blinked. It was not a question. The thought of the maids who scrubbed her rags telling the empress was so excruciating, she did not know what to say.

'If you bleed, you are a woman. But you need not assume a woman's duties after your marriage.'

'You mean . . . ?' How could she say it?

'Yes.' Agnes heard, rather than saw, the empress's tidy smile. 'We shall respect the innocence of your years. You and Alexios may live apart for a while yet. You are pleased. You may kiss me.'

She turned her head away so that Agnes could touch her lips to this woman's cheek, scented with orange-water and something darker. Marguerite-Constance lay back and closed her eyes while Agnes's mind raced.

She certainly wasn't looking forward to doing *that* with Alexios, but doing *that*, if she understood *that* as well as she thought she did, would make him a little more hers and a little less his mother's, which meant she wanted to start doing *it* as soon as possible.

'Marguerite-Constance?'

The empress's eyes flickered open, the whites suddenly visible against the painted rims.

'You wish to say something?'

'Yes,' Agnes began, feeling the heat rising in her voice. 'I do.'

But she broke off and forced herself to lean in against

Marguerite-Constance's shoulder, the golden ridges of her embroidered robes digging into her face.

'I wanted to thank you for this and all your kindness to me,' she whispered.

Marguerite-Constance stiffened, and Agnes decided to stay put, nestled close as any chick under its mother's wing. No need to exhaust herself arguing when she'd already had an idea.

'Thank your lucky stars her vapours got you out of it,' said Murzuphlus.

Theo frowned. He'd only talked to her that one time on the boat, but she really hadn't seemed the fainting type. He wasn't going to tell Murzuphlus that he thought she'd faked it, though.

'Yes, thank God women are so delicate.'

'What do you know about women?'

'More than you. You wouldn't know a real woman if she— Ah, greetings, kaisar.'

Renier was lolloping towards them.

'Oh, don't mind about all that,' he said, brushing aside the honorific. 'Wanted to say you're not half bad, Theodore, isn't it? Wish I'd had a go. You did drop your lance a bit in the second bout, but—'

'I did not,' said Theo. 'The other fellow . . .'

Murzuphlus rolled his eyes. Theo cuffed him. Renier grinned. And together they wandered out of the Great Palace to have, Theo hoped, the kind of fun three young men could only have in the Queen of Cities.

Back in her room, Agnes started composing a letter – in verse and in Greek. It wouldn't be very good, but she hoped its shortcomings might be part of its charm. She'd nearly finished copying out a fair version when a hand swooped down and grabbed it. She jerked round.

'What are you doing here?' she demanded.

'I heard you'd called for paper,' said Constantinos. 'Why? I

48

asked myself. Let me see . . . Your scansion's awry at line four. And you want epsilon here, not êta. Rosy gates? Hackneyed, my dear. Altogether, though, a most creditable effort for a novice of our noble tongue. But I recall setting you some pages of Demosthenes as homework, not a love poem begging a youth to defy the will of his parents and take his beloved in his arms. Agnes, please enlighten me.'

She looked at the eunuch.

'Marguerite-Constance does not want Alexios and me to be . . . to be . . . properly married.'

'But from this letter it seems you are almost indecently keen to be *properly married*. This is most strange. Scarce an hour has passed since the emperor told me that you broke down in tears before his wife and begged most touchingly to be excused the duties of the marital bed until you were older.'

'That's a lie.'

'I thought it might be. I wonder why she . . . No, don't tell me. I can see plain enough for myself.' He turned his back and stared out the window, his hands behind his back. 'You are properly a woman?'

'Yes.'

'You understand what I mean? If you are not, it is sacrilege.'

'Of course I understand. I have been *properly a woman* for nearly two years. Look, I have—'

'Yes, my thanks, Agnes, it is not my eyes I have been deprived of.' He turned back to face her. 'The emperor was reluctant for you and Alexios to remain separate. He wants his son to become *properly a man*, shall we say, but he was willing to delay out of consideration for you.' He nodded a few times. 'I shall tell him there was a misunderstanding. You shall have your wedding night.'

He was halfway out the door when she remembered.

'Constantinos, you still have my letter.'

'Can I not keep it? A souvenir?'

'Put it in the fire this instant or I swear I'll never speak to you again.'

'That, Agnes, would be your loss, not mine.' But he smiled and threw the papers into the grate.

'Thank you,' she said. 'For that and for . . .'

'Helping?'

She nodded.

'I have not helped you. Your interests have merely overlapped with those of the City.' A quick nod. 'A baby boy lying in a cradle in a Porphyry Chamber would be very reassuring. A straight line, father to son, father to son. Men do so like nice straight lines.'

The Porphyry Chamber, built of purple marble, hung with purple silks, was where her husband had been born – Maria too. That made them porphyrogenitos and porphyrogenitê, born-in-the-purple, a crazy title, but accurate. Agnes had first seen it when Maria showed her around the Great Palace soon after she arrived. Even though she'd just seen the crown of thorns, the lance that had pierced His side and the phial that held His blood, it was the imperial birthing room she'd most remembered. It was like being inside a flower, a cold dark rose. Or maybe it was like what a baby saw inside its mother's belly – dark purple blood.

'Constantinos,' she called after him. 'One more thing. Who is Cousin Andronikos?'

'Why do you ask?'

'They were all talking about him. Arguing about whether he should come to the weddings.'

Constantinos's face registered a flicker of interest. 'Tell me, my dear, who wanted him to come?'

'Maria. But who is he?'

'Maria. You're sure of that?'

'Of course I'm sure. Who is he?'

'Who is Andronikos? I wish I knew.'

'Don't be Delphic.'

'*Don't be Delphic.* My dear, that expression was in vogue at least three years ago. All right, all right, don't throw that at me.'

Agnes realised she did have the ink pot in her hand. She put it down.

'Andronikos was the emperor's rival – and also his friend. Some say he is the greatest hero of his generation. Others say he is the greatest villain.'

'But which is he?'

'Either. Both. You'd have to meet him yourself to decide.'

2 March 1180

Theo scrambled on top of a covered caravan that was waiting for permission to enter the City and gazed north and west up the road to Hadrianopolis. His father was cutting it fine. The wedding was set for noon that day, and even the great general Branas, bulwark of the west, couldn't afford to be late. They'd had word to expect him soon after dawn, and Theo's mother had packed him off to the Gate of Charisius while it was still dark. *No dawdling now – fetch him straight home for feeding and washing.*

The gatekeepers weren't letting many into the City that day. The local farmers' carts, stacked high with cress, mangold and orache, the first greens of spring, were waved through fast enough, but the clumps of milling travellers – pilgrims, mercenaries, merchants – were having less luck. Theo watched an uppity western knight haranguing the guards in tavern Greek.

'Why no enter? Why no enter?'

'Imperial wedding, mate. Come back tomorrow.'

The knight stamped off, easy prey for the throngs of implausible souvenir sellers – *hem of the Virgin's birthing robe*, that was a new one – and agents, as they liked to call themselves, who were no doubt promising they'd win the guards round for a hefty consideration.

The religious-looking travellers were more relaxed, content to be so close to breathing the holy air of the City. They sat cross-legged by the roadside, gazing up at the immense double walls, white stone studded with layers of brick, that stretched north and south as far as the eye could see.

There he is.

His father didn't travel rich, that wasn't his style, but nevertheless the crowds were falling back before a score of horsemen who were covering the final stretch of road at a smart military trot. Theo tumbled down from his perch, much to the surprise of the merchant's wife who was setting up a stove by the side of the caravan, and ran to meet him.

They embraced. It had been more than a year since they'd last seen each other, and Theo hoped his father would notice how much taller, how much broader he was. But if he did, he didn't mention it. At least Mikhail, his father's body-servant and Theo's old friend, treated him differently, kissing his cheeks and calling him by his right name rather than squeezing his balls and calling him *titch* or *you poxy runt.*

Theo fetched his horse and together they passed straight through the gates, the sound of the crowd booming and echoing under the stone arching, and plunged on to the northern branch of Mesê, the forked thoroughfare that led into the City.

'How's your mother?'

Theo grinned. 'Fretting. The deer I shot for you was too young. The fish eggs aren't the right shade of black. The—'

'Stop, stop.' Branas held up his hands in mock surrender. 'I'll hear it all a dozen times over when we get home.'

'If we get home,' replied Theo. 'The traffic's horrible up ahead.'

It hadn't taken them long to canter through the outlying reaches of the City, past prosperous vineyards and scattered houses, to where the Church of the Holy Apostles, smaller only than the Holy Wisdom itself, marked the start of more populous districts.

But they were soon stuck behind a dozen men who were cursing God, each other and the spring rains while they laboured to dig an ox clear of a stinking mire that had swallowed the road. The animal was buried up to its armpits, snorting and bellowing, and the men were hauling on a rope about its shoulders, a losing game of tug-of-war.

The foreign knight, who'd evidently greased his way into the City, appeared behind them. Two of his escort spurred towards the men and their ox, whips raised, cursing them for worthless peasants and ordering them to clear the road.

Branas gave Mikhail a nod and the soldier rounded on the Latins with great enthusiasm.

'Remember whose fucking City this is.'

They backed up fast when they saw his sword – they'd had to leave their weapons at the gate.

'If you're in such a bloody rush, get off your horses and help,' Mikhail growled. 'Digging an animal out of four foot of shit is rough enough without a bunch of foreigners giving you a hiding for it.'

The knight looked at Mikhail, then at Branas, and gestured to his men. They shouldered the rope and started to heave.

In a small side room off the Trullan Chamber in the Great Palace, Agnes waited. She'd been told a hundred, a thousand times how to stand, how to bow, how to sit, how to pray, and she was going to do it all perfectly. They'd see.

But there was Constantinos, bearing down on her, a tablet and stylus in his hand, more helpful advice – probably on how to *breathe* – at the ready. Her eyes glittered.

'I *know* how to do this. What exactly do you think I'm going to get wrong?'

'That, Agnes. Just that.'

'What? *What?*'

'That. You look too real. I can see you thinking and feeling. Do neither, please.'

'Don't be silly.'

'I am never silly. Listen, Agnes, today, for the first time, you will appear before the people – and they require a little bit of magic. Something beyond the grasp of their senses. A slice of the infinite.'

'You're still being silly.'

He pointed out of the window, to the world outside that was gilded with spring sunshine.

'Look at the Bosporus. Tell me what colour is it, please.'

The great waterway, she knew, could be as blue as the sky or as grey as the Styx, but that morning it was . . .

'Gold,' she replied, reluctantly. 'But it isn't really.'

'Precisely,' said the eunuch. 'You and I both know that beneath the surface black currents lie – black currents and sunken ships and sunken men and God only knows what else, but we can't see them, can we?'

Her guards were starting to line up by the door. The women who would follow in her train were hovering close at hand. Agnes wanted Constantinos to shut up so she could run through the ceremony in her head once more.

'It is the same with your family,' Constantinos continued, and she was surprised by how serious he sounded – surprised enough to listen. 'God's light shines bright upon the Komnenoi. His grace transforms them. That is what the City sees. That is what it *must* see.'

'But what about me?' she said. 'I . . . I am too close. I can see . . .'

She stopped. Constantinos was shaking his head.

'Don't look so hard. Enough.' He raised a finger in acknowledgement of somebody at the door. 'It is nearly time.'

Washed, combed and dressed in their finest, Theo and Branas strode into the great domed chamber and were discreetly directed to their places by one of the army of protocol officials. Theo didn't envy them. Herding the most powerful, fractious and self-important aristocrats in the City was a fiendish job, and the eunuchs, gliding to and fro across the stone floor, were pink-eared with concentration.

They were late, very late, so they had to squeeze past members of every clan that had ever made it big in the City, from greybeards who normally kept to their beds to soft-headed cousins who were usually kept out of sight. There were dignified Palaiologoi, wily Kamateroi, handsome Kantakouzenoi, as well as countless Doukai and of course, most important of them all, the male-line descendants of the first great Komnenos, the fortunate few who bore that name.

This was a big ceremony, with iron rules of etiquette, and everybody was behaving. They had several hours ahead of them, several hours of standing still and respectful, but that didn't mean they couldn't talk – through the sides of their mouths, with little hand gestures or flicks of the eyes.

Theo and his father found themselves standing next to the Angelos family. His mother could have told him exactly how they were related, but all he knew was that the Branades and the Angeloi had a similar-sized trickle of Komnenos blood in their veins.

Angelos was Admiral of the Fleet, an empty title if ever there was one; the closest he'd come to seafaring was probably a seagull shitting on his head. They were nothing but City men, court men, and Theo did not like them one bit. Not the father, all purple-nosed bluster, not the urbane, diffident elder brother, and certainly not Isaakios, the younger one, who somehow managed to lounge while standing on two feet.

But Theo knew that although the Angeloi might appear amiable, well-fed and nothing more, their ambition was polished to a mighty sheen. His own father, on the other hand, had brought him up to despise ambition. *Do your duty, and have a good time doing it,* that was what he said.

Theo glanced at Branas. He was looking about him, smiling broadly – doing his bluff soldier act, as if he were a nobody fresh from the provinces, not one of the great men of the City. Or maybe it wasn't an act. After all, he *was* a bluff soldier.

'How's the front, General?' whispered Isaakios, making *front* sound like a dirty word and *General* sound like an insult.

'Quiet, lad, very quiet.'

'Must be a thrill being back in the City. We see so little of you. But we've all loved having little Theo around.'

Theo groaned. *Little*, for God's sake. Isaakios wasn't so very much older than he was. He told himself not to get riled. Riling people was what Isaakios did for a living – riling, and kissing Komnenos arse.

'Hush, Theo,' Isaakios murmured. 'Here comes our emperor, may God grant him health and a very long life.' He rocked on to his tiptoes. 'We don't have terribly good places, do we? I wish I had a better view. I do so love a nice wedding.'

A slight frown wrinkled Branas's brow. At first Theo thought it was because Isaakios was irritating him, but then he realised that he was no longer paying attention to him. He was looking at Manuelos.

After the ceremony was over – and Constantinos's brief nod told her she hadn't put a foot wrong – Agnes mounted a platform that looked out over the Augusteion, the old marketplace in the shadow of Holy Wisdom. At her side stood her husband and below her, packing the square, hurling the ritual phrases of benediction into the heavens, stood the people.

She told herself the roars were cheers, the flailing fists salutes, the bared teeth harmless grins. She told herself that although she was besieged by the meat-and-sweat stench of thousands upon thousands upon thousands of people, the ranks of guardsmen stationed at the foot of the dais meant nobody could touch her. She told herself that even if the Varangians uncrossed their axes and gave way when the crowd next surged, the people did not want to hurt her. They would fight to kiss the hem of her robe, nothing more.

They loved her, she told herself, or tried to. That noise was love.

But the closer she looked, the more frightened she became. She saw faces broken and beautiful, faces laughing and deranged. She saw fingers pointing, mouths mocking. She saw glamour down there, and disease. She saw, or thought she saw, women staring at her with rapture or hatred or both. She saw men weighing her, worshipping her, wanting her. She saw children screaming with unformed excitement while their fathers tried to keep them aloft, safe above the heads of the throng.

This was the world outside the palaces. It was there, every day, and she never saw it.

She flicked her eyes to Alexios. He was unmoved. *If he can do it, so can I.* She tilted her gaze upwards, adopting the steady stare of a statue whose painted eyes take in rooftops, clouds, the endless horizon, oblivious to whatever might lie at its feet.

And then their time was up. Alexios was turning, she was turning, and behind them officials were weaving through the crowds, distributing largesse, making sure that for years to come every man, woman and child in the Augusteion would remember their marriage as a great day.

A great day. My day. That was what she kept telling herself, although her crown felt very heavy and she felt very small.

Theo and his father had processed from the palace into the hippodrome, the glory ground and killing field that hugged the western walls of the Great Palace, the most important place after the Holy Wisdom where the people and their rulers came face to face. Except that day, of course, the people were not invited.

The columns that ran down the central spine of the arena were garlanded with spring flowers. The statues of ancient gods and heroes were wreathed with bright green boughs. Fresh sand had been scattered underfoot. Theo could still see the rake marks.

'You didn't tell me,' said his father.

'Tell you what?'

'How ill he is.'

'Who?'

'Fuck's sake, Theo. The emperor.'

'Ill?' said Theo, defensive. 'I didn't know.'

'It's plain as day, son.'

'I thought he was just . . . old.'

His father shook his head. 'That's not old. That's dying. No wonder these weddings have been rushed through. No wonder I've seen imperial messengers on all the roads. Good God, it's going to be messy.'

Theo tore his attention away from the food and drink that heaped the tables.

'What's going to be messy, Father?'

'Who follows him.'

'But surely? Won't it be . . .' Theo frowned and looked pointedly at Alexios. His father cuffed him.

'Of course, idiot. But who—' and here his father actually lowered his voice '—who will be regent? Can you at least tell me that, Theo?'

They were approaching the long tables where the highest-ranked men were taking their seats. Theo looked left and right, hoping the answer would come to him.

'You're looking the wrong way, Theo.'

His father put a hand on the back of his neck and swivelled him so he was looking at the women's tables.

As she took her seat, Agnes saw him, Theo, standing in the bright light, his hair that funny shade of deep dark red, his face burnt and freckled. She saw another man limping after him, clapping him on the back, urging him forward. That must be his father. Father and son. They were very alike – the same nose, broken; the same set to the jaw – but everything that was rough about Branas was polished in his son, like a grubby tunic that had been scrubbed and hung out to dry.

'It's a miracle you didn't faint,' Maria whispered in her ear as she sat down heavily beside her. 'Slip like you. All that raw humanity. You wobbled, sweetie, didn't you?'

'No. I didn't. I don't *wobble*. And I certainly don't faint,' said Agnes, and smiled.

Maria smiled back.

'No. All right. You don't.' She leant back. 'But I still say you look a bit peaky. Got a whiff of all the animals who've died here? All the people, too? Or is it this evening? The *first night*? There's nothing to it, sweetie.' She winked. 'How did you manage that, by the way? I thought it was all off.' She broke a piece of bread. '*Fertile*, are they, your family? Am I going to have a fat nephew gurgling in the Porphyry Chamber nine months from now?'

Agnes shot a look at her.

'I shall pray to be blessed.' She might have said more – she was tempted to ask whether Maria's children would have the right to be born in the purple – but Marguerite-Constance slipped into the chair on her other side.

'Here we all are then,' she said.

'Yes,' said Maria. 'Here we all are.'

Two lines – *men do so like nice straight lines* – began to form in front of their table, men wanting, Agnes assumed, to pay their respects to her, the bride. So busy was she making sure she tilted her head the right amount to acknowledge the precise status of each man in turn that she almost didn't notice it – and when she *did* notice it, she almost dismissed it as chance.

The men approached either from Maria's side, her left, or from Marguerite-Constance's, her right, speaking a few words to whichever of the two women they came to first before moving to congratulate her. Then they returned to their seats. The number of men who spoke to both women, both

Marguerite-Constance and Maria – those she could count on the fingers of one hand.

Some hours later, Theo was one of a phalanx of grievously drunk and badly behaved groomsmen who were escorting Alexios to the nuptial bedchamber. The dignity of the day had drained away and the eunuchs in charge were moving from disapproval to outright despair – not that they could do much about it if the best young men of the City had decided that even an emperor-to-be couldn't escape some ritual – and thoroughly un-Rôman – groom-baiting.

After much feasting, Theo was very unsteady on his feet. He and Murzuphlus were staggering along at the back, bickering about who was propping up who.

Ahead of them, the Protosebastos had an arm wrapped around his cousin's shoulders, giving him gulps of unwatered wine, stooping to whisper bedroom advice in a voice designed to be just loud enough for the others to hear. The Protosebastos might look like an elongated corpse, but he was filthy and funny, and everyone was snorting with laughter that they tried – not very hard – to stifle whenever Alexios turned round to see what was going on.

As the others bundled into the groom's robing chamber, Theo leant his forehead against the wall to stop everything spinning. The stone was cool. He took a deep breath and swivelled round, willing his legs to hold him up. A flash of gold through a door opposite and suddenly the world was sharp again.

Agnes, the bride – but very different to the trussed-up doll he'd seen at the feast. She was in a funny formal nightgown, her feet and forearms bare, her blonde hair shockingly loose. Her back was to him, but he could see her face in the looking glass.

Theo knew how girls, especially girls so very young, were meant to look on their wedding night – scared, pale, trembling.

61

Not Agnes, though. She looked determined, like she was concentrating, like a man before a big speech or a battle. She turned round and started to call out.

'Why is the door . . . ?'

She stopped – she'd seen him standing there. Their eyes met. Theo's mouth gaped, the wine hammered in his skull – then a handmaid holding two enormous hairbrushes appeared behind her and hurried to shut the door. He stumbled back towards the male laughter in the other room.

Agnes was furious. That boy, drunk doubtless – she could hardly fail to hear what was going on in the groom's room – had been gawping at her as if she were a tart in a brothel doorway. No, that wasn't quite right. There'd been something else on his face, something almost worse. What was it? *Pity.* Pity from a wine-soaked lout.

Two more maids came in to finish dressing her – not Blanche; there'd been a huge row earlier about whether she was experienced enough, which Marguerite-Constance had won – and with a jolt, Agnes realised that they all had the same look on their faces.

Pity.

She wanted to tell them not to feel sorry for her, but they were probably enjoying themselves – a nice story to tell their friends. *I prepared that poor little Latin girl for her wedding night. A slip of a thing. No mother, no sisters. So very far from home.* Agnes kept her eyes down, her hands folded – if that was to be her part, she might as well play it well – and when they were done, she whispered her thanks in her shyest voice. The women curtsied and backed out of the room, their heads tilted to one side with concern.

Now all she had to do was wait.

At last she heard the men leave her husband and caper away down the corridor. Then came silence, followed by the sound of Alexios leaving the anteroom and entering the main chamber. His footsteps approached the door to her room and swiftly retreated. She heard a rustle of material as he sat down on the bed, but he must have sprung up straight away because the footsteps started up again. This time they stopped at the far end of the room. She heard the clink of glass and something being poured.

She entered.

'Husband.' She spoke as he was lifting the drink to his lips.

'M-my lady wife.' He started towards her, then realised he was still clutching the glass and put it down on the table – carelessly as it turned out. It caught the gold-painted edge of a plate of spiced fruit and overturned. Red wine poured across the white tablecloth. He frowned, helpless, as it started to drip on to the floor.

He picked up a bell and was about to ring it.

'Why are you doing that?' Agnes asked.

'To tell them to come and clear it up.'

'There's no need. Honestly.'

And she picked up one of the napkins and began to mop up the spill.

'See?'

He watched her, amazed.

'B-but we have servants.'

'I know we have servants.'

'Then why . . . ?'

'Do you want them back in here? Laughing at us? Enjoying themselves at our expense?'

'They wouldn't d-dare.'

'Of course they would, silly. They all think it's hilarious. Two people making love for the first time is always hilarious. Especially when those two people are your master and mistress. They've all done it, maybe hundreds of times, and we haven't – so they've got one over us.'

She paused. Maybe his father had sent a kindly woman to the boy's rooms.

'You are a virgin, aren't you, Alexios?'

His blush was the only answer she needed.

September 1180

The City thundered its acclamation as the imperial household, the men, of course, took their seats high above the hippodrome. The women gathered behind the thinnest of drapes, which let in sunlight and dancing dust and the noise of tens of thousands of people high on race-day excitement, animal blood and dizzy dreams about the tight, tight clothes the tumblers wore.

Previously, Maria had taken Agnes to watch from the balcony of St Stephen's, a view every bit as good as the one from the kathisma, the imperial box. From there, Agnes would try to copy her sister-in-law's intense interest, her profound pleasure as chariot wheels locked, horses screamed, skulls smashed, winners howled and the crowd roared and roared – although the noise that shook the stones turned her stomach, made her feel sick and besieged. And then Maria would smirk at her unease and point out some little detail she might have missed, perhaps a snake of intestine dangling from the jaws of a lion.

But Maria hadn't suggested St Stephen's that afternoon. That afternoon, she had eyes only for her father.

A brisk wind stirred the drapes, giving Agnes and the other women occasional glimpses of the emperor, wrapped in a heavy cloak. Marguerite-Constance had insisted he wear it; Maria had said it would stifle him. Manuelos looked relieved when Renier offered him his arm, and walked as fast as he could, which these days meant a painfully halting shuffle, to their seats, where Alexios, who was watching the gate through which the charioteers would enter, was already waiting.

Agnes watched Manuelos lift his right hand and place it on

his son's leg. It was still there when the drapes next swirled aside, and she saw her husband staring at it, embarrassed. Agnes knew what that hand looked like. Yellowing, dry as leaves, the skin flaking away, the nails thick and furrowed.

She heard the *oohs* and *aahs* as the rope-walker, a warm-up act, danced above the arena. The applause intensified. She must be juggling up there, or standing on one leg, or pretending to nearly-nearly topple, saving herself at the last moment – teasing her audience, who loved nothing more than to see an acrobat fall.

As the cheers faded to an expectant drone, Agnes sensed something – an uncertain stir out there in the imperial box. Maria leapt up, but Marguerite-Constance was ahead of her, darting forward, tugging the drapes aside.

The emperor was on his feet, staring out over the crowds. The people hadn't noticed, not yet, but it wouldn't be long before they'd all be looking up at him, expecting an announcement, the proclamation of some kindness. Manuelos glanced behind him, blind and bewildered, then he swayed, teetered, and Agnes waited for a roar of surprise and fear as the City witnessed its emperor, God's anointed man, collapse.

But God's hand saved him. God's, or His servant Renier's. His right arm whipped out and stopped his father-in-law falling. Swiftly, gently he bore the emperor under cover.

'Father . . .'

'Husband . . .'

The two women crouched over Manuelos even as his guards tried to hold everyone back. A physician appeared – although there'd been no time for anyone to have sent for him, and Agnes realised that one must always be at hand. He ordered the emperor on to a makeshift litter, a door torn from its hinges, and the guards bore him away, Marguerite-Constance and Maria at their heels. Alexios might have followed too, but the Protosebastos put a hand out and stayed him.

'You fear for him,' Agnes heard him murmur to her husband. 'We all do. But for his sake, I advise you to stay in view until the races are done and the victor is crowned. The people will not watch in peace if they see that father and son are both absent. Back in there. Back, I beg you. You too, Renier, you too.'

And his arms went up and out and he propelled them both before him into the kathisma. Alexios glanced back at Agnes. If she'd expected him to look anxious, fearful, she was mistaken. She saw that his father's illness excited him. She turned from him and chased after Marguerite-Constance and Maria.

The main entrance to the emperor's apartments was thronged not with men of God or medicine, but with droves of astrologers, strange faces from many places, faces both shifty and plausible, an all too familiar sight since Manuelos had begun to ail.

Agnes forced her way through their ranks, the air about them rotting-sweet or rank with sweat, fearing she would find the door already barred. But Marguerite-Constance and Maria were both standing on the threshold arguing with the chief physician, white-bearded and resolute.

'Forgive me, basilissa, kaisarissa, but we must attend him in private,' he was saying. 'I will admit you as soon as we have made him comfortable.'

He slipped inside and Agnes heard a bolt clank across. Marguerite-Constance settled on a stool, but Maria was already prowling left, right, left, right, her fists tight with emotion.

'Soul-eaters. Useless pack of magicians,' she yelled suddenly at the astrologers. 'Away with you. Away. You've been lying to him. Lying!' She grabbed one of them by the collar and shook him, the rusty chains around his neck jangling. 'I'll have you all flayed if you set foot in here again.'

The astrologers, even the ones who had seemed locked in a mystical trance, nimbly vanished. Maria stood still, panting.

'A dignified performance, daughter.'

'They've been tormenting him with hope.'

'Hope – a torment?' Her voice was mild, her tone pious. 'I would rather call it a blessing.'

'A blessing for you – not for him. He is dying. *Dying.* He should be preparing for what is to come. Preparing himself and us, the empire. And instead you coddle him with—'

'With prayers, Maria. We pray. Should a wife not pray with her husband for health and long life? But maybe your ambition would have it otherwise?'

'How dare you? How . . .' Maria brought herself back under control. 'Oh, you think you can play me, do you? I love my father—'

'So you keep telling us.'

'—but to you he is nothing, *nothing* but a dying old man. And he sees it, he knows it. You can fool everyone else, but you cannot fool him. I won't let you. I—'

The doors opened and attendants rushed out, carrying basins of bile – or worse. The physician emerged next.

'Basilissa, kaisarissa.' He bowed. 'We have settled him and sent for the patriarch. He wishes to be inducted before he goes. But first he asks for his family.'

Agnes slipped behind the two women into the room's unreal twilight. Outside, a bright autumn day blustered, but in here everything smelt fusty, decayed. There he was. On the bed. He looked already more than half with God.

'Where's my son? Where's Alexios?'

That was what he was trying to say, but the words came out strange.

'He will come.'

'He is coming.'

For once, Maria and Marguerite-Constance were united. Neither of them needed the boy there.

'I can send for him,' Agnes piped up. The other two women scowled at her, but she spoke again, louder. 'I can bring your son here, basileus, if you will it.'

68

His eyes fluttered open, and to her surprise, they found her. 'My dear,' he said. 'Come here.'

She drew closer, although she could feel the other two hating her for it. He reached for her hand and she tried not to flinch away. There was something horrible about being touched by a man so close to death, even if he meant to be tender. And the smell was even harder to bear. Old milk. Old men and babies smelt the same. Curdled.

'I am leaving you earlier than I had hoped. You will be well, though. You are happy? You love my son?'

You love my son? A question? Or maybe it was a command. *You love my son.* Either way, there was only one answer.

'I do, basileus.'

'Good, good, good . . .'

His eyes shut. Pain or ghosts or dizziness – something took him away from the room. She didn't know what to do. The hand of the greatest man in the world was clenched around hers. For a moment, she feared he was dead already and the stiffness had taken him and they would have to cut his hand free – or hers. But his eyes opened and he released her. With great effort, he motioned to his body-servants to prop him up.

'You three,' he said, as if noticing them all for the first time. 'I am glad you are here. Mother, sister, wife. I entrust him to your care. He – my son – he is not strong.'

So he can admit it.

'He needs your help. You will keep him safe. You will help him grow into a good man, a good emperor. You promise? You swear?'

Marguerite-Constance chose a nod and silence, as if there could be no doubt, but Maria knew no such restraint.

'Father,' she began, too fast, too fervent. 'You are dying.'

Blunt words, but Agnes saw the distress on Maria's face and knew how weak it made her. Love, any kind of love, was dangerous. It made you vulnerable.

'You must decide,' said Maria. 'You must appoint a regent. A true Komnenos, Rôman-born. Someone who loves the empire.'

But Manuelos's face had hardened.

'Must, must, must,' he murmured.

Marguerite-Constance moved to crouch over her husband. She took his head in her arms and swayed softly.

'You are not dying. You shall get better,' she said, a sing-song croon. 'Your son, our son, will come to the throne in his prime. Beloved. Ready—'

'Don't lie to him. Stop lying. *Stop!*'

Maria shouted and her father choked. A paroxysm swept over him, his eyes popping, his skin darkening blue. Agnes expected Marguerite-Constance to order Maria from the room, to hiss *look what you've done*. Instead, she loosened his collar, mopped at his mouth, which was overwhelmed by spittle, and held water to his lips.

'Easy, easy, drink this, my poor darling.'

She didn't even look at Maria. But Manuelos did.

'Leave . . .' A word. A croak. 'Your impertinence. I cannot. Today . . . enough.' He rallied. A little colour returned to his cheeks. A very little. 'We shall talk of this later.'

'But Papa, I beg you—'

'Was your father insufficiently explicit?' the empress murmured.

Agnes watched Maria look to her father, beseeching.

'Leave us, daughter. Now. I command you to leave.'

Pink spots started on Maria's cheeks.

'But—'

'Now.'

She ran from the room, and Marguerite-Constance turned to Agnes.

'Do you possess even the most rudimentary manners? Permit a wife a private moment with her husband.'

Agnes followed Maria, to console her, to commiserate. The anteroom, however, was empty. Maria had fled. She could go after her. Or return to the imperial box. Or—

Then she saw that the door had not shut behind her. She knelt down and peered through the opening. Marguerite-Constance was leaning in close, speaking soft. Agnes had seen her sisters talking that way when they wanted their littlest children to do something but knew they would meet defiance if they pressed too hard.

'What will they say? . . . A woman . . . a westerner . . .'

Her words were faint, the emperor's fainter.

'Yes . . . yes . . . When I am going . . . So . . . so many things . . .'

'It would be safest, my darling.' Marguerite-Constance's voice was becoming more assured. 'Safest, and easier for you. To find your peace with God. That is all that matters. Your peace. Your God.'

She sank yet lower, her lips grazing his face. Nuzzling. Or nibbling. Agnes did not know how she could stand it. How *he* could stand it.

Suddenly Marguerite-Constance stood up and disappeared to the other end of the room. Agnes shifted, trying to see where she had gone. The empress returned, a writing tray in her hands. Reaching deep inside her robes, she pulled out a roll of paper. She laid it on the tray, weighting it open, and then seemed to forget about it. She opened a book – an exquisite thing, encased in what looked like ivory – and read to the emperor, quiet words of religion and prayer. She broke some fruit and held it out to him, beseeching him to eat, eat just a little.

'A spider's patience,' whispered a voice behind her.

Agnes jumped and nearly gave herself away, only relaxing when she saw it was Constantinos. He put a finger to his lips and joined her at the door.

They saw Manuelos's hand closed around a simple reed pen, and Marguerite-Constance guiding both pen and hand across the paper. The hand was released, the pen returned to its

71

stand, the tray put aside, and she began to run the backs of her fingers down the side of his face, humming, shushing. Manuelos submitted. He slipped down the bed and his eyes closed.

Constantinos tapped Agnes on the shoulder and beckoned her away from the door. She ignored him and watched Marguerite-Constance, who had been so slow, so tender, suddenly snap upright. She snatched up the paper, blew on it, read it through, once, twice, smiled, rolled it tight into a tube and—

Agnes scarcely had time to join Constantinos behind a screen before the empress swept past. At the same time, coming from the opposite direction she caught a glimpse of her husband and the Protosebastos, the patriarch and the physician, all four rushing to witness the emperor's soul crossing the threshold from life to death.

'Constantinos?'

'Yes?'

'What was that?'

'What?'

'What she left with.'

'Ah, that. That, Agnes, was her heart's desire. A chrysobull.'

'A what?'

'An imperial order naming her regent until your husband reaches his majority.'

'But that's . . .'

'Years away. Yes.'

'But that means . . .'

'Yes. Once the emperor is dead – which I imagine he will be before the sun sets – your mother-in-law will wield power over us all.'

The Second Emperor

Names, thinks Alexios, are odd.

His mother was called Marguerite-Constance until she married his father, then she was re-baptised and became Empress Maria, even though that was the same name as his half-sister. Having two Marias was so confusing, though, that in private she was always called Marguerite-Constance. But after his father died and she became a nun out of grief and piety, she took another name: Xenê, the foreigner, the stranger.

Of course, none of that makes any difference to him; he calls her Mother – or Mama if they are alone – and he always will.

He wishes his wife understood about names. Now that they are married and he is emperor, she is meant to be called Empress Anna. Agnes is a peculiar name and she ought to realise that, but she doesn't and refuses to answer when he calls her Anna. His mother told her that Anna was her name, end of discussion.

Agnes – Anna – went very quiet after that.

His name, on the other hand, will never change. In fact, he is the only Alexios amongst the hundreds of Alexioses in the City, the thousands of Alexioses in the empire, who is just plain Alexios. Everyone else is which-Alexios? Or Alexios-who? Take the two men sitting in the room.

Alexios-the-Protosebastos – see? – is his father's nephew. He's the head of the regency council, his mother's right hand in everything, and Alexios likes him very much.

He's less sure about Alexios Branas, who's been droning on about King Bela and the Magyars all morning. Alexios wishes he'd just ride off and defeat them like generals are supposed to. Now he's

talking about unfair Italian trade concessions and the need to curb
western influence and anger brewing on the street and a whole raft
of other stuff that's making his mother look out of the window and
the Protosebastos pick his fingernails.

'Basileus, what do you think?' Branas is looking hard at him. 'I
would know your mind.'

Alexios coughs. He doesn't like being looked at like that.

'I shall be guided by Mother and by the Protosebastos. In this as
in all things.'

There. That was real imperial dignity for you. His mother smiles
at him reassuringly and the Protosebastos gives him a friendly wink.
Branas gets the message – he stands, bows and leaves.

'At last,' says his mother. 'Men forget their manners if they spend
too long in the field.'

And all three of them laugh.

The spring of 1181

Agnes rode out under the trees, the air flecked with growing things swirling in the light. The branches above her head were sprinkled with buds and tiny leaves and the afternoon sun filtering through them was soft and gentle. The season was young. Everything was uncurling, unfurling, preparing for the future – everything except her.

She was holed up in a stupid country palace, miles from everything that mattered, stranded with a husband who'd pretend his own nose wasn't stuck on the front of his face if that was what suited him.

Don't be too long, my love. Mother is coming to visit us this evening. She wishes to consult me about some important affairs of state. We must be ready for her.

That was what he'd said before she set off – the latest in a long, long string of statements so naïve, so blind, so stupid that she could no longer listen to him without wanting to stick her fingers in her ears, scream *la la la* or pelt him with anything that came to hand.

It had begun straight away after Manuelos died.

Marguerite-Constance announced that her son's colour was poor, his wheezing worrisome, and sent for a glittering pack of physicians who put their heads together and decided the young emperor needed better air. And better air turned out to mean banishment to Philopation, a pretty prison buried in woodland beyond the north-west walls of the City.

Agnes had tried being subtle.

77

Alexios, husband, is not your place in the City where all your ministers can find you easily?

Mother says the empire depends upon my health. I must not risk it.

She'd tried being direct, tried proving to him that his mother wanted him out of the way, but it was like punching a swamp. He wouldn't argue back. If she said something he didn't like, he'd pretend not to hear. That was his trouble. He'd never wanted for anything, so he couldn't admit his life wasn't perfect. It meant there was a blankness about him – like some of the immaculate rooms in the Blachernai Palace that felt like they'd never been lived in.

She'd tried being cruel to shock him into understanding, but he liked her cruelty. The angrier she was, the more he revelled in it. He looked wan, wrote her poems, brought her presents – impossibly rich, impossibly beautiful, impossibly stupid presents. Flocks of birds that covered her room in shit. Mounds of flowers that rotted and stank. Jewellery so heavy it rubbed her skin raw.

She sighed as she turned her horse for home.

He was probably thinking of some ridiculous gift now. After he'd told her Marguerite-Constance was on her way, she'd snapped something about *that old cow coming to gloat* before marching off to the stables. She knew she was becoming careless – in spite of everything Constantinos had said to her.

He'd knocked on her door a few days after Manuelos's funeral and told her he was being reassigned to a minor clerical post in a minor town in a minor province. He said he'd come to wish her goodbye and good luck. She'd laughed.

I wouldn't be laughing if I were you. You're going to have to watch your back, Agnes. And what you eat and drink.

She'd asked if he was joking, but he said he wasn't.

She won't poison you. Not straight out. Most likely she'll drug you and you'll know nothing of it until you wake up naked with a pretty little serving boy in your bed and poor Alexios staring down at his adulterous bride.

A black something buzzed past her, tangling for a moment with the fringes of her headdress. She whisked her head from side to side and it vanished. Then she saw it between her horse's ears, a massive bristling insect, a hornet. She flashed at it with her sleeve. It returned and she batted it again. It whirled in madness and burrowed into her horse's neck. The animal squealed, shied and bucked her off.

She wasn't hurt. She was fine. She brushed aside her attendants and told them to forget about it, but soon after she reached her rooms, Alexios rushed in.

'They told me what happened. I said you should not ride. I said it was dangerous.'

'It's perfectly safe. A fly bit my horse and it threw me. It's nothing.'

Once upon a time, she'd have loved being fussed over. She'd probably have turned the accident into a drama that would have kept her at the centre of attention for days, but now the prospect of Alexios's tender ministrations was too exasperating.

'It's nothing,' she repeated. 'Really, I'm fine. Look, they've laid out food. Join me.'

'Thank you, yes, in a moment I shall,' he said and vanished.

She shrugged and started to pick at the meal in front of her. Which meal was it? There were so many. Too much sweet food and never enough plain bread and meat. She never felt the stab of hunger that made a meal worth savouring, not when she was constantly tempted by little treats – almond and honey cakes, plum jam to eat straight from a spoon, things she'd have killed for when she was little.

She prodded her arms. She was turning into a fat petted animal, its teeth and claws filed down, its coat clipped close, a tiny silver leash about its neck.

A servant appeared and begged leave to escort her into the emperor's presence. His face was absolutely impassive and she knew there was no point asking what it was about, so she traipsed along the corridors and out into the courtyard.

She stopped, stared. There in the slanting sunshine, her horse lay in a growing pool of dark red blood, a sword stuck upright in its throat. Alexios stood at its side.

'What have you done?' she gasped.

'I did it for you. Nothing shall harm you. Ever. I give you my word.'

He opened his arms to embrace her. There was a smudge of blood on his cheek. He must have wiped his hand there. He was sweating, from exertion, from excitement, she did not know.

'Thank you, husband.'

'Shall we retire? It grows hot. We should rest before Mother arrives with the court.'

Shall we retire? That was his cue for lovemaking – or his version of it. An hour of fondling sighs that led nowhere. Had the sight of blood made him think of it? Or the thought of his mother? She was about to find a way to refuse him, but then she thought she'd rather have everything sweet when Marguerite-Constance appeared. She wouldn't give her the satisfaction of thinking they'd quarrelled.

An hour later, Agnes crept out from under the sheets, tense, sticky and determined to forget about everything that had happened that day. *A bath, yes.* Her body-women would rub aloe salve into her limbs, coil her hair and paint her eyes. They would clasp golden jewellery, beaten as thin as her own skin, about her wrists and throat, and hold up the looking glass, which would be as kind and reassuring as ever.

She did it all and enjoyed doing it. Who didn't like the feel of silk, the look of gold against their skin? But as Alexios escorted her into the dining chamber, a relatively intimate affair with couches for no more than two score and ten, she knew she need not have troubled herself, not that evening, not ever again.

Nobody gave her a second look.

A few guests – the dullest, the most leaden – knelt before her, but even their eyes swerved away, hunting her mother-in-law. Marguerite-Constance – or Xenê as they all called her now – was wearing plain-spun, shapeless, colourless clothes with a pious manner to match, and the men loved it. She was besieged not only by aristos from the old Rôman families, primped and perfumed, but also by a new breed of courtier – westerners who cut their hair short and talked loudly about killing filthy Saracens.

Marguerite-Constance didn't flirt, of course she didn't, but Agnes watched her allot each man a moment in the sun before turning her back and smiling her pure, serene smile at the next man and the next.

She saw Alexios leave his mother's side and weave through the crowd towards her. She ran out into the night without looking back.

She wasn't sure where her feet had carried her until she stumbled across the stablemaster, down on his knees, scrubbing at the red stain on the ground. He looked up – maybe he'd heard her coming – but he was in a pool of torchlight and she was in darkness. She darted into the stable block and sat down in an empty stall.

For once, nobody knew where she was.

The thought cheered her immensely. She kicked her legs out. She rubbed some mud on the back of her hand and looked at it. She splashed the water bucket and talked a few filthy words of Latin. It felt good – until she heard footsteps and wondered what she'd say if a pair of grooms found her sitting there. Hopefully they'd go somewhere else. Hopefully they'd . . . but no, they were coming closer.

'This one's empty,' a man's voice said. Not a groom. An aristo voice.

She saw two silhouettes as they passed inside. One a man, very tall. The other a woman. Agnes's cheeks started to burn.

There was only one reason why a man and a woman would creep into an empty stable. The scent of horse and hay vanished, replaced by something that she knew and hated. Orange-water.

It was Marguerite-Constance.

They did not speak. The man bent Marguerite-Constance over a manger and began to thud backwards and forwards. It was love, she supposed, but like animals. The noises Marguerite-Constance made were animal-like too. An animal surprised or in great pain. Suddenly, with no change in rhythm, the man – who had been silent as the stars all the way through – gave a low grunting moan. They broke apart and Marguerite-Constance laughed, a deep, rich, happy sound that seemed to come from another woman entirely.

They had barely left the stables when Agnes was seized by a bout of giggling. She had to bury her face in the straw to stop herself crowing out loud. As soon as she'd calmed down, though, she knew that what she'd seen was, above all else, useful – if only she knew who the man was. She began to pick the straw from the hem of her dress, picturing the men at the party and trying to conjure up their voices.

Straw.

She hurried back to the hall.

'Where've you been?' Alexios was dithering near the entrance, obviously looking for her.

'The . . . the chapel. Forgive me, I remembered it was my mother's name day and I wanted to say extra prayers for her.' A sinfully bad lie, but one she knew he'd like to believe. 'Come, husband, let us sit over there. In the middle of the room. I do not think I recognise all of our guests. You can tell me their names, all about them.'

In the end she didn't need his help. She didn't know who she was expecting to see with a little mud and straw clinging to their indoor boots, but when she spotted him, it was a shock.

The Protosebastos. Marguerite-Constance's nephew – not by blood maybe, but her nephew nonetheless. It was more than a scandal, it was an abomination.

She shut her ears to Alexios and thought furiously. What should she do? Should she tell someone? Who could she tell?

Maria. I'll tell Maria. She's my friend. She hates Marguerite-Constance. Agnes glanced at her husband. *But she hates him, too.*

She weighed the choice like a stone in her hand. She could lay her knowledge aside and return to her life of spoon-sweets, silk cushions and suffocating boredom. Or she could act.

The autumn of 1181

The Magyars were on the run.

Theo wished he'd had a hand in it, but his father had kept him out of the main engagement – and Mikhail had collared him when he'd tried to sneak away from the command post. *Orders, boy.* Theo ducked, but the clip round the ear didn't come. *You're too big to hit, I reckon,* said the soldier with a grin that Theo refused to return. And now his father was ringed by his aides-de-camp, each trying to outdo the next with their congratulations.

'We showed those upstart dogs, General.'

'The barbarian oath-breakers will rue the day, General.'

'Bela's barbarian tail is between his barbarian legs, General.'

The fight, Theo knew, had been more personal than the usual border policing. Manuelos had fostered the Magyar king as a boy. The emperor had raised him, educated him, *civilised* him. Once, there'd even been talk that Bela – the same barbarian dog they were all so busy cursing – would wed Maria and become the old man's heir. But that was before the empress had her boy and everything changed. Instead, Bela accepted Marguerite-Constance's half-sister as a bride and promised not to make trouble. He'd filled his wagons with enough gold to make even the most cynical think he might keep his word.

But he didn't.

He'd tried to take a bite out of the empire's northern marches, where they bordered his own lands, and he might have succeeded, too, if it hadn't been for General Alexios

Branas – who, Theo realised, was now standing right in front of him.

'Off you go, then.' His father was pointing down at one of the reserve units, a light-armed cavalry tagma, a band of mopper-uppers. 'Ride with them.'

Theo didn't need to be told twice. He vaulted on to his horse, the way he'd always imagined he would, and set off in pursuit of stragglers. His father must have reckoned the Magyars would be running too fast for his son to get into trouble, but Theo had other ideas.

He set his sights on a rider who was falling behind a pack of fleeing enemy fighters. One of the horse's hind legs was lamed, and however frantically the rider brought the flat of his sword down on its rump, the beast had nothing more to give. For the first time, Theo felt blood hunger in his throat.

You're mine.

Ahead, the Magyar chanced a look over his shoulder, and Theo caught a flash of his face. A boy, no older than he was, beardless and terrified. Theo hated him for it. He wanted his first kill to be a man.

His own horse, crack-trained and fresh, held its gallop, but the boy's was beginning to stagger. Theo didn't want him to fall and break his neck before he could kill him, so he pushed himself high in his stirrups and swung his sword – too soon. The momentum of his hasty stroke nearly whirled him out of the saddle.

The Magyar pulled ahead. *You've got to want it more, Theo.* That was what his father always told him. *Wanting tips a fight.* He kneed his horse onwards. *I want it, I want it.*

His blade landed between the boy's shoulders. There was no chain under the shirt, only a bit of leather that gave way immediately. The boy arched and collapsed on to his horse's flank, pulling it round into Theo's path. Before he could slow down, before he could turn, the animals collided.

He must have been flung clear, otherwise he would be dead.

That was all Theo knew as he scrabbled in the mud. He hauled himself to his knees, to his feet. He was shaking. His legs were weak. The screams of a dying horse were loud in his ears. The boy was tangled between its hooves. His own mount was nowhere to be seen. The screaming. He had to make it stop. He hacked at the beast's throat until there was silence.

Tears started in his eyes and he breathed in and out, hard and slow, horrified at how close he'd come to death, how easily it might have been him lying broken in the dirt.

He turned and saw – thank God – a pack of riders on the ridge above him. He waved, hallooed – and dropped his arm almost as soon as he'd lifted it. The riders weren't Rômans. They were Magyars, three of them, the dregs of Bela's army. They must have been hiding out until the imperial troops had dispersed, and were now heading for whatever shelter there was in these scrublands.

Had they seen him? Even if they had, would they bother to turn aside? For two heartbeats, Theo thought he might be safe. The two lead riders were past him, heads down, driving their animals hard. But the third wheeled round and bore down on him, pike aloft. Running was futile. Theo dropped to the ground, balled himself against the dead horse and squeezed his eyes shut, a childish impulse he despised.

The pike split his side. He gasped, tried to control the pain, the panic – the need to make it not have happened – and then he could control himself no more. He howled and thrashed –

– and must have lost consciousness.

Suddenly, it was night. His body was stretched out before him, silvered by the moon, so for a moment he thought he was looking at his own ghost. Only the pain made him real. Clutching his side, made squeamish by what he felt there, he lumbered to his feet. He begged his legs to move. He had to drag himself back to the camp – or bleed to an end right there on the plain.

Singing. A halo of light and voices in the night air. He feared that meant the end until something scalded the inside of his nose. *Latrines.* Angels didn't dig latrines. Of course. The singing was the trisagion, the evening hymn to the Trinity. He was nearly there. He bit down on the stench of shit. Leant into it. Bathed in it. Gulped it into his guts and covered the last fifty paces to the camp gates.

'Password?'

The night curfew had begun.

'Holy Cross?' he croaked.

'That was yesterday's, mate. Kip down there till dawn. Your commander can vouch for you then.'

The sentry gestured to where half a dozen men were lying wrapped in horse blankets near a fire. Theo knew that if he lay down, nobody but the saints would be able to vouch for him. The urgency of his pain had gone. All that remained was a dangerous submissiveness.

I'm dying. That wouldn't impress the sentry. Men died. Especially no-account mud-caked boys caught on the wrong side of the palisade at nightfall.

'I . . . I'm son to Alexios Branas.'

The man thrust a torch at him.

'So you are.' A grin spread across his face. 'The old man'll be pleased. Word was you'd gone down. Here—' that to a dozing messenger boy '—run to the general's tent.'

'I can go . . .' Theo tried to speak.

'No you can't. No offence, mate, but I don't think you're going nowhere.'

Three days later, or at least three long sleeps later, it might have been longer than three days, Theo lay – *out of mischief,* as Mikhail said – on a makeshift bed screened off in a corner of his father's tent, comfortably reeling in and out of thought.

Victory, a victory he could claim to have played a part in, victory and his first proper wound, very different from any

87

of his previous knocks and bruises. His side complained most satisfyingly whenever he twisted and turned under the blankets. It had been poulticed and bandaged and he fancied he was going to have one spectacular scar once he could unwrap it.

From his bed, he'd heard his father saying Bela had got what he deserved. That was in public, though. In private – and private meant when sitting quietly at Theo's side – Branas said he didn't blame Bela or anyone else for trying to take a bite out of the empire. Of course everyone – north, south, east, west – had agreed that the boy Alexios would rule unopposed, but they might as well have been promising that elephants would dance on the Column of Justinian. It just wasn't going to happen.

There'll be more like Bela, Theo, more and more – so long as the boy looks weak.

Theo wasn't sure whether to be pleased or not. Another campaign would keep him fighting, which of course was what he wanted. It would also keep him away from the City, which might be what his father preferred, but Theo was starting to realise that maybe he wanted something different. The City fogged his head, confused him. He didn't know its rules, but it also excited him.

He swung his feet out and stuck them in a pair of boots, then pulled back the curtain, an invalid no longer.

He was confronted by a very unmilitary object – a portly man, bundled up in layers of clothes, coughing delicately and sipping what looked like his father's last bottle of proper Chios wine.

'Theo, this is Constantinos. I thought he was doing penance in the east. It seems, however, that he's here.'

Theo nodded. A court eunuch. Precisely the kind of person who made the City so confusing.

'Thank you for your warm welcome, Branas. Yes, I am here. Although why you fighting men have to conduct your business in such inaccessible and—' he coughed '—inclement corners of the world remains a mystery to me.'

'Don't try that on me, Constantinos. I know you can ride as hard as any scout. And on less food too.'

'Maybe,' said the eunuch with a twitch of a smile. 'But don't let on to anyone, will you?'

'So, what brings you here? Out with it.'

'As you said, officially, I am in the east. Unofficially, I have an important message for you.'

'You've been busy.'

'I am always busy in the service of the empire, Branas, the same as you. First things first. This is your boy? You trust him? He doesn't talk?'

Theo bristled, but his father calmed him. 'He is my flesh.'

'Very well. I am here to tell you what's been going on in the City while you've been doing its work far away. The men of the court have been like hogs at a trough, clambering over each other, fighting to show the beautiful widow a good time.'

'We'd heard all that,' said Branas. 'My wife writes. She said Marguerite-Constance would have none of them.'

'Wrong. She's been screwing the Protosebastos.'

'*Him?*' Theo pictured the tall, pale, languid man – with resin plaques where his own teeth had rotted away. 'Why'd she take him?'

'I can only suppose he has his membrum virile to thank, Theo. It's priapic. Everyone has their weakness. I never imagined this would be Marguerite-Constance's, but there you have it. The empire's being run from the bedroom of a man whose chief qualification is the length and breadth of his cock. Not good, Theo, not good.'

Branas put his hand up. 'But how the hell did anyone find out? She's not stupid. I'd have thought she'd have been more careful.'

'Maria got wind of it,' said Constantinos, 'but she refuses to say how.'

'A spy in her household?'

The eunuch shook his head. 'All the people close to Marguerite-Constance came with her from Antioch. I have my suspicions, but no more. Nevertheless, Maria has worked fast and worked thoroughly. She's gathered enough proof and is ready to blast her stepmother's reputation.'

'And the boy – the emperor? Does he know?'

'He does not. He hunts. Or tries to. And moons about after the Empress Anna. A man in love with his own wife. It's comic.'

'What about the administration?'

His father meant the bureaucrats, the shadowy men who ran things – with pens not swords.

'The administration will weigh up—'

'You mean they will dither,' Theo interrupted.

Constantinos raised an eyebrow.

'We can't all be brisk and decisive like you soldiers, boy. The administration thinks in terms of decades, not days. They raise the taxes that fund your adventures and they make the City a marvel for you to admire on your return.'

'And they dither,' said his father.

'Granted. But they are not emotional. They will not turn their backs on Marguerite-Constance because she climbed into the wrong bed. What would they say? *Manuelos ordered Marguerite-Constance to act as regent and technically she hasn't arrogated unto herself any powers not judicially apportioned.*'

'That's fucking ridiculous,' said Branas.

'It is, and that is why I am here.'

'To ask me to fight? I cannot leave the front. I cannot put the empire's security at risk. I won't do it.'

'You won't have to,' said Constantinos. 'As it turned out, the province I was exiled to shared a border with Paphlagonia.'

He left a significant pause. Theo had no idea why. Branas looked blank, too, but not for long.

'Ah. So you are, in fact, here on behalf of . . . ?'

'Exactly. He is ready. He only needs your assurance that if he marches, it will be with your approval. He remembers your friendship. He does not want you as an enemy.'

'And Maria, does she know about this?'

'She does. She sent to him herself. But I fear she misunderstands his intentions.'

'I see,' said his father.

I don't, thought Theo.

'Maria has taken to reminding all and sundry that it would not be the first time a daughter followed her father on to the throne. Historically speaking, that is perfectly accurate.'

Theo's father shook his head decisively.

'Exchanging sister for brother so soon after their father's death. No. It would not play well on the frontiers. Nor in the City.'

'I agree.'

'A new regent, on the other hand . . .'

'A better solution by far. But he needs your blessing.'

'My blessing . . .' Branas frowned. 'Give me a moment alone, Constantinos. I need to think without your eyes needling me.'

The eunuch smiled, bowed and withdrew.

'I thought I'd never see him again,' his father said. 'Seems I thought wrong.'

'Who, Father? You neither of you said who.'

'Of all the men in the empire, he is the boy's best hope. But he is—'

'Who, Father? *Who?*'

'Andronikos.'

Theo stared. Andronikos was a legend, the hero of all the best stories. Even better, he was a hero who had disappeared from the City before Theo had grown up, so he did not know the man, only his reputation. And it was a reputation every boy wished to have as his own – a great fighter, a great rebel *and* a great lover.

His father smiled. 'You look pleased, son. You would follow Andronikos?'

'Rather him than Marguerite-Constance.'

'I agree with you. Constantinos!'

The eunuch returned. 'Brisk and decisive as ever. What is your answer?'

'My answer is yes. On one condition. Take my boy with you and recommend him to Andronikos.'

'You want your own eyes and ears at court, Branas?' asked the eunuch.

'I want my son to learn what Andronikos can teach.'

The spring of 1182

'Where is she? Where's the Latin whore?'

Agnes hurtled into her room and shut the door behind her as quick and quiet as she could. *They don't mean me. They don't mean me.* Panting hard, her back pressed to the wall, she listened to a dozen pairs of boots thundering up the hallway. *It's her they're looking for.* Agnes could tell herself that as many times as she liked, but she was still terrified. *Don't panic. Hide.*

She looked about her. Behind the washstand? In the chest? The crash of a something being upended in another room sent her diving under the bed. She wriggled as close as possible to the wall and peered out. *No good. You've got to do better than that.*

She reached forward and tugged the bedspread after her, hoping it'd screen her from the soldiers – at least she assumed they were soldiers, although they looked nothing like the grand regiments she saw about the City – who were running amok through Philopation. She sneezed – it was dusty – and nearly screamed at the sound of something heavy shattering on the marble floor outside.

She lay still and – when she wasn't busy praying that nobody would think to look under the bed – wondered whether telling Maria about the Protosebastos hadn't been a colossal mistake.

And it hadn't even been easy.

Marguerite-Constance kept her so secluded that it was Ascension before Agnes had her chance. She and Maria had been processing side by side down streets scattered with pine and hung with wreaths of ivy and bay, myrtle and rosemary. The scent made her bold.

What are you going to do, Maria?

Oh, you may be sure I'll do something. It might take a while, that's all. I need time to think, and these sorts of wheels can turn slow. Then she'd looked at her strangely. *Why did you tell me, Agnes?*

Her. I want her . . .

Dead?

No! No. I want her out of my life.

And what about your husband? My little brother? Do you want him out of your life as well?

A slow, steady thump of fear – fear for herself; fear for what she had done – had drowned out the noise of the crowds and she'd seen that behind the cross she was carrying, a beautiful cross woven out of roses, Maria was laughing.

Don't worry, Agnes. I'll take good care of you. You see if I don't.

And that was the last she'd seen of her.

In the weeks and months that followed, there'd been clues, hints that something was brewing, and Agnes knew that Marguerite-Constance sensed it too. Her mother-in-law might try to hide her unease, but a host of tiny imperfections – stale breath, ragged thumbnails, a sore weeping on her lower lip – betrayed her.

Outside the voices grew louder, uglier, and Agnes pressed herself to the floor.

'Bitch can't hide forever.'

'Sniff her out, sniff her out.'

Maria's move had come at last.

The merchant ship Theo and Constantinos had hitched a ride on in Thessalonikê was hove to a few hundred yards off the docks that lined the Golden Horn.

The sun, not far off setting, sent their spindly shadows teetering down the deck and only the lightest breeze ruffled the ripples that slapped the boat's side. A perfect dusk. Peaceful, radiant — the sort of homecoming a soldier deserved after months of fighting in the wilderness. The Great Chain that barred the harbour entrance in times of trouble was nowhere to be seen.

Theo was about to turn away and gather his few belongings while the crew readied the boat to stand in to shore, when Constantinos put a hand on his shoulder.

'Look.'

He followed Constantinos's finger. A pall of smoke hung above the masts and rooftops, but it wasn't the haze of hearth and forge. The merchants' quarter, the string of warehouses and wharfs owned and run by westerners, was ablaze.

'Coincidence?' Theo ventured, although he knew it wasn't.

'He moves fast. It has begun.'

An uncomfortable thought struck Theo. 'How did he know my father would agree?'

'Andronikos has a habit of guessing right. That is why he is Andronikos.'

Crash!

The door to the room Agnes was hiding in burst open. But instead of thick-soled nailed boots, she saw painted cowhide slippers pattering in circles out on to the balcony, back inside, over to the chest. It was her husband, scurrying about like a cornered dormouse.

'Barricade the door,' she hissed.

'What? Who?'

'The door, block it, quick.'

'Agnes?'

'Yes. Me. Under the bed.'

'What are you doing under there?'

'Hiding, you idiot.'

'Agnes. You shouldn't speak to me like that. I'm the emperor and—'

'You're about to hide in a chest. I'll call you what I like. Come on, help me.'

She squirmed out from under the bed and started to shove the chest in front of the door, fear bubbling in her throat.

'Stop, Agnes, it's too heavy.'

'Well, what's your plan? God help us, you're not even armed.' She glared at him. 'Where's your sword?'

'It's . . . it's in the armoury.'

'That's no use! What are we going to do when they find us? Chuck cushions at them? Come on – help.'

Together they lugged the chest in front of the door, flinching as it screeched and scraped over the floor. They took a step back.

'We need to get out the window. We need to get away from here.'

'Where to?'

'I don't know. Anywhere there aren't armed men running around smashing everything to pieces. What's going on? Are they after us? Or are they just looting? What's happening?' She was shaking him by the shoulders. 'What's happening?'

But all he could do was shake his head. 'I don't know. I don't know. I swear to God I don't know.'

As the sun sank lower, Theo watched boat after boat, from little coasters to deep-hulled merchant ships as big as the one on which he stood, peel off from the dockside and strike out into the Bosporus. Every one was crammed, heaving with westerners clinging to the rigging, to ropes trailing astern, scrabbling up the sides, trying to clamber on deck.

He couldn't believe it when he heard their captain giving orders to make for shore – he hadn't pegged him as a hero. Then almost immediately he laughed at himself. The captain wasn't a hero; he was a man of business. Anyone he plucked from the harbour would have fistfuls of gold stashed under his cloak, and he'd be able to take a hefty cut once he'd got them safe out to sea.

The crowd saw that a boat was approaching and surged towards it, a blur of desperate faces. Theo fought his way to shore, clearing a path for Constantinos, trading punches, whatever he had to do to stop them being pushed back on board. Together they dodged through the harbour gate and out on to the main thoroughfare behind the sea wall.

Immediately a man, a City tanner by the smell of him, had Theo by the shirt front, roaring red-mad filth in his face and trying to drive a dagger into his belly. Theo caught his wrist, disarmed him and spat good Greek curses in his face.

'What the fuck is going on?'

'Bit of spring-cleaning, brother. There's an army here doing for Manuelos's Latin bitch, and we're wiping out the rest of the Latin scum. Grasping miser merchant roaches.' The man wrenched free from Theo's grip and ran off, roaring over his shoulder, 'Join us! Slit open their money bags and make them choke on their gold.'

Theo looked round, expecting to find Constantinos in serious need of help, but two City men lay writhing at his feet and a third was running away fast, one arm hanging at a hideous angle.

'You can fight?'

'Don't look so surprised, boy. I was born on rougher streets than these. I'd have you begging for mercy if it ever came to that.'

Theo was about to tell him he was ready any time when a woman's screams erupted behind them. She was being dragged out of a house by two men, her clothes ripped, her face bloody. The house had been torched and flames were roaring into the twilight sky.

Theo charged and kicked the two men off her. They ran for it – plenty of easier prey. He started to help her to her feet, but she bit his wrist and darted back through the burning doorway.

A face appeared at a window on the second storey, a little storeroom, a safe hiding place. It was a boy, no more than five or six. His mouth was open, shrieking and shrieking for his mother. Then he disappeared and there was nothing in the window but flames. A gnawing, wrenching, splitting sound and the house collapsed, burying the woman, the boy and God alone knew who else inside. Theo started towards it.

'Don't be a fool.'

The eunuch was pulling him away.

'Get your hands off me.'

'We have to get out of here. Right now. Come on. You've seen worse. You're a soldier, aren't you?'

'It's not right. Here in the City. It's not right.'

'It's war, Theo, war like any other.'

Thud!

A boot – or something else heavy – battered the door. The wood splintered but the chest stopped it opening. Men cursed each other. *In the fucking way . . . the fuck rid of it . . . hurry the fuck up.* Agnes just had time to see an axe-blade appear through the back of the door before she grabbed her husband and hauled him under the bed.

For a moment everything went quiet outside – she and Alexios might have been playing make-believe – but then the door split open and a dozen soldiers burst into the room. They started grabbing things, her things, shoving anything of value into sacks, chucking clothes, linen, whatever they didn't fancy on to the floor. Agnes held her breath. Maybe they'd take what they wanted and leave, move on to the next room. Maybe she'd be all right.

One of them stopped right in front of the bed, breathing heavily. She could see the toes of his boots. Was he going to look down? Was he going to find them? No, she realised he must be looking at the icon, the Theotokos, the Mother of God, hanging above her bed. It was beautiful, painted, real, a piece of His beauty and grace, a wedding gift from Manuelos. *She will watch over you.*

The man stepped up on to the bed to rip it from the wall. Agnes tensed as the bed creaked under his weight. He jumped, but must have missed. He swore and jumped again. The planks gave way and his boot plunged between them. Agnes screamed, Alexios screamed, and all three of them were tangled in a mess of broken wood, sheets and limbs.

The other men reacted fast. Two pinned Alexios against the wall; another hauled her clear of the debris, gripping her elbows. She shook him off, but he grabbed her tighter, twisting her arms behind her back.

'Ow!' she screamed. 'Get off me, you brute.'

If they were going to kill her, fine, but they'd have to get on with it – she wasn't going to be manhandled by an oaf who stank. She squirmed, furious, but that only made him laugh, so she stopped fighting and went completely limp, as if she'd fainted. His hold relaxed and she flopped to the floor. She counted to five, then sprang up and darted towards the door.

I'm through. I'm through.

But a man was blocking her way, a tall man who took her arms easily and whose grip did not slacken no matter what she did. His face was in shadow, but she could tell he wasn't another soldier. He let go of her hands and she backed away into the room. He followed, stepping over the wreckage of the door.

A pair of grey eyes looked her over. Grey eyes set in the most perfect face she had ever seen. Eyes the colour of iron, a shade or two darker than the slate-grey of his hair. She was standing open-mouthed, stupid as a peasant girl gawping from a hayfield when the comte's eldest son rides past. She pulled herself together.

'Who are you and what on earth gives you the right to march into my chamber?'

It was a ridiculous thing to say when the room was already full of sweating, grimy intruders.

'You'll learn that I have every right,' he replied, and turned to Alexios, who was cringing like a puppy. 'Cousin, well met!' Her husband practically yelped as he found himself caught up in the man's embrace. 'But forgive me, family feeling has overridden protocol. Allow me to kiss your hand and call you my emperor.'

'Y-your emperor?' Alexios stuttered.

'Yes,' said the man. 'You are Alexios Komnenos, are you not? Son of Manuelos, son of John, son of Alexios? You'd better be. I'd kill any other man before I bowed my head to him.'

'I am. Yes, I am.' Alexios looked like he wanted to deny it all and run from the room.

'Splendid. I am sorry that my misunderstandings with your father stopped us meeting sooner, but I am here now and I shall fulfil my oath to him.'

'Y-your oath?'

'If anyone dishonours you, I am to destroy them – or words to that effect. The original was rather more delicately expressed.'

Agnes's eyes widened.

'You're Cousin Andronikos!'

'Indeed.'

Alexios, if anything, looked even more desperate to bolt.

'But who,' Andronikos said, swivelling towards her, 'is this? You keep strange company, cousin. This creature has no manners and speaks our noble tongue like a barbarian.'

'Like a *what*?' Admittedly, her Greek wasn't perfect, but she was proud of how fluent she'd become. 'You are the barbarian – yes, you. So these soldiers are acting on your orders, are they? Ransacking the palace, mauling the emperor. You . . . you ought to be ashamed of yourself.' She paused. 'And I'm not a creature. I am the Empress Anna, and you'd better start kissing my hand as well.'

She thrust her right arm into the empty air between them.

'Agnes,' Alexios squeaked, 'don't, for God's sake. Andronikos, cousin, please meet my wife.'

'Your wife? I see you really are in need of my guidance. Even in the most elementary matters. You should never have stood by while I insulted her.'

His words were cold and Agnes knew immediately why men feared him. But then he smiled and the moment vanished, as impossible to remember as seasickness once you were safe ashore.

'Empress Anna,' he said, 'forgive me. The heat of the moment. You are of course right to insist on the correct courtesies.'

And he bent his head over her hand and kissed it. She felt the faintest scrape as his beard brushed her knuckles. Involuntarily her left hand clasped the right as he stood back up.

'Now that the introductions are over, to business. Stephanos!'

A truly hideous man walked in. His face was eaten up by some pox which a straggly beard, such an ugly yellow that it looked almost green, failed to hide. Half of his nose had been hewn off, so he looked like a malevolent pig, and he had a rag pressed against a fresh cut down one cheek. Andronikos laughed at their faces.

'Meet Stephanos Hagiochristophorites. He isn't pretty, I admit, but you'll get used to him. Remember the Lord Jesus Christ kept company with lepers, so who are we to judge? Well, Stephanos?'

The man smirked. 'We've got her, boss.'

'Put up a fight, did she?'

Stephanos rubbed his cheek and looked at the blood that came off on his hands. 'You can say that again. Sharp nails and not afraid to use them.' He looked over at Alexios. 'Can't say I see much of a family resemblance.'

'W-what do you mean? Who've you got?'

'Good news, Alexios,' said Andronikos, clapping him on the

shoulder. 'The pernicious whore who has been working night and day to undermine you is in custody.'

Alexios looked blank. 'You mean Maria?'

'No,' said Andronikos. 'I do not mean Maria. Maria was a devoted daughter, remains a loving sister and will always be a loyal servant of the empire.'

Alexios's brow furrowed. Andronikos was obviously enjoying waiting for him to understand, but Agnes couldn't bear to look at his stupid, baffled face any longer.

'Your mother, husband, he's talking about your mother.'

The whole City was looking for Andronikos, but nobody knew where he was. Nobody apart from Constantinos. Theo listened as he asked questions of men and women they passed, some great, some insignificant, and their answers seemed to guide him.

'How do you . . . ?' Theo began.

'The City is easy to read if you only know how. Men who stand to gain from trouble have a keener nose than your aristo who is worried about what he is going to lose. Fear makes men flap. And it's hard to think and flap. Never flap, Theo. Think. Always think.'

And so it proved. Theo saw familiar faces rushing south to the Great Palace or turning aside to Blachernai, but Constantinos led them out through the gates to Philopation. The chaos in the courtyard and outer chambers lessened as they wound towards a room on the second floor guarded by a dozen soldiers. The eunuch exchanged a few words with their leader, a man with a blighted face, who opened the door and followed them in. Theo saw the back and broad shoulders of a tall man.

'Andronikos,' said Constantinos.

He turned and Theo took him in. Was it wrong to be so struck by another man's looks? Wrong or not, Theo immediately knew why so many women – the greatest beauties, the richest heiresses – had disgraced themselves and their families for his sake. It wasn't his height – other men were as tall. The unrepentant years showed themselves everywhere. His eyes were not wise. His mouth was not kind. But his presence was undeniable. He possessed the air around him – as totally as he now possessed the City itself.

'Constantinos.' A nod. No other pleasantries. 'Tell me, friend, what word from the general?'

Theo had prepared a small speech, a nonchalance. He wanted this man to be conscious of the honour his father, the Branas family, did by pledging their support. But the words evaporated unspoken. He did not know what to say.

The eunuch made a small introductory gesture towards Theo.

'Here is his answer.'

Theo felt Andronikos's attention pass to him.

'Ah, it is good news, I see.' Andronikos placed a hand on his shoulder and smiled, excluding the other two men in the room. 'I don't need to ask who you are, young man. You are Theodore. It's like I am a boy of eighteen again and Alexios Branas is standing before me. I am glad to know you.'

What had he been worried about? Of course this man valued him and his father. Theo's heart glowed and the words – the *right* words – came easily.

'My father recommends me to you,' he said, 'and asks that you take me into your service.'

'Nothing would give me greater pleasure.'

Andronikos tipped his head to one side and looked more closely at Theo.

'What? Out with it. There's something else you want to say.'

Theo swallowed.

'Still mind-reading, Andronikos?' murmured Constantinos.

'I read men, not minds,' he countered. 'Which is why you remain a happy enigma to me, Constantinos.'

The eunuch chuckled.

'You're right. The boy's aching to tell you something.'

'Andronikos, sir . . .' In an empire of titles, he had no idea what to call this man. 'I thought I should tell you. The City mob is ransacking the docks. They're after Latin blood. I would be happy to take a detachment of your troops to restore order.'

He hoped he sounded manly and decisive, but Constantinos rolled his eyes and the other man snickered. Only Andronikos nodded as if to say *yes, yes, absolutely, I understand*, and for a wild and happy moment Theo thought he was going to agree. But when he spoke, it was regretfully.

'There are one or two problems with that, Theodore. Firstly, I don't really have all that many troops.'

'But how . . . ?'

'I have a ragtag collection of huntsmen and blacksmiths from the lands where I was passing my exile. I used a bunch of old tricks – tricks I learnt from your father, I might add – to fool the City into thinking I had ten times the number of men I do.'

'I could assemble a detachment of guards to stop them.'

'You could, you certainly could. But the question is, do we want to stop them? And the answer is no. Don't look so surprised. The life of a poor man, Theo, is an unpalatable cocktail of resentment and pride. He hears that Marguerite-Constance favours westerners and he hates them. He wants to take from them, hurt them, humble them, but under normal circumstances he cannot. Today, however, he can.'

The ugly man gave Theo a nudge in the ribs.

'What the boss is trying to say is that men feel a hell of a lot better once they've fucked a woman who can't say no. And what's more, they'll love the man who gives them leave to do it.'

'Ah, Theodore, meet Stephanos. He does have a point. Sometimes bread and circuses alone will not satisfy the people.

They need something meatier. Something they can get their teeth into. I'm sure you understand that.'

Theo nodded. He did understand, didn't he? Of course he did. This was what running an empire was all about. Difficult decisions. Yes, of course he understood.

'Excellent. Now, I have some delicate family business to attend to. Gentlemen—' and Theo was pleased to see that he was included along with Stephanos and Constantinos although he wasn't sure how either of them counted as gentlemen '— shall we?'

Andronikos led them to a room where Emperor Alexios and Empress Anna sat, as rumpled and worried as children in disgrace – children watched by two dozen Varangians.

He has the guards as well. That was Theo's first thought. *By God, she looks a mess.* His second. *In a good way.* His third.

The curls in Agnes's hair were at least two days old and her face was unpainted. She looked like the seasick girl he'd met on the boat, not the perfect, poised creature he glimpsed at court. But she didn't look scared, he'd give her that.

She looked at him – she'd seen him looking at her – and frowned. She was probably trying to work out what he was doing there. Well, she'd have to get used to it – she'd be seeing a lot more of him. He gave her a small smile – why not? – but before he could see whether she smiled back, the guards crashed open the doors and Marguerite-Constance stood on the threshold.

Theo's eyes popped. The old empress really was giving it her best shot.

She wore a nun's habit, her face hidden behind a veil, her hands lost in long sleeves and – a nice touch – her feet bare. As she walked past, Theo realised she must have borrowed the clothes from a nun who hadn't bathed in years. Her quadruple guard looked absurd. She was nothing but a woman, small, powerless, encumbered by her beauty.

Alexios darted to her side and lifted the veil. She dropped smartly to her knees and pressed his hands first to her mouth and then to her forehead, as if seeking his blessing. Alexios pulled her to her feet, kissing her cheeks warmly in return.

'Mother, thank heavens you are safe. It's chaos. I don't understand, I don't understand . . .'

Marguerite-Constance looked up at Andronikos, and Theo saw her eyes harden before she could blink the hatred out of them. She reached for his hand, kissing it with reverence.

'Illustrious friend. A friend in need. We all so longed for your guidance . . . your experience . . . your much-vaunted wisdom . . .'

She was laying it on a bit thick, but Andronikos let her soldier through a magnificent ode to his great qualities. When he finally spoke, it was in the conversational tones of a farmer who'd bumped into an old acquaintance at one of the City's markets.

'Been a long time, hasn't it?'

The casualness was cruel, but also clever. It made a mockery of her passion – of the drama she was playing out for her son. It was a yawn – as if at an old ham. Theo couldn't help liking him a little bit more.

'Tell me, basileus,' Andronikos said, glancing at Alexios, 'how do you like your new father?'

Alexios stared. Everyone looked at their feet, at the ceiling. Nobody was going to meet the boy's eye.

'Cousin? What do you . . . ?'

'Andronikos, please, don't . . .'

He spoke at the same time as his mother. Neither finished. They stood looking at one another. Andronikos spoke again, airily.

'A nun with a lover. The stuff of lewd jokes.'

Silence.

'How was the Protosebastos, Marguerite-Constance? I am curious – did you dress like this for him? Some men, I know, find the brides of Christ alluring. Or do you still wear your purple silks beneath the sackcloth?'

His eyes flicked back to Alexios.

'Forgive me, is this new to you? None of your advisers told you that your mother has debased your father's name, his memory, his honour?'

The young emperor sat down on a stool, but so distractedly that it wobbled and nearly fell underneath him. His face, never firm at the best of times, trembled as he gazed up at his mother.

'Mama, tell me it isn't true.'

She was back on her knees, his hands clasped in hers. She reached up, a suppliant, and stroked his cheek.

'Son, don't listen to these lies. I would never betray my husband, my beloved Manuelos. His memory is as sacred to me as it is to you. My darling boy, don't listen to them. This man's a monster. He'd tell you anything, anything. He wants to drive us apart. But he'll never . . . never . . .'

Her voice dropped to a hypnotic murmur, but there was desperation in it, an intense need for him to believe her. Alexios shook her off − not unkindly, but as if he had forgotten who she was, why she was there − and came to Agnes's side.

'Agnes, is it true?'

'Yes, Alexios.' Her eyes were cast down, but Theo could swear he saw a glint of pure pleasure in them. 'I'm sorry. Yes it is. Every word.'

'You little . . .' With an almighty shriek, Marguerite-Constance lunged for her, a frenzy of hatred, nails gouging at her eyes, fingers ripping at her earrings, twisting at the necklace about her throat.

Alexios was shouting, 'Mother, Mother, stop, please, stop,' but he didn't move.

Theo glanced at Andronikos, who nodded, and leapt forward. Marguerite-Constance writhed in his grip, a Fury, a hissing, spitting Medusa, until Andronikos signalled to the guards to take her away.

Agnes struggled to her feet, coughing, holding her throat. Theo could see the marks where her gold chain had cut into her windpipe. She put her hand up to her right ear. It was red, sticky – blood oozing.

'This is not the circus,' she snapped. 'We are not wild beasts to kill each other for your sport.'

Andronikos tore a piece of silk from his sleeve and held it against her ear, then touched one finger to her throat.

'I am sorry.'

That was all he said, but Agnes, Theo thought, suddenly seemed much less angry.

'Alexios.' Andronikos turned from wife to husband.

The boy was still staring at the door through which his mother had disappeared.

'Alexios,' he repeated.

'W-where have they taken her, cousin?'

'To a prison cell, where she belongs. You object?'

'N-no. I . . . I . . .'

'You?' Andronikos prompted.

'I-I am grateful to you. But w-what happens now?'

Andronikos frowned and left a pause so eloquent of his perfect power and the boy's perfect helplessness that for a moment Theo thought that Alexios's days as emperor were done.

'Why, dear cousin, I shall remain here to safeguard you and your empire. No, do not thank me. It shall be my pleasure to serve.'

As the new regent sketched a bow, Theo heard a woman's voice growing louder in the corridor outside.

'Where is he? Is he here? Where's Andronikos?'

Maria burst into the room.

'Cousin, I bid you welcome. I hear you have already—'

She stopped as she saw Andronikos straightening up before her brother. Other than stand perhaps a little too still, she did nothing to betray herself. But Theo – remembering his father's conversation with the eunuch – could not fail to see that she was mortally disappointed.

The late summer of 1182

The imperial family, far from prying eyes, was lounging in the shade of a plane tree. The air, which smelt of warm earth, was criss-crossed with bees, tiny white butterflies and sudden stripes of light. It was long past midday, closer now to night. Soon the sun's rays would steal below the branches and paint the shade orange. But for now, they were all enveloped in a green torpor.

They had travelled a little way out of the City to pray at a shrine close by the grave of Andronikos's father. Agnes had prepared herself for the quiet of fasting and worship, and in some ways she'd been looking forward to it — after all, she had a great deal to thank God for. But this trip, like so much else with Andronikos, had turned out more festive than devotional.

The remains of a gargantuan lunch, which had drifted into an equally sumptuous dinner, lay before her. She had drunk more wine than she was used to, which, combined with the heat, the cushions and the food in her belly, was making her drowsy, but also somehow expectant.

On the other side of the loose circle, her husband burst out laughing. Andronikos had been larding him with attention all afternoon, murmuring small asides in his ear, addressing his tallest tales to him, and Alexios was lapping it up. He was so besotted with his cousin that he'd forgotten he was meant to be madly in love with his wife. Something else to be grateful to Andronikos for.

No doubt — he had set her free. He'd been shocked, perhaps

even genuinely, at how little she'd seen, how few people she'd met since arriving in the City. *Cousin,* he said, *you must not hide the empress's light.* And so being empress suddenly meant trips and parties, plays and poetry . . .

'What happened next?' Her husband's voice, piping, breathless. 'Tell us, cousin, how ever did you come to escape from the City's dungeons?'

. . . and watching the men at court, the young men anyway, cluster round Andronikos, tripping over each other to wow him with war talk, begging for adventure stories – other sorts of stories as well, she'd bet, when the women weren't there.

It was the same when they travelled through the City. The people sang as he passed, songs about his life, bawdy rhymes set to popular tunes, belted out with gusto. There was one she'd heard dozens of times about all the starchy City wives who'd secretly loved him through his years of exile trying to batter down his bedroom door. *But who's in there?* That was the refrain.

He'd had a mistress, back east. He'd even been married, once upon a time. But nobody knew who shared his bed now. And nobody was likely to find out, because first they'd have to get past Constantinos, Stephanos and three pink-eyed, slobbering dogs who crouched in front of his door and never shut their eyes so long as he was inside, if what she'd heard was true.

His story was reaching a climax. Not that he was telling it himself, not exactly. The men already knew it. They were telling it and Andronikos was just shaking his head when their version became too preposterous.

He caught her eye, and his mouth, one side of it, twitched. Now he knew she'd been looking at him. And why not? If he'd seen her looking at *him*, that meant he'd been looking at *her*. And he *did* look at her – although she worried that his glance was often more amused than anything. He paid her compliments, too, elaborate tributes to her youth and beauty. *Agnes, our budding rose. Agnes, our pinkest pearl.* That sort of thing.

Charming words, but insincere. They had a ritualistic, almost mocking edge. She'd detected the same tone in his voice at court – and even, shockingly, at prayer.

She sighed, aloud, less guarded than she'd meant to be. He noticed. He spoke.

'Not enjoying yourself, Empress Anna?'

He was looking at her, and so was everyone else. Everyone always looked wherever he did. Previously, she might have politely disagreed. She might have said a light, bright nothing about the food, the sun, the company. But something that afternoon made her change her tactics – or maybe play a different game altogether.

She shrugged, sulky, not caring, took to her feet and wandered away, stretching her hands behind her back, rubbing her fingers into the hair at the nape of her neck.

Time moved; the light changed. She watched a pack of wasps prowling through some lavender.

'Here I am, Agnes. Following you as you wanted. What's on your mind?'

She tilted her head up to look at him.

'You, Andronikos. You are. You *know* I'm thinking about you. It's all anyone ever does, although they all pretend they're not. And now I'm doing it too. Do you not get bored?'

'With what, Agnes?' There was a lighter shade to his voice.

'With all this *attention*?'

She gestured to where everyone else was sitting under the tree. They'd started a game of dice, but Maria, her husband, even Renier, they all kept glancing towards them. She knew that only Andronikos's back kept them at bay. He was not a man you approached uninvited.

'You wouldn't find it boring if you were loved by the entire City,' he replied. 'I imagine you'd probably rather like it. I confess I do. Should I not?'

'But you're wrong,' she said. 'The entire City doesn't love you. Some of them, they hate you.'

111

'I am hurt, Empress Anna. Who could hate me?'

'The Protosebastos hated you. Until you ordered his throat cut.'

'Who else?'

'Marguerite-Constance hates you, wherever she is.'

He nodded, meaning *of course, go on.*

'And . . .' she began, and stopped. Maybe she was about to go too far.

'And?'

'Maria. She hates you too.'

A flash. A glint in his eye of . . . what? Surprise, maybe, or appreciation. But she was more pleased by his reaction to those five words than she had been by anything else in her life.

'I know that,' he said. 'But how do you? She's doing her best to hide it.'

'But her best isn't good enough, is it?'

'No. But *why* does she hate me? Tell me that, clever little Agnes.'

Clever little Agnes. She tried to quash the exultant crowing in her head.

'She didn't only want Marguerite-Constance gone, did she? She thought Alexios was going too. She thought you were going to be her man. But you're not, not one bit. And now it's eating her up that you're being so nice to him – to my husband – when she doesn't understand why.'

Agnes paused. She didn't understand why either.

'Go on,' said Andronikos.

'She wants you to admit it's all a joke. That you and she know better than the rest of us. And so she tries to treat you with . . .' She paused; how to describe it? 'With a sort of stupid man-to-man frankness. But you're not playing along, are you? You're polite, but you treat her as the sister of the emperor, nothing more.'

'Is that all?'

'No. She misses her father. She thought you might be like him. But you're not. She hates you for that, too.'

'Not like the great Manuelos? But what am I like?'

'A . . . a charioteer. A very successful one.'

He laughed. And for a terrifying, giddy moment, she thought she would only ever be happy listening to that sound.

'Hey – what's going on?'

She looked up in time to see Maria lob a plum at her. Andronikos's hand snapped out and caught it before it hit her. He walked back over to the table, placed it carefully on a plate and began to skin it with a tiny silver knife.

'Come on, Agnes,' said Maria, as she too returned to the shade. 'What was that tête-à-tête about?'

Agnes paused a fraction too long before answering.

'I was telling Andronikos what a lovely day I've had and how much I'm looking forward to going to bed.'

'What utter nonsense. And you can't go to bed. Not for hours. If you go to bed, Andronikos might say I have to as well. He might say it's not *seemly* for me to sit alone with all these men. Even if one of them is my husband.'

'I didn't think Andronikos worried about that sort of thing,' Agnes murmured.

They were looking at each other, but Agnes knew they were both speaking to Andronikos. He, however, was concentrating on the plum in his hand.

'You would have thought so, wouldn't you?' said Maria. Agnes could see that the lines at the edge of her mouth were tight. 'Play with me, sister.' She rattled the dice-bones in her hand. 'If I win, you will tell me what you were really talking about. You can even whisper it in my ear. I won't tell a soul.'

'No. I know you'll win,' said Agnes.

'You ought to have more faith in your luck, Agnes,' said Andronikos.

He speared a slice of the plum and held it out to her on the point of his knife. She took it and ate it without looking at him.

'If you say so,' she replied, 'but Maria always tells me it's a game of skill. And I have no skill at dice.'

'Our Agnes doesn't like playing games she doesn't think she's going to win. It's insufferable,' said Maria.

Agnes knew Andronikos's eyes were on her.

'Is that so?' he asked.

She met his gaze.

'Maybe.'

Something arrived under the table. Dice. He placed the two bones in the palm of her hand and closed her fingers over them. She looked at him in surprise.

'Play,' he said. 'As a favour to me.'

Maria hadn't noticed.

'I shall pray for luck,' Agnes told Andronikos.

'I don't think God altogether approves of prayers of that sort,' he replied. 'Maybe best not to let him know what you're up to.'

He was always saying things like that, things that would have turned her brother Philip purple with righteous horror. She tried to pretend they didn't make her nervous.

'Excellent,' said Maria. 'Now what shall I wager?'

'If you lose,' said Andronikos, 'you will escort this child to bed and retire yourself.'

'You see, Agnes? If I had a more suspicious mind, I might think he didn't want me around. Do you know what I call that?'

Agnes shook her head, although she knew the answer.

Ingratitude.

'Ingratitude,' said Maria.

'Ingratitude?' The word slipped soft and dangerous from Andronikos's mouth and everyone stopped what they were doing.

Everyone except Maria.

'Exactly. If *I* hadn't bade you return, you wouldn't be here at all. You'd still be doing whatever it was you were doing in your dusty little . . .'

'Damp, Maria. Paphlagonia was very damp.'

'. . . little outpost. So I hardly think you are in a position to tell me what to do. If Agnes wins, she shall choose my forfeit. Not you.'

She smiled and patted Agnes's arm proprietorially.

'Let's play, Agnes. Best of five.'

But every time Maria threw, Agnes defeated her. Three perfect scores. Her sister-in-law snatched the dice out of her hand.

'Where did you get these? They are not the ones Renier was playing with.'

'My lucky dice,' said Andronikos, pocketing them. 'I thought our young friend could use a little help.'

Maria took an angry gulp of wine.

'She doesn't need help. She knows exactly what she's—'

'M-Maria, y-you leave Agnes alone.' Alexios stood up so fast that his chair fell over behind him with a crash. 'Andronikos is right. You sh-should go to bed.'

Agnes felt rather than saw the looks passing between everyone around the table. Alexios standing up to his sister – it was unheard of.

'Should I?' asked Maria, amused, unthreatened.

'Y-yes. I think the way you're behaving is s-squalid and inappropriate.'

'D-d-d-d-do you, little brother?'

'Yes, I d-d-d . . .' He was too agitated. The words would not come.

'You know what I think is squalid and inappropriate?' said Maria.

She rose to her feet and took a step towards Alexios, but at a nod from Andronikos, Agnes saw two of his men – Theo and Murzuphlus – appear out of the shadows and, taking an elbow each, walk her indoors, followed by Renier and a flurry of servants.

Agnes hesitated. Suddenly, she wanted desperately to stay. But Andronikos was behind her.

'Bed, little one,' he murmured. She felt his thumb – so gently she almost did not believe it – rub the nape of her neck, below her hair.

She lay on top of her sheets, trying to work out exactly what was going on. She'd left Andronikos pouring Alexios more wine. Over her shoulder she'd seen other men coming to join them now that the women had left. Something was definitely up. Or several somethings.

But what?

The next day

When she woke, the sun was already high in the sky.

Alexios was sitting up beside her, staring out of the window. His right hand was trembling, fluttering about before him. She reached forward and stilled it.

'What? What is it? What's happened?'

He looked odd, pale. His eyes were raw, smudged purple underneath. He was more than distracted. There was a wildness to him that she had never seen before.

'What is it?' she repeated.

'I came to bed too late. I don't feel well.'

She sighed. He'd drunk too much. Again.

'You hate me, don't you?'

'No.'

The denial came automatically. What else could she say to a husband, an emperor? But then she realised it was true. She'd wasted months despising him for what he wasn't. Now she pitied him for what he was. An anchorless, rudderless boy.

'No,' she repeated. 'I don't hate you, husband. I . . .' She paused. There was no room for the truth. 'I think you should get dressed, and then we can take a little air before we breakfast. That'll make you feel better.'

She touched his shoulder, but he flinched away.

'Don't touch me. Don't even look at me.'

'Why on earth not?' Almost a snap. She was trying to be kind.

'I'm a monster.'

'You have a hangover. It's not that bad.'

'Yes, yes it is. I am a sinner.'

'We're all sinners, Alexios.'

'We are not all matricides.'

Drinking was bad enough, but the self-pity that followed it, that was unbearable.

'You are not a mother killer,' she told him. 'She did wrong. She has been punished. She will live out her years in the convent. God could see no sin in that. Indeed, he would welcome it.'

He laughed at her. He was sort of acting. A hollow laugh.

'You see this hand? I wish that I could cut it off. Let the fire eat it away. Let wild beasts—'

'Stop, Alexios. Stop.' She stilled him, tried to sit him down. His breath was coming in fast wheezing bursts. Tears streamed from his eyes. 'What are you saying? What's happened?'

'After you and Maria went to bed last night, I sat up with Andronikos and his – my men. I wish I had gone to bed with you, but I didn't. Andronikos was telling us stories – great stories. He made us laugh. He poured more wine, always filling my cup first. We talked about the empire, its future, our plans. What was important.'

The words spilled forth, faster and faster. A confession.

'I was so impressed. The way he talks. I drank more than usual. I do not drink well, you know that.'

'I do.'

'The talk turned to money, finances. It was . . . a bit boring. I stopped concentrating. Then I heard Stephanos say something about my mother. I didn't hear it properly, but everyone laughed. I asked what he'd said, but he pretended not to have heard. So I stood up and ordered him to tell me. And he smiled, you know how horrible it is when he smiles, and he said . . . he said that the Protosebastos had been knocking off the imperial treasury along with my mother, those were his words. He said he was up to his b-balls in both. I was so angry.'

'With him?'

'With him. With her. I don't know. I only know I was angry. Andronikos told Stephanos to hold his tongue. He said I loved my mother and I was grieving. He said it quietly. I wasn't meant to hear, but I did. That made me angrier. I wanted to show them all that she was nothing to me, nothing. I was so angry . . .'

'So you said.'

'No, no, you don't understand. I cursed her. I cursed her for a huh-huh . . .' His throat made a horrible clicking, sucking sound. 'For a whore. Andronikos was nodding all the time. He wasn't saying much, but he was agreeing with me. I felt so lucky to have such a good friend, somebody who understood me. My own father never listened to me like that.'

Suddenly his eyes disappeared and his mouth twisted into a groan and he sobbed, once, twice, then stopped with a great gasp.

'I said I wished she was dead. Andronikos said I didn't mean it and I swore that I did. I said I was emperor and had power over all men, all women. I don't remember anything after that. I don't remember how the night ended. I don't remember how I came to be here.'

He grabbed a cup of water and gulped it down.

'I woke. I . . . I was sick. Forgive me, but I must tell you everything. I was sick. It felt like I was coughing up my soul.'

Agnes was very still.

'You fear that you've . . .' She found she could not say it out loud.

'Maybe. I don't know. I don't know.'

'Then we must find out. Let us send for Andronikos.'

'No!' Alexios looked startled that he had shouted so loud. 'No,' he repeated.

'Why not? You're probably imagining things. Your mother is probably quietly at her prayers in her cell.'

'H-he will laugh at me. I made a fool of myself.'

'So what? You're not the first young man to stumble over unmixed wine.'

Her voice was light, but there was a painful tightness in her chest and throat as she sent for a servant and told him the emperor wished to see his cousin at the earliest possible convenience.

'Come, husband, come.' She stroked Alexios's head. 'Dry your eyes. You mustn't be crying when he comes. Here. It'll be fine.'

She sat beside him and he buried his head in her lap, hugging her knees tight to his chest. That was how Andronikos found them.

'Ah, young love,' he said from the threshold. He was carrying letters. Carelessly dressed. A busy man. 'I remember when I, too, found time for a wife amid my duties. I am charmed. Charmed.'

Alexios hurtled to his feet.

'Cousin, I . . .'

'No, no, don't mention it. It happens to us all,' he said. 'You are refreshed? Recovered? Rejuvenated? At your age, you bounce back fast from nocturnal adventures. It's not the same for us older fellows.' A rueful laugh, warm and rich as sunshine.

Alexios was visibly relaxing. The pain was leaving his face.

'So, everything's all right?'

'Of course. Absolutely. Was there anything else?'

He was turning to go. He was nearly gone. Alexios hadn't dared ask.

'His mother . . .' Agnes began.

Is she alive? Have you killed her?

Andronikos looked at her.

'What about his mother?'

'Is she . . . ?'

'Is she what?'

'Is she dead?'

120

He laughed. The question was clearly absurd. Agnes relaxed too. But then he spoke.

'Of course she's dead. Such was the young emperor's particular command. I presumed he'd asked me here to make sure I had obeyed. Cousin.' He bowed. 'Forgive me if I was not clear. The appropriate officials approved your order. Justice is done. Your mother is dead. Her body has been disposed of. You are pleased?'

His hands fingered something in the folds of his tunic. Out it came. A letter. He turned it over a few times in his hands.

'But of course you are pleased. Here is your signature. I was a little reluctant, I admit. No man executes a woman lightly, no matter how serious her crimes. But you made me see sense.'

Agnes realised she was holding her breath. She breathed in, fast. A gasp. By her side, Alexios swayed from foot to foot. Tears stood in his eyes. She could see that he was trying – hard, painfully hard – not to let them fall. One hand brushed one away, another, but then they began to spill, unstoppable, pouring down his face. He stumbled to the washroom, keeping the pain inside him. Only when he was hidden – from sight, if not from hearing – did the retching sobs begin.

'Leave,' she told Andronikos. 'Leave. I can't bear to look at you.'

It was a stupid thing to say, seeing as she was staring right at him. She tried again.

'Leave. I must tend to my husband.'

She tried to turn away, but he caught her by the hand and pulled her back.

'*My husband.* You say that a lot. A big word. Does he deserve it?'

'Don't talk about him like that.'

'We both know I can talk about him however I like.'

There was nothing playful in his voice. Fear prickled. He was very close to her, his eyes hard on hers.

'I'm surprised you're not better pleased, Agnes. It was plain that you loved Marguerite-Constance little enough.'

But then he smiled, and she knew his words were an invitation, of a sort. All she had to do was return his smile. To say, *yes, I am glad.* But she wasn't ready to do that – even if it was the truth.

'How could I be glad a woman is dead? *Dead.* I am not a monster. I'm not.'

He cocked his head.

'You don't look like one, but one never can tell. Monsters come in the strangest guises.' He gestured towards the washroom. 'Keep an eye on him. Don't let him do anything stupid.'

She nodded, and he looked at her again, appraising.

'Not a monster, no, but not altogether good. I'm glad.'

And he was gone. *I'm glad.* And she was glad he was glad. What was wrong with her?

Silence from the other room. She found Alexios huddled in a corner, balled like a baby, arms about his head. She touched his shoulder and he started to rub furiously at his face.

'I'm fine. I am, really. The woman was punished as befitted her crimes. Thank you, cousin. Thank you.'

'He's gone, Alexios. You don't have to pretend to be pleased.'

The early autumn of 1182

Very little light penetrated the women's baths at Blachernai. The curved ceilings, low enough that a tall man – not that a man would ever set foot in there – could reach up and finger the mosaics that looped and curled from wall to wall. Blunt-nosed dolphins leapt through waves, fish wriggled through sea plants, and boats, small, without captain or crew, gave chase. It was a fanciful scene, intimate. The craftsman relaxed and free after some grand project.

Agnes's toes edged towards the cold pool where green water lapped over the brim. She handed her wrap to an attendant and slipped in, sinking all the way to the bottom, the chill making her more alive, more alert. Once, she'd hated bathing all together. Then she had only liked to be soaped, warm and lazy. But now it pleased her, how *ready* she felt, after the bite of cold water had done its work.

A little push from her feet and she surfaced. Even before she had the water out of her eyes, she knew from the change in the silence that somebody other than the servants was watching her. She was right. Maria, dressed for something other than bathing, was propped in an alcove, arms folded, legs crossed.

'You've grown up a lot, haven't you, Agnes? You're all woman now.'

Involuntarily, Agnes glanced down at her body. Above her head, little windows of coloured glass let in the light, and the reds, the greens, the blues patterned her limbs. Maria hadn't taken her eyes off her. Agnes held up her arms, a signal, and two attendants came forward, patting her dry, pulling a shift over her head. They sat her down and began to dry her feet.

Through a grille came the smell of outside. The gardeners were burning leaves. But now all she could smell was some sickly new incense that clung to Maria's clothes. The women hovered, ready to assist the kaisarissa but she waved them away.

'Leave us. All of you.'

They gathered up ewers, discarded clothes and vanished.

'You wish to speak to me, Maria?'

'No need to sound so surprised. Or do I mean defensive? I always want to speak to you, Empress Anna. Don't we all? What does Andronikos call you? *Our clever little Agnes.*'

'Don't be silly. He doesn't call me that.'

Maria's head shifted out of the coloured light and Agnes thought she looked strangely bloodless under her make-up, her eyes glassy.

'You've no idea what he calls you when you're not there. But let's not talk about him. Let's talk about us. I am sure we used to be better friends. Were we not once better friends? Time was I even fancied you looked up to me as a sister, a wise, kind sister. Or was that only until *she* was gone? Well, she is gone, isn't she?'

And Maria sniggered like a small boy confronted by something very painful or very shameful.

'They say she offered to bed the men who came to kill her. Stephanos and Dadibrenos. They say they had her and killed her anyway. They laid her over a barrel and had their pleasure, both of them, one after the other, and when they'd filled *that* hole, they tried the other, and when they'd finished, they pushed her head into the water until she stopped kicking. What's wrong, Agnes? Too much for you?'

'You're making it up.'

She had to be. That was more truth than she could stomach.

'Am I? She deserved it, Agnes. She deserved everything. And it's partly thanks to you, you know. You can be proud of yourself, really proud. Once so innocent. Not any longer. Your hands are dirty now. Grubby little doll's hands.'

'It had nothing to do with me. Nothing.'

'That's right, Agnes. Nothing.'

'It was Andronikos.'

'Yes, you have to hand it to him, don't you? I'm sorry I missed it. Getting my little brother to order his beloved mother's death. It's really rather comical when you think about it.'

Maria flinched, as if somebody had said something unkind to her, and stood up suddenly.

'But what's going to happen next? That's what I ask myself. And you should be asking too. Seeing as your husband won't.'

She walked a few paces to the left, a few to the right, haltingly.

'Are you all right, Maria?'

'Oh, hush . . .'

She doubled over, and Agnes rushed forward.

'Don't play nursemaid with me, chit.' She took two, three slow breaths. 'I'm fine.'

But Agnes could see she wasn't. Maria had never been good-looking, but there was something strong about her face. That morning, though, it was pinched, diminished.

'What's wrong, Maria? Tell me.'

'What's wrong? Do you want to know my secret, Agnes? Of course you do. All City women love secrets. But first you have to tell me something. A little something. You will tell me, won't you?'

'Of course.'

She'd decide whether or not to answer after Maria had asked.

'Agnes, are you with child?'

That wasn't what she'd expected, and she hesitated. Her

hand went to her belly, a reflex, but before she could answer, Maria had gripped her wrist.

'What? Are you? Tell me. Tell me this instant.'

Maria's face was too close, the glands in her neck protruding.

'No, Maria, *no*, I'm not. And let go. *Let go.*'

Maria dropped her arm, turned aside fast and bent over a basin. Agnes stepped aside, closing her ears to the sound of gagging and spitting. She hated looking after people who were ill, and told herself Maria wouldn't want to be seen looking weak. Slowly, too slowly, the sounds subsided.

'There,' said Maria, her voice hoarse, snagging in her throat. 'That's my secret.'

She covered the distance between them and tugged Agnes's hand towards her belly.

'In there. My father's grandson. A Komnenos.'

She smelt rank, like over-boiled meat, and Agnes had to force herself not to shrink away.

'You? With . . . ?'

'And why not? Surely I am not so very old?' Maria was laughing, almost. 'Old for my first, maybe, but that's what happens when you marry late.'

'How do you know?'

'I have all the signs, my women say. No bleed. And I feel sick all the time, and tired, with these appalling headaches. No taste for lovemaking. A few weeks more and it should be plain.'

My father's grandson.

'Congratulations.'

A rival.

'Thank you. I shall pray for him at the Bathys Ryax rites. Will you come with me?' She pressed Agnes's hand. 'You and Alexios must come with me. We shall pray together for my son's future. I am happy. Truly, truly happy.'

'I am glad, Maria.'

Agnes's mind whirred. She thought she knew why no child had begun to grow inside her – although she would have found it hard to put into words if anyone had asked her such a thing.

Alexios . . . *struggled.*

That was what she called it. How else to describe the spilling, the shame, the anger? She soothed him and stroked him – and was relieved. Once babies started coming, they'd never stop, and then she'd look like an old woman; worse, she'd turn into one, groaning about mysterious ailments and worrying. There was plenty of time for all that later.

Except maybe there wasn't. A smile lifted Maria's face.

'Clever little Agnes. Don't worry. I'm sure your turn will come. It's just that my turn's coming first.'

Her sister-in-law made to go, but as she turned, something unseen butted her in the stomach. She dropped to the floor and started to convulse.

'Help me.' Her hands snapped out. 'Help me.'

'Maria! Is it the baby? Maria?' When she got no answer, Agnes ran to the door, flung it open and yelled, 'Help! The kaisarissa is sick. The kaisarissa is sick. Help!'

Attendants rushed in, plucked Maria from the floor and laid her on a bench. Her movements were less wild, but she was still twitching and jerking horribly. Some of the women were calling for the palace physicians, others were trying desperately to usher Agnes away, but she shook them all off and knelt at Maria's side.

'Maria.' She squeezed her hand, the fingers swollen fat and stiff, but felt no pressure in return. 'Maria.' She shook her – too hard, probably. 'Maria.'

'Renier.' More a gasp than a word. 'Find him. Tell him . . . It's . . .'

But although her lips continued to move, only a thin, green, foul-smelling bile came out. Agnes stepped backwards, staring aghast at the mess in front of her, then turned and sprinted from the room.

Theo and Renier were fencing back and forth.

Theo was delighted. Normally Renier bested him – he had

a couple of years on Theo, a longer reach, and the power of an ox – but lately Theo's speed had meant he could last the bout, even if he still struggled to find the killer blow. This morning, however, he was pushing Renier back and back.

He liked Renier. When he'd asked him what he made of the massacre of the westerners, Renier had shrugged. *People die. It is hard, but it happens.* Theo couldn't decide whether that was great wisdom or great stupidity, but either way it made him feel a lot better. They never talked much about politics again.

The big man always sweated hard when they fought, but today it was sheeting off him. His usually cherubic face was blotchy and misshapen, his neck had turned puce and white spittle specks were drying around his mouth.

'Too much to drink last night?' Theo called, easily batting away Renier's counterattack.

'Ate some bad oyster,' Renier grimaced, stumbling as Theo advanced.

'Blame what you like, man,' Theo grinned. 'I've got you.'

And he did have him. Renier's sword was on the ground, his back was against a pillar and Theo's blade was tickling his throat.

'I'll have my revenge next time.' Renier tried to smile. 'Sorry. Water. Moment in the shade.'

'Take it easy, friend.'

Theo clapped him on the arm – the skin was clammy, like snow-chilled meat – and left him to it. He wasn't unsympathetic. He'd suffered enough himself after big nights as part of Andronikos's cabal. They drank hard and they drank late and it was a lot of fun. But it was tough getting up in the mornings.

A burst of wind whirled the leaves in the courtyard and he wandered over to watch Murzuphlus parry a feeble thrust from Alexios and launch what was obviously meant to be an equally feeble counterattack. But he'd overestimated the emperor's ability to wield a sword, and the blunt point of his practice blade caught Alexios under the armpit. Alexios looked crestfallen – and a little surprised.

'You've bested me.'

Murzuphlus remembered at the last minute to look pleased rather than irritated. 'A lucky stroke, basileus.'

Theo grinned and went over to offer them some water.

'I'll take over,' he muttered in his friend's ear. 'I'm much better at fencing badly than you are.'

'That's because you *do* fence badly.'

'Wrong. It takes a truly great swordsman to fight worse than him. Watch me.'

And Theo bobbed and wove, making a great show of nothing, floundering and flapping and opening his guard and mis-hitting and tripping over his own heels. Alexios wore his best fighting frown and Murzuphlus was cheering him on.

Out of the corner of his eye, Theo saw Renier doubled over. At first he thought the idiot was laughing – much too obviously – but when he looked again, Renier was hunched on the floor and Murzuphlus was leaning over him, shaking him, calling his name. Theo put up his sword.

'Done in, Theodore?' snickered Alexios.

'You'd tire out Heraklês himself, basileus. But look – Renier is not well.'

Alexios gave a worldly shrug.

'He probably drank too much last night. He always does.'

Theo shook his head.

'Forgive me, but that's not wine. By your leave?'

'What? Oh, you wish to tend to him? Go ahead. I shall retire to my chambers. Get Andronikos to knock up one of his purges. They are legendary.'

As Theo approached, he saw that Renier's face was green-grey, like rot. The whites of his eyes were pink as a mouse's. His pupils flickered wildly.

'Damn it, where are his people?' said Murzuphlus. 'He needs a physician.'

Theo looked around for help, but the serving men who should have been posted at every entrance had vanished. He tucked that information away somewhere, and gripped Renier under his arms.

'You take his heels,' he told Murzuphlus. 'We'll get him back to his room.'

It was hard work dragging Renier along the corridors, harder still hoisting him on to his bed. While Murzuphlus fumbled about looking for a flannel, a pitcher of water, Theo laid his ear on Renier's chest.

'He's breathing. Just. You go and find—'

But they were interrupted by a hammering at the door. Theo barely had time to open it before a small figure was shoving and pushing, trying to get past him.

'Renier, where's Renier? I must see Renier.'

'Empress Anna!'

Her hair was wet. She was wearing what he supposed was some sort of bathing robe. Bare feet, bare ankles. It was shocking, indecent and – he stamped on the thought before it could go anywhere dangerous – painfully arousing.

'Empress Anna, you can't go in there. You know you can't. What are you—'

'Let me in. Maria, she wants to see Renier. He's got to come quickly. Theodore . . .' for the first time she seemed to take in who she was talking to. 'The kaisarissa is sick. Really sick. She thinks she's . . . she's pregnant, but I think it's some vile plague.'

The kaisarissa is sick.

Theo didn't need to hear any more to know what was happening.

Why didn't he tell me?

But he had no time to worry about feeling slighted. He had to deal with Agnes, stop her scandalising the palace, stop her ruining whatever the hell was afoot.

'Thank you for delivering your message, Empress Anna. I will tell Renier. I beg you, withdraw to your chambers and . . .'

Put some bloody clothes on. He didn't know how to say it without drawing attention to the fact that he could see her breasts curving where the material of her shift was wet. His attention faltered and there she was, trying to push past him again.

'Stand aside, Theodore, I said I would bring him myself.'

He grabbed her arm to stop her.

'You can't go in. He's lying down.'

'Get him up, then. Get him up and bring him out here. At once.'

'For God's sake, Agnes.' He stopped and lowered his voice. 'For God's sake, don't you get it? He's sick too.'

Their eyes met. Understanding turned her cheeks red, then white. She carried on staring at him, accusingly, very quiet, very still, her hands clenching and unclenching at her sides.

'Both,' she muttered. 'Both sick.'

He put a hand out, unthinking, to touch her shoulder. He was trying to act like he knew what was going on. Like he understood it all.

'You should go to your rooms augustê. Stay there. Until this is . . . is over.'

She shook him off.

'I am *not* going to my rooms. I am *not* going to hide. I . . .' she hesitated, but only for a moment, 'I'm going to find Andronikos.'

Her assurance was ridiculous. He wanted to laugh.

'You think you can change his mind?'

'I'm going to try.'

'Don't be stupid.'

'Don't call me stupid.'

He took a step towards her.

'I'm trying to help. Don't get mixed up in this.'

'I am mixed up in this.'

She turned from him and would have flown down the corridor, but he caught hold of her arm and held her back.

'Let go of me. Let go!' She rounded on him, anger burning her face. 'I suppose you think this is funny. The little empress, the last to know. Go away and laugh. Laugh with *him* and all your friends. Laugh because you're so big and clever.'

'I'm not laughing.'

His words cracked as they came out. Something in them stilled her.

'You didn't know either, did you?' she said, almost in a whisper.

She was shaking her head, backing away from him. And this time he let her go.

Agnes found Constantinos sitting behind a desk in the antechamber to Andronikos's ever-growing network of rooms.

'Don't open that door.'

'I don't care how busy he is.'

She flung open the door and immediately leapt backwards. Three dogs were chained on the threshold. One leapt and snapped at her face. The other two crouched low on their front paws and growled.

'You . . . you should have warned me.'

'I did. You should have listened.'

He looked back down at his papers.

'Constantinos . . .'

He looked up. 'My dear girl. Go to your rooms. The advice Theodore Branas gave you was good. Go to your rooms. Stay there.'

'How do you . . . ? Your spies. It makes me sick. Is there anything you don't know?'

'I don't know why you're being a nuisance. I thought,' he lowered his voice, 'you had more sense. We all did.'

'You're killing Maria.' She was shouting, she couldn't help it. 'You're killing her. Have you seen her? If you'd only seen her, you'd stop it. She thinks she's pregnant. She's happy and she's dying. It's cruel, cruel, cruel—'

Constantinos slammed his pen down.

'That's enough! If you act like a child, I'll lock you in your room like one.'

She looked at him. There was no joke there.

'Did you think it was going to be happy families from now on? No. Maria has not given up the throne. Far from it. We uncovered a plot on your husband's life. And on yours.'

'You're making it up.'

'I'm not.'

'I'm her friend.'

'You're not. And you know it. Maria fancied she was going to have Alexios – and you – butchered when you attended the rites at Bathys Ryax next year. Blunt. Inelegant. Very Maria.'

Agnes was silent. *The rites at Bathys Ryax*. Maria had said something about them, but that didn't mean anything. Not necessarily. Did it?

'I don't believe you.' But she knew her voice was less firm.

Constantinos sighed. 'Do you want her to be empress? Very well.'

She heard a small click as a compartment opened in his desk. The eunuch placed a vial in front of her, a beautiful thing, red glass stoppered with fine-wrought bronze.

'Go on. Take it.'

'What is it?'

'The antidote.'

A pause. He laughed and put the vial away.

'That's not fair,' Agnes gasped. 'I was about to take it. You took it away too fast.'

'Agnes, little Agnes . . .' and she heard a little, a very little, of the old warmth returning to his voice. 'Peace, you must understand, comes with a price. Sometimes that price can be paid in gold, but more often blood is the only currency that will serve. A little blood for the sake of the empire.'

'For the sake of the empire? We both know for whose—'

She broke off. Andronikos had entered the room – when,

she did not know – and was leaning against the door frame.

'What? What do you both know?'

His eyes flicked to Constantinos. The eunuch put up his hands, palms out. *Nothing to do with me.* Andronikos's attention flicked back to her.

'What's this, Agnes? Silence? I'm surprised. You seemed to have so much to say.'

He turned back to the eunuch.

'Constantinos, be a good fellow and find the emperor for me. I want to let him know that his sister and brother-in-law have been taken ill after eating some mushrooms the kaisar gathered while out hunting. The poor boy is unfamiliar with our native fungus. Tragic. Not you,' he said as Agnes made to follow him. 'I want to talk to you.'

The door shut. One of the dogs yawned and crossed its front paws.

'Your dogs – I thought that was just talk.'

'It was. But I heard the talk and thought it sounded like a good idea. Stephanos found them for me.'

A pause.

'If I were you, Agnes, I'd work on making myself so small that nobody noticed me.'

'No you wouldn't.'

He laughed. Even then, with death everywhere, it was still something to make him laugh.

'No. You're right. I wouldn't. I never could make myself small. I didn't know how, and maybe you don't either.' A look. 'That's the trouble with girls like you. Or do I mean women like you? No matter. Girl, woman – you, Agnes, are quite hard to ignore.'

Agnes felt a warmth spread across her face that was neither fear nor shame.

'It's your certainty that does it. Enjoy it, that certainty. It doesn't last for ever.'

Another pause.

'Have you ever really wanted something, Agnes? I don't mean dolls and dresses?'

He was close, very close.

'I know what you want,' she said, suddenly bold.

'And what is that?'

'Power.'

'I do?' He shook his head. 'I do not want to rule. I want to watch your husband grow in stature and become a great emperor of this great empire. And I want to watch you standing loyally and lovingly at his side.'

It was a grotesque speech. A challenge, more than anything else.

'Don't lie to me.'

'Lies are nicer, Agnes, much nicer. Believe the lies.'

'I won't. You want my husband's throne.'

'So my enemies claim. Are you my enemy, Agnes? Don't be my enemy. You would regret it – and you are young, far too young, to have regrets.'

The menace was there, cold and unmistakable.

'Don't look so alarmed,' he said. 'Or rather, do. There's something rather lovely about your face with a little fear on it.'

And then, suddenly, they were no longer alone. Constantinos and Alexios were standing in the room beside them. She was relieved. Their arrival meant she could look away from Andronikos without surrendering. She could look away and pretend she'd known what to say, what to do next.

'Your sister. Your poor sister,' she said, quickly at her husband's side.

She caught the man-to-man look Alexios gave Andronikos, and at once grasped its meaning. *My little wife. She doesn't understand.* She recalled Maria's pleasure at Marguerite-Constance's death and now saw it mirrored on Alexios's face, and she felt sick and hateful. *It's you who doesn't understand, husband.* That was what she wanted to scream.

* * *

135

Theo paused. Voices: Andronikos was not alone. He nudged the door open and saw that he and the boy were mid-conversation, all smiles and bonhomie, while Agnes stood apart, white-faced, sullen. He tried to catch her eye, but she pushed past him, out of the room. Constantinos joined him, a question on his face.

'It's over,' said Theo, quiet.

Two small words to describe a man's passing. The eunuch nodded, and Theo was about to take his leave, but he saw Andronikos's finger raised slightly. *Wait here.* He waited, sick with his new memories.

Renier crying. *Write to my brothers, will you, Theo? Boniface and Conrad. Tell them what happened. You're my friend, aren't you? Tell them what happened.* Renier slipping into whatever western tongue he'd spoken as a boy. Renier thrashing. Renier dead.

A hand on his shoulder. He turned and saw that only Andronikos remained in the room.

'Excellent. You're here. Stephanos?' he called, and the man emerged past the dogs from his chambers. 'Can I leave you two to do whatever tidying up is needed? Come to the House of Michaelitzês when you're done. I think we'll all need to unwind. Until later.'

He was about to leave when he took another look at Theo and frowned.

'Theodore,' he said, 'I do not see a happy man before me. What's wrong?'

'Nothing. Nothing is wrong.' A boy's voice, surly.

'You're sure?'

A simple enough question, but Theo couldn't make himself say *yes*.

'I . . . I didn't know that you – that we were planning to kill Maria and Renier.'

'No. You didn't,' Andronikos said, equably. 'You and Renier were of an age. You seemed to enjoy each other's company. I thought it might be hard for you to do what was necessary.'

Theo flushed. He'd been told he couldn't be trusted. He'd

also been told he'd sat back and watched a friend die. The sting of the insult made him bolder.

'Why?' he said. 'Why . . . ?'

He regretted speaking immediately, and stuttered to a halt. Another man altogether stood before him, his face pure ice.

'You, Theodore Branas, have yet to earn the right to question me. If you for one moment doubt me . . .'

This was not like his father angry – a big noise, a big blow, all over. This was like standing in front of a snake, weaving left, weaving right. He would do anything, say anything to make it stop.

'I do not doubt you, I swear it.'

'What I do, Theodore, I do for the good of the empire.'

'For the good of the empire,' Theo repeated.

'Are you man enough, Theo, to do what is necessary?'

Andronikos had no weapon in his hands. And yet Theo felt as compelled as if the other man had both hands tight about his throat.

'Yes. Whatever is necessary. For the good of the empire.'

Andronikos smiled, and the ice melted.

'Good. I want us to be friends, Theo. But a man in my position needs to be sure – very sure – of his friends. *Whys* make me nervous. And I don't like to be nervous. Don't make me nervous again.'

He left.

'Where d'you leave Renier, then?' asked Stephanos. 'Lead on.'

Theo hoped that was all he was going to say as they walked through the palace, the corridors full of people trying to act aggressively normal, but Stephanos was feeling talkative.

'You look like you've seen a ghost, sunshine. First time you caught the wrong side of the boss? Surprised you, did it? Don't blame you. He can get edgy all right. And when he does, believe me, it's no fucking picnic. Better when he's sweet. Better when he gets what he wants. Better for everyone.'

They found Murzuphlus still on guard outside Renier's rooms.

'Where's this corpse, then?' Stephanos laughed at their faces. 'Aristos,' he said. 'So delicate. You wait here while I get him wrapped up.'

He disappeared into the room.

'I don't like what's happening,' said Murzuphlus, slowly. 'I don't like where this is going. I'm getting out of here. I don't care where.'

'You mean you're running away?'

'Call it that if you like. I'd rather say I'm going to find a way to do my duty as an administrator in some corner of the empire. You should do the same. Sit this out.'

'*Sit this out?*'

'People are dying.'

'It's hardly the first time that's happened. It was necessary, I'm sure.'

'Oh well, if you're *sure*, Theo . . .'

'I am.' He had to be. 'This is life at the top. If you don't have the stomach for it, then pack your bags.'

'Exactly what I plan to do.' Murzuphlus grimaced. 'It's only a matter of time before he goes for the boy. You know that, don't you?'

The autumn of 1183

But Murzuphlus was wrong. A year passed, and the boy lived on – although Theo would have chosen death, any death, over Alexios's darkling days in Andronikos's long shadow.

Theo looked on as Alexios was robed for church, robed for processions, robed to distribute golden trinkets to ambassadors, silken cloth to courtiers, copper coins to the poor. Alexios spoke the appointed words, prayed the appointed prayers and signed whatever Andronikos told him to sign. He ate when they bade him eat, small, perfunctory mouthfuls, chewing over and over as if the palace cooks had dished up baked cow hide, not silken livers. He drank, too, whenever he got the chance, whenever Andronikos did not stay him, tossing back goblets of wine until purple stains spread about his neck.

Alexios reminded Theo of the magical toys which filled the Great Palace, the golden automata, the mechanical marvels that had dazzled barbarian guests for generations. Ruby-eyed birds that flapped slender wings of silver. A gilt throne that hovered above the floor. Truly wondrous things they were – from a distance. But only the gullible, the irretrievably naïve could fail to hear the click of the cogs, the whir of the pulleys.

Alexios's face grew pinched. His arms jerked. His legs twitched. But he did not stop. He kept going. He did what had to be done because Andronikos made him do it.

Click. Click. Whir. Click.

And then, sometimes, Andronikos let go of the levers. A Pisan ambassador or a City senator might ask a question – something banal and formulaic, nothing taxing – and

Andronikos, who normally managed everything, deferred to Alexios. The boy baulked and stuttered, hedged and blundered, sounding idiotic, mentally deficient rather than merely young. Andronikos let him flounder – but not for too long, not so long as to appear cruel – and then intervened. *What the emperor means is . . . What the emperor wishes to convey is . . .* Smooth, kindly, apologetic. But the message to everyone was plain.

The boy's no good.

Slowly, Alexios withdrew – or rather, Theo helped him withdraw. Those were his orders. *Keep him busy.* And so he provided Alexios with a wholesome diet of race-going, polo and whorehouses until one very short, very early-morning conversation with Andronikos told Theo that his days playing boon companion to the young emperor were fast drawing to a close.

'I want him out of the City all day, but bring him back by dusk, no later. Understood?'

Theo nodded, and when Alexios summoned him, he suggested they go hare-hunting near Philopation. The boy was pleased. He never could land a spear on a moving target, but he liked setting his dogs on small game.

The hares the gamesmen had flushed out bounced and ran, twisting sideways, turning sudden invisible corners, so fast that there was nothing for the dog's jaws to close on. Theo looked at the emperor's face. He was giggling. Delighted. Flushed. Away from Andronikos, he was often like that, confiding and reckless, trying so hard to have fun.

A dog jogged up to Alexios, the first kill of the day kicking feebly in its jaws. Alexios dropped to his knees, petting it, calling it by some made-up name. He loved the dogs. He brought them bones, played favourites.

'My beauty. Beauty girl. Tomorrow we shall hunt something better than hares, shall we not? I long to find the boars on the plain. Or mountain cats. Where do I find a good mountain cat? My beauty deserves better than these jumping rats.'

Theo was suddenly angry. Why was Alexios so stupid? Animals knew a predator by sight, by sound, by smell, and they knew to run. They tried to save themselves. Why didn't the boy do the same? He's like an insect, thought Theo, a brightly coloured insect busy on a leaf, oblivious of the child's fingers itching to crush it.

'Theo? Theo?' Alexios returned to his side, a gamesman's bag stuffed with hares slung over his shoulder. 'Is there to be a celebration tonight? I saw preparations. I like Andronikos's parties. What is the occasion? Theo?'

But before Theo could even begin to answer, Alexios's attention was caught by a tussle between two untrained pups over a ripped-up carcass. He waded in kicking, stick flashing, and by the time Theo suggested they begin the ride back to the City, he seemed to have forgotten the question.

What would he do if Theo told him? The occasion, basileus? Oh, nothing much. Only that Andronikos takes your throne from you today. Not take, Theo corrected himself. That wasn't a word Andronikos liked to use even when only his innermost circle were listening. *I do not like to take things. I prefer to be given them. Willingly. Some men like the making, the force. I prefer gentler means.*

But Theo knew what happened when people did not give things willingly. He knew that the jails were starting to fill with men who were not giving. They filled and emptied again as those who didn't make it eloquently clear that they had come round to Andronikos's way of thinking were executed, quietly and efficiently. The way Andronikos ran the empire. He called it being tidy. Stephanos called it sorting out a handful of stuck-up donkey-fuckers who had a fucking problem with the boss.

Theo suddenly realised that Alexios was riding in silence. That was odd. Normally he had to put up with a flow of irrelevant chatter. He looked at the emperor's face – tense. His posture – tense. And Theo understood then that Alexios knew what was about to happen.

He struggled with the idea that Alexios was being brave. No, being brave meant getting your sword out and sticking it into the man who was trying to hurt you, not waiting around like some fucking martyr.

As they passed through the gates, Alexios flung a few coins to the beggars gathered there, who shouted their thanks up at him.

'The emperor loves you,' called Alexios gaily.

'And tell Andronikos we love him too,' one, witty, called out.

Theo wondered whether Alexios had heard. He knew he ought to send a man to punish the beggar. A few kicks to the head. But, all things considered, it didn't really seem fair.

They clattered into the main courtyard at Blachernai.

'The servants say there's supper ready in the Polytimos Chamber, basileus.'

'M-maybe I'll retire, Theo.'

'Have a bit to eat first, basileus.'

'V-very well, Theo.'

The door to the chamber – far too big and grand for a hunting supper – was open. Beyond it lay as homely a scene as one could ask for in the Blachernai Palace. A simple table. Andronikos reading a book to himself. Andronikos standing and bowing. Andronikos offering Alexios the best seat. Kind enquiries about the emperor's luck in the field. Servants coming forward with bread and wine. A discussion about the merits of cross-bred hunting dogs. Theo fading into the background.

And then the noise began.

Andronikos and Alexios both pretended to be surprised. Men tumbled into the chamber – Theo saw Isaakios Angelos, his brother behind him, a couple of Kantakouzenoi, a clutch of Makrodoukai, everyone really. They all fell to their knees and begged Andronikos to take the throne.

'Guard Alexios!'

'Guide Alexios!'

'It is God's will!'

'It is what Manuelos would have wanted!'

Andronikos motioned for quiet and aimed an apologetic shrug at Alexios.

'This is very embarrassing, dear boy. But maybe, after all, it is for the best?'

It was Constantinos who brought the news to Agnes in the women's quarters.

'Your husband begs your forgiveness, but he will be celebrating the accession of his co-emperor tonight.'

'What? That's ridiculous. You can't have two emperors.'

'You can, respected Empress Anna. In Old Rome they were obliged to have two senators. We in New Rome can choose to have two emperors. For balance.'

'And how exactly will Andronikos balance Alexios?'

'The silver of wisdom shall complement the gold of youth. It is perhaps more usual for the younger man to follow the elder to the throne. The son joins the father, the nephew the uncle. But we cannot ask Andronikos to be usual, can we?'

'I don't see why he doesn't just—'

'I'd restrict your remarks to *God give them both long life,* Agnes. Don't wait up.'

Don't wait up.

She listened as his footsteps echoed down the passageway. Her part of the palace was too quiet. The empress's rooms ought to be bursting with chatter, quarrels, schemes, crowded with women seeking preferment or political insight, but men were reluctant to send their wives and daughters to her. After all, the wife of Alexios could advance no career, broker no marriage, secure no mercy, and so the aristos avoided her as if her powerlessness might be contagious. She ran a finger down the tapestry at the head of her bed. Dust. Even the servants tried to keep away. *You'd think my walls were hung with plague shrouds, lepers' bandages.* She shivered. When death tracked close, you couldn't fail to feel its fingers, even if they were not groping for you.

She sprang from her bed and crept to her husband's apartments. Servants came in to bank up the small fire, to turn his sheets, but hurried out backwards when they saw her sitting there. *They probably know more than I do.* She wanted to shout after them that she wasn't stupid, that she knew what was happening, even if she couldn't stop it. It was only Alexios who was blind to the pitying glances, the averted eyes. Deaf, as well, to the chants that were becoming popular in the City, the ones that laughed at him even as they lauded Andronikos. And Agnes was starting to hear the same tunes hummed in the corridors of the palace that were sung on the streets.

The door opened. It was dark in the corridor, so at first she couldn't make out who was coming in. Then she saw her husband draped over Theo's shoulder. Like her worst dreams. Death blossoming at her feet. She gasped.

'He's not . . . ?'

'No.' Theo shook his head. 'He's not.'

Yet.

The unspoken word boomed in the dark.

'He's drunk too much,' said Agnes. 'I wonder why, Theo?'

He couldn't meet her eye. Of course he couldn't.

'We've been celebrating—'

'Oh, shut up. I know what you've been celebrating.'

Theo shifted Alexios off his shoulder and tried to set him down, but the boy's legs wouldn't hold him.

'I . . . I should go. I didn't know you'd be . . .'

'Waiting up? Worrying? No. What on earth have I got to be worried about?'

They stared at one another.

'All right,' she said. 'Put him on the bed and then go wherever it is you go.'

He reddened. She'd made him angry. Or ashamed. Either was good. He hesitated, and then carried Alexios over the threshold. As he laid him on the bed, the emperor's outer tunic gaped and it was plain that he was wearing no underclothes.

'Theo, what . . . ? Oh, don't trouble to tell me. Girls.'

Theo coughed. 'There were. But you know, he doesn't, not really . . .'

'Oh, I know very well he doesn't. *Not really*. And what about you?'

Theo did more than cough. He choked. 'Me? I . . .'

'How about him? Andronikos? Does *he*?'

'He . . .'

'No, I don't want to know about that either. Well, I hope you all had fun, because I'm sure my poor husband didn't. And he used to enjoy it so much. All that drinking and laughing and boasting. Not any more. His eyes go funny and he can't speak.' She leant over Alexios. 'He stinks. Can you smell it too? It's fear, Theo, fear seeping through his skin.' She straightened up. 'Pull his boots off, then. I'm an empress. I don't pull off boots. Even an emperor's.'

She wasn't sure that he would, but he did. He placed them by the side of the bed. Neatly.

'I'd better go back.'

She nodded, and he was about to leave. But something about his face, his eyes, the way he looked at her and looked away and looked again, something made her call him back.

'Theo, don't go.'

'Empress Anna?'

'Agnes. Please, call me Agnes. And please . . . Nobody talks to me. I can't bear it. *I can't*. I haven't spoken to anyone for days. Weeks. Apart from him, and he's . . .' The truth of what he was threatened to overwhelm her. 'You don't know what it's like. He's falling and I'm tied to him. I can't make him stop falling and I can't untie myself and . . . Oh God. I'm raving. I sound like I'm mad. But I know what's going to happen to him and I don't want it to happen to me. I don't. *I don't.*'

A nameless thing was squeezing her chest, blocking her throat. She'd felt it before, but never this bad. Breathe, she had to breathe, and it would pass.

'The waiting,' she whispered. 'It's driving me mad. Please, Theo. Tell me. I know it's going to happen, but tell me when.'

He shifted, but did not speak.

'Tell me.'

'I don't know. But I do know that you won't . . . that you'll be . . .'

'Fine?'

He nodded. 'Fine.'

'*Fine* like Marguerite-Constance was fine? *Fine* like Maria was fine?'

'No, no, you see, he . . . he likes you.'

'He does?'

'Yes. Yes, he does. I'm sure he does. He often says things.'

'What sort of things?'

'Oh, you know. *I wonder what little Agnes would make of this. Little Agnes said the funniest thing.*'

'Oh.'

She didn't know what else to say.

'Anyway, you have nothing to fear. I swear it.'

She looked at him. He meant it.

'And him?' She was about to touch her husband, but pulled her hand away. 'What about him?'

They looked at each other over the body of the emperor. The answer was in Theo's eyes.

'When?' she asked. 'I want to know when.'

He shook his head, violently. 'I don't know.'

'And if you did know, you wouldn't tell me.' Suddenly she was angry with him and his eyes that did not lie. 'How do you find it? What you're doing? What you've done?'

'What I've done?'

'Helped him kill everyone who stood between him and the throne.'

'I haven't—'

'Oh, you have. And you know it The Protosebastos. Marguerite-Constance. Maria. Renier. Your friend, Renier.'

'Stop it.'

'Do you pray? You must pray really hard.'

'Stop it.'

'Why should I? It's true. It's all true.'

She expected him to argue. She *wanted* him to argue, to say pompous and stupid things that she could shout down. But he didn't. Instead, he reached over and took her hands.

'You'll be all right,' he said, his voice quiet and urgent.

She was so surprised that she forgot to remove her hands.

'Yes, you will,' he repeated, as if she'd contradicted him. 'I know it. I've always known it. On the boat. Your wedding day. That night when Andronikos arrived. Any other girl would have wept and screamed, but you didn't. And now. You say you're afraid, but . . .'

'But what?'

From some strange, faraway place, he conjured a smile.

'I think you're more angry than afraid.'

She ripped her hands away.

'Don't joke. How can you joke when—'

'I'm not. I'm sorry. I was . . . I was trying to help. I'm sorry if it didn't come out that way.'

'I know. You are helping. You're being kind. It's . . . Thank you, Theo. All right? Thank you.'

There was an odd pause. A dangerous pause. She looked down. Somehow he was holding her hands again. She looked up. Suddenly, there were a hundred things she wanted to tell him, but she didn't know where to begin.

'Thank you,' she repeated, and she might have said more, might have done more, but Alexios stirred on the bed. His head lolled to the other side. Little animal noises came from his throat.

'I must go,' said Theo. 'I've been too long already. He said he needed me back.'

He said. He said. Her anger returned.

'To pour his wine? Cut his meat? Plump his pillows? Undress his—'

But she was interrupted by the sound of Alexios's stomach heaving.

'Go,' said Agnes. 'Go. You attend one emperor. I'll attend the other.'

She turned her back. Once she heard the door close behind him, she began to stroke her husband's hair, tucking it behind his ears, brushing it away from his forehead. He liked her doing that.

'You don't have to accept it, Alexios,' she whispered. 'You could try to stop it. You could run away. Go into exile. You could seek asylum. You don't have to end like . . . like the others. You could . . . we could . . .'

She stopped. He was mumbling something. She leant in.

'Shuddup.'

That was not what she'd expected to hear. She persevered.

'Alexios, stop pretending, please. You must—'

'Shut up, I said.'

And he gripped her hand hard.

'My sister was a traitor and my mother was a whore.' He was glass-eyed, sweating and thick-tongued. 'They deserved to die. Andronikos is loyal. He was my father's truest friend until enemies began to whisper tales about him. And now he is *my* friend. And if you whisper about him, I'll tell him and then you'll get what *you* deserve.'

She opened her mouth. How could he be so *stupid*? How could he not *see*?

'He's going to kill you.'

As soon as she spat the words at him, he struck her, a weak blow, but shocking. Nobody had ever raised a hand to her before.

A matter of days later

Theo looked down from the balcony that ran under the dome of the Holy Wisdom. From up there, he could, he supposed, be watching over any coronation from the last hundred – two, three, four hundred – years. From up there, all he could see were the heads of a worshipful congregation, their white mantles shot with gold, and two emperors shrouded in sacred mystery.

A bird's-eye view. God's view. The view of a young man who'd been told to keep his eyes peeled for trouble. A view he shared with a dozen sparrows, the giant faces of the saints, their dark eyes opaque, unfathomable – and Stephanos, who was leaning on the balustrade opposite Theo, scanning the ranks of aristos beneath them.

Theo struggled to believe anyone would threaten Andronikos. The penalty would be an elaborate death, unimaginable pain. But then, he'd never imagined he'd carry so much as a needle in the Holy Wisdom, yet there he was, a dagger in each boot, a sword beneath his cloak. Usually, he liked the feel of a blade at his side. It completed him. But there, with the saints gazing down on him, it weighed heavy.

A man shifted and Theo was all alertness, but he was only switching a walking stick from one hand to the other. *Don't be so jumpy.*

Everyone looked the same down there. He couldn't see a man's bearing, a woman's beauty. He certainly couldn't see the bruise on Agnes's face that everyone knew was there and that no one mentioned because there were only two men in the empire who could have given it to her, and who was going to tell either of them who they could or couldn't hit?

It made him angry, though. He could be angry, couldn't he, even if there was nothing he could do about it? He wished his father were there. He wanted his father to tell him that what Andronikos was doing was right. That what *he* was doing was right. But his father was miles away, where he belonged, doing what he did best. Defending the empire. And Theo, what was he doing?

The ceremony was coasting to a climax. Andronikos was on his knees, praying on the porphyry slab in front of the silver gates of the iconostasis. He was dressed in robes that had been given to the first emperor of the New Rome by angels. Soon he would be seated on a golden throne and crowned, and every man there would pay him homage, prostrating themselves before him.

He'll enjoy that, although he'll pretend it's nothing.

It was over. Stephanos nodded at him, and together they made their way to find Andronikos in a side chamber, a robing room. The patriarch was leaving as they entered. He'd just administered the sacraments. The heavenly Body was crumbs on Andronikos's mouth; the precious Blood was wet on his lips. He wiped his mouth with the back of his hand.

'Hello, you two.'

Stephanos pressed himself to the floor, the obeisance an emperor demanded. Theo was about to copy him when Andronikos flung a crimson buskin at Stephanos.

'Get up,' he said. 'You look fucking ridiculous. Never mind all that. Not in private, anyway.'

He tore off his headdress; one of the strings broke, and pearls skittered across the floor. 'Keep them,' he told the serving boy who was gathering them up. 'Now get out.' When the boy was gone and the three of them were alone, Andronikos stretched, yawned.

'Gentlemen,' he said. 'I know you want to celebrate, but first you have a little job to do.'

A gag in her mouth, a sack over her head, her arms pinned behind her back. At first Agnes thought it was another nightmare. That was how they all began. But then she felt the ropes twisting round her wrists and ankles, and she knew she was awake and it was real. She couldn't see. She could hardly breathe. Next to her, panicked gasps, scuffling, muffled protest. The men, whoever they were, had Alexios too.

Somebody picked her up and dropped her over his shoulder, her head hanging down his back. She knew there was no point resisting, but she arched and wriggled all the same. It didn't help.

The men didn't talk. A few grunts and they set off through the corridors. She could see a lamp through the coarse weave of the sacking. It was smoking badly and making the man carrying it cough.

Where were they going? Outside. Cold air and the smell of damp stones. The man slipped and stumbled and put the hand that was holding her out to break his fall. She fell hard on her shoulder and cried out in pain.

'Watch it.' A voice she knew. *Theo.*

Suddenly, she was furious. How dare he be part of this? She tried to say something, but the leather band between her teeth made it impossible.

They were going down steps, down a narrow passageway, walls close at hand. It must be slippery underfoot – the man carrying her was treading carefully. It stank of decay and dying things and worse. Drops of foul water splashed on to her. A sewer, maybe. She could hear water running under their feet.

A new sound, a new smell.

The sea.

The men stopped.

'Where's the boat?' Theo again.

A laugh from the man holding her – Stephanos, unmistakable.

'There's no boat.'

'But I thought . . .'

'Change of plan. Dead is safer. Simpler.'

Silence.

'Her too?'

'Yes, her too. Come on, he's fainted. Do her first.'

Do her? Kill her?

She struggled.

It was real it was going to happen it was real.

She struggled and Stephanos laughed, and the more she struggled the more he laughed. He let go of her and she ran, hit a wall, ran the other way. Arms grabbed her, held on to her. Somebody ripped the sack off her head and there was Theo staring at her.

'Still, be still. See where you were about to run. Look.'

She looked. Two more steps and she would have toppled off the lip of the tunnel and down into the blackness below – into the Golden Horn with her hands bound. She shivered.

'What you up to, boy?' Stephanos had stopped laughing. 'You should've let her fall. Job done.'

'She's not meant to die. She doesn't deserve this.'

'Sometimes they do, sometimes they don't. It makes no difference to what happens to them.'

'I thought we were seeing her to a convent.'

'Orders change. And orders, Theo, is orders. Get on with it.'

She looked at Theo, looked right at him, deep into his eyes. He wouldn't hurt her. But then she saw his eyes slide away from hers and heard the scrape of a dagger leaving its sheath.

Why hadn't she flung herself into the sea? Then it would be over. Instead, it was about to happen. She was about to die. She willed herself to faint, but she couldn't. She had never felt more alert, more alive. She could see every stone, every patch of weed, beautiful and precious. The last things she'd see.

She could also see Stephanos. She wished she couldn't. There was too much blood in his lips, too much heat in his eyes. He came close. For a horrible moment she thought he was going to kiss her, but instead he reached behind her, plucked the blade from Theo's hand, cut her bonds and undid her gag.

Then he clapped Theo on the shoulder.

'We were worried you might lack the stomach for the harder parts of this job. Seems we were wrong. A man who would draw a knife on such beauty is committed. Well done. And well done to you, Empress Anna, I've seen a lot of men think they were about to die, and few enough had your courage.'

Agnes fell forward on to her hands, then sprang to her feet and turned to look at Theo. Such was the self-loathing on his face that for a moment she pitied him. Then she spat in his face. He didn't even wipe it away.

Stephanos gave an abrupt laugh. 'Doesn't always make you friends, this business, Theo, but you must know that by now. Now for the boy. No reprieve for him. You might want to shut your eyes, Empress Anna.'

Of course she wanted to shut her eyes, but she wasn't going to do what that man told her. She fixed her gaze on the bundle that was her husband.

'Please yourself. There are some as love to look. Come closer if you like. Maybe you're pleased to see him go. Are you?'

Theo grabbed his shoulder and shook him. 'Shut up and do it.'

Suddenly, Alexios stirred. After a brief struggle, his head emerged from the sack, a child woken from sleep, baffled, clutching the front of his nightshirt.

'Do you want to say goodbye, Empress Anna? Any last words? A parting kiss, perhaps? No? Then I'll get to it.'

What could she do? Nothing. She reached a hand out. Why?

To show him he was not totally alone. To show him that despite everything, she was not truly part of this.

Stephanos leant down and wrapped something, a bowstring maybe, around Alexios's neck. He didn't resist. He didn't do anything. His body started to jerk, his face turned red, bulging, devoid of all thought, like he was about to climax. Agnes screamed and buried her head in her hands.

'There. That wasn't so bad, was it? An emperor is no different from other men after all.'

Stephanos stuffed a dozen stones into the sack, followed by Alexios. He secured the sack with whatever he'd used to kill him and kicked it over the ledge. A short wait, and then a splash. He was gone. Neither she nor Theo had moved.

'Right. He's waiting. Let's go.'

Agnes took a step, but fell over. Without a word, Theo picked her up and started to stumble back up the tunnel after Stephanos.

Put me down.

She tried to speak, but there was something wrong with her jaw, her tongue. It was as if she had been floating for days in freezing-cold water.

Murderer.

'What?'

'Murderer.'

'Murderer.'

She was fighting him, but he clung on to her. He wanted to hold her tight. She'd be safe with him, if anywhere was safe.

'I am not a murderer,' he muttered. 'I'm not. I wouldn't have . . . I didn't . . . I'm not . . .'

He was talking quietly, into her hair. She twisted around to look him full in the face.

'What are you, then? A hero? For God's sake, put me down. I can walk.'

'Are you sure?'

'Down,' she yelled. 'Put me down.'

He put her down, as carefully as he could, and she fell into step behind Stephanos. They strode back into the palace, a bizarre trio, Theo trailing behind the other two, wretched, confused. A girl terrorised with a knife. A boy strangled and thrown into the sea. That was who he was.

'You go in and report,' he told Stephanos once they reached Andronikos's antechamber. 'I'll keep an eye on her.'

Stephanos didn't bother to hide how funny he found that, but Theo told himself he didn't care.

'Please, sit down,' he said to Agnes once they were alone. She was standing in the middle of the room, breathing fast and shallow. 'You're safe.' He tried to lead her to a chair, but she pushed him away.

'I trusted you. I actually trusted you.'

'You can—'

'I can't. How can you even pretend it? What you just did. It was . . . it was . . .'

'It wasn't. You don't understand. Listen—'

'You think I'll listen to you? After you betrayed me.'

'It wasn't me. It was Andronikos who—'

But she was shaking her head, furiously.

'That's different, and you know it. He never promised me anything. I actually thought . . .'

'What, Agnes? What did you think?'

Her head came back up, wounded and defiant.

'I thought you liked me. There, I've said it. I thought you were my friend. *My friend*. What an idiot. There are no friends in the City.'

'Let me be your friend now. Please, Agnes.'

'No, it's too late. I know what you are. You're weak. A man says kill, and you'll kill. That's no good. That won't help me.'

He looked at her face, pale and shimmering. He saw a

fierceness there, a determination that was new and different. It alarmed him.

'I need . . . I need . . .'

But before she finished, the door opened and there were Andronikos and Stephanos.

'What do you need, child?' Andronikos didn't even look at Theo. This man he would have killed for didn't even look at him. 'My poor girl. You look dreadful. Come with me.' And Theo had to watch, impotent, as Andronikos ushered Agnes away.

'Let's sit you down. You need something to eat. A fig? No, something stronger.'

It was still before dawn, but Andronikos didn't seem to have been pulled from bed. Nor did he look like a man who had been awake all night. He poured her something syrupy and potent.

'I don't want that.'

'Nonsense. Drink up. Do you good.'

She drank. It was some kind of wine, doctored with herbs and spices. It warmed her blood. It reminded her she was alive. She flung the cup to the floor.

'You killed my husband.'

'I did. But please don't make a big scene about it. You didn't love him. You could hardly bear to be in the same room as him. You're probably quite pleased he's dead. Or you will be when you've calmed down.'

'Calmed . . . ? You almost killed me.'

'Not true. I pretended to almost kill you. There's a big difference. I needed to learn more about Theodore Branas, and that was the best way to do it.'

'He's a coward.'

'No, he's not. Being ready to kill you to please me makes him my man, not yours. It doesn't make him a coward.'

'What if Stephanos hadn't stopped him in time? I'd be dead.'

'Yes, you would be. But Stephanos did stop him – and in plenty of time, didn't he? Stephanos is very, very good at his job. I had no fear for your life. But I am sorry if it was difficult for you.'

'Difficult? Do you have any idea what it's like to think you're about—'

'To die? Oh, Agnes, I have every idea. The feeling is as familiar to me as breathing.'

Her need to live was starting to sound ridiculous, even to her. She forced herself to change tack.

'Why?' she said.

'Ah, questions.'

'Why kill him now? Why wait all these months? Why didn't you kill him when you first got here, if that was what you meant to do?'

'I am sure you can answer that all by yourself.'

And he was right. She could. If he'd killed Alexios immediately, it would have been bloody assassination. By waiting until there wasn't a man in the City who didn't believe Andronikos was a thousand times the man Alexios would ever be, he looked like a deliverer. It was a matter of presentation.

'Why am I not dead? Why did you spare me?'

'I'm not callous. I do not kill for pleasure. Your death was not necessary.'

'Lucky me.' She forced herself to smile.

'Lucky you.' He smiled back.

'What happens to me, if I am not to die?'

'Finally. That is what I wanted to talk to you about.' He grimaced. 'The convent. That is what happens to imperial brides whose usefulness has passed. I believe there is a great deal of needlework. Needlework and prayer. It's a healthy life. Good plain fare. If you're lucky, you might have three score years to look forward to.'

She didn't know what she'd expected, but it wasn't that. A

life immured. He couldn't do that to her. She wouldn't be able to bear it. That wasn't meant to be her life.

'You can't. Don't. Please, don't.' She raised her eyes to his, imploring. She realised she was crying – she who never cried. 'I beg you.'

He shook his head. 'I'm sorry.'

'Don't say sorry when you're not.'

'But I am sorry. Nevertheless, that is what must happen. You'd be too useful to my enemies.'

'Send me home.'

'And insult your family? No. You will ask to enter God's service and I shall grant your request. What nobler path for a widow?' He reached forward, brushed the hair out of her eyes, smoothed the tears from her cheeks. 'You are unhappy. I would not have you unhappy. But Agnes, this is your road. There is no other.'

An idea that had been hovering out of reach landed fully formed in her head. She seized it like a soldier scrabbling for a dropped blade.

'There is. Marry me.'

'To whom?'

She stamped her foot. 'Don't be obtuse.'

'Obtuse. That's a fine word.'

'You know what I mean.'

'I don't. You have lost your heart? You wish me to sanction your marriage to some young swain?'

'No. Don't play games.'

'But I love playing games.'

'I don't. Marry *me*. You need a wife. Emperors need wives. Marry me.'

'Am I to understand that you, a child, young enough to be my son's daughter, widowed this last hour, are demanding to be wed to me? *Me*?'

'Yes.'

He laughed, joyfully, uproariously.

'Oh, Agnes, I spent some of the happiest days of my life seducing girls like you. The tears, the talk of honour, the oaths never to see me again – and the rapture when they relented. But never, never have I been propositioned so boldly by such beauty.'

'You think I'm beautiful?'

The words were out before she could stop them. He took a step towards her – and paused.

'You're too young to be truly beautiful. You won't be that until you've lived a little, suffered a little. Already you are closer to true beauty than when first we met. But you are ravishing, certainly you are that.' He smiled. 'Were you worried I had not noticed?'

'I never gave it a moment's thought,' she lied.

'Liar,' said Andronikos. He took her hands in his. 'I had no idea I had touched your young heart.'

She removed her hands. 'You haven't.'

'That's a pity. I like to be loved.'

'You don't deserve love. You . . .' She stopped herself. Better not to think about what Andronikos deserved. 'This is – what do you call it? – a transaction. I do not want to go into a convent.'

'I see. And what – if there is to be no talk of love – is in it for me?'

She took his hands again, placed them around her waist and pressed herself close. She felt a small shudder run through his body, and she thought she must be winning.

'I don't have to marry you for that,' he said, and kissed her.

For long, long moments she could not pull away. When she did, it was hard to remember what she wanted. It was hard to remember anything.

'You do have to,' she said and, with great effort, pushed him from her.

'I don't, Agnes. I really don't.' But he came no nearer. 'Some will say I would do great dishonour to bring a rosy-fingered, bud-mouthed maiden into my bed.'

'I'm not a maiden,' said Agnes, perhaps a little too sharply.

'No, you're not, are you?' he said. 'Although that is a true maidenly blush.' He took her hand and kissed it. 'You're not scared? You know what became of them all — those deaths, those grisly, necessary deaths — and yet you do not run away. The reverse, you draw near. If I were your friend, Agnes, I might advise you to bow out while you still can.'

'What the hell's going on in there?' said Stephanos, circling the room. 'How long does it take to tell a girl to pack up and go?'

He had a point. Theo had been so busy castigating himself, he hadn't noticed how long Agnes and Andronikos had been talking.

'Maybe she's not packing up,' said Constantinos, who'd just walked into the anteroom with his breakfast on a tray as if it were a day like any other. 'If I know Agnes as well as I fancy I do, I doubt she'll be sleeping on a convent pallet tonight.'

'But the boss said—'

'I know what he said. Agnes might disagree, that's all.'

'Oh, come off it.'

Theo stared at them both. What were they talking about?

'Come in, gentlemen!' A shout from Andronikos's room.

Theo followed Stephanos and Constantinos inside to where a strange sight greeted him. Strange and, he realised, terrible. Andronikos's arms were around Agnes. She was smiling up at him. She turned and looked at Theo — with what? Hatred? No. Defiance? Pride? Even pleasure. He couldn't tell. On Andronikos's face, however, there was only amusement.

'Congratulate me, gentlemen. I am, it seems, to be married.'

'Fuck,' said Stephanos.

'Congratulations,' said Constantinos.

A pause, in which Theo tried and failed to think of the right thing to say.

The Third Emperor

Andronikos Komnenos is not looking at Dadibrenos, but Dadibrenos — a man constructed on so vast a scale that he could surely stop a stampeding hippopotamus with his little finger — is looking at the emperor. His face — flat, square — is confused, almost affronted. He stands accused of abusing the hospitality of a household of peasants on a tour of inspection. Without quite daring to say that peasants are as fair game to him as the hare is to the hound, he is protesting that he has done nothing wrong.

'No?' says Andronikos. 'Nothing? Let me see . . .'

He nods, and the eunuch Constantinos unrolls a piece of paper.

'He ordered the farmer's lambs butchered, saying he only ate young, sweet meat. He proceeded to drink so much of his wine that, amongst other acts, he emptied his bladder into the crib where the man's six-week-old son lay asleep and bedded the man's orphaned niece, who is, I understand, thirteen years old.'

Constantinos rolls the paper back up again and returns to his desk.

'Does that sound familiar, Dadibrenos?' Andronikos enquires.

Dadibrenos squirms.

The emperor turns to Stephanos Hagiochristophorites, now better known in the City as Stephanos-the-Antichrist.

'Well? He's your man. What have you got to say for him?'

Stephanos shrugs.

'He thought it was business as usual. I've heard worse. I've done worse.'

'Ah,' says Andronikos, 'but it isn't business as usual, is it? A new emperor is on the throne. A good emperor who will punish the greedy and comfort the indigent. And this peasant has heard all about it. His

second cousin tends the palace gardens, and this worthy man is betrothed to the woman who makes the honey and rose-water cakes my wife is so devoted to. Do you know what that means, Dadibrenos?'

Dadibrenos shakes his head. He does not even know what indigent means.

'It means, Dadibrenos, that you are going to be flogged within an inch of your life.'

The man smirks. Nobody has flogged him since he grew taller than his father when he was ten years old.

'You think I'm joking? You are going to receive a dozen lashes from the roughest bull-hide whip Stephanos can lay his hands on, wielded by a man skilled enough to open up your back before you've heard five-six-seven. Stephanos — make it happen. And bring me his shirt when you're done.'

The emperor and the eunuch are left alone.

'A man who loves me enough to enjoy thrashing his friends,' says Andronikos, nodding after Stephanos. 'The perfect servant. Don't make that face, Constantinos. He does love me.'

'Talking of love, how's married life treating you, Andronikos?' asks Constantinos.

'Don't be so fucking insolent.'

'Very well. Then tell me more about this good emperor . . .'

And Andronikos says that while he lived in exile, he saw how tax collectors devoured the people. He says that he is going to pay governors properly so they don't squeeze the provinces. He says that farmers will work harder if they know their harvest isn't going to pay for a new statue of some petty bureaucrat in their local forum.

'The empire is rotting, Constantinos. It looks nice and plump, but so does a dead cow with a belly full of gas. The aristos? They are cretins. Inbred imbeciles who live and die by backhanders and back-scratching. I'm going to change it all.'

Constantinos nods. 'There's not a word you've said that I don't agree with. But the aristos won't like it. If you rip the bone out of a dog's mouth, it'll bite.'

'Then we must rip out its teeth as well.'

The spring of 1184

One morning, some six months after her second marriage, Agnes rolled over and was surprised to find Andronikos still beside her in the grey of a day not yet begun. Normally he had to leave her bed in the middle hours of the night, roused by a discreet knock.

He'd moved the court from Blachernai – *far too many mosaics of Manuelos, my darling* – down to the Great Palace, which made it all too easy for anyone to get hold of him at any time of the day or night. When she'd complained, he'd told her he wanted to keep an eye on the barracks and jail cells, the counting houses and coining presses that were as much part of the Great Palace as its halls and porticoes. But she guessed there was another reason. He also needed to be close to the hippodrome, the Mesê, the Holy Wisdom – the places where the people of the City gathered.

Occasionally, no knock came and he might linger, lying on his back, his hands behind his head, staring up at the silk drapes louring above them like giant butterfly wings. Then she'd lie on her side, watching him, waiting for his eyes to close, wondering what his face might betray at rest. But sleep always stole over her first, and when she woke, the room was dark and he was gone.

But there he was – all hers.

She looked at him, carefully, cautiously, as the birds started calling to each other outside. The half-light blunted his age, leaving only the impossible lines of his features. Her fingers wanted to touch the turn of his jaw, trace the rise of his cheeks.

His eyes opened.

'Don't pet me,' he murmured, not unkindly.

His hand moved and took her wrist, his thumb running back and forth over the tiny bones close to the surface of her skin. A pounding began in her belly. No, not in her belly. Lower, deeper. He knew it. And liked knowing it. She shifted a little towards him. He smiled and closed his eyes again, but his grip did not loosen.

The very first night, the night they wed, she'd been disappointed by how offhand he'd been. He'd strolled into her chamber, flung himself on to a divan, poured some wine and told her to undress. She'd turned away to hide the angry flush she knew was stealing up her cheeks and told herself only an idiot would be surprised — after all, she was the hundredth, no, probably the thousandth woman in his life.

That didn't matter. She'd show him.

But Andronikos had looked — she could admit it now; there was only one word for it — *bored* when her hands flickered near him.

'No,' he said, and stopped her. 'If I want a whore's tricks, I'll go to a whore. Don't look so offended. Some women, Agnes, do this for a living. You could live to be a hundred and you still wouldn't match them, so don't for God's sake try. Besides . . .' a smile, 'I'm not here for my amusement. I'm here for yours.'

She'd thought that was a joke, and not a very funny one. But of course he hadn't been joking. Not in the slightest.

Had he fallen asleep again?

The grey outside was turning blue. Warmth was already stealing through the shutters. For a moment, she allowed herself to be intoxicated by life's sweetness.

'I love you,' she whispered.

She didn't know whether it was true, but she wanted to hear how it sounded.

'No you don't.' He sat up, yawned and stretched. 'What we

have isn't love. It's much better than love. But don't confuse the two.'

'Oh, what do you know about love?' she said, rolling herself up in the sheets.

'A great deal more than you.'

'You've never been in love.'

He looked amused.

'Haven't I?'

'When? Who?'

She shouldn't care. But she did.

'When I was young. Not much older than you.'

'That doesn't count. Young men are in love all the time.'

'If you say so.'

'What about afterwards? Since you were a boy?'

She was surprised when he answered her seriously.

'Yes, there was a woman.'

'What happened to her? Is she dead?'

'No, Agnes. She's alive, but she's a long way away. She did not want this. What I want. What you want.'

'You mean . . .' she said, gesturing vaguely at the sheets, their nakedness.

'No.' He smiled. 'This she liked. I mean the world outside. The world that calls to me from beyond this room. That she did not want. And that was something we could not agree on.'

Agnes had time to think *what a stupid woman* before a knock sounded at the door.

'What is it?' Andronikos called.

'Branas's boat has been sighted. If the wind holds, he'll dock within the hour.'

After he had dressed and gone, Agnes walked out through the palace gardens, down a tree-lined avenue and into a shady courtyard that looked out over the Bakoleon and the Propontis. The sun was turning the waters below her a thousand different colours, and the breeze was making the ripples dance. Fishermen

169

swept past, trawling on the current, and she wondered how it could be so warm so early in the year.

She pictured herself as one of the goddesses in the old poems, gazing down from a mountaintop, wreathed in clouds of gold, infinitely more glamorous than Mary, Mother of God.

She flushed.

That was his influence, making her think thoughts like that. It was the sort of thing he said – things about God that were both wrong and exciting. He'd even laughed at Mary's virginity, and said something about the old gods having a much better idea how to live.

The crunch of little stones on the walkway scattered her thoughts. She looked up and saw Susa walking towards her, her baby on her hip, pursued by a cluster of nurses.

Susa was her new friend, maybe her first friend. She couldn't remember ever having had a friend before, only sisters and servants. Susa was married to one of Andronikos's two sons – well, one of his two legitimate sons; she was sure there were countless others. He was, inevitably, called Manuelos, and he cut a slight, insignificant figure beside his father.

'What are you smiling about?' Susa asked as she settled herself beside Agnes.

'Nothing. Everything. The sunshine. Yes, I think the sunshine.'

Susa smiled, a smile that seemed both to guess what Agnes was thinking and promise to ask no more.

Agnes had been wary of her at first – actually, wary was an understatement. A sharp needle of jealousy had pricked her chest when she first saw Susa's dark hair, dark eyes and soft face. She was little, quiet, perfect. And when she spoke Greek with a shocking barbarian accent – she came from somewhere called Iberia, and she had no more heard of Paris than Agnes had heard of her home city, Tbilisi – everyone thought it was enchanting and it did not occur to them to sneer.

Agnes had feared a rival, but she realised quickly that Susa had only one focus – her son.

They fell to talking, gossiping, dangling strings of glass beads for the baby to grab hold of, bouncing his toy horse against his nose. The nurses hovered nearby, cross that they were not needed, suggesting a snack, a sleep, another layer, or maybe a bonnet. Susa ignored them, picked Alexios up when he grew fractious and stood looking out to sea, swaying, singing something in her own strange, spiky language – so at odds with her face – until he fell asleep. Agnes, meanwhile, shut her eyes and allowed the sun to warm her thoughts.

Once, she had asked Andronikos whether he wanted a child.

I have children, Agnes.

But do you want my child?

No, my love. Once you have a baby, your blue eyes will no longer follow me around as they are wont to do.

'Look.' Susa's voice came to her quietly, so as not to wake Alexios. 'Boat.'

Agnes stood up and joined her looking down at the imperial dock where five years – or a lifetime – ago she had first landed in the City. As she watched, Andronikos appeared with a suite of his men at the top of the steps. That was unusual. He'd obviously been waiting.

'Who are the men coming from boat?' asked Susa.

Two men were walking up the steps, two men with unmistakable hair and burnt, freckled faces.

'The older one is Alexios Branas. The younger is his son, Theodore.'

Agnes knew that Susa would be waiting for her to say more. Normally she loved telling her about the people of the City, but she didn't know where to begin with Theo. She should try to see him as others did.

He's a big player, Susa, a coming man – he and his father are very close to Andronikos. He's a big catch, too – lots of women want

171

to marry him. But I met him when we were both little more than children. We became friends – or I thought we did – but then he held a knife to my throat.

No. She mustn't say that. She mustn't even think it. Suddenly, the weight of all the things she mustn't think threatened to overwhelm her.

'They . . . they are important men from Hadrianopolis. They have some Komnenos blood through a grandmother,' she said, knowing that Susa would think she sounded strange and stilted. 'They've been in Bithynia as far as I know. They're fighting men. They . . .'

She broke off and looked more closely at her husband. To an outside eye he might appear unruffled, but she'd learnt to be sensitive to his moods and she could see that something was very wrong. She gave Susa a quick kiss on the cheek and set off towards his rooms, where she guessed they would all be heading.

'Where do you go?' Susa asked. But she wasn't really looking at Agnes. She was looking at baby Alexios, who had woken up and was trying to stuff her shawl into his mouth.

'Back soon,' Agnes said, silently asking to be spared children for a while longer. If they stopped you concentrating, they weren't safe.

'Agnes,' Susa called her back. 'Be careful, heh? You're not afraid – of him?' Agnes realised she might have underestimated her. 'My husband is, you see. Afraid, I mean. Why is he? I wonder to myself. Andronikos is only kind to me. So I thought I would ask you, his wife.'

'He can be . . . ruthless, if necessary. But only if necessary. And a lot has been necessary.' So few words to cover up so many dead. 'Do you understand, Susa?'

'Understand? Maybe. The necessary can be very frightening, that I know. But you do not answer me, Agnes. You – are you afraid of him?'

'No, I'm not. I cannot be. Because otherwise . . .'

But she could not say any more. Fear made people tense and grey and jerky, and he wouldn't want her if she looked like that. No, she was not afraid of him.

'What about you, Susa?'

A smile, rueful and incredibly pretty.

'I fear everything. I fear that bee there may bite my little Alexios. I fear he swallow one stone and his breath stop. Andronikos. Pah. I have not time to fear Andronikos.'

She heard his voice long before she could make out what he was saying. He wasn't raging nor breaking things, nothing like that, but something about his tone made her hesitate to enter. She stood outside the door to listen.

Don't tell me you think I should have humoured that sack of dough?

You could have been more diplomatic. We need them. A new voice, calmer, close by the door.

We do not need them. And since when were you a fucking diplomat, Branas? I will give them nothing – nothing, you understand. You heard what Isaakios Angelos said. 'It's a big pie, basileus. We can all have a few crumbs, basileus.' No. Fuck him. Fuck all of them. They need to understand I am their God on fucking earth and they do not dare fucking haggle with me.

The other man – Branas – started to talk quieter, too low for her to make out. She pressed her ear to the door, trying to hear.

'I'd keep clear if I were you, Empress Anna,' said a voice behind her. 'He's in a filthy mood.'

It was Theo. He was about to go past her into the room.

'That's why I'm here, Theodore. He's my husband.'

'*He's my husband.*' Theo aped her words. 'You think that's what he needs right now? A wife?'

'I happen to know he finds my company very congenial.'

'He doesn't want congeniality. He wants men who can help him keep a grip on the empire.' He cocked his head and gave her a meaningful look. 'But I forget, you won't have heard.'

She wouldn't ask him what was happening. She wouldn't give him the satisfaction. She wouldn't . . .

'Wait. Stop. Theo. What's happening?'

'Don't worry, Empress Anna. It's all being taken care of.'

'I didn't ask whether it was all being taken care of. I asked what was happening.'

He looked down and she realised she'd grabbed his arm. She dropped it.

'Tell me. I demand that you tell me, or I'll . . .'

Before she could finish, he bowed.

'Oh, but if the empress commands it, I shall, of course, tell all. Nicaea. Prusa. Lopadion,' he said, naming three of the great cities of Bithynia. 'They are threatening to rise.'

Agnes flipped through what she knew of them.

'But they're . . .'

'Ve-ry big and ve-ry close,' he said, stressing each syllable as if she were a halfwit.

'Don't talk to me like that.'

He did not reply, only bowed again, much lower than was necessary, an insulting bow. That was too much. She forgot who he was, who *she* was, and instead only saw an idiotic boy with a pleased look on his face.

'You have no right,' she found herself hissing, 'no right to treat me with that little respect.' She wouldn't hold back. She'd give it to him. 'You . . . you should feel ashamed after what you did. Shame. Remorse. Some Christian feeling.'

'I do feel remorse.' There was no mockery there. 'But I feel it before God—' one finger jabbed up in the air '—not before you.' The same finger came within a whisker of poking her in the chest.

'How dare you!'

'*How dare I?* Oh, stop trying to make out I'm a worm and you're some kind of angel.' His stately tone had vanished. 'You're no better than me. *What I did?* You – you'd have held that knife to my throat if he'd told you to. Don't pretend you wouldn't.

Instead, you did what you had to do. You got him to marry you. That wasn't part of his plan. It was your idea, all yours.'

'Yes, and I don't deny it. Why should I? It *was* my idea, and a very good one too. I'm very happy.'

'Are you? Are you really? You don't look it, you know that?'

That blow landed.

'Of course I'm happy. What a ridiculous thing to say. Don't make that face. It *is* ridiculous. *Happy*. Ha! Who cares about happy? You can't eat happy. You can't wear it. For all I know, the woman who poured my bath this morning is happy, but that doesn't mean I want to be her. *Happy.*'

He was looking at her more and more strangely, but she carried on regardless.

'What's it to you anyway, whether I'm happy or not? You've got bigger things to worry about, soldier,' she said, relieved to find herself back on the attack.

'Yes, I do, and that's why I—'

Their angry, urgent whispers were growing louder and louder until Andronikos's voice from behind the door – *Where's your boy with those reports?* – stilled them.

'Go on,' she whispered. 'You go first. I'll follow in a moment.'

Theo did as she said, but returned almost immediately.

'He says to come in.'

'But how . . . ?'

Andronikos appeared behind Theo in the doorway.

'Young Theodore always has the same look on his face after talking to you. Preoccupied. I can spot it a mile off.'

There was something beneath his words, an implication, an insinuation, that was so unsafe she refused to let it crystallise in her head. Instead, with nothing but her husband in her mind, she went to his side and took his hand.

'I saw you at the docks. You looked like there was bad news.'

He squeezed her fingers.

'It's nothing, Agnes. Go back to the gardens.'

'Tell me. I'll worry if you don't.'

She nestled close. Sometimes he liked her sweet. She hoped this was one of those times.

'How could any man resist you?' he said with a slightly theatrical sigh. 'Come on in, then. Have you met Alexios Branas? He shall tell you.'

The general made a very correct bow – not obsequious, not casual, just right, and she liked him for it. He had the clear eyes and clear manners that spoke of a life spent far away from the City with its intrigue and politicking. They were warm and kind and they made her a little uneasy. They made her wonder what her own eyes looked like.

'Empress Anna, a group of aristo families have banded together in revolt. The Angeloi, the Kantakouzenoi, many others. The ringleaders have fled the City and are gathered behind the walls of three cities in Bithynia.'

She frowned and turned to Andronikos.

'But I thought the Angeloi supported you when you arrived.'

'Exactly. Well remembered. And that's what makes their current behaviour all the more vexatious.'

He was acting more like himself, less like the man she'd heard behind the door, not too serious, always in control, but it didn't quite ring true. Every muscle in his face was set rigid. He was livid.

'What do they want, husband?' she asked.

'Oh, what men always want. More power. More money. More, more, more. They were grateful enough when I rid them of Marguerite-Constance, but now they are conspiring to be rid of me. Every one of them.'

'Not all of them. Some . . .' Branas tried to speak, but Andronikos talked over him.

'Every one, I said. They're spreading rumours that I am not the true emperor, Agnes. There's an amusing tale abroad that your much-missed first husband escaped my clutches and fled to Sicily to take refuge with the Norman court.'

'Sicily! Why, husband, he'd have to be a very good swimmer.'

Silence.

What had she just said? How could she have joked about that?

But then Andronikos started to laugh, and Branas and Theo joined him. Her husband pulled her to him and kissed the top of her head. She tucked herself under his shoulder and stayed there.

It was the safest place to be.

Also in the spring of 1184

Something unpleasant dripped into Theo's eye. He blinked hard, but it didn't shift. He rubbed his face against his shoulder and it came away as a smear on his jerkin. Where was it coming from? He looked up – and immediately regretted it, as another dollop splattered on his face. The soldier next to him chuckled.

'Won't do that again, will you, boss?'

Theo grimaced. Rank intestinal ooze was seeping through the slats of the battering ram shelter above his head. It was covered with a triple layer of steaming fresh goat hides – an unlucky shepherd's flock that had been requisitioned, butchered, the meat tossed in pots, the skins draped over the siege engines. It was revolting, but it would protect them from the arrows and fire pots the rebels were hurling over the walls of Nicaea.

Theo's squadron had charge of the section of the walls between the lake and the gate at the end of the road that led back to the City. His father's instructions were simple. *Let no man in, no man out.* Easy enough, he thought, and wished he'd been trusted with a longer stretch.

But that was before he'd spent five days, scarcely daring to eat or sleep, breathing down his soldiers' necks as they stood guard over the postern gates. These weren't actual gates, but gaps in the walls no wider than the span of a big man's arms, little dog-leg tunnels that kinked left then right to an opening on the far side. The Nicaean soldiers, surprise on their side, used them to stage sorties, rushing out, roaring, ramped up, ready to bag a handful of easy kills – and to take cover as soon as Theo's men drew blood.

The only advantage of the relentless strain, Theo told himself, was that he had no time to wonder whether he was on the right side of the walls.

The night before, he had left his post to attend a council of war. The emperor he knew from the City, cool and elegant almost to the point of unmanliness, had transformed on the march into a credible warrior. His breastplate was pitted, his sword notched – they'd done more than ceremonial duty – and his tent, although comfortable, was far from luxurious.

'We'll beat them,' his father was saying.

'Of course we're fucking going to beat them,' Andronikos interrupted, 'but I dislike the waiting. I dislike it immensely.'

'The rebels have more money and more men than we expected.'

'Isaakios Angelos is a toad. Kantakouzenos is a cockerel. They are not men.'

'Nevertheless, they can't hold out for long, basileus.' His father was treating Andronikos very carefully. 'We need to dig into their water supply. We need to transport more ships so we can blockade the lake side more effectively. We'll have them before the next moon.'

'Too long, Branas. I can't wait. Nicaea is a beacon for other malcontents. We need to finish this soon.'

'We shall.'

'And by soon, I mean now.'

The two men stared at each other, but it was his father who dropped his eyes first. Here, he was the second in command.

And so as dawn lifted over the hills, Theo was grunting the battering ram forwards in the fetid dark. If he looked down, he could see the shadows of the walls cast by the bright spring sunshine, but he might as well have been festering in one of the Devil's sulphur pits. He said a small prayer to ward off that thought and steadied for another backswing. They had to be through soon.

An unholy scream darkened the morning air, a noise so loud and powerful that he could almost see it – white and bright before his eyes like lightning. The men to his left, on the other side of the ram, were on fire – the fire that did not go out. The soldiers around him were too big and war-bitten to know much about fear, but they abandoned the ram and started to run back to their own lines. Theo joined them, waiting for the searing pain to tear through his jerkin and rip down his back, waiting for his skin to be scorched clean off his bones.

He stopped, panting. The back of his head prickled and he swatted it with one hand.

'You're all right,' said the man next to him. 'You're clear.'

His fear subsided and he felt ashamed to have run, although every man had done the same.

A bugle sounded the emperor's approach, quickly drowned out by the insults hurled down at him by the exultant defenders.

'Priapos! Tithonos! Kronos!' yelled an imaginative few. 'Ram-cock! Dog-balls!' yelled the rest.

Andronikos had been overseeing the assault on the northern gate, but now he was bearing down on Theo, oblivious to the din above.

'Why the fuck have you retreated? Answer me, boy, or by God I'll . . .'

His sword was up, and Theo took two steps backwards rather than wait to see whether Andronikos really would lop off his general's son's head instead of waiting for an explanation.

'They have the fire that doesn't go out, basileus. The fire that clings. They came out of the posterns. Look . . .'

'That?'

Andronikos was clearly unimpressed by the sight of two dozen charred bodies screaming their last under the walls.

'That's not true sea-fire. That's a few balls of well-aimed naphtha.' He paused. 'But it's irritating, I admit.' He stopped again and laughed a little. 'All right. If they want to be creative, so be it. Theo, I want a good rider. Your best. Now.'

Morale, which had plummeted after the failure of the assault, rose fast as word spread that Andronikos had sent to the City for a secret weapon of his own. Real sea-fire, some of Theo's men said hopefully. Others said no, that wouldn't knock down walls. It would be something else, something nobody had ever heard of, an invention from the east that Andronikos had learnt about on his travels. They all assumed that Theo knew and wasn't telling, but in truth he was still in the dark when, five days later, a pair of camp-boys he'd sent to collect their rations came running with the news.

'It's here . . .'

'The weapon . . .'

'It's arrived.'

Theo ordered his men to stay put, and hurried towards the baggage wagons, where he found a gaggle of men gawping at a covered cart, deep in speculation, while a dozen guardsmen hefted their axes from hand to hand to make sure nobody got any ideas about coming too close.

'What is it?'

'It can't be very big.'

'Maybe it folds up?'

'Maybe it's poison?'

'Ooh . . .'

'Look . . .'

A patrician woman emerged from behind the drapes. Her face, which was neither young nor beautiful, was not painted, but she was dressed as well as only such women could dress. After a moment's indecision, she permitted one of the guardsmen to hand her to the ground. Theo pushed the soldiers aside and bowed; she was definitely the sort of woman you bowed to.

'May I be of service, sebastê?' he asked.

He detected relief in her eyes at the sound of an aristo voice.

'Yes, young man, you may. You can explain why these brutes snatched me from my breakfast three mornings since and drove me here like an animal, although—' she peered about her '—I remain unclear as to where exactly *here* is. Well? Can you enlighten me?'

'He can't, but I can.'

Theo looked round and saw the soldiers backing away as Andronikos jumped off a horse. He tossed the reins at one of the guards, strode forward and put an arm round Theo's shoulders.

'This, Theo, is my secret weapon. And those, my lady Euphrosunê Kastamonitissa Angelina, are the walls of Nicaea.'

Theo blinked. Isaakios's mother. The sort of lady who was much praised as the moral backbone of the City, and much avoided for the same reason. She'd observe every saint's day, make countless small pilgrimages and do a great deal for lepers and orphans. His own mother invited women like her by the dozen to long, boring afternoons reading the lives of the apostles and doing embroidery under her fruit trees. That was where she belonged; not here.

Euphrosunê Angelina, superbly calm amid the smoke and dung, looked down her long nose at the emperor.

'Always making trouble, Andronikos.' A tut. 'As a boy, as a man, and now, nearly in your dotage, you remain a thorn in all our sides.'

He bowed his head, as if to admit that every word she said was true.

'Tell me, Andronikos, why have you brought me here? Do you plan to hold a sword to my head and make my boy open the gates? It won't work. I am old, and with God's grace, I am ready to die. Believe me, I'll throw myself on your sword before I allow him to yield to you.'

'Bravely said. But that is not what I had in mind.'

'No?' Her voice faltered.

'No. I know Isaakios would not scruple to hide behind the

walls and watch me butcher you. No, you shall make yourself useful another way.' He smiled. 'Theodore. Where are you? Come here.'

Theo stepped forward.

'Basileus?'

'Let me see. This—' he pointed at one of the stock of battering rams '—this will serve. Strap her on top. Make sure Isaakios can see her face. Send word when you are done.'

Theo's mind was already running over the practicalities, his eyes hunting for a suitable length of rope. Obedience to the emperor was a reflex, after all, like breathing. But something – his heart; his conscience; the sudden ease with which he could picture his own mother standing before him – something betrayed him, and he heard himself utter one startling word.

'No.'

'Say that again,' said Andronikos, more amused than angry.

'I won't do it.'

'You are disobeying a direct order from your emperor? Why am I even asking?' He turned to the guards. 'You – lock him up. You – deal with the woman.'

Three men stepped smartly forward and began to lay her awkwardly on her back. She winced as the knots tightened about her chest, hips and legs, but she did not cry out. She did not weep, scream, plead or curse. She did not even close her eyes. Instead she lay looking up at the sky, whispering what Theo assumed were prayers of absolution.

That was the last he saw before they dragged him away and thrust him into a makeshift dug-out cell.

Later that day, or maybe the next, he'd lost track of time, his father came and untied him. He sat down beside him and, without acknowledging where they were, began to tell him what had happened.

'His plan worked, you know. It even had me fooled. I thought he was using that woman to give our ram time to breach the walls, but that wasn't it. He didn't want to get us in — he wanted to get them out. He wanted them to get so riled by the sight of the old lady that they'd open one of the gates and attack. Brilliant, really.'

Theo scowled. The last thing he wanted to hear was his father telling him that Andronikos was brilliant.

'Kantakouzenos led the charge,' Branas continued, 'but his horse tripped and he landed on his head at Andronikos's feet. Dead as a doornail. It spooked the rest of them, bad luck like that, and it didn't take us long to finish them off. Isaakios is already talking terms with the emperor.'

'You mean grovelling,' said Theo.

'Call it what you want, he's a fucking virtuoso at it. He organised a real show. The archbishop in his finest robes, on his knees, begging for mercy. The women and children, too. Bare heads, bare feet, all of them waving olive branches.'

'Andronikos fell for that?'

'He likes to be entertained. Isaakios's apology — it tickled him. He's letting him go back to the City — although I doubt the rest of the aristos are going to be so lucky.'

He stopped talking and stood up. When he spoke again, he sounded like a different man.

'You see how it is, Theo. Andronikos is in a good mood. Apologise and it'll be forgotten. I told him some tale about that woman being kind to you as a boy. Apologise, son.'

Theo set his teeth. 'It was wrong, Father. Wrong.'

'It was a legitimate military tactic.'

'Legitimate? Tying an old woman—'

'What if it had been an old man? What if it had been Isaakios's pompous prick of a father? What if it had been his little boy? Where do you draw the line? It wasn't pretty. Of course it wasn't pretty. But that's war.'

'An old woman . . .' Theo repeated doggedly.

'It's still war, Theo. Old women die by the dozen. Or is it

because she's well-born? What if it had been some scrawny hag? What then? And anyway, she's not dead. God spared her. She's probably delighted. What a story to tell the other good matrons back home.'

But Theo remembered Euphrosunê Angelina's grey face and the stain of piss about her skirts. He searched out his father's eyes, trying to find the man he loved behind the general's bravado.

'Do you really believe that, Father?'

'It's done.'

'That's not an answer.'

'It's done. We've won.'

'Who's *we*?'

'Who the fuck do you think *we* is?'

'I don't know what to think any more.'

'Don't fucking think then. You've embarrassed me, Theo. Not with one of your boyhood idiocies. This is serious. You disobeyed an order from the emperor. I'm going to have to have you whipped. But it needn't turn out any worse than that – if you apologise.'

'I won't apologise. I'm right.'

'Right is not good enough.'

That was not his father speaking.

'Is Andronikos the man you thought he was?' Theo asked, his voice low so he could be sure it wouldn't carry. He needed his father to be able to answer truthfully.

'What's that? Speak up.'

'You heard.'

His father tugged his helmet off and scratched at the grimy red patches where it had lain tight across his scalp.

'The aristocracy is trying to unseat him. He's not going to survive by being fucking nice.'

Andronikos entered, rubbing his hands.

'No. I'm not. But Isaakios will. He's been extremely nice to me. And now it's your turn, Theo. A little bit of niceness from

185

you and we can all get out of here and go and enjoy ourselves. Come on, let's hear it. I'm all ears.'

But Theo shook his head.

'Order me another thousand times, and I would still refuse.'

It was his father who hit him round the face.

'Some fucking soldier you are.' *Punch.* 'Let's go, Andronikos.' *Punch.* 'He'll come to his senses overnight.' *Punch. Punch. Punch.* 'We'll deal with him in the morning.'

They left him coughing and spitting on the floor, but Theo was smiling, almost laughing. His father had pummelled and bellowed precisely long enough for Theo to pluck the dagger from his belt – and stopped the moment Theo was on the floor with the weapon hidden safe beneath his belly.

Now he only had to wait for nightfall. He was armed. Everyone would be drinking. He would escape.

Two days later

Theo was sure he'd ridden his stolen horse fast enough to outstrip word of his escape. But even if Andronikos had set soldiers on his tail, they'd presume he'd make for the comparative safety of his family lands in Thrace – not for the City. They'd never think to look for him in the bowels of the Great Palace, deep in the lion's den.

All he needed to penetrate the multiple layers of security was a purposeful stride, a dusty cloak and a dispatch bag over his shoulder. Most of the palace guardsmen knew him by sight if not by name, and all of them knew he was as close to the emperor as his own shadow. And so they waved him through from the outer gates, to the inner courtyards, to a quiet, unremarkable corner of the palace gardens.

'There's the empress, sebastos,' said the guardsman, pointing.

Theo stared. Agnes was playing with the Iberian princess and her little boy. He saw a toy house, a sort of tent on a wooden frame, little flags fluttering on top of it. The boy, little more than a baby, was poking his head in and out of the flaps, giggling madly. The two women were pulling silly faces at him and laughing.

It was such an ordinary, peaceful sight. What had he expected? To find her alone, abject, sobbing? He turned to the guardsman.

'My message from the emperor is for the empress alone. Can you . . . ?'

The Varangian nodded, and Theo stayed out of sight while he murmured something to Agnes. The man's back blocked his view, though, so he couldn't see how she reacted, only that the boy was cross at being told to go inside. Theo shrank into the shadows as Susa walked past. He couldn't understand what she was saying, but he knew the tone – she was cajoling the child, promising all sorts of treats to make up for his game ending.

Agnes was alone now, looking about her. He wanted to stay where he was, out of sight. The low sun, slanting between two stone pillars, wrapped her head in gold, casting her face deep into shadow.

'Empress Anna.'

He strode towards her, hoping he looked manly, purposeful.

'Theodore Branas.' She came towards him and the halo vanished. 'This is . . . surprising. A little irregular, no?'

He had prepared what he wanted to say. *I did wrong. I am here to put it right.* He wouldn't talk about the old woman on the ram. Nor about Renier dying. Nor about a little boy's face in the window of a burning house. She didn't need to know any of that. All she needed to know was that this time, he was going to get it right.

But on her face, instead of a gratifying smile of welcome, there was a small frown. She had no idea what was in his head. She only saw the emperor's man, standing stupid with mud on his boots.

'What are you doing here?' But then her expression softened into concern. 'Your face, it's . . .'

He touched his cheek, where his father had hit him.

'Horrible?'

'Does it hurt?'

'No, not . . .' He caught her sceptical look. 'Well, maybe a bit. Actually, quite a lot.'

She lifted her hand and touched his face. It was shocking, as cool as moonrise. He could feel himself starting to shake, not his arms or legs, but his insides, his being.

'Empress Anna, I . . .'

Then he saw what he should have seen earlier. They were

not alone. Constantinos was standing visibly invisible at a door leading into the garden.

'Will you walk with me, basilissa? My message is for your ears alone.'

She glanced at the eunuch, and although Theo could see nothing in his face that either gave or withheld permission, she nodded and walked ahead until they were standing under the branches of a plane tree. She was looking at him, but also looking back the way they had come.

'Well?' she said. 'What word from my husband? Theo?'

He took a deep breath.

'You were right, Agnes. I was weak. I betrayed you. But I've broken with him, and you can too. You can come away. Now, this minute. I'll—'

'Wait. Stop. What are you saying? You're going too fast. You've *broken* . . . ?'

'Yes, yes. I should have done it before. But it's not too late. You must—'

'Come away? With you?'

'Yes, yes, away. With me.'

She did not ask where or why. He poured more words into her silence.

'You said I should feel shame for what happened that night, and you're right. I do. But I am here to make amends. You are not safe. You know you're not safe. You—'

But she was shaking her head.

'Look at these walls. I am the safest woman alive.'

'The same walls held Marguerite-Constance. The same walls held Maria. You must understand—'

'Theo!' His name cracked out, loud, angry, silencing him. 'Theo,' she repeated, and he saw that she was controlling herself only with enormous effort. 'I understand everything all too well. That is why I am alive and they are dead. And I want to stay alive.'

'That is why you must—'

'Stop telling me what I must do. You want me to be safe? Then leave. Leave now! I don't know what madness brought you here, but . . .'

Something caught Agnes's eye. Spear tips, the men holding them hidden from view, moving up the terrace walk below. She knew the slow, steady tread of the palace guards. This was different. These men were running, stones flying. They were after someone.

'Run, Theo!' she gasped.

But there was no time to run. And nowhere to run to. One of those spears would be in his back before he made it under cover.

'Quick. Hide. In there, quick. *Quick!*'

She pushed him, too stunned to resist, into Alexios's little tent, and started to scream.

'Help! Guards! Help!'

She saw mistrust burn across his face, and feared he was going to leap out and ruin everything. But then the first men emerged up the steps and at their head was . . .

'Stephanos! Thank God you're here.' That sent Theo ducking under the canvas. 'He went that way. Up on the walls. He must be running for the docks. Get him. Get him.'

Stephanos barked a few orders and his men fanned out – but he did not follow them. Instead he joined her.

Don't look at the tent.

'He's a bloody genius,' he said with a low whistle.

'Don't swear. Who's a genius?'

Don't look at the tent.

'The boss. He had a hunch the boy would be here. I said I doubted it, but if such was his pleasure, of course I'd take a look. Shows what I know. Seems I got here in the nick of time. What did Theodore Branas want from you, Empress Anna? Out with it.'

'He tried to abduct me.'

190

Don't look at the tent.

'Did he now? Thought he could rescue Persephone from Hades. Sweet.'

He must have caught her surprised look.

'Oh, I know all the old stories. You can't spend time with the boss and not pick up a little learning. We all learn something from him. Wonder what you've learnt?'

'You should be trying to catch him, not standing here talking nonsense.'

Don't look at the tent.

'You know what he did, Empress Anna? He told the boss to go fuck – sorry, I'll mind my manners – he told the boss he disapproved of certain of his actions. Didn't think he had it in him. Maybe he was trying to impress someone. You got an opinion on that, Empress Anna? People like to square up to the boss when they've got something to prove. They always regret it, though. I make sure they do.'

He rooted at the grass with the butt of his spear.

'So. Young Theo was going to kidnap you, was he? I hope he wasn't expecting you to walk out of the palace with him? That would have been far too easy.'

'Of course not. He had a . . . a ruse.'

Don't look at the tent.

'A ruse, did he?'

'Yes. He said my husband wanted me to join him in Nicaea. He said he was to accompany me. Of course, I asked for proof. And when he had none, I called the guards. Now, would you be so good as to escort me inside? I don't feel safe out here.'

Don't look at the tent.

A pause.

'All right. In we go.'

She turned to the side entrance to the women's quarters. Stephanos was half a pace behind her. It cost her everything she had not to rush, not to look round. They were ten paces

191

away, twenty, thirty. Relief flooded her limbs. Stephanos stopped suddenly.

'Fuck. Fuck, he's in the fucking—'

He spun round and was back beside the tent in a few bounds, his spear levelled at the entrance. Agnes bit down a scream as Stephanos jammed the weapon into what had to be Theo's head. But it came out with a toy horse dangling from its tip.

'Alexios will be awfully upset,' Agnes called. 'He dotes on that horse.'

She was almost crowing with relief. But where was Theo?

Theo had been staring at a rag horse with cloth flowers plaited into its mane, so tormented by the knowledge that he was about to die that at first he hadn't heard what Stephanos was saying.

The boss is a bloody genius.

And then he forgot about dying because there was something even bigger to think about. *I love her.* Of course he loved her. That was why he was there, wasn't it? Why else? *Duty. Amends.* Who was he trying to fool? He was suffused with happiness, and then he remembered he was about to die.

Would you be so good as to escort me inside?

He loved her even more. She was keeping her head. She wasn't stupid. She'd draw Stephanos away, and then—

He rolled, powered by some instinct deeper than thought, rolled underneath the flap of the tent and on to the path. His eyes snapped left, right. Stephanos was nearly in the shadow of the colonnade. A low wall ran around the rim of the garden, before the land dropped away to the next tier closer to the sea. His body rippled over the wall and fell on to some paving. Two statues peered at him, silent, disapproving. He pressed his back to the wall and listened.

He dotes on that horse.

*   *   *

Stephanos walked her to her rooms, speechless with anger, leaving two of his men outside the door and one in sight of every window. It was against protocol, but she wasn't going to argue the point.

She was shaking, pacing. He'd come. He understood. She did have a friend. A friend who'd taken a great risk for her. A stupid, dangerous risk, maybe, but how bold. To break with *him* . . .

She forced herself to stop pacing. That would give her away. She sat down and tried to look bored. *No.* Somebody had tried to abduct her. She should look a little bit scared. She stood up. Maybe pacing was right after all.

A knock. Constantinos came in. He looked so bland and unassuming that she knew at once he must have something important to tell her.

She widened her eyes and tipped her head. *What?*

A small shake of his head. A purse of his lips. *Wait.*

She beckoned a servant to pour some cordial, while he selected some papers. Outside the window she could still see Stephanos's goons.

'Dispatches, Empress Anna. An account of how your husband dealt with the traitors in Bithynia.'

He handed her some pages – reports. She whispered the words as she read them. What she saw, smudged black on dirty white, was grotesque.

'*Andronikos left the dead drying on the walls. He pruned prisoners' fingers like grapevines. The fruit trees buckled under the weight of those he hanged. Men were im-paled* . . .' She looked up at Constantinos; she didn't know the Greek word.

'A spike, like a spear, but blunter, through a man's guts,' he supplied.

'. . . *impaled on spikes like scarecrows in a cucumber garden.*'

'The writer has a nice turn of phrase, doesn't he?' said Constantinos, and took the pages back. 'When I hired him, he told me he wanted to be a poet, but one must earn a living somehow.'

'This is . . . these are . . .'

'Yes.' Constantinos nodded. 'I am sure they deserved it.'

'My husband does what he must.' A shrug, dainty and dismissive.

Constantinos picked up a pen and scratched out a few words. *Something in him breaks. Maybe it has already broken.* A pause. More scratching. *Beware.*

21 May 1184

She had no warning.

One sunny morning, the feast of Jesus's ascent into heaven, Agnes was breakfasting alone. Soon she would bid her maids robe her and set out to worship, as prescribed by custom, at Pege, a little wooded sanctuary sacred to the Virgin, a pleasant place where it would be easy to imagine things were other than they were. But first she would try to manage another bite of bread, another sip of—

Something made her turn, and he was there, leaning against the door frame. She gave a yelp of surprise, which at first seemed to please him, and then maybe not.

In the days since Theo had ghosted into the City and out of her life, news, ever bloodier, had stalked the palace. Andronikos had warped in her imagination, his return a thing of dread. Every day she expected him; and every night he arrived, monstrous, in her dreams.

'Behold, your husband, the conquering hero,' he said, and struck an ironic pose.

She'd rehearsed this moment. She leapt up, ran to him, flung her arms around his neck.

'Thank God you're safe.'

He held her to him. Where was the fiend? He looked down and kissed her. He wasn't a fiend. He sat and ate the remains of her breakfast while telling a funny story – it really *was* funny – about the skipper of the boat who'd brought him back across the Propontis. To all appearances, he was a man mild, even-tempered, courteous, bent on discovering how she did.

He yawned.

'I think, Agnes, that God will forgive us if we forgo Pege this once.'

She said nothing. She didn't like to think about what God might or might not forgive.

'But I do want to get out of the City. Too many weeks close-quartered with my soldiers. What do you say to a trip to Philopation?'

They approached in a litter, incognito apart from a dozen outriders. Although the blinds were drawn, she could tell there was far more traffic than usual on the road. Maybe the pack of petitioners that trailed an emperor everywhere had word he was bound to the country palace. They must be pretty desperate, she thought, to seek out a man rumoured to have—

'Preoccupied, Agnes?'

'The road is so busy. I'd hoped we wouldn't be disturbed. That's all.'

'Forgive me.' He gave her a smile of what could have been charming apology. 'The emperor has no leisure.'

The main courtyard at Philopation was indeed crowded, but not with the merchants and guildsmen she might have expected. Instead she saw men from the best families in the City, the sort who would not normally come begging for favours so openly. Andronikos caught her look of surprise as the guardsman handed her out of the litter.

'My business interests you, does it? Come, then, and see for yourself.'

He led her forward. The crowd fell back before them. She heard mumbled congratulations as one by one the noble foreheads touched the ground. Once they had been desperate to attract his attention, now they longed to avoid it.

In the middle of the courtyard stood two men, grey-faced, swaying on their feet. Agnes guessed that only the ring of spears levelled at their chests stopped them collapsing.

'Who . . . ?'

'Their names are Constantinos Makrodoukas and Andronikos Doukas, but that is of little importance. What is important is that they are here to be punished. They are here to die.'

'What did they do?'

'Does it matter what they did? I say that they deserve to die. Does that not make them dead in your eyes?'

'What did they do?' she repeated.

Andronikos smiled, and she knew it was because she had dared ask the same question twice, something none of the men in that courtyard would have done. But although he smiled, he did not answer, and she knew only a fool would ask a third time.

'Come,' he said.

As she followed him inside, she looked over her shoulder at the two men. *The dead men.* It was an uncomfortable sight. *Uncomfortable?* That's what she would once have said about a necklace chafing her throat.

Andronikos led her through the main chamber and up to the second floor, to a smaller room which had a balcony overlooking the courtyard, a pretty place where she'd often sat during her days of semi-exile with Alexios.

There were refreshments laid out, fruits and honeys. Constantinos appeared with a sheaf of papers – something about troop deployment, a deposition from the eparch, a senator's bequest. She'd spent many afternoons like this in his company, always wishing he'd finish. That afternoon, listening to the subdued throb and scuffle of the people outside, she hoped he would work for ever.

'Agnes . . .' He spoke without looking up. 'Why did Theodore Branas visit you?'

Dread landed like a stone in her stomach.

'To try to make me leave the City. To leave you.' She paused, and he raised his eyes to her face. 'I said no.'

He smiled. 'I'm touched.' And stopped smiling. 'Would you

rather be with him? A boy to call you sweet names. A boy to moon over you. Is that what you want?'

'No.'

'No?'

'*No.*'

'Good. Understand one thing, Agnes. I don't like sharing what is mine.'

She nodded.

'Theodore Branas is a traitor. Down in the courtyard, another two await their end. Some are already dead in Bithynia, but there are more, still more. How many, I do not yet know, but I shall find them, and I shall kill them.'

He stood up, his chair scraping over the floor.

'Don't worry, Agnes, we shall outlast them all.'

He pulled her from her chair, holding her hand tightly – too tightly – and marched her out on to the balcony. Looking down, she took in the double line of guards surrounding the palace, their tufted helmets like clumps of flowers. Fear tacked through the crowd as each man looked up and saw her husband.

'Stephanos,' he called. 'Read the charges.'

Constantinos Makrodoukas and Andronikos Doukas dropped to their knees and raised their eyes to the sky, both tracing the sign of the cross again and again in the empty air. They would listen to their crimes, a story woven out of truths and half-truths. They would listen and deny it all, hoping against hope that they might yet be spared.

Stephanos stepped forward, and Agnes saw at once that he had no paper, no list, nothing to deny. Instead, he plucked a large stone from the ground and flung it at Constantinos Makrodoukas's head.

It hit him between the eyes, ripping a small flap of skin and sending a gush of blood coursing down his face. Agnes watched the man, portly, pleasant-faced, touch his forehead, astonished, as blood dripped and pooled in his hands. He held up his sleeve to stem the flow, looking more embarrassed than anything, as if he'd been struck by a nosebleed in church.

'Traitors,' said Stephanos, a statement, factual, measured, not a shout of accusation.

He picked up another stone and pitched it at Andronikos Doukas. The younger man's reflexes were better and he dodged in time, but his sudden movement made him lose his footing and he came down hard on his behind.

'Traitors.' Stephanos called the word a little louder, and looked at the men assembled in the courtyard. 'Traitors.' It was an invitation.

Agnes glanced to her right, to where Andronikos was standing, his hands resting on the stone balcony. He was quite calm.

'Traitors!'

The cry came from deep within the crowd, and then everyone was shouting at once. A stone flew, and another, and then a hundred men began to rush in circles, levering up bits of paving, scouring the ground for something to throw.

The two prisoners were huddled on the ground and Agnes realised that unless the men grew bolder and bloodier and dashed the biggest slabs straight on their heads, it would take an unbearably long time for them to die.

'Enough,' called Andronikos. 'Restrain yourselves, gentlemen. Your devotion is unimpeachable, but we shall leave the rest of their punishment to the professionals.'

As he turned and went back inside, Agnes saw two of Stephanos's dogsbodies scurry forward and roll the quivering, pulpy – but very much alive – bodies in blankets.

'They're to be impaled, Empress Anna,' said Stephanos, who'd looked up and seen her still standing there, too numb to move. 'Have you seen that done?'

Stephanos's laughter pursued her as she hurried after her husband. She found him slumped on a chair. The blood, their subjection, his power, none of those things had excited him; instead, he looked curiously defeated.

'You've seen the comet in the sky, Agnes?'

'Yes.'

'You know what people are saying?' He didn't wait for a reply. 'They're saying that a serpent is coiled above us, its jaws agape, dripping poison, thirsty for blood, ready to swallow the world. They're saying I am that serpent.' He stretched and put his feet up on a stool. 'Is that what you see, little one? A snake?'

She sat beside him and put a hand to his cheek. For a moment he leant into it and closed his eyes.

'The people don't think you're a snake,' she said. 'The people love you. The people have always loved you.'

He did not open his eyes.

'What about you, Agnes? Do you still love me?'

'I—'

'No. Don't answer.'

He pulled her on to his lap and held her tight, his face against her chest. Suddenly, she thought that maybe she could make it right, whatever was wrong with him, maybe she could bring him back. Her arms came up and cradled his head and she whispered,

'Are . . . are you sure?'

'Mmm? About what?'

'That you are truly in as much danger as you fear. You have defeated your enemies. The people, the aristos, all obey you. You are safe.'

He pushed her away from him and his eyes opened slowly. The whites were heavily veined, purpled with blood.

'*Safe.*' The word came out flat, dead. 'Who told you to say that? Who? Give me his name. His name, this instant.'

'Nobody. Nobody, I swear it.'

She'd scrambled to her feet and was trying to get as far away from him as possible – which wasn't very far in that little room. Without thinking, without knowing what she meant to do next, she made for the door.

'Stop,' he said.

She stopped.

'Sit,' he said, pointing at a seat beside him.

She sat.

'*Safe*. I am not safe, Agnes. My enemies have scattered, that is all. Some south to Saladin's court. Some west to the Normans in Sicily. They will try to stir up trouble there, beyond the empire's borders.'

His left hand, lying on the arm of his chair, was trembling. He stilled it angrily with his right.

'*Snake*. I am no snake. They are the snakes. A hydra, a many-headed hydra. I cut one head off; back it grows. I cut off another; another grows. It will be a mighty battle, but I am equal to it. I'll cut off every head, cauterise every stump until my enemies are nothing, nothing but a bloody carcass at my feet.'

His eyes focused on her.

'*Safe*. Only an enemy would say that.'

'I am not your enemy. I am your wife.'

She turned away from him.

'Oh, don't look so hurt. Sorry. I was angry. For God's sake, don't look hurt.'

He kissed her, much more roughly than he had ever done before. His teeth bit into her lips. His hands tugged hard at her hair. She cried out and tried to pull away. But he didn't let her go.

He'll never let me go.

When he had finished, when he had left, she walked on to the balcony and stared out. A bank of spiky flower heads cast their shadows on the stones. As they thrashed in the wind, they looked like dozens of Nile crocodiles, snapping their jaws in the empty air.

The summer of 1185

Theo and Murzuphlus stood on the walls of the acropolis, the city of Thessalonikê falling away into the gulf at their feet. Before them lay tiled roofs and gilded domes, sun-browned treetops and the jagged dirty-white rectangle of the walls, while in the far, far distance a thin strip of cloud leant on the shoulders of Mount Olympos. The sun in the southern sky was fierce – white, not yellow – and so bright it remained on the back of Theo's eyelids long after he looked away. It had turned the sea into a sheen of beaten metal, a piece of silvered iron.

Murzuphlus was talking a great deal, the kind of talk designed to cover the wariness that existed between friends after a long parting.

'The governor here's a Komnenos, just about, called David. He has an easy job. Everyone in Thessalonikê makes a lot of money – he just sits on his fat behind and creams off every kind of tax, tariff, toll, you name it, and sends a crumb or two back to the City. He's petrified Andronikos will find out, but he can't stop himself. It's an obsession. Piling up money.'

'Dare say you've stashed away a bit as well?'

Theo thought he might have offended him – and maybe he'd meant to – but Murzuphlus only shrugged.

'What else am I meant to do? We hear what's been happening in the City.' He paused. 'Why are you here, Theo? I thought your father was tight with Andronikos, but you stumbled in here like a vagabond. You've worn those clothes too many days and too many nights, and that beard would do justice to a monk on Athos. You're reserved, Theo. Since when were you reserved? Come on, talk to me. Where've you been?'

'On Athos, actually. They gave me shelter over the winter.'

'What the hell were you doing there?'

'We quarrelled.'

'You and Andronikos?'

'Me and Andronikos.'

'Then you're lucky to be alive. I thought he was more thorough. Half the City dead, half fled, half in prison . . .'

'That's three halves.'

'Don't joke, Theo. It's beyond a joke. You heard what happened to Mamalos? That tubby little man who never had a thought in his head other than how to keep his wife from finding out about his mistress? Andronikos decided he was the mastermind behind some great conspiracy. Ludicrous fucking idea, but Mamalos was dragged into the hippodrome anyway, stripped and hobbled like a goat. Then a huge fire was lit and they pushed him in. He leapt out, and they shoved him right back in, again and again, until there was no leap left in him. They say people were in tears, Theo. Hundreds of grown men sobbing.'

'I'd wager hundreds more were loving the show.'

'Theo, don't tell me—'

'No. Sorry. I like it as little as you do. I hadn't heard that one. But I've heard others. Even if half of what you hear is made up, the other half is bad enough. But who's going to stop him? The City loves him. And the army.'

'Your father?'

Theo shook his head.

'He serves him still. I don't know why.'

He was grateful when Murzuphlus changed the subject.

'I suppose I should feel honoured that you've chosen my hearth as your sanctuary. But what if people come looking for you? Am I to deny all knowledge of your existence?'

'Worried about your own ugly hide?'

'It's the only one I've got. I need to take care of it.'

Theo laughed and leant over the wall. He realised something about the view was bothering him.

'Why is the fishing fleet returning? It's barely past noon.'

'That's odd.' Murzuphlus frowned. 'It's much too early.'

'That's not . . .'

'What the . . . ?'

And they were both racing down the steps, colliding with other men who had seen the same thing. A massive navy was bearing down on Thessalonikê, the second city of the empire.

'A wife who cannot bear to be parted from her husband? I am moved, Empress Anna.'

Andronikos turned his back and walked down the marble steps to where a boat was waiting to take him to one of the summer palaces on the far shore of the Bosporus. That was how he always talked now. Light words, polite and courtly, but spoken with flat, unblinking eyes.

'Empress?'

Stephanos was behind her. She ignored him.

'Empress?'

He held out an arm and offered to hand her down the steps and into the boat, smiling with lips too small for his teeth. She tried not to flinch. It was no longer his face that troubled her – she'd got used to that a long time ago – it was everything else about him. She leant on his arm for as little time as possible, but that was still long enough for him to whisper something in her ear.

'I've been watching you. I've been wanting to tell you something. You're doing well. Better than I expected.'

He nodded to the stern of the boat, where Andronikos was sitting.

'You and me, we know how to manage him. That makes us partners.'

'It makes us nothing of the sort.'

He laughed as she pulled away from him.

'Know what I like to ask myself, Empress Anna? What you'd have done if he'd looked like me?'

He was still chuckling as she took her seat beside Andronikos.

'Vexed, Empress Anna?' he said.

In the bright sunlight, he was starting to look closer to his true age. The whites of his eyes were yellow and a small vein lumped up blue on his left hand.

'That man. He . . . he displeases me.'

'He is useful.'

'You mean he kills for you.'

She waited for the old look to come into his eyes. The look that said she amused him – the look she strove for. It did not come.

'Men like Stephanos are very precious and very rare, Empress Anna. Soldiers are easy to find, but people who like to kill even when their blood is unheated by war or wine, I have met no more than two or three in my whole life.' A pause. A smile. 'It's a shame he does not please you. You, I know, please him very much indeed.'

'I cannot bear that he should think of me at all.'

'You would have me forbid him to think of you? Stephanos! Come here!'

She turned from him and watched the City slip away astern.

'Ah, Stephanos, my lady has a command for you. Empress Anna, beloved wife, your servant is waiting.'

She looked down into the water, at the waves slapping the hull.

'Empress Anna, beloved wife,' he repeated. She looked up. 'Tell him your command.'

Stephanos bowed. She did not speak.

'No? Shy, suddenly? Then I shall tell him myself. Stephanos, you are no longer to look at my wife. You are no longer even to think of her. She does not like it when you do. Is that clear?'

Agnes did not like what she saw on Stephanos's face. He looked hurt, but his desire to hurt her looked stronger.

'There, my dear.' Andronikos draped an arm about her shoulders. 'Never let it be said that I am not the most attentive, the most devoted of husbands.'

'We must send to the City. We must send to the emperor.'

'Yes, Murzuphlus.' The governor, David Komnenos, pursed his lips. 'That is an option, certainly. But is it the *right* one? That is what I ask myself. I am the governor, and as such I have been charged by the emperor to manage things. Better to manage them quietly, I say, rather than trouble him with trifles.'

Theo cut in, unable to listen any longer.

'Murzuphlus is right, governor. If Norman soldiers have sailed from Sicily, Thessalonikê needs help.'

'And who might you be, young man?'

The question sounded genial enough, but it oozed a kindly condescension that set Theo's teeth on edge. His reply was curt.

'I am Theodore Branas.'

'Well I never,' said the governor, lifting his eyebrows. 'We heard you were away from the City, but presumed yours was the eternal absence the emperor has of late been so eager to mete out. I must say I am extremely surprised you should want to alert him to your existence.'

'It's not about my existence. It's about Thessalonikê being under siege.'

'Let us not get over excited. This is a trading city, a peaceful place where men delight in nothing so much as making one another a little more prosperous. We have no flair for the affairs of Mars.' He chortled, pleased with himself. 'But rest assured, Theodore, we are first-rate negotiators.'

'You're deluded if you think you can buy them off.'

'My word, Murzuphlus,' David said in a mock whisper, 'I'm not surprised Andronikos tired of this young man. His frankness is overwhelming.'

'Totally fucking deluded,' Theo repeated. 'Use your eyes. That's not a raiding party. That's an invasion force. The city needs proper reinforcements. You must send to Andronikos.'

'Really, there's no call for that sort of language. Besides, I have already sent to Andronikos. I have told him that he is not to worry about a thing.'

'But that's a lie.' Theo turned to Murzuphlus, but his friend only shrugged. *What did I tell you?* Fighting the urge to grab David around the neck and strangle some sense into him, he tried one last time. 'Tell him the truth. Please. For Thessalonikê's sake.'

'The truth?'

For the first time the governor looked him in the eye, and Theo thought he might be winning, but the man's face clouded and the jocular tone returned.

'And have one of Andronikos's dogs at my door at dawn, ready to part me from my testicles? No. Best to sit tight, eh? It'll turn out all right. We are Rômans, are we not? And the Normans, who are they? Vagabonds from the north.'

'Vagabonds who've taken land after land. England. Italy, for God's sake. Vagabonds who've . . .' He stopped. The governor was staring vacantly out the window. 'Are you listening?'

'No, dear boy, I'm not. I could hear a harangue coming on, and it is a point of honour with me never to listen to a harangue.'

Theo took a deep breath. 'What will you do if they won't negotiate? What will you do if they attack? Tell me that at least.'

'Oh, I'm sure we'll manage somehow. And now, if you'll excuse me, gentlemen, I believe the archbishop is waiting for me.'

And David Komnenos sailed from the room, leaving Theo cursing and his friend laughing.

'It's not funny, Murzuphlus.'

'I know, I'm sorry. It's the opposite of funny. But if I didn't laugh, I'd have lost my mind months ago. You see how it is now? He's so scared of Andronikos, he'd rather spend the rest of his days in the belly of Jonah's whale than attract his attention. He fears our emperor more than all the Normans ever spawned.'

'This is ridiculous. We must do something. Can you get a letter out? While the eastern road is still open?'

'A letter to Andronikos? You'll struggle to find a man willing to carry it. He has an unhealthy reputation when it comes to bearers of bad news.'

'Not a letter to him – a letter to my father.'

Hundreds of servants must have worked hundreds of hours to prepare the feast at Meloudion, a little palace with grounds fronting on to the water.

Fish lay by the dozen over cook-pits, their flesh melting, their skin crisping, their tails curling up to escape the heat. Kids turned above their own fires, spits poking out of their open mouths while their hooves jutted like trees stumps after a forest blaze. Pigeons, threaded on to sticks of slow-burning wood, dripped gobbets of fat into the flames.

Another boatload of revellers pulled up to the pontoon. A gangplank landed with a thud and Agnes watched men and women stumble ashore, gripping each other's shoulders and laughing too loudly. They'd probably been drinking on the way over, maybe for fun, more likely to bolster their nerve. She found it hard to believe people were still willing to risk their lives for her husband's favour, but with so many of the old families in ruins, fathers dead, sons in exile, she supposed it might be tempting to close one's eyes to danger.

Beside her, Andronikos's gaze was returning again and again to one of the dancers. She was not young, not slender, but dark and alive. Her hair curled down to her waist, its tiny span dwarfed by her breasts and hips. She was painted, but even paint could not hide the mobility of her face. Her features danced and her body told a thousand stories. Agnes watched

Andronikos watch this woman and like what he saw. He did not gawp – of course he did not gawp – but his eyes acquired her. It reminded her of something he'd said in the early days, back when lovemaking turned him confiding.

Everything I want, I have the moment I want it.

'Don't be sad. His interest doesn't last long. You are his wife. He'll come back,' said a voice soft in her ear.

It was Stephanos. She held still.

'I'll make sure he does, Empress Anna.'

She felt his fingers circle her upper arm. It was too much. He should not dare.

'Let go,' she hissed, and when he did not, she said the words again, louder – loud enough for Andronikos to hear, which was not what she had intended. He turned towards them, and at once Stephanos's fingers released her. She smiled at him, but her smile slipped when she saw that he was amused, not angry.

'I want to go home,' she said.

'You can't. The boatmen are all drunk. Have a drink. And eat something, for God's sake. I cannot bear a woman who hungers and sulks.'

The thought of meat sickened her, so she took a peach from one of the platters and tore away its skin. As she parted the flesh where it reddened at the core, the stone – or what she had thought was the stone – dissolved, and a dozen earwigs scurried across her hands and disappeared into the shadows.

The fighting had split Theo and Murzuphlus from the other troops manning the acropolis, so they had no idea whether Thessalonikê still stood. But that didn't matter. They were no longer soldiers defending a city. They were two young men trying very hard not to die.

A band of Normans, armed with spears that far outdid the reach of their swords, was herding them backwards, grinning, taunting, poking at their legs, making them scuttle and jump like wild pigs being driven into a pit.

Theo risked a glance over his shoulder and saw the low walls of a stable rising up behind them. There was a door a few paces to their right, and he just had time to leap sideways, hauling Murzuphlus after him, before the Normans closed round them. They slammed the door, fumbled the bar across and stood panting in the dusty gloom.

'What the fuck are we going to do, Theo? They'll torch it. We'll fry.'

'No, they're coming after us. Quick, up here.'

The walls were rough-built, studded with rings and hooks for horse gear, which – combined with his very real fear – gave Theo the climbing skills of a cat. He swung on to a rafter beam, shinned out over the empty air and crouched, ready to pounce. Murzuphlus was balancing on the next beam, his sword in his right hand, a dagger between his teeth.

Theo fought to control his breathing as he listened to the sounds coming from outside – threats, oaths, the scrape of something heavy being dragged towards the stable door. *Thud.* They exchanged glances. *Thud.* The planks wouldn't hold long. *Thud.* With a sharp crack, the hinges ricocheted off the stone floor and, a heartbeat later, the door splintered. Half a dozen men tumbled inside, spears pointing in all directions as they sought their prey.

Theo caught Murzuphlus's eye. *Ready?* A nod.

With a howl they flung themselves to the ground. Two of the attackers were dead before they'd even got to their feet. That made the odds two to one.

Theo grabbed a horse blanket with his left hand and used it to beat away the spear thrusts, whirling it in tight circles. He spied a spade, caked in horseshit, and dropped his sword. The balance was ugly, but at least he could get past their spears.

'Theo, your back . . .'

The words were hardly out of his friend's mouth before Theo felt danger prickle the nape of his neck. He pirouetted, swinging the spade in a wide arc, and watched it slam into the face of the Norman who had been about to attack. His blow knocked the man to the floor, flattening his nose across his face.

Theo ducked a thrust coming from the right, tumbled to the dead man's side and snatched up his spear. His first jab caught the other soldier's nosepiece and he nearly lost his grip, but his next – one of the luckiest he'd ever made – took the man full in the face, ripping open his cheek. Theo left his dagger in the man's throat and turned to help Murzuphlus.

One soldier was dead at his feet, but the other was midway through a wild backswing that might have finished his friend if Theo hadn't blocked the spear before the blow landed. Surprise made the Norman lose his footing, and Theo stamped his weapon from his hand. There was no room to thrust with his own spear, so he settled for a one-two punch to the face, then he took two steps backwards and drove his spear into the Norman's thigh. When he dropped to the floor, Theo kicked off his helmet and ended it with a swift stab to his neck.

He turned round to see Murzuphlus doubled over, groaning. It didn't look good. Theo hauled his mail shirt over his head and unbuttoned his coat. There was no blood.

'I'd say you've got more ribs broken than not, but you'll live. I'm going to see what's happening.'

He poked his head outside the stable. Below him, a dozen fires were belching black smoke into the blue sky above the city, and a terrible noise – part slaughterhouse, part smithy – rose up from the streets. The gates of the acropolis were shattered and the banner of the Norman kingdom of Sicily dangled from a post above the walls. He ducked back inside.

Murzuphlus was sitting against a wall, his head dangling between his knees. At the sound of Theo's footsteps, he looked up.

'Well?'

Theo shook his head. 'We've lost. The city's fallen. It's over.'

211

'It can't be . . .' Murzuphlus tried to get up, but Theo put a hand on his chest and stopped him.

'It's over,' he repeated.

He was trying to sound matter-of-fact, but in truth he could hardly believe it himself. The empire shouldn't lose a whole city, not in a matter of days. He swallowed hard. Never mind about empires and cities. How the hell were he and Murzuphlus going to escape the catastrophe alive?

The night darkened.

Girls everywhere. Tiny and perfect, with pale faces and loose black hair. In the shadows under the trees, Agnes could see couples locked together as if they were wrestling, not making love.

'What is your name?' Andronikos said to the dancer, beckoning her over.

'Maraptikê, basileus,' she replied, her bright eyes on his.

'My wife is sad, Maraptikê. She does not wish to be here. Perhaps you can make her happy?'

The woman bent over her and began to stroke her face, teasing her hair through her fingers. The scent of winter roses and the darkest cinnamon filled Agnes's nose. She tensed and tried to push the hand away, but Maraptikê only laughed, leant in closer and—

'The emperor. Where is the emperor?'

A man's voice – urgent, sober – in the dark. Agnes sprang to her feet. For an insane moment she'd thought Theo was striding towards her, but it was his father, the general.

'Thank God I've found you,' said Branas.

Andronikos reached out, took Maraptikê's hand. She coiled both arms round his neck. Kissed his jaw.

'Basileus, I must speak to you.'

A pause during which Agnes watched her husband slowly, deliberately caress the dancer's thigh where it emerged from her creamy tunic. Then, abruptly, he pushed her aside. She sauntered away, throwing Agnes half a smile over her shoulder.

'All right, Branas,' said Andronikos, leaning back in his chair. 'Get on with it.'

The general came close and spoke so that only the emperor and Agnes would be able to hear.

'The Normans are at the gates of Thessalonikê. The city may already be under attack.'

'That? What's that to you?' Andronikos did not trouble to lower his voice. 'The governor speaks of a raiding party, nothing more.'

'He is lying. I've had word that the situation is more serious than he'd have you believe.'

'You've had word.'

If Branas heard the danger in Andronikos's voice, he chose to ignore it.

'Yes, I have – and I ask your leave to muster a relief force. The troops stationed at Kypsella could march tomorrow.'

'I see. You are well informed.'

'It is my duty to be. You will give the order?'

Andronikos did not reply at once. The men and women closest to them were pretending to think only of their wine.

'Tempting, isn't it?' said the emperor at last.

'Tempting, basileus?'

'To be at the head of an army.' He stood up. 'You want me to give you an order? Here's one. Leave. Now.'

Agnes willed Branas to obey, but he didn't move.

'Andronikos. Please.'

'Still here, Branas?'

'I must go to Thessalonikê.'

'If I were you, Branas, I'd choose my words with more care.' He drew closer to the general until barely a hand's span separated them. 'You've been waiting for this moment, haven't you? Your chance to move against me?'

Branas shook his head. 'You know that is not the man I am. You know I am loyal to you and to your throne.'

'Why, Branas? Why are you loyal? No one else is.' A laugh. 'You're a good man, Branas. If I were a good man, I wouldn't be loyal to me. Why then are you?'

The general leant towards Andronikos, but he spoke too quietly for Agnes to hear. She only caught the tone, soothing but firm, like a stablemaster might use to a horse in distress. It didn't work.

'Lock him up.' Andronikos snapped the order to Stephanos, who conjured up half a dozen guardsmen out of the darkness.

'Husband.' Agnes was on her feet, a hand on his arm, before she had time to think what she was doing.

'What, wife?'

'The general is sincere. He wants to help you.'

'What do you know? You know nothing. Thessalonikê will not fall, because I say it will not fall. Death to any man who says otherwise. Away with him.'

Theo and Murzuphlus emerged from the stable at sunrise after a long night with no food and only the dregs of a bucket of musty water to drink. They'd stripped off their armour and most of their clothes, wrapped their feet in bits of sacking and covered whatever parts of their body weren't already filthy with flaking dung.

Leaving the acropolis and its Norman guards behind them, they made for the shadow of the houses at a shuffling run, Murzuphlus clinging on to Theo. They wove downhill through the streets, planning to give the agora, the central square, a wide berth before getting out of the city by whichever of the eastern gates looked least well guarded.

The dead were everywhere. A white-bearded man lying in a gateway, his face cut almost in two. The twisted body of a woman who had obviously jumped from a rooftop – a death of her own choosing. It was only as they passed close by that Theo noticed the child in her arms, its head broken open.

At that moment, they saw a Rôman, still wearing good

boots and a belted surcoat, hurrying away from the agora, a gang of twenty Normans on his tail. Theo and Murzuphlus shrank into an alleyway and watched the soldiers surround him.

First, they motioned for him to strip. The man obeyed as eagerly as if it were his wedding night. Next, one of them hacked off his beard, taking a chunk of cheek with it. Two more stabbed at his feet with their spears, ordering him to dance. He shifted himself into a lumbering jig. *Clap your hands*, they mimed. *Above your head.* He did as he was told. He dropped his arms. *Up, up.* They jabbed him again. He tried to keep going, but they were growing bored, and when his arms collapsed a third time, they killed him.

Nobody would carry his body away. The kites, wheeling and shrieking overhead, would have his eyes by noon, his nose by nightfall.

Theo and Murzuphlus crept onwards.

In the shadow of the walls, a small party of soldiers was standing in a circle, dead drunk on looted wine, howling with delight at something out of sight at their feet. A woman, probably. The soldiers would be taking it in turns. But then the men parted and Theo saw what it was. Three Normans, weak with laughter, were arranging corpses into monstrous shapes. A man fucking a dog. A donkey fucking a man.

They stared – a mistake. One of the Normans turned, caught sight of them and peeled off from the group.

'Whuzh youse?' he snarled, shaking Theo by the shoulder.

Theo had no idea what he was talking about.

'Youse? Youse? Gowd. Sivver. Sivver n gowd.'

'Fuck's sake, Theo, it's Greek,' Murzuphlus hissed. 'He wants to go to our house and get his hands on our stuff. Silver and gold.'

'Oh, we can help him with that,' Theo said, and twisted his face into what he hoped was a humble and ingratiating smile. 'This way, sir, this way.'

The man grinned and beckoned to two of his companions, who stumbled after them.

'Which is ours, d'you reckon?' said Theo, peering at the houses lining the prosperous side street. He knew he couldn't keep them waiting long. 'Here we are, sirs, in here.'

He had plumped for a house where the gate had already been ripped open, and led them inside, hoping his instinct would guide him to something that might plausibly house valuables. They entered what looked like a steward's room, and Theo, to his relief, saw an iron strongbox housed in a niche behind a desk.

No key, he mimed, twisting his hand back and forth, and pointed to the man's mace. Two of the soldiers set about the box, and Theo hoped it would hold long enough for him to work out what to do with the third man, drunker than the others, who was leaning against a wall, supposedly guarding them.

Theo pointed into the fireplace, rubbing his fingers together. *More money. Up there.* The man leant over, supporting himself with one hand on the smoke-stained brickwork, and peered up into the gloom, expecting to see sacks of gold strung up like onions.

Theo brought a poker down hard on his head.

The others were so busy pulverising the safe that they had not heard. Theo chucked the Norman's sword to Murzuphlus, but his friend's reactions were slow and he missed – he should have thought about that – and it clattered on to the stone floor. The two soldiers turned round and saw Theo armed with a poker, and Murzuphlus scrabbling for the blade, which had skittered under the desk.

Theo bounded up on to the table and leapt on to the bigger of the two men, flailing his poker, hoping that surprise would win. The man fell beneath him, but he was quickly up and fighting, backing Theo against the wall, mace whirling.

He brought the weapon down hard on Theo's hand and he

dropped his poker, leaving him unarmed. The man grinned, and Theo felt the certainty of death paralyse his limbs. But the Norman wanted to hurt him before killing him. His first blow was a sharp upper cut between Theo's legs. Thought vanished and Theo howled on the floor.

When the pain retreated enough to allow him to open his eyes, he saw that the Norman was dead and Murzuphlus was standing over him, rocking with silent laughter.

'What's the fucking joke?' Theo wheezed.

'You – rolling about like a bad tragedian.' He gulped and offered his hand, then howled in pain himself when Theo struggled to his feet and embraced him.

'Sorry, I forgot about your ribs.'

'Bollocks.'

'I did. Honestly. How did you kill yours?'

'Honestly? He did most of the work for me. He went for the sword under the table as well and cracked his head on the edge. That stunned him and I finished him off. Yours was easy – he was so busy enjoying your display.'

'Thanks.'

'Don't mention it. I hope everyone we ever have to fight is as drunk as they were.'

'Amen to that,' said Theo. 'Come on, let's get their gear on.'

'Another disguise?'

'I'd rather be a stinking Norman than a stinking beggar.'

'We can't speak whatever it is they speak.'

'Most of them can barely talk. Just slur and grunt. You'll sound fluent. If anyone challenges us too close, pass out on the floor.'

'Might pass out anyway.'

Theo looked closer at Murzuphlus. His voice was light, but his skin was darkening from white to grey. They needed to clear Thessalonikê and find food and shelter fast. He wrapped an arm about Murzuphlus' waist and half pushed, half carried him towards the gate that would take them out on to the Via Egnatia, the long, straight road to the City.

'Courage,' he said whenever Murzuphlus stumbled. 'My father will have mustered the armies. We'll find him. He's probably only a mile or two down the road. Come on. Keep hold of me. Come on . . .'

September 1185

Agnes woke in the dead of night. At first she thought that Susa's new baby, Davit, must have jarred her awake. She was used to hearing the insistent clucking, a quick squall, then silence as the baby fed. Normally she rolled over and went back to sleep, but tonight she was already wide awake.

Maybe it was the heat. The late-summer days were thick and stuffy. Even the afternoon storms that swept overhead were not enough to thin the air completely. Sometimes it felt as if she were sleeping with a hot wet towel draped over her mouth. She shuddered. The image was unnerving.

Agnes felt the palace writhing with ghosts. Manuelos, Marguerite-Constance, Maria, Renier, Alexios, they all walked the corridors, skimming a hand's breadth above the flagstones, whispering in her ear before sleep, breathing quietly from a corner of her room when the dawn light was the same colour as the shrouds of the dead. Sometimes she even thought she could smell Marguerite-Constance's scent on her pillow.

She opened her door and slipped outside. There would be no more air in the courtyard, but maybe the sound of the water, the sight of the stars would do her good.

An abstract design of vines swirled under her feet, blending with the tendrils that coiled up the columns of the portico. The moon beat down, so bright and clear it was almost blue. The fountain – the gulping mouth of a fish frozen mid-jump – spilled endlessly, a peaceful sound, like a mother shushing everyone to sleep. She sat down, trailing her fingers in the water, and jumped when something moved. She had startled one of the carp, ungainly, lugubrious, that were lurking in the dark.

He rarely visited her at night, but slept with the other one, Maraptikê. Or with one of half a dozen other girls. But mainly with the other one. If they were still awake, she'd be able to hear them from the courtyard, the squeaks and sighs. She stilled her breathing to listen.

Silence. They were asleep.

But then the sound of footsteps came on the still night air. She sank to the ground behind the fountain to let them pass. Leaving her room at night wasn't forbidden, but nor did she want to be found. It was probably a servant delivering food, a maid returning to her own room. The footsteps stopped.

A shape – large – settled into one of the alcoves around the portico. It was a hooded man, a man who stank, a man whose breath wheezed beneath his ribs like a pair of bellows. He waited – but not for long. Two more shapes joined him.

'It is auspicious?' That was her husband's voice. 'Well?'

'He does not speak.' That was Stephanos.

'What the Devil use is he if he doesn't speak?'

'He only speaks the will—'

'Of God?'

'Let us call it God.'

'What does he call it? No. I mind not. He has sight. Sight is all I need. Come, Stephanos. I need answers. Answers. And I need them now.'

The three men swept out of the courtyard.

What sight? Answers to what?

Agnes followed them across the palace grounds towards an open space where a cauldron was set upon a tripod. Beneath it, logs smouldered a deep, impenetrable red. They were three figures in the moonlight. Three figures standing in a rough circle. The strange man stepped towards the cauldron and peered into it, but then he stopped, turned in her direction, and produced a high-pitched bark.

Stephanos sprang towards her. She could not hide. Her white gown would glow, a splash of phosphorescence under the gloom of the trees. He'd probably love to chase her and wrestle her to the ground, but she wouldn't give him the pleasure.

'Andronikos.' She ran towards him and tucked her hand in his. 'I had a fearful dream. Then I heard footsteps. I feared . . . I know not what I feared.'

She buried her face in his shoulder.

'Little ghost in white. She rises like a wraith from the sea. Don't be scared, little wraith. Stay here awhile,' he murmured into her hair.

She could hear Stephanos begin to protest.

'No, she stays. It is her life as well. If I die, so does she.'

If I die, so does she.

He held her tight under one arm.

'Begin, soothsayer.'

The man dug deep into his robes and flung a handful of herbs on to the fire. The flames changed colour, sparked, cracked and made her staring and dizzy. The water was bubbling hard. Vapours rose into the sky. The soothsayer was chanting, babbling words from every language and none, building to a gibbering frenzy. Suddenly, he flung off his cloak, lifted his fists to the heavens and plunged both hands into the cauldron, deep, to his elbows. A hideous hiss. Agnes screamed.

'Still, child, he won't come to any harm.'

And it was true. Or at least his arms came out in one piece. Maybe he was in agony, the same as any man, but he had the power to hide it. Agnes's only comfort was that Stephanos looked appalled as well.

Silence.

The soothsayer was staring into the water while his fingers, their nails long and hooked, traced slow patterns in the steam. He let out a low, whistling sigh and aimed a kick, surprisingly swift and sure, at the cauldron. It tumbled over, the water vanishing into the flames.

'It is done,' he said.

'Tell me, Seth,' said Andronikos. 'What did you see?'

Agnes was surprised this man could have a name. But maybe all men did, no matter how lost to God, to light and life.

'I saw a sigma in the shape of a half-moon, and before that an iota.'

The Greek letters took shape in Agnes's mind. An *S* and before that an *I*.

I-S.

'What does it mean?'

'It is the name of your successor. The name of your destroyer.'

'Isaakios.'

Andronikos's grip on her shoulder tightened. She bit her lip to stop herself crying out.

'When?' he demanded. 'Tell me when, or by God I'll—'

The soothsayer's poise did not falter, but his answer came fast.

'Within days of the Feast of the Exaltation of the Cross.'

At that, Andronikos threw his head back and roared with laughter. He marched over to where the soothsayer stood and embraced him.

'My dear fellow, my dear fellow. You nearly had me there. But how in the Devil's name do you do that trick with your arms? It's quite brilliant.'

His expression hardened.

'But you are also a fool. The feast day has already passed. Is Isaakios marching on the palace even as we talk? No! You have overreached yourself. Were you going to demand half the treasury to grind toads and emeralds together to make a spell to save me? Come, I'll give you a second chance. Admit you've made all this up.'

The soothsayer shook his head.

'I cannot change what the moon writes in the water.' He paused. 'And nor, Andronikos, can you.'

'Can I not? What if Stephanos drags Isaakios from his bed and cuts his throat? Will he still sit on my throne?'

Say no, say no.

'Yes. That is what is written.'

'You lie. My enemies hired you to confound me. I'm done with you.'

'How shall I do it?' Stephanos asked.

'Quickly.' Stephanos looked surprised, and Andronikos smiled. 'This man loves pain. We shall not indulge him with a slow death.'

The soothsayer did not seem to understand what was happening. Even when Stephanos jammed his knee into his stomach to make him double over and drew a knife smartly across his throat, he still looked surprised.

Andronikos gave a brisk nod. 'Good. And now, find Isaakios and finish him as well.'

'It'll be my pleasure, boss, but this one's a liar,' said Stephanos, pointing at the body that now lay twitching softly on the ground, one hand dabbling in a pool of blood. 'Isaakios is no threat to you.'

'Of course he's no threat. But why did your soothsayer say that name? Somebody must have put the idea into his head. No, I spared him once. A moment of weakness. I shall not do so again. See that he does not live another night.'

Stephanos bowed and disappeared under the trees, leaving Agnes alone with the mad emperor and the dead magician.

'Who do you see on my throne when I am gone?' He pulled her towards him. 'Do you think they will take you into their bed as I took you into mine?'

'You didn't take me into your bed,' she whispered. 'I asked to be taken. Remember?'

He frowned. She had made a mistake. That was not the girl he wanted.

'Are you already winking at them, offering to spread your legs for the first one to clamber over my dead body? No. You'll have none of them. You are mine. Mine.'

He was going to take her on the floor with the stench of the dead soothsayer rich in her nose. She could have been anybody. He wanted to empty himself, pour his black bile into her.

She wanted to stop him. But stopping him — even if she could — would be more dangerous than letting him do what he wanted. *Don't. Don't. Please, please don't.* The words screamed in her head while she tried to make her body move, tried to make her hips rise to meet his, tried to arch backwards. *Don't. Don't. Please, please don't.*

'Don't. Don't.' The words were no longer in her head.

'Don't? You're telling me *don't.* Me?'

He stopped.

'What's wrong with you? You used to like this. You used to like me. It used to be like dancing with a nymph new-born from the glade. You were worth a poem or two. Now all I can see is a red-faced child. Where is my nymph? What have you done to her? I want her, not this snivelling wretch.'

He hauled her up roughly and touched her face with a finger.

'There's my nymph. How did you find yourself here, little one? Do you wish you were still at your father's hearth, waiting for your marriage to a little duc? Safe in the woods of the west? Do you?'

She looked him in the eye. *Brave, be brave. He eats weakness.*

'No. No, I don't. But nor do I want to die.'

'What makes you think you're going to die?'

'You. Your face. Soon you'll have nobody left to kill. And then you'll kill me.'

Three days after the Feast of the Exaltation of the Cross

When the land walls of the City rose up before them, Theo was too exhausted to speak. It had been a long road from Thessalonikê, a long road with too many close calls. He stopped and nudged Murzuphlus, who'd been trudging, head down, a few paces behind him. His friend lifted his eyes long enough to take in the glorious sight before their eyes before resuming his slow shamble.

'C'mon, Theo. God's sake, keep going. If I stop, you won't be able to start me again.'

Originally, they'd struck out along the coast, following trails made by generations of fishermen and goatherders, hoping they'd dodge the invaders if they gave the Hodos Egnatia, the straight road to the City, a wide enough berth.

But bands of Normans were prowling in a wide arc all around Thessalonikê, and on the second day a raiding party spied them before they had time to hide. The Normans chased them through the trees, more for sport than anything else, and they only escaped by clambering over the cliff edge, clinging to the scraggy trees that grew out of the rocks.

On the fourth day, they met no Normans and risked turning north to the road again, where they merged with a long line of refugees, all hunting a place of safety – a garrisoned town, a distant relative's village in the hills, anywhere that might keep them alive when the Normans advanced. And all the while rumours snapped at their heels.

The Normans have razed Thessalonikê; the Normans have

roasted babies to eat; the Normans have reached Neapolis; the Normans have sprouted wings and pointed teeth; the Normans are marching on the City; the Normans will take the City; the City will fall; the City will fall.

But no soldiers overtook them, and Theo guessed the Normans' love of plunder would keep the City safe for a while longer. The conquerors must be taking their time. After all, they'd found themselves masters of some prime country, juicy, fat and ripe for pillage. And with no hint that the Rômans were planning a counteroffensive, they could pick Thrace's bones at leisure.

Theo and Murzuphlus covered the final distance to the walls, and stopped, aghast. Men and women were flowing freely through the Golden Gate, milling about between the double walls. A couple of lads had even scaled the ramparts and were larking about on top.

'Where the fuck are the guards?' muttered Theo.

'Something's up,' said Murzuphlus.

'No shit. Come on.'

They collared a few people as they passed through the gates and asked what the hell was going on, but they were all strangers, people who'd fled from the west and were as surprised and troubled as they were to find the City so exposed.

As they hurried towards the Mesê – as best as two weary men could hurry – the outlying districts were eerily quiet, but they could sense an almighty buzz of agitation building before them. Dozens of men were overhauling them, spilling out of tenements, wine-shacks and workshops.

'Armed,' said Murzuphlus. 'They're all armed.'

It was true. There wasn't a man on the streets who wasn't holding something that could kill. Not swords, not spears, not soldiers' weapons, but soot-blackened pokers, sawn-off beams and squat butchering knives. As for the City's women, they had all but vanished. Theo saw one bundling two boys into a doorway, boxing their ears as they tried to wriggle free. He approached and asked what was happening, but she shrank from him, screaming to leave her alone.

Ahead of them, the Forum of Theodosius was pandemonium. They hesitated, reluctant to surrender to the crowds, but before they could turn aside, those in front surged backwards, other men clustered behind and they were sucked into the mass, as powerless as sheep in quicksand.

But here, at last, Theo began to grasp what was happening.

'The Normans are coming . . .'

'The emperor is mad . . .'

'The army does nothing . . .'

'Keep moving, damn you . . .'

'Death to Andronikos . . .'

The cry was taken up all around them.

'Death to Andronikos! Death to Andronikos! Death to Andronikos!'

Death to Andronikos!

'The City's rising, Murzuphlus. The City's fucking—'

But a heave in the crowd ripped his friend from his side. He caught sight of him a few more times as they were borne further and further apart, and then he vanished in the flood.

Theo had never seen, never imagined, anything like it. Tens of thousands of men who normally ate and slept, bought and sold, fought and fucked in parallel had come together with one purpose. They weren't men any more; they were a mass, unstoppable. And he was one of them.

He had no choice. Already he'd felt soft things underfoot and knew they were men who'd tried to resist. He had to run as everyone ran – or fall and be trampled. As soon as he gave himself up to the inexorable flow, he felt strong, part of something remarkable, part of the City. He ran, and he was glad to run.

Death. Death. Death to Andronikos.

Was he shouting it? Or were the cries so loud they seemed to be in his own throat as well?

The mob poured between a forest of columns into the hippodrome, stone-cut seats rearing up all about them. Ahead stood the walls of the Great Palace, and they could go no further.

'Death! Death! Death!' thousands of voices chanted as one.

They had come as close to their prey as they could, but Theo knew the walls would not stop them now. Nothing could stop them; not even themselves. The City had shrugged, month after month, as Andronikos tore through the ranks of the aristos. It had cheered him, claimed him as its own – and now it was going to have his blood.

And still Theo did not truly understand why.

A figure appeared in the imperial box, one man standing alone, raining arrows down on the crowd. It was impossible to take cover, and Theo heard howls of pain rise above the din.

'Death! Death!'

It was Andronikos. The man he had last seen high on victory in that little cell outside Nicaea had transformed into a black demon, dancing above the heads of his people, deranged, berserk, a sickening marvel.

'The gates! The gates!'

The men lunged forward, surged backwards, a living battering ram, and then an exultant roar tore through the crowd. Somewhere, a gate had burst, and Theo was swept up in a murderous charge.

A column rose before him, twin serpents writhing round each other up to a point high in the sky. The mob parted to flow round it, and Theo saw his chance. He flung himself at it and hung on, wrapping his arms and legs about it like an octopus clinging to a rock in a storm.

Gradually, the press thinned. Theo opened his eyes – not remembering when or why he had closed them – and let go. His heart was whirring and his breathing was hoarse and ragged. He looked down at his hands. They were shaking so hard he had to clench them to make them stop. He wasn't hurt. No man had threatened him. But his body was behaving as if he had been a moment from death. He was free, though, and he could think, a man again. And his first thought . . .

Agnes is behind those walls.

Her eyes flicked open.

What's that noise?

She listened. Nothing. There was nothing. Was there? No, nothing. She was oversensitive – jumpy – paranoid. Of course she was. The night before . . .

And then you'll kill me.

Those words. And then he'd leant forward and – and kissed her. Gently, on the forehead. Kissed her and told her to go. She'd backed away, not wanting to lose sight of him, expecting a joke, a trick, something, anything other than escape, but he turned, forgetting her, and she fled, running, running, up the slopes, through the gardens, sure that someone – or something – was following her. But when she risked a glance over her shoulder – nothing. No Stephanos. No Andronikos. No black shape. Nothing but grey air and grey stones.

She'd stumbled into her chamber and buried herself under her sheets as dawn was breaking. *I'm safe. I'm alive. I have lived through another night. And by God I will live through this day too.* Those words played on her lips, her teeth chattering with tension, fear and a chill that had nothing to do with the still air of sunrise, until she slept – or blacked out. And now, hours later, she was awake.

What's that noise?

She started from her bed.

The angle of the light coming through her drapes told her it was mid-morning at least. But nobody had woken her. There was no tray of food at the foot of her bed. And something else was wrong.

The quiet. The palace was never quiet – too many people

lived and worked within its walls. And there was that noise again. A strange whisper, a new sound, one she couldn't place.

Still in her muddy nightgown, she hurried into the corridor. It was empty and aggressively still. Then came the sound of footsteps – one pair – pattering fast towards her. She tensed. The person would appear at any moment. Shrinking back into the doorway, she saw a kitchenmaid – her hair flying, flour spilt down her apron – run past.

'What's . . . ?' Agnes began, but the girl was already past her, running, fleeing, flying.

The whisper was getting louder and louder. Suddenly, Agnes knew what it reminded her of – the hippodrome, the City roaring blood and victory. Except it sounded too close for it to be that. Much too close . . .

More footsteps. Two mop-women, older, sisters probably. Both stumbling, shoving each other on.

'Stop! Please, tell me . . .'

This time, one looked over her shoulder, recognised her.

'Run, basilissa, run. They're coming. They're coming.'

'Who? The Normans? *Who?*'

'Not they. Not they.'

'The people . . .'

'The people are coming . . .'

'For him, for him.'

The people.

For a moment, it made no sense to her. The people? Which people? But she found herself running all the same, running even before she fully knew why.

The people.

And then it was all terrifyingly clear. The diabolical whisper was the roar of the City.

On she ran, following the other women, away from the richer parts, out, out, towards the kitchens. The people mightn't come there. Nothing to steal but pots and pans.

Maybe they knew a way out, a small cellar door, overlooked. She could slip away. A nobody in a dirty white dress.

Her breath was gulping, her chest burning. Her legs were confused, rebellious. She never ran. Only pretend races with Susa's little—

Susa. Her boys. Andronikos's grandsons. Somebodies.

Where were they? They might all still be asleep. Susa slept late after long nights with baby Davit. She must at least try, mustn't she? Try at least to warn her. She swerved round and ran back towards the imperial quarters.

She shook Susa's door open.

'It's me! It's me! We must get out. They're coming, Susa! They're . . . !'

She was shouting at an empty room. Was she hiding?

'It's me. Agnes. You can come out.'

Why was she yelling? The room was empty. Empty, but not quiet. The roar was getting closer, breaking up into distinct voices. *Think. Think.* But she couldn't think. The animal panic that had made her run, made her know which way to go, had abandoned her. The noise was too great. It stole her senses. She ran backwards and forwards in the room, wringing her hands, sobs of terror writhing in her chest. *Think. Think.*

She plunged out of the door, knowing it was hopeless, knowing they'd be on her. And then she was writhing for real, fighting in the grip of some man, some City madman.

'Still. Be still.'

That wasn't a street voice. That was . . .

'You!' she exclaimed.

Theo shouldered some discarded weapons, a hand-axe, a staff, and chased towards the broken gates with a few other stragglers. The odds of finding her were tiny, but he'd try. He had to try.

Before he'd covered twenty paces, a man with a lopsided face and wandering eyes bowled into him and clung on, gabbling nonsense. Not quite nonsense. A word or two emerged.

'An angel. An angel.' His face was rapturous, repulsive. 'An angel in the Holy Wisdom.'

Theo tried to shake him off, but the man had lunatic strength in his fingers.

'Zakius. Zakius. Zakius the basileus. Zakius. Zakius. Zakius the basileus,' he chanted.

Theo was about to bring the staff down on the man's skull, hopefully not hard enough to kill, when the words *Zakius* and *Angel* sounded once more in his head.

'Isaakios Angelos?' he demanded. 'Is that what you're saying? Isaakios Angelos? What about him?'

The man gibbered and jabbered, too thrilled by the sudden attention to get the words out properly. Theo threw him off and the man stumbled and landed on his back, staring up at the sky.

'Long live the angel! Long live the basileus!' he cried, squirming in ecstasy.

'I'd sooner see you basileus, friend, than Isaakios Angelos,' shouted Theo over his shoulder as he made for the palace.

But his way was blocked by two heavies. No, four. Make that six.

'What's your problem with Isaakios Angelos?' said one.

'None. He's a moron. But that's his problem, not mine. Now get out of my way.'

'Hear that? He's insulted our emperor, boys. What do we do to people who insult our emperor?'

'I'd love to find out,' said Theo, levelling the staff at them, sword-style, using the axe to guard his left side.

He was in no shape to take on so many, but they didn't know that. Hopefully they'd decide he wasn't worth the trouble – not when there was a palace to be sacked. It looked like it was working. He saw a couple of the littler ones exchange glances, shrug. *Fuck it.* But no, the biggest one, the one who'd spoken first, was looking at him with new interest.

'Here,' he said, 'I know him. It's Branas's boy. He looks like shit, but listen to that posh voice. And look at that devil hair. Come on. The Angel said to deliver any aristos we find to him.'

The others looked doubtful.

'There's gold in it,' the man urged. 'You seen how much he's got with him in the church.'

Theo wasn't going to wait around to see whether he persuaded them. He had to get past. He had to get into the palace. He sent the axe spinning into one man's belly, whirled the staff high and fast and clubbed two others to the floor. Shifting to a two-handed grip, he thrust the staff high above his head to block a fencing post that was about to smash his skull. He caught the blow in time but his staff splintered, leaving him with nothing but his fists.

Before the man could heft the post into the air for another go, Theo buried his left hand in the man's belly, his right in his nose, and watched him go down. That left two. The big ones.

'Scrapper, isn't he?' remarked one.

'Plucky fellow,' said the other, reaching down in time to snatch the post that Theo was about to grab.

'Come on, pal. You're coming to see the emperor. Up to you whether you do it conscious or not.'

'I'll see your emperor in hell,' said Theo, as cocksure as he could muster.

But he was worried. The fight had already squeezed what tiny reserves he had, and he reckoned these men, seasoned bruisers, could tell.

They split, one at his front, one at his back. One mock-lunged with an old pike. Theo leapt aside. The other gave him a shove in his back. Both laughed, hefting their weapons. Theo abandoned any idea of beating them and turned to make a run for it. But they must have seen him tense, because they jumped him before he'd got clear.

Boots to his head. Blackness.

Agnes was staring into that face. Still perfect. That perfect, hated face.

'It's like our first meeting, isn't it, my love? I remember our eyes locked while all around was chaos. You feel the romance of it too?'

'Get off me,' she hissed. 'I'm not your love. Get off me.'

He released her.

'There. I'm off.'

His voice, mild, mollifying, brought her up short. She darted a look of surprise at him, but nevertheless made to run. She didn't get far.

'Not that way, fool. That ways lies half the City. What will they make of the pretty little empress, her clothes so provokingly awry? A nice prize. You'll be snapped up and spat out.'

She sank her teeth into the arm that was holding her. He winced, but did not let go.

'Teeth won't keep you safe from the mob. Your way is this way – with me.'

'I'm not going with you.'

'Go that way and you're dead.'

'I don't care. I'd rather die than—'

'No you wouldn't. You're not that kind of girl.'

She screamed, 'Help! Help!' and with a brute strength she'd never have guessed she had, ripped herself free.

'Idiot,' he snapped. 'You'll bring them—'

But they were already there. At the far end of the corridor she saw a pack of men advancing on them. She looked at them, at their red faces, their black eyes, their blunt weapons. They looked back, recognised the emperor and his empress, howled and gave chase.

She fled. Of course she fled.

Every heartbeat she expected a hand, many hands, to seize her, but she and Andronikos had one advantage. They knew the palace; the men behind them did not. She sidestepped left into a little chapel and slipped behind the iconostasis. From there a ladder led out on to the roof where the eunuch boys sunned themselves between lessons. Andronikos was close behind her.

'Nice idea,' he said. 'Now where? It won't take them long.'

The men were blundering about the chapel below, trying to work out which way their quarry had gone. Agnes looked about her. She hadn't thought how they'd get down. Andronikos peered over the edge.

'The coast's clear.'

He dropped in a loose sort of crouch and rolled when he hit the ground. *Come on*, he beckoned. *Jump*. It was a long way down – the height of a small tree. She wriggled off the edge, hanging by her fingertips. Even then she might not have dared let go, but she lost traction, felt the sharp scrape of stone against skin and landed badly, jarring her left foot.

Already he was pulling her along.

'Wait,' she gasped. 'I can't . . .'

'Of course you can.'

He plunged into a guardhouse, opening doors, kicking over piles of blankets, shields, looking for something.

'Somewhere here. There's a passage to the harbour. The Varangians use it. Where the—'

'Wait,' Agnes said, fighting for breath. 'They can't search everywhere. There must be a place where we can hide.'

'There isn't. Wherever we hide, they'll find us. Anyway, I won't cower in the dark.' He darted into a storeroom, hauled aside a few sacks and cried, 'Got it.' He ripped up a trapdoor. 'This way. The Varangians built this for times of trouble.'

'Where are they now, then?' she said, climbing after him.

'What?'

'Where are your precious Varangians? Shouldn't they be saving you. Dying at your feet?'

He looked up at her, and she saw something, some loss, on his face, but all he said was, 'I don't know. Now pull it shut behind you.'

It was dark, but he set off confidently enough. The way led through storerooms, cellars, gardeners' sheds until they came on to the open ground above the Bukoleon.

'There,' he said. 'See down there. We'll get away yet.'

He pointed to the harbour. She could see three boats chasing each other up to the dockside, fighting to squeeze into a spot between two imperial galleys. They were snub-nosed and barrel-bottomed and, to her eyes, very, very small.

'Who . . . ?' she began.

'Fishermen. They'll have got wind what's afoot. They're smart men. Slip in by sea. Grab what they can. Slip out.'

Half a dozen men scrambled off each boat and plunged up the marble steps into the palace grounds. Agnes made to hide as they hared up the path not a hundred paces from where they stood.

'Wait,' said Andronikos, gripping her arm. 'They don't come inside the City walls. They won't know us. Not in these clothes.'

It was only then that she took in what he was wearing. The roughest of clothes, woollen and simple. They softened him. She was used to seeing his face framed in gold. And he was right – the fishermen didn't look twice at a young woman in nothing much and a tall man in grey.

'Your ship awaits, wife. Come on. We're nearly safe.'

'But who will man the oars?'

'Not the galley, empress. Not today.'

And she saw that he was busy unlooping one of the lines the fishermen had fastened around the mooring posts.

'It's perfect,' said Andronikos. 'Hop aboard.'

'That?' gasped Agnes. 'It's a bathtub.'

'You can expect much of me, but I can't sail a galley on my own.'

'You have money?'

He laughed.

'That's more like it. You're starting to think practically. Yes, Agnes, I have money – more than most men see in a lifetime.' He opened his cloak, and she saw heavy-stitched brown bags slung on some kind of cross-belting around his body. 'I have money – and I have friends in faraway places. Which means we have a future.'

He jumped down, and the boat rocked beneath his weight. As he started to haul up the sail, the ropes lifted off the deck and flogged in the breeze. One lashed across his face and ripped a weal of blood. He didn't seem to notice. He held a hand out.

'Wife? My empress? Agnes? Will you come with me?'

What was she doing? Why was she even considering it? She didn't have to obey him. Not now. Not any more. She'd run. Find her own bloody way out. That was what she'd do. Run.

Run.

And she was going to do it, she really would have done it – if hundreds of men hadn't charged out of the palace and on to the marble steps. She had to choose. She had to stay where she was and take her chances, or go – with him. She hesitated. Andronikos held his hand out, but she backed away.

'They've no reason to hurt me,' she said.

'But they will, Agnes, you know they will. I can offer you something better than being raped by half a hundred men.'

A cry came from up above them and the men started to thunder down the steps, howling blood and murder.

Theo stared blearily at the mosaic above his head. He'd seen it a thousand times. The Virgin sat with the Child in her lap; to her left stood Constantinos, the first emperor, offering her his city; to her right was Justinian, holding out the Holy Wisdom, the cathedral he had built. They were men who were great enough to stand beside the Son of God and give His mother gifts. They were emperors.

But the fat, florid man walking towards him, smoothing his hair with one hand, was he an emperor? Theo felt something very like fear trickle through him. Not for himself, but for every man, woman and child in the City.

'Hello, Theo, old chap,' said Isaakios Angelos. 'Good to see you.' He was acting as if they'd met at a summer hunting party. 'Thought you were hiding out in the west.'

'What the hell is happening, Isaakios? The people are calling you emperor.'

'They do seem to have taken it into their heads that I am their God-allotted leader, yes. Strange beast, the crowd. Still, the people know best, don't they? Or they did in Athens. I'm not sure about this lot. But I think for now we'd—'

'Shut up for a moment and listen. I don't know why these idiots dragged me here, but I need to—'

Before he could get any further, one of Isaakios's new friends – who looked like he'd been badly stitched together out of slabs of ox – stepped forward.

'This gent was speaking bad about you, Exalted One. We brought him here for your judgement. Shall we kill him?'

Isaakios chortled happily.

'No, my good man, no. Thanks all the same. You may stand down.' He winked at Theo. 'See? You'll have to mind your manners. Come to think of it, you should probably be kneeling if you're talking to me. Or maybe lying flat on the ground?'

He caught sight of Theo's face.

'No? Not keen? Well, we can save that for later. Perhaps once I am properly crowned. This—' he tilted the thin band of gold on his head to a jauntier angle '—was something of a stopgap measure. Still, I fancy it is rather becoming.'

'Very becoming.'

'Aren't you going to ask me how I came by it?'

Theo couldn't bear it. He was exhausted. Half-starved. Worried about his father and Murzuphlus – and terrified for Agnes.

'Isaakios, please, I cannot stay here. I must—'

A boot landed square in his back and he collapsed to his knees.

'If the Angel wants you to ask him something, you ask him.'

Theo didn't want to pander to a play-acting clown. But the clown was ringed by very large men.

'Please, Isaakios Angelos, please tell me how you came by it.'

'That's more like it. Well, last night – I can hardly believe it was last night – Andronikos's in-est-im-able servant Stephanos appeared at my gatehouse. It seems I had somehow incurred the wrath of our beloved emperor – or ex-emperor, as I think we may now safely call him – and he had sent his minions to kill me. I acted, if I may say so myself, Theo, with great dispatch, with great decisiveness, with a boldness and steeliness quite worthy of one of the heroes of a far nobler age than ours, dear boy.'

Isaakios paused and frowned.

'Theo, this is my first opportunity to relate my tale to a man of birth. You should be honoured. And yet I have the most uncomfortable impression you wish to be elsewhere.'

'I . . . I am concerned about the women of the palace household, that is all.'

'Theo, you are a true hero, but I am sure the good men of the City will show them every courtesy.'

'That's fucking ridiculous and you know it.'

Isaakios sighed as the man clubbed Theo to the floor again.

'Now, where was I? Ah, yes. I mounted my horse, my noble steed, donned my armour and girded myself with my sword, and when that rapscallion Stephanos kicked in my gate, I charged him. I have never been so terrified in my whole life

– you won't tell that to a soul, will you, Theo? Terrified, and yet also a little exhilarated. I believe I was under the influence of what soldiers call *bloodlust*. Is that the right phrase? I was so full of it that I believe I could have ripped the flesh off Stephanos's bones with my bare teeth. Luckily, it did not come to that.

'I hit him. Struck him with my sword. I clove his head in twain. Or is it cleft? No matter. It was in two very distinct pieces on the floor. I don't believe I have ever killed a man before. In fact, I know I have never killed a man before. And if there was to be a first time, I am so very glad it was him. He was a bad man, Theo.'

'He was. His death does you credit.'

Isaakios beamed.

'Such praise. Such comradely approval. Thank you, Theo. Now, let me tell you the rest. After the red mist had lifted, I realised I was still in very great danger. I decided I would throw myself on the mercy of the City. I rode my horse here, to the Holy Wisdom. I told the people what had occurred. I asked their forgiveness for my mortal sin. I cursed Andronikos. I begged their aid. And before I knew what was happening, I was hoisted upon their shoulders and acclaimed as emperor.'

'And now you are holed up here until they finish off Andronikos?'

'If you mean am I taking spiritual succour while my servants dispose of a tyrant, yes, Theodore, that is what I am doing.'

'I don't get it. He was a hero to them. How could they throw him over for you?'

'I'll ignore what you're implying, Theo. It's hardly flattering. You want to know why? They're scared, dear fellow, scared stiff. Not because he's killed all those aristos. No, I doubt that's troubled their bloodthirsty little hearts. But what they've heard about the Normans terrifies them. And when people are terrified they can turn very, very nasty.'

'Like you did.'

That made Isaakios titter.

'Exactly so, just like I did. Stephanos and his knife made me ever so nasty. And, by God, what we've been hearing about Thessalonikê is enough to make Herakles himself quake in his lionskin. Blood-curdling stuff, Theo, blood-curdling . . .'

The man who'd been guarding the gate was racing towards them, waving his arms and shouting.

'Great One. News. News of Andronikos.'

'Dead? Is he dead?'

'No, Great One. He's not dead. He's escaped. He's set sail in a boat bound east.'

'Pursue him. Bring him back alive – *alive*, do you hear me?'

The man was nodding, bowing, turning to go, but Theo stopped him.

'Tell me, did he go alone?'

'No, they say his wife went with him.'

She was alive. *Alive* – but still in his power.

'What ails you, Theo?' Isaakios was looking at him curiously.

'Nothing. Nothing. I . . . I pity her. That is all.'

'Don't we all, dear boy, don't we all?'

Agnes lay in the bottom of the boat, seawater swashing around her, making her cuts sting. She sat up, shivering, bruised – and furious. She tried to stand, but realised that ropes bound her to the deck.

'They were for your own safety,' said Andronikos from behind her. 'Better than rolling overboard. The knots should be easy enough to undo.'

She began to work herself free, pausing every so often to glare at him.

'Don't look at me like that,' he said. 'You knocked yourself out when you jumped. Either that, or the sight of our illustrious citizenry caused you to faint.'

'I don't faint,' she said, gnawing at the rope. 'I must have hit my head.'

He smiled and said no more.

Behind them, the sun was starting to sink, and she suddenly felt very small. She was used to being dwarfed by the domes and pillars of the City, but this was different. The hills on either side of the Bosporus were out of reach. They were alone with the sea and the sky.

'Welcome to exile,' said Andronikos. He was braced at the back of the boat, the steering oar wedged under his arm.

The moon broke out from behind the banks of clouds and shone on his face. She hardly recognised him. It was as if whatever madness had possessed him had passed.

'Andronikos?' she said.

'Yes?'

'Why did you bring me? Honestly. Why didn't you leave me there?'

'I told you. The mob . . .'

'I don't believe that.' She paused. Was it really safe to speak?

'Yes?'

'So many have died. You . . . you've killed so many. What difference would it make if I had died too?'

'No great difference to this world of ours, but a little difference to me. I like you, I always have, you know that. Besides, adventures are always more fun with a beautiful woman at one's side.'

'I'll run away, you know *that*. The first chance I get, I'll run back to the City.'

'And I promise I won't stop you. But you might find you like me a little better, away from all that.' He waved a hand at the darkness behind them. 'Besides, do you really want to live under Emperor Isaakios Angelos? I know I wouldn't. And you'll find the Rus are a delightful people. Their furs will become you.'

'The Rus?' Despite herself, her eyes widened. 'You can't mean to sail us to their lands in this?'

He laughed.

'No, even as a young man I would not have attempted that. Once we've cleared the straits, I'll put in at some port and hire something more appropriate to our majesty.'

He said no more, and for a while she watched him steer the little boat before the wind. Above her, the sail was as flat as the face of the moon. They seemed to be going very fast. It felt like the waves rolling up behind them were racing them, trying to outrun them, romping like dogs chasing a chariot.

'Andronikos, why are you so happy?'

'Because the wind is with me.' The boat lurched and he grabbed the side to keep his footing. 'That's the race off the headland. It'll set the boat dancing for a while yet. It's going to be a rough night. But that's good.'

'Good?' Agnes didn't know much about boats, but she knew enough to be sure it was madness to be at sea on a night like this. Already she was drenched. She had no feeling in her fingertips, none in her toes. Salt stung her eyes and her face smarted with the cold. 'How is that good?'

'Isaakios's men can't be far behind us. The wilder it blows, the better the chance we have of losing them.'

'Do you know what you're doing?' she shouted into the wind.

'Yes. Yes I do.'

She stared up into the sky. A few moments ago there had been stars, now there was nothing, only night. She listened to the water boiling and fighting, to the waves exploding out of the darkness behind them.

The outline of the hills, black against black, was changing. They were clearing the headland and heading out into the open waters, where the wind blew stronger. And the motion of the boat was changing, too. The waves no longer rolled underneath them, but gripped the stern, lifting it up, hurling the boat forwards, while Andronikos fought to keep it under control.

Suddenly, something bright white exploded to their left. A breaking wave reared out of the blackness. It sounded like a thousand trees falling, a thousand people roaring, and then she could hear nothing at all, because the wave had buried them.

Her arms clung to a tangle of ropes, but the water was churning, sucking, snatching at her clothes, and she was slipping away. Voices whispered, soft and kind.

Let go. Breathe. Breathe, let go and say goodbye.

She was no longer cold. A warmth, a great heat was building around her heart, shooting down her limbs. She only had to let go for the heat to be hers for ever and ever. Bright figures danced out of reach and—

The boat burst above the water and she was back in the world. A cold, mad, deafening world.

The mast. The mast had gone. Or rather it hadn't gone, but it was hanging over the side of the boat, trailing in the water, the sail a stone dragging the boat down.

Dragging the boat down.

Andronikos lay motionless, his arms wrapped around the steering oar. She fumbled inside his cloak, found a dagger at his hip and leapt on the ropes that still held the mast to the boat, hacking, slashing, sawing. The first two parted quickly. She attacked another, pausing only when a wave nearly tipped the boat back on its side. Another rope. And another. And then the weight of the water tore mast and sail free. She watched them whirl away behind her, a few fragments sticking above the water, then nothing.

Everything was unexpectedly calmer. The boat still reeled and danced, but it was one with the sea, like a leaf or a stick, spinning on a river current, too small to sink.

A rending sound came from behind her, and for a dreadful moment she thought the boat must be breaking up beneath them. But it was Andronikos, sobbing uncontrollably in the bottom of the boat. At first she couldn't hear the words, then they came, strangled, bloated with tears.

'Wrong. This is wrong. This is not meant to be my end.'

He stumbled to his feet and stared back the way they had come.

'Behold, Agnes, your salvation.'

Just inside the horizon, a small fleet was bearing down on them, tall ships with tall masts from which boys would be scanning the waters, hunting the emperor and his wife.

'Your salvation,' he repeated, 'and my doom.'

Before she could think to stop him, he snatched his dagger out of her hands and lifted it high in the air. She froze. Was he going to kill himself? Kill her? But with a strange, rueful smile, he brushed the tears from his eyes and tossed the blade into the sea.

'No. Many things they may say about me, but never that I was a coward.'

His voice was stronger.

'Come, Agnes, let us sit on the other side of the boat. I take no joy watching them approach. And see, it is a beautiful evening.'

It was true. The wind was easing fast. It still blew hard, but there was no longer any vice to it. The seas, which had been so steep, so short in the shadow of the hills, were lengthening into billows, and the clouds had thinned enough for the setting sun to turn the light to gold.

Agnes heard the thump of drums, then the bosuns' shouts, and finally the grunts of the oarsmen. She glanced over her shoulder, and looked away fast.

'I said it was best not to look,' Andronikos said. 'Don't worry. I'll tell them I made you come.'

'That,' she said, 'is the very least you can do.'

He laughed, as she'd meant him to do. He took her hand and kissed it.

'I'm sorry,' he said. 'For everything.'

He did not let her hand go, and she found that, despite everything, she did not want to take it away. Behind them there was a yell and a crash as a grappling iron buried its teeth into the deck.

The Fourth Emperor

Isaakios Angelos is gloriously dressed; the best way to feel like an emperor, he believes, is to look like one. He has a delicate visit to pay and he wants to play his part well.

He pushes open the door to the prison cell.

Alexios Branas is leaning against the far wall, where a gap in the stonework, smaller than the palm of a child's hand, lets in a grey trickle of sky. His eyes are open, but hunger and waiting have deadened them. He's been preparing himself for death, looking at it from every angle, so that when it comes it will not be able to surprise him. He has never done anything he was ashamed of, and he does not want his death to change that.

'What are you doing here?' The general's voice is a croak.

'Manners, Branas,' Isaakios says with a little laugh.

'What the fuck are you doing here?'

Isaakios sighs and nods to one of his escort. The man knocks Branas to the floor, picks him up, punches him down again, stamps on his hand and returns to his place by the door.

'I am your emperor.'

'You're out of your mind.'

'No, my dear fellow, I am not. A very great deal has happened since that godless lunatic tossed you in here.'

'He is a hundred times the man you are.'

'I'm hurt, Branas.'

'I mourn the change that came over him. But nothing can lessen what he once was — what he should have been.' A pause. 'What has happened to him?'

'You are neighbours, so to speak. Listen.'

Branas finally allows himself to hear the grunts and thuds he has been carefully ignoring all morning.

'Do you wish to share his fate?'

'Stupid fucking question. Of course I don't.'

'Why should I spare you?'

'If I were you, I wouldn't spare me. I don't like you. You know that.'

'Shall I have you killed?'

'Be my guest.'

Isaakios turns away to hide his irritation. The conversation is not playing out according to the plan in his head, according to which Branas should be clutching his knees, cursing Andronikos's name and pledging his undying loyalty.

But one of Isaakios's greatest strengths – his only strength, maybe – is that he has no illusions about his own shortcomings, chiefly, that he is no soldier. To keep his throne, he needs to defeat the Normans. And to defeat the Normans, he needs to keep Branas.

'I shall pardon you.'

Not a word in reply. He might as well have said the general was to have an extra spoonful of porridge for his supper.

'I shall pardon you, and you, Branas, you will fight the Normans for me.'

'I'll never do anything for you.'

'For the empire, then? Let's say you're doing it for the empire?'

A nod.

'All right.'

'So you'll do it?'

'For the empire.'

Branas stands and walks past Isaakios and out of the door, leaving Isaakios staring at the empty cell. A shiver races down his spine, a memory, a dream, a premonition, he cannot say. He hurries back into the daylight world where he is the most powerful man to breathe God's clean air.

September 1185

Agnes stared at the sampler, watching her fingers push the thread in and out, in and out. She drove the needle into her thumb and watched a droplet of blood balloon from her skin, but there was no pain.

Her face hurt from showing emotions she did not feel. Her throat ached from saying words she did not mean. She thought about acrobats who could stand on one leg for hours at a time. They might look at ease, but she knew that somewhere, deep down, they must hate it. But they had to do it – it was their living. The same as pretending was now hers.

Nobody must ever know that she'd chosen Andronikos above the blameless life of the convent. Nobody must even guess that at first, and for longer than she could now bear to admit, she'd . . . what? Not loved him, no. Wanted him to love her? Maybe. Desired him? Certainly that. She put her thumb in her mouth and sucked hard to stop the blood flowing.

Her feelings now were hard to place, but she knew they were not what they should be. She remembered all that he had done – and forced herself to name it evil. But it was hard. *It was not he who did those things*, something in her wheedled. *He was not himself. A demon is to blame. A demon, not him.*

Most of all, nobody must ever suspect that at the end, there on the boat, when she had him back, the real him, hers, all hers, she had longed to escape with him, longed to wear the furs he promised.

A sigh escaped her lips and her needlework dropped from

her hands. The palace women – the new palace women – took that as a signal to rush to her side.

'There, there, you can tell us, there, there.'

That was Dora, Isaakios's younger sister, a mouse-haired ninny who worshipped her brother with a pagan zeal that would have been funny if it wasn't so sickening. She looked like him too, fleshy, button-nosed and simpering. And now she was covering Agnes's face with kisses, no doubt hoping she would crumple into gratifying sobs.

Agnes sat stiff and dry-eyed.

Dora mouthed *in shock* at the other women and patted her like a two-year-old who'd scraped its knee.

'My dear,' she said in a whisper pitched for all to hear, 'you must be brave now. We are bade into my brother's—' she tittered, clapped a hand over her mouth '—I should say *the emperor's* presence.'

The women, Angelinas by birth or marriage – little birds who'd never dared dream they'd one day perch so high – cooed with delight. Only one, plain and stooping, rolled her eyes behind Dora's back, a perfectly timed signal for Agnes, and Agnes alone.

'Euphrosunê,' said Dora, spinning round with an intuition that warned Agnes she was perhaps not quite as foolish as she appeared, 'I suppose you had better accompany us.'

'You honour me, Theodora.'

Euphrosunê. Agnes's brain woke up. She was wife to Isaakios's elder brother, Alexios Angelos. Agnes was fairly sure he had fled south, maybe to Alexandria, after Andronikos crushed the rebellions in Bithynia. The family she'd been born into, the Kamateroi, were not renowned for looks or courage, but they did have a reputation for great resourcefulness; shiftiness, their enemies would call it.

Before they'd gone far, it was plain that Dora didn't know the way to the throne room. She hesitated at every turning, peering down long corridors, squinting into sunlit courtyards, but Agnes wasn't going to flaunt her imperial pedigree by telling Dora she was leading them straight to the servants' latrines, and she sensed that Euphrosunê wasn't going to either.

At the sight of a Varangian captain, orange hair plaited beneath his helmet, bearing down on them, Dora quickened her step.

'Stop, sebastê. Stop,' he called.

Dora pretended to ignore him, and Agnes realised with the briefest lightening of her spirits that the big guardsman scared the emperor's sister witless.

'Beg leave, sebastê.' He lengthened his stride to match her bustling half-run. 'Basileus, he this way, sebastê.'

'Oh,' said Dora. 'Yes. Very good. Of course.'

The Varangian escorted them to the throne room, where a press of people already blocked the entrance. At a few words from him, the aristos fell back.

Agnes saw one young man, Constantinos Raoul she remembered his name was, frown at being ordered to make way for a woman he did not recognise, but when his companion mouthed *Theodora Angelina,* his expression shifted from irritation to courtesy to what had to be a simulation of desire, eyeing her like a dog does its dinner. Dora, Agnes realised, must still be unwed.

Ahead of them, Isaakios lounged on the throne, fingering the filigree on one of the arms. Agnes knew him by sight, of course – she'd received his obeisance at the side of one or other of her husbands enough times – but she wouldn't be looking at the top of his head today.

'Brother!' trilled Dora.

Isaakios, who was listening with immense satisfaction to the overcooked compliments being dished up by the men clustered about him, looked up.

'Dora, best of sisters. Euphrosunê, my brother's second self. And Agnes . . .'

That was her cue. She dropped to her knees. Her hands touched the floor by his feet. Her forehead would have followed, but she felt him touch her shoulder, raising her up.

'Nay,' said Isaakios, 'you shall not kneel to me. You came to our lands when you were scarce more than a child. You were entrusted to our care, but we betrayed you. You have suffered an ordeal, a fearful ordeal. On behalf of every man in the City, I beg your forgiveness.'

The words were good – she remembered that he'd always had a nice turn of phrase – and the people about them applauded.

'My saviour, my deliverer,' she whispered, as bashful as she dared. 'Words . . . I have no words . . .'

'And none are needed. Make yourself comfortable. We have a little treat in store for you.'

Agnes took a seat up on the dais with the other two women and composed herself for whatever lay ahead. Below her, the aristos were gathered in loose family groups, although Andronikos's reign had left their ranks patchy, like a bed of flowers after a freak hailstorm. Dozens of pairs of eyes looked her over, some with pity, but many more with hostility. On the faces of those who'd actually seen her laughing and joking with the man who'd murdered their husbands and brothers, their fathers and sons, there was hatred.

Isaakios stood up and the room fell silent. He nodded to a guard at the foot of the dais, who strode to a side door and – a little self-consciously; the scene felt rehearsed – rapped hard on the wood.

The doors swung open to reveal Isaakios's treat. Andronikos. Agnes was grateful that everybody would be looking at him, not her, because she couldn't keep the horror off her face.

He was bowed and hunched, as if half the bones were missing from his back. His cheeks had collapsed, and it took her a moment to realise that somebody had knocked out most of his teeth. His beard was shaven, his head shorn, but it had been done so badly that his skin was criss-crossed with cuts. Her eyes drifted lower. She shuddered. His right hand was missing.

Around his neck hung a massive iron collar, the kind used to control the bigger beasts in the animal games. From it dangled two chains, and two more shackled his feet. If Isaakios wanted to show him broken and beaten, the clanking metal was a mistake. It made him look unspeakably dangerous.

The room was perfectly still, the men and women motionless in a semicircle. Andronikos made a little gesture – it was hard to define – but Agnes read it as *well, if you're all just going to stand there, I may as well get back to my dungeon.*

Then a woman, Agnes did not know her name, hurled herself at him with a cry that you would have sworn came from a ghoul if you couldn't see her sweet, puffy, motherly face.

'You monster, you monster,' she howled, and began to shriek one name over and over again.

The trance was broken. The room pounced, men and women, everyone fought to get close enough to throw a punch, land a kick, to hurt the man who'd hurt them all.

Isaakios glanced at her. A quizzical flick of the eyes, nothing more, but she knew she had to act, and act fast. She shrieked out some words, she knew not what, leapt down the steps and threw herself into the whirlpool of people. By some instinct, they let her through until she was close to him. Next to him. Alone with him.

She sought his eyes and saw no reproach there, only understanding. He took a step towards her. He was making it easy for her. She saw – or thought she saw – two silent words form on his lips.

Do it.

She screamed and spat in his face. She scratched his cheeks and pounded his chest. If somebody had handed her a dagger she would probably have driven it between his eyes.

'Enough! Enough!' A battlefield voice silenced the room. 'This lessens every man here.'

Agnes spun round and saw a commotion spreading from the far door as people fell back before Alexios Branas. Before she had time to be pleased he was alive, her stomach contracted. A man who had been that close to Andronikos must be as good as dead.

'You forget yourself, Branas.'

Isaakios was on his feet, eyes popping, finger pointing, but then his face relaxed.

'But perhaps you have the right of it. It is not a pretty sight, is it, our ladies turning into vultures before our eyes?'

'Execute him and have done.'

Isaakios sniffed.

'Mere execution will not suffice. He does not deserve a tidy death. I shall throw him to the people. I am sure they will contrive something fitting.'

Guards formed ranks about Andronikos. Agnes was about to rush after him, propelled by a stupid, dangerous desire to say some final word, but a pair of hands gripped her, holding her back. She turned round and found herself looking into a face she had never thought to see again.

The brown of his eyes was a little less bright. His hair had faded, lost some of its fire. But it was him, Theo – a smile in his eyes, a twist to his lips – and she knew that whatever had happened to him since he'd escaped from Stephanos, he had not forgotten her.

They broke apart.

Andronikos had gone.

Theo was walking to join his father, and Isaakios was embracing them both, declaring them to be brave men who had done their best to serve the empire in the most difficult of circumstances. It was all a big show, Agnes could see that, some sort of deal. Isaakios was playing the game more enthusiastically than Branas, but the general was putting in a great performance compared to Theo, who looked wooden and surly. Instantly, she felt better.

She might be cosying up to Isaakios to save her skin, but at least she wasn't the only one.

The next day

Theo found himself outside the gates to the Anemas prison, not in disguise, not exactly, but he wore nothing that would mark him as anything other than an off-duty soldier. He'd spent the last half-hour shouldering his way to the front of the crowd until there were thousands of men behind him, but only a score in front – hard-faced brawlers who Theo knew wouldn't give way without a fight.

The men of the City were warming up, tasting their strength, turning into a pack. Chants ripped through their ranks, hippodrome songs, waiting songs. A man to his left – thin, rangy, maniacal – caught his eye. Theo knew how to look back. Not scared, not confrontational, but ready. Hungry. The same as the rest of them.

Somebody shoved him hard in the back and he jerked round.

'What the . . . ?'

He obviously looked menacing enough, because the man backed up with a grunt of apology. Theo caught a glimpse of his face. He couldn't place him, but he knew him from court. An aristo, then, who'd borrowed his doorman's spare tunic. Theo wondered how many more men of birth were mixed into the crowd, waiting for the jailers to throw the lion to the jackals.

He caught that thought and cursed himself. *Lion.* Why did Andronikos still get to be a fucking lion?

He suddenly wished he hadn't come, that he was still at home. His mother and father had been breakfasting when he left. His mother had put a hand out, asked him to sit with them, but he'd shrugged her off, said he was going out. She hadn't asked where – where else would anyone be going? – but Theo told her anyway, to prove he wasn't ashamed.

It's important to witness his death, I think.

Witness. A snort from his father. *What a load of bollocks, Theo.*

Husband . . . His mother had silenced him with one of her smiles.

Up front, something was starting to happen. The men behind him sensed it and pushed forward, even as some of those closest to the prison lost their nerve and tried to drop back. The gates cranked open and half a dozen guards, armed with pikes, thrust their prisoner out on to the street.

A hush fell.

For a terrible moment, Theo thought Andronikos might speak, might find the right words and survive, but then he pitched on to all fours. There he remained, head down, and Theo realised he lacked the strength even to stand.

'He's all yours,' shouted a guard.

The gates slammed shut.

'Up, up, up,' roared the crowd.

Four men charged forward and plucked Andronikos from the dirt, dragging him away from the prison, away from the palace, racing towards the heart of the City as if they were worried that the emperor – the new emperor – might suddenly change his mind.

Theo followed them.

A roar of laughter, thunderous applause, and Theo saw Andronikos, twenty paces away, swaying on top of a camel, a roll of scabby fur clenched in his remaining hand. He wasn't looking at the people chanting at his feet, but up – up to the church domes, the birds, the clouds, the sun.

The mob reeled on to the Mesê. The City was theirs; there were no soldiers on the streets. But they ignored every temptation in their path – the great houses, the rich monasteries.

They were hounds; one scent alone burnt in their noses. Onwards, through the Forum of Theodosius, into the Forum of Constantinos.

Somebody was fighting their way through the press with a shovel heaped high with cow dung.

'Nice one.'

'Let him through.'

The man yanked Andronikos towards him with one hand, and with the other scooped handful after handful of filth and smeared it all over his face. He clamped a hand around his jaw, forcing it open, and stuffed more shit inside his mouth, holding it shut.

'Swallow! Swallow! Swallow!'

People were laughing hard, wheezing, weeping, clutching strangers, pointing, exclaiming. Little boys who could see nothing were racing round in circles, punching each other, shrieking with the bliss of abandon.

A horse careered into the crowd and stopped, whinnying, staring, a stream of piss thundering from its cock. Some drunk soldiers tried to catch it in their helmets and nearly got trampled. The horse crabbed away, bucking, but it had given the crowd an idea.

'More. More. More.'

One of the soldiers tugged his own cock free, but with hundreds watching, nothing came out. Two little boys wanted to try, but a butcher, his apron bloody, his hands big and white, slapped them out of the way.

'Too sweet!' he roared, and filled a helmet to the brim.

The butcher tried to lift it to Andronikos's mouth, but he batted it away with his stump and the man was drenched in his own urine. For a moment, everyone found that funny – the butcher cursing, rubbing at his eyes, spitting – then it made them angry.

They pulled Andronikos off the camel, and when Theo saw him again, he was unconscious. His body was jagged. His face was lost behind blood or mire. His eyes were gone. Ripped out.

They tried to drape him over the camel, but he slid off. So they tossed him into a cart, a vending barrow really, and wheeled him into the hippodrome. Many, many men were already waiting on the seats. Theo glanced up. The imperial box was empty. Or looked empty. Who knew who might be peering down? Some bureaucrat would be watching, recording. Somebody would need to tell Isaakios. After all, this wasn't mob rule. It was official, sanctioned by the emperor, sanctioned by God.

There was a strange hiatus. Nobody knew what was going to happen next. Except that Andronikos was going to die.

It could be me.

Temptation fizzed in Theo's limbs.

It could be me.

But he didn't move. He didn't want to kill a dead man. He wanted to turn back time.

Two men emerged from beneath the stands carrying a great coil of rope. Two more hefted a pair of ladders. Theo told himself to leave. He took a few steps backwards, but he couldn't make himself go any further. He watched them string Andronikos upside down between two columns, his arms dangling the height of a man above the ground. His tunic flopped down and hid his face.

One man climbed up a ladder and cut his clothes away. Tunic, undershirt, leg coverings, it all came off. Only his boots were still on, the ropes around them. His pale flesh mottled with bruises. His ribs stoved in. But his chest still moved.

With a jolt, Theo realised that Andronikos had not once screamed. He had not once cried out. But now his tongue, black in his mouth, was working and working. He was trying to speak. One man leaned in and put an ear close to his face.

'What's he saying? What's he saying?'

'Lord have mercy.' The man shouted Andronikos's words to the crowds. 'Lord have mercy.'

261

They didn't like it. It wasn't a curse. It wasn't a plea. It had nothing to do with them. It was what any man who was about to die would say to his God.

A woman ran up and emptied a pot of boiling water over his face.

He screamed then.

A man plunged a sword into his guts and shoved and twisted it until it came out of his throat. He left it there, like a knife stuck in a joint of meat waiting on a table to be carved. The body swung. Short of chopping up the corpse and eating it, there was nothing left to do.

It was over.

Theo had time to think, *Agnes is a widow*, before he was suddenly, violently, repeatedly, shamefully sick.

A knock, discreet.

Dora went to the door and Agnes heard her talking to some official. After an eternity, she returned, pink with delight at her knowledge.

'Ladies, a message from my brother. It is over.'

She was mobbed, delicately.

'What happened?'

'Did they say how?'

'Naturally – but I am sure you would rather I spared you the details.'

Everyone nodded, looking prim, proper and immensely disappointed. Euphrosunê burst out laughing.

'Their poor faces. If recounting this day's valiant deeds troubles your womanly sensibility, Dora . . .'

'My *Christian* sensibility, Euphrosunê.'

'. . . then I am happy to indulge our friends' curiosity myself.'

'But you haven't heard what happened.'

'Haven't I?'

'But my brother only just—'

'Told you, yes. But that doesn't mean I don't know.'

'Why didn't you tell me earlier?'

Euphrosunê smiled.

'You didn't ask.'

Dora's face was warring, transparent.

'Maybe I shall tell them,' she said, superbly. 'It is fitting for all to learn the fate of sinners.'

A murmur of assent and anticipation. Agnes locked her hands together, staring at her knuckles as Dora began to talk, accompanied by a chorus of squeals and groans.

'No!'

'They didn't!'

'Stop! Stop!'

Agnes couldn't block it out. She could only try to send her mind floating far, far away, to a place where everyone she knew did not always die horribly.

'Agnes! Agnes!' Dora was flushed. 'You must be delighted to hear the punishments meted out to your tormentor. Come here, come closer. I am arriving at the part where they cut away his . . . his . . . God bless me, but I do not know how I shall say the word aloud.'

She turned to her audience and mouthed *his manhood*, which made them all grimace prettily.

'Agnes?' said Dora. 'Does my story not divert you? Agnes? Are you not attending? Agnes?'

A dozen faces turned to her. A dozen mouths open. *Speak.* But she couldn't.

'This meat is too rich for Agnes.' Euphrosunê's broad back landed between her and Dora. 'For me, too. A quick thrust of a sword in his cell would have served.'

'You are not defending Andronikos?' asked Dora.

'I am defending every one of us. Andronikos was the emperor, and that title needs to be revered throughout the empire and in every land beyond its borders. But who will value it now that the lowliest man has been given licence to piss in the emperor's mouth?'

'Are you criticising my brother?'

'No, Dora, you know I would never do that.'

Agnes stood up. She meant to slip away, but there was something she desperately needed to know.

'What happened to his body?'

Everyone was looking at her.

'What happened to his body?' she repeated.

'It's in the pens under the hippodrome,' said Euphrosunê. 'Where they toss the animal carcasses after a show.'

'Hah. He can rot there with the wild beasts,' squeaked one of Dora's acolytes.

Agnes turned and left the room. Dora must have made to follow her, because she heard Euphrosunê saying,

'For God's sake, leave her be.'

She lay on her bed and stared up at the ceiling.

Sleep came, but it brought no release, instead she was looking down into a pit full of tangled limbs, and in the middle of them, a face, his face, whole and unbroken, but turned a ghostly silver in the hellish half-light. It crumbled, rotting into a mask of death, and then arms with no bodies began to creep towards her, blind fingers seeking to drag her down, down into the abyss.

She sat up, gasping for air, sweating and trembling, a cloying, sticky smell in her nose and throat, and she knew that if she didn't act, that face and that dream would haunt her waking and sleeping for the remainder of her days.

That night

She'd never left the palace by herself.

She was worried it was going to be hard, but in fact all she had to do was cover herself against the cool autumn dusk and walk out. The guards' job was to question people coming in; it would never occur to them that anyone other than a serving woman would prefer the City streets to the warmth and light of Blachernai.

A cursory inspection, to make sure she hadn't stolen anything. A stern warning. *No re-entry till dawn, miss.* That was all.

She'd expected more people to be abroad, but the road was very quiet – not peaceful, but eerie, menacing. The City was sated for now, sleeping off its orgy of violence, but to Agnes it was a monster that might stir at any moment.

Braziers at the front of the larger houses cast red pools of light that faded to orange and disappeared. Scufflings and scamperings sounded down dim alleyways, and she gave them a wide berth, imagining strange hands grabbing the hem of her cloak and tugging her away into nothingness. Every dozen paces, her resolve wavered and she nearly turned back.

'Need a lift?'

She pressed herself against a low wall. Out of the darkness, she saw a small cart, laden with what smelt like hay, trundling slowly up behind her. She shook her head and walked on, but the man laughed, his donkey keeping pace.

'Hop up. Road's no place for a woman on her own. I won't try any funny business. But there's plenty others who might.'

She hesitated. Of course, he was right. As a compromise, she ignored the seat next to him and climbed awkwardly on to the back of cart, her feet dangling over the edge.

'Suit yourself,' said the man, and told his donkey to walk on.

As they drew closer to the centre of the City, they began to pass odd groups of men, drunk, laughing. Huddled deep in the hay, Agnes allowed herself to stare at them. Which of them had been there? Which of them had watched? That man there, maybe his was the last face Andronikos had seen before they took his eyes. That one, maybe he'd struck the blow that killed him.

Once they'd crossed the Forum of Theodosius, she muttered a thank you and jumped down from the cart. It was full night now. She hoped the light of the old half-moon, already high in the sky, would be enough for her to find the house she needed. A few blocks to the east, a little past the Church of Forty Martyrs, and it should be there, on the right.

She left the Mesê confidently enough, but hesitated at an unexpected fork in the road. A woman, walking briskly, a boy lighting her way with a torch, was disappearing down one path. Agnes decided to follow her – her receding bulk looked matronly, unthreatening.

As she passed through the flicker of a watchfire outside a new tenement block, an old man staggered out of an alleyway and stopped to stare her. She quickened her pace, but heard him limping after her, hooting and cackling, calling her *titbit* and *pretty little sparrow*.

Just as she was about to break into a run, the woman turned round. She marched past Agnes, straight up to the old man and jabbed a finger into his chest.

'Take yourself off home this minute, or I'll see to it that your daughters give you nothing but milk and cabbage for a week.'

He shuffled off, muttering to himself.

'Thank you,' said Agnes.

'Thinks he's still a lad of sixteen, the old . . .'

She broke off, took the torch from the boy and peered at Agnes more closely. She realised it hadn't been a good idea to open her mouth.

'And what are you doing out so late, missy?' the woman asked.

Agnes mumbled something about an errand, something about her mistress, horribly aware of her lingering western accent, her too-fine Greek.

'Who's this mistress, might I ask?'

'The . . . the wife of General Branas.'

At that, the woman laughed.

'No she's not. She's *my* mistress. Which means I know you've never worked in her kitchens, no, nor in the bedrooms neither.'

'You . . . you know where her house is?' said Agnes, before she had time to think better of it. 'Will you take me there? I have a message for her.'

'You do, do you?' The woman gave her an appraising look. 'You sure it's not young Master Theo you've a message for?'

Agnes was about to protest, but she realised that that was the perfect excuse she'd been trying – and failing – to come up with.

'Well, yes, yes, maybe you're right.'

The woman chuckled.

'I knew it. Whenever pretty girls appear near our gates at this hour, we always know to let them in.'

'Does he often . . . ?' Agnes broke off.

'Best I don't answer that, wouldn't you say, dearie? Come on then, follow me.'

They passed the main gate of the house and a sleepy doorkeeper let them in by a side entrance. The woman led her through a courtyard, through the kitchens, scrubbed clean and silent, and up a set of small stairs. As they left the servants' quarters and entered the part of the house where the family's rooms must be, a voice, sharp but not unkind, halted them.

'What have you got there, Agathê?'

The woman began to spin some story about a niece come to visit from up country, but her mistress – she had that tone – interrupted her.

'Honestly, how many nieces am I to believe you have? Now, who—?'

She stopped as the light from the lamp she was holding caught Agnes's face.

'Empress Anna! What in God's name are you doing here?'

She didn't look angry, only surprised.

'I'm not Empress Anna, not any more.' Agnes smiled – or tried to. 'I'm nobody.'

Nobody. She'd meant it as a feeble sort of joke, but once the word was out of her mouth, she realised that it was absolutely and irrefutably true. *Nobody*. The wave of desolation that swept over her must have been all too obvious, because both women immediately stepped forward to console her.

'Sorry. It's nothing.' She tried to shrug them off. 'It's just that it's been . . .'

She started crying, for the first time, actual tears, and she found that however much she wanted to, she could not stop them.

The woman – Theo's mother; *Anna*, she remembered her name was Anna – handed the lamp to Agathê, pulled Agnes to her and held her while she sobbed. Everyone else's sympathy had been unbearable, but for some reason this woman was different.

'You've had a terrible time, haven't you? What you've been through – with nobody to help you. No wonder you're upset. There now. You cry.'

That made Agnes cry even harder, but slowly, as Anna stroked her back, her sobs stilled. She rubbed at her tears with her sleeves.

'Sorry.'

'You've no earthly reason to be sorry.'

Agnes hiccuped a small laugh.

'That's better,' said Theo's mother. 'Now, do you want to tell me why you're here? Is it to see my son?'

Agnes caught a look fly between mistress and servant, but she didn't have time to work out what it might mean.

'No. Not exactly. I wanted . . . I wanted to see your husband. I thought he might be able to help me. He was Andronikos's friend before he . . . before he changed.'

'He was.' She nodded. 'And so was I. How can we help you?'

Now that she had to say it, what she had in mind sounded so preposterous, she couldn't make the words come. Anna would never ask her husband. In fact, she'd order Agnes from her house, and she'd be right to. What she was asking was impossible.

'Tell her, sweeting,' said Agathê. 'She won't bite.'

'I . . . I want him to find Andronikos's body,' Agnes told the floor at her feet. 'I want him to bury it.' Panic rose in her throat. Her chest felt too tight. Everything – the walls, the ceiling – was pressing in on her. 'Please. Please ask him. Please, or I'll never sleep again. If he lies unburied, I'll always be down there with him – in those animal pits. I have to be free of him. Please. I have to be free.'

Silence.

'I'm sorry. I've disgusted you. I don't know why I came. I was being stupid. I . . .'

Agnes heard a door open and saw a candle – Branas. Another door, another candle – Theo. They were both looking at her. They'd both heard.

'Get dressed, son,' said the general.

'Father, we're not actually going to . . .'

'We damn well are. The girl's right. We shall do our duty by his body. His soul, that is in God's hands.'

* * *

If Theo had hated Andronikos before, his loathing reached new levels after spending the last watch of the night picking through decomposing animal carcasses. They'd both bound wash-cloths tight over their faces, but a man would have to be dead himself for the stench, slip and squirm of whatever lay underfoot not to turn his stomach. So when the flicker of his father's torch finally lit up a boot, a leg, the emperor's empty body, Theo found himself looking at it with relief rather than revulsion.

'What next, Father?' he said as they rode slowly home after leaving the body – and a bag of money – at a monastery near the western walls.

'We tell the girl it's done and have a bloody big breakfast.'

'That's not what I meant.'

His father sighed.

'I promised Isaakios I'd rid the empire of the Normans. So that's what we're going to do.'

'And after that?'

'Theo, you're making my head ache.'

They covered the rest of the way home in silence.

After scrubbing their hands and faces, they rejoined the women as the first hint of day was starting to show through the windows. Both Agnes and his mother were still awake, although they had let the fire burn very low. An uneaten plate of bread and cheese lay on the table.

'It's done.'

'I don't know how to . . .'

'It's all right. You don't have to,' said his father, giving her – to Theo's surprise – a quick, clumsy hug.

His mother took his father's hand, in the way that she always did when she had something very particular to ask.

'Alexios,' she began, 'this poor girl needs a place to recover. We simply can't let her go back.'

But Agnes was already shaking her head.

'You're kind, truly kind, but I can't stay here. Isaakios, Dora, they want me under their wing. They won't let me go, especially not to you. In fact—' she stood up resolutely '—I should get back to the palace before they miss me.'

His mother looked at his father, appealing, but he too shook his head.

'She's right. She knows how these things work. Isaakios would probably take her for himself if the church allowed third marriages. But even though he can't do that, he'll still want to keep her close. You know too many secrets, don't you, Agnes?'

She nodded.

'Maybe in the future we can do something – once the dust has settled – but not yet. I'll send for someone to take you . . .' He faltered, coughed. 'No. Perhaps best not to involve the servants. Theo, why don't you see Agnes back to Blachernai?'

Dawn

Side by side they walked through the grey morning. Gulls screeched overhead and the smell of the day's bread baking drifted through the air. The night was behind her. In front lay the road to Blachernai. And beside her was Theo. Who was not speaking. Who was not even looking at her.

'Theo . . .' she began, tentative.

'I'd have left him to rot,' he cut over her. 'But I suppose you know that anyway.'

'I do.'

She watched him stop and kick a stone.

'Why?' he asked. 'I only wish I understood why.'

'Why I wanted him buried? I—'

'Oh, I heard what you said to my mother. *I have to be free . . .* All that. You could tell me the same thing a hundred times and it still wouldn't make any sense.'

She threw up her hands, angry.

'So you hated him. All right. I get it. Good for you, Theo. But you could hate him from a distance. You had that luxury. I couldn't hate him, could I? Not if I wanted to live.'

He walked on, still sullen. She followed him.

'Are you glad I'm alive, Theo? Because you're not acting like you are.'

He stopped.

'Don't be an idiot. Of course I'm glad you're alive. But are *you* glad he's dead? That's what I want to know.'

'Of course I am.'

'Of course?'

'*Yes.*'

'Swear it?'

'Isn't *yes* enough?'

'No. No, it's not.'

'All right. I swear it. Satisfied? He's dead and I'm glad. He can't touch us – either of us – ever again.' She hesitated. 'Theo, that night in the sewers . . .'

'I don't want to talk about that.'

'But you don't know what I'm going to say. Andronikos—'

'And I definitely don't want to talk about *him.*'

She glowered at him.

'Shut up and listen. Andronikos could make people – men and women – do things they wouldn't normally do. You were young. We were both young. I'm not saying what you did was right . . .'

'No, it wasn't. I've never been so ashamed of anything. Ever.'

'. . . but I'm saying I understand. And I might have done the same thing. Truly, Theo.'

A pause.

'Thank you, Agnes. That means a lot.'

He looked happier, and that made her happier than she could ever remember feeling.

'I . . . I did things I should not have done as well,' she said. 'I didn't kill anyone. Or *nearly* kill . . .'

She glanced at him and they both laughed. *Laughed.* That was the power of dawn, the power of sunshine. It banished Stephanos's face and the drip of the sewers, gone like spume on a wave.

'I killed nobody. But in some ways I was as bad as him.'

'As bad as *him*? Don't be absurd.'

'I was, Theo, I—'

'You're not bad, Agnes. You're just not.'

'I'm not all that good, either.'

'No.' He grinned. 'But if you were, I probably wouldn't . . .'

He flushed, and stopped.

'Wouldn't what, Theo?'

'Wouldn't love you, Agnes. These long years.'

Men had looked at her in many ways in her life, but never like that, so open, so naked, and yet so fierce. She had never seen the truth, so undisguised, in a man's eyes before, and it lit something deep inside her.

'You've had a funny way of showing it,' she said, but she was smiling.

'And so have you.'

'Who says I love you?' Still smiling.

'I say you do. You do. Don't you?'

She looked at him. As an experiment, she took his hand, to see how it felt. It was warm and callused. She laced her fingers through his and their palms closed together. She might have expected him to kiss her then, but he stayed still as walls.

She took his other hand and brought it to her mouth without looking up at him. His fingers smelt of soap and horses and leather. Alexios's had smelt of sandalwood and Andronikos's – *no, don't think about him.*

She breathed in deeply, trying to imagine a simpler life. If she had been born a Rôman girl, her father a Palaiologos, a Kantakouzenos, they would have known of each other since childhood. She could have whispered to her mother that she liked him. If her mother was as nice as Theo's, she would have helped them wed.

Stupid dreams.

She looked up and found his eyes on her own.

'Don't you?' he repeated, painfully quiet.

'I do, Theo, but . . .'

'Don't say but. Just tell me that you love me.'

'I love you, Theo, but . . .'

'Come with me now,' he said. 'Be my wife, Agnes, please be my wife.'

'No.' She was shaking her head. 'You've forgotten what your

274

father said. I've been married twice already. I cannot wed a third time.'

For a moment he looked downcast.

'So we cannot marry, but who cares? I do not. You have no family here. No brothers, no father. We can do—'

'No, Theo, no we can't. Isaakios would never allow me to live with you.'

'Isaakios is an idiot.' Theo no longer looked happy. 'I hated to see my father serve Andronikos. But Isaakios is worse. A man who is worth nothing . . . nothing.'

They looked at one another.

'Agnes, I cannot foretell. I only know that he cannot last long upon the throne. It's a horrible accident. A hoax like the old gods played on their Achaeans. It can't be long before the wheel turns again, and when it does . . . Will you wait for me?'

'Yes.'

'You swear? Men will try. I know men will try. You are—'

'Quiet, Theo, I know what men are. And I know what I am. I swear. I shall be a grand dowager. Distant. Aloof. How about that?'

She smiled, inviting him to smile too, but he looked contorted.

'Don't joke. Please, not about this. I couldn't bear it if you . . .'

'I won't. Don't worry. I won't.'

'Because this is different, Agnes, isn't it? You're not pretending, are you? I've seen you pretend with the others, with everyone. You're not pretending with me, are you?'

'No, Theo, no. I promise – I swear by everything I have ever held dear, by Mary and all the saints, that I am yours, that I shall always be yours.'

He touched his forehead to hers, their eyelashes brushed and they dissolved into a kiss that made the City disappear.

* * *

They parted. Not with grief, with hope. More than hope – with confidence. They were blessed. She was sure of it.

But she had not gone far when a hand landed on her shoulder. She turned, hoping he'd followed her for a final farewell, a smile of welcome on her face. But it wasn't him. It was—

'Euphrosunê!'

'Hello, Agnes. What are you doing out and about at this hour?'

'I might ask you the same.'

'Yes, you might. But I would have a plausible explanation. What's yours I wonder?'

Agnes knew she could not justify herself, so instead she went on the attack.

'You've been spying on me.'

'I have,' Euphrosunê agreed. 'I was worried you might do something foolish, so I set a couple of men to watch you. You should be thankful that I did. One of them spared you a most perilous walk.'

She waved towards a man lounging under the awning of a grocery shop. He tipped his hat and grinned.

'Hop up,' he called.

'You?' Agnes said, her eyes widening.

The man gave her a wink.

'Didn't you think that the cart was perhaps a bit *too* convenient?' said Euphrosunê. 'You've led a funny sort of life if you expect obliging drivers to pop up out of nowhere like that.'

But Agnes wasn't in the mood to be teased.

'Why would you do all this for me?'

'Don't look so suspicious.'

'Of course I must look suspicious. Will you tell Dora?'

'Insult me! No. I would sooner scrub her undergarments than tell that imbecile anything.'

Agnes couldn't help smiling at that.

'That's better,' said Euphrosunê. 'We're in the same position, you see, Agnes. My husband is somewhere in the south. He should be back in a year, but who knows? I need a friend to keep me sane while Dora rules the roost. Pure self-interest. Nothing more.'

She tucked Agnes's arm through hers.

'Had you thought how you were going to get back in? No? I thought not. Come, I have transport. We have been attending matins at . . . well, we can decide which church on the way.'

Euphrosunê did not speak again until they were sitting side by side in an unremarkable sedan, drapes screening them from view.

'Now, what do you say to breakfast in my rooms? We can get better acquainted. I would love, for example, to learn how your skin looks so fine. Do you have some secret ointment, or is it just the after-effect of Theodore Branas's sweet kisses?'

'You didn't . . . ?'

'Oh, I most certainly did. I am delighted to learn you are such good friends with the Branades. That, Agnes, might prove exceptionally useful in the months ahead.'

'What are you implying?'

'If you don't know, I shan't tell you. But I rather think you do.'

November 1185

The Normans had spread over the Thracian plain like drunk men straggling home from a feast. Some had remained in Thessalonikê, flies clinging to a bloated corpse. Others had prowled north and east towards the mountains, stealing what they could carry, torching what they could not. Still more had followed the main road, the road to the City, but they had stalled on the rich Strymon river plain.

One band alone had forged east and reached Mosynopolis, which was but a few days' march from Kypsella, the base to the west of the City where the Rôman army was mustering.

Theo was chewing on a chunk of paximadion, the toasted barley bread which soldiers ate on campaign, while watching a second army of servants unpack the emperor's baggage train. Thick tufted rugs passed before his eyes – rugs, linen towels, flax-blue cushions, wine coolers, a silver table service that must have needed its own wagon, a collapsible bath of red-dyed ox hide, and finally, a pair of gilded chairs.

'They're chamber pots,' said Murzuphlus, who'd appeared by his side.

'What?'

'Those chairs. They're actually chamber pots. Neat piece of design.'

Theo grunted.

'What's wrong with a fucking hole in the ground?'

'Nothing. But why shit in a hole when you can shit in a gold pot? And why, Theo, are you eating that sawdust when we still have fresh bread?'

'There's nothing wrong with paximadion.'

'No,' said Murzuphlus equably. 'But there's not a lot right with it either. There's no need to eat it just because you'd rather the emperor travelled light.'

'Isaakios the Emperor. Isaakios the Saviour. Isaakios the fucking Hero. He spilt the blood of one crook, and now he's on the throne. Luck, blind luck. And they—' he gestured vaguely over his shoulder to the aristos '—are all sniffing his backside as if it smelt sweet as Easter violets.'

'If it wasn't for him, Andronikos would still be emperor. Fact.'

Theo snorted.

'He didn't confront him. He'd never have dared. He's too much of a coward. The one time he could have fought him – at Nicaea – he chickened out. He was meant to be leading a rebellion, but all he cared about was saving his own skin.'

Murzuphlus raised an eyebrow.

'But he did a good job of it, didn't he? And not just his own skin, either.'

Theo didn't like the way this argument was going.

'Didn't he?' Murzuphlus repeated, an annoying smile hovering around the corners of his mouth. 'Andronikos let the Nicaeans live. He let the city stand.'

'But the aristos who'd come to Nicaea to fight, he flung them from the walls. And the mercenaries – the ones Isaakios hired – he stuck them on spikes.'

'What about Isaakios? No spike for him.'

Theo shook his head grudgingly.

'No, no spike for him.'

'Sounds like a clever man to me. Anyone who crossed paths with Andronikos and survived must know something. Look at you and your father.'

'If you weren't my friend, I'd knock you down for that.'

Murzuphlus's smile grew broader.

'So, you admit it's true.'

Theo landed a blunt blow across Murzuphlus's jaw.

'Sensitive subject, Theo?' said Murzuphlus, slumped on the ground, rubbing his cheek. 'There's no shame in being alive. I know I'm glad I am. There's plenty enough who aren't. You think you'd feel better if you'd died at Nicaea? At Thessalonikê? If Andronikos had ripped your guts out and burnt them in front of you? No. You wouldn't feel better. You'd be dead. End of story.'

He spat out a mouthful of blood and, Theo saw, a tooth. No wonder his knuckles hurt.

'You talk like a coward.'

He might have expected Murzuphlus to take objection to that, but his friend only shrugged and held up his hand for Theo to pull him to his feet.

'*Coward.* A word, nothing more. Remember what Achilles said when Odysseus visited him in the underworld? *I'd rather live as a labourer than be king of the dead.* Achilles said that. *Achilles.* The perfect warrior. Doesn't that tell you something, Theo? Odysseus wasn't a perfect warrior, but he lived, didn't he? Well, maybe Isaakios wanted to live too.'

Theo was silent, and Murzuphlus pressed on.

'Seems like Isaakios has a nose for power like some men have for wine. He'd no more stand in its way than he'd dangle his cock over a snakepit. So he bent. And guess what? It worked. And now he's emperor and you and I are going to have to kiss his boots.'

'I'd sooner kiss . . .'

But Theo got no further. His father was picking his way towards them.

'You two look like you could use some distraction. Come on. Follow me. Council of war. Sit at the back and keep your traps shut.'

The scene in his father's tent did little to improve Theo's mood.

Very many well-born, well-moneyed men had come out of their rat-holes after the fall of Andronikos and were now competing to prove their worth to the new emperor. Titles, jobs, marriages – there was a lot to play for. And that meant too many men who knew too little about the business of campaigning crammed into one place bandying flimsy arguments derived at best from centuries-old fighting manuals, or at worst from the bloodier bits of Homer.

'Thessalonikê! We must retake her for the empire,' puffed a portly Palaiologos – Theo wasn't quite sure which one. 'The mortification! One of the brightest stars in our emperor's firmament in barbarian hands. It must not be borne, Branas, it must not be borne.'

Of course that was hard to disagree with. Nobody was about to say it was a *good* thing that Thessalonikê was in Norman hands.

'Well, Branas, speak up, man. I am sure the emperor would like to know when we march.'

'We are not marching on Thessalonikê,' his father replied.

Theo thought his father's words were impressively restrained, but the man's crimson face made it clear he was not used to being told he was wrong.

'You would allow . . . ?'

'Yes, I would. The Normans hold Thessalonikê, and they will be prepared to defend it. They command the sea, so we cannot starve them out. And anyway, marching on Thessalonikê is exactly what they will expect us to do. We must do the unexpected.'

Many of the men were now nodding along with his father – just as they had been nodding along to that other man. *Ah, yes, the unexpected, just so.* They all made Theo sick.

'We must show them we can still fight – fight like real men, like men who have something to lose. Their forces are split and we must do the same with ours. Harry them. Pick them off a few score at a time.'

'It's beneath the dignity of the Rôman army to fight like bandits,' said the Palaiologos, but he was looking increasingly isolated.

'Better bandits than fools.'

A blast of cold air, followed by the sharp tang of myrrh, and Isaakios, fresh from his bath, entered the tent. Everyone dropped to their knees, a few even pressing their heads to the dirt, even though court etiquette was normally relaxed on campaign.

'Good, good, good.'

There was a stir, and for a moment Theo thought some of the aristos were going to petition Isaakios to tell his father to lay siege to Thessalonikê, but the emperor waved them into silence.

'Gentlemen, we shall do exactly as my esteemed friend Alexios Branas bids. He is the expert in these matters. Upon him I bestow all my power and authority. When he speaks, imagine it is I, your beloved emperor, who commands.'

Theo was pleased his father would have his way, but he resented – hated – the fact that it was Isaakios who could make it happen.

'Cheer up,' said Murzuphlus as they filed out of the tent. 'You'll be fighting soon. Time for some heroics.'

Despite himself, Theo smiled. His friend was right. It would be good to start killing Normans.

Two weeks later, Theo and his detachment of Alan mercenaries – horsemen from the Caucasus mountains who seemed to fight for pleasure and pride, not gold – trotted into the Rôman advance camp at a place called Demetritzes.

His men, and other light cavalry units like them, had scoured the land behind clean of roving Norman bands, but the enemy had regrouped, and was now stationed on the eastern bank of the Strymon river.

The equinoctial gales had blown most of the leaves from the trees and the first rains had churned the waters thick and muddy. The birds had scattered and the landscape they'd left behind was quiet and uninviting. Fog clung to the hollows, clouds lay heavy on the hilltops and a haze hung over the sea to the south. Winter was coming, no doubt about that, and so Theo was not surprised when he found the camp buzzing with the rumour that the Normans were asking for a parley.

'Begging, more like,' said his father when he found him.

'You're not going to agree, are you?' Theo asked.

'Not a fucking chance.'

Theo grinned.

The evening hymn had been sung, curfew had begun, and Branas was in his tent putting the final touches to his battle plan when a messenger – young, panting, self-important – arrived from the emperor, who was still at least a day's march away.

The boy handed the message to the general, who grew very still, then very white. He ripped it into a dozen pieces and very carefully set each one alight with a candle. He ground the ash under his boot.

'Somebody, Theo, and doubtless I'll never know who, has sent a fast rider to Isaakios with word that the Normans are ready to talk. And you know what Isaakios says? He says I am to accept their generous offer.'

'But the initiative is all ours. If we . . .'

His father stilled him with a hand on his shoulder and turned to the messenger.

'Boy. When did you arrive?'

The messenger plainly thought he deserved fancier words than those, and his answer came slowly.

'Why, but a moment since. You can see I have not stopped to wash the mud off my . . .'

His father nodded at Theo.

'Let me help you out,' Theo said, putting an arm round the messenger. 'You're still on the road, right? You're not going to get here until at least noon tomorrow, right?'

'But . . . but I was ordered to ride as fast as I could. I was

ordered to deliver the emperor's message. He'll be angry if
I—'

'Not half as angry as the general'll be if you don't shut up
right now.'

The boy shut up.

'Now, young man,' said Branas, 'let's try again. When did
you arrive?'

'I . . . I haven't arrived. I am on the road.'

'Good lad.' He turned to Mikhail, who was lounging in a
corner. 'See he has some edible food and a decent bed. And
don't let him out of your sight. Not even when he takes a shit.'

The boy left with Mikhail, and Theo was alone with his
father. Branas sat down on a stool and stared at the plan in
front of him.

'Know what I don't like?' Branas said at last.

Theo shook his head.

'I don't like being told how to fight by a man who has spent
every night of his life tucked up safe in bed. Under silk sheets,
for all I know.'

Theo grunted. There wasn't much you could say to that.

'Know what I like even less?'

Theo shook his head again.

'I don't like being told *not* to fight. Not by any man. And
least of all by him. We attack tomorrow. No warning. No
heralds. No fucking talk. I'm going to smash those Norman
bastards and drive them into the sea.'

A gap opened at the southern end of the Rôman infantry line,
and a detachment of Cuman horse archers cantered in a flowing
arc, firing swift rounds over their left shoulders into the
Norman ranks. As they swerved to their right in front of the
enemy lines, guiding their horses with their thighs alone, they
increased their pace to duck back behind their own lines,
loosing a final volley over the animals' rumps.

It was a skilled manoeuvre that Theo himself had never

dared try, and it left the Normans in disarray. They had taken the field in a hurry when the Rômans advanced soon after dawn, and now they had too many horsemen too close to their front line, and the animals were bucking and skittish under such concentrated fire.

The Norman commander didn't wait for another assault by the archers before ordering a cavalry charge. Immediately, the imperial front rank, the Armenian heavy infantry, dropped to one knee and raised their pikes, grounded in butts. But the Normans had misjudged the distance, barely accelerating out of a canter by the time they closed on the Rôman lines. It might have looked ugly to a man who'd never seen a fight before, but Theo knew that for all the screaming of the men who'd taken a hoof in the face, the enemy had barely dented their defences.

His father held up his hand. Now it was Theo's turn.

For the first time, he was to ride with the kataphraktoi, the heavy-armed cavalry formed up in a blunt wedge behind the infantry. The front line of the charge was where the best men, the bravest, fought.

His father's hand dropped and they exploded forwards. Theo's lance was down. The other men were fanning out behind him, twelve ranks deep. Ahead of him, a gap in their own lines opened up as the foot soldiers made way. Theo overtook a wounded Norman, running for safety. The man disappeared under his hooves and the enemy front line rose up before him. It was thin, but not as thin as he'd hoped. He could see their faces, and prayed they were not men who were going to stand.

When he was ten strides away, he hurled his lance, and saw it take a man full in the chest. He swept a mace from the holster on his saddle and brought it down, crushing a man's skull, his upswing catching another man's shield and driving it into his face. He was deep in the melee now – fighting on his own, not as part of a pack – and he felt vulnerable. In his giant's armour, it was hard to manoeuvre, hard to see, nothing like the nimble fighting he was used to. His first mace was long gone; an unwise sideswipe catapulted the second from his grasp. He drew his curved sword, his favourite, and met the next man, and the next.

Suddenly the field was alive with Rômen koursôres, agile fighters, many foreign. They'd done it. Their charge must have scattered the Normans enough for his father to dispatch his lighter troops. That was Theo's cue to retreat.

The Rômen line closed behind him and he sat on his horse, panting, his chest and limbs burning. He wanted to pull his helmet off, but his arms, weighted down with metal, weren't up to it.

Murzuphlus rode up beside him – he was in the field as Branas's adjutant and would only fight if things got desperate. He gestured to Theo to turn round and tugged a spear-tip free.

'Just under your shoulder blade.'

'Remind me to buy my armourer a drink. Get my helmet off too, would you?'

Theo wiped the sweat out of his eyes and nostrils and ears and took a proper swill of water. All that metal had been starting to make him feel trapped.

'What's happening, Murzuphlus. How are we . . . ?'

But before his friend could answer, they both caught sight of Isaakios riding towards them.

'Theo, my dear chap, I seem to be in the midst of a battle, not a parley. We found this little fellow in a latrine in the camp—' Theo saw the messenger from the night before cowering behind the emperor '—and he has the most extraordinary tale to tell. I find it hard to credit. Where is your father? He has some explaining to do.'

'He's up there, basileus.'

'Escort me, Theo.'

They arrived on the mound from which Branas commanded a good view of the battlefield.

'You'd better have an explanation, Branas.'

Isaakios was being unusually blunt.

'I do, basileus, I do.' And his father was being unusually cheerful. 'Behold the retreat of the Norman invaders.'

It took Isaakios a moment or two to make out what Theo could see immediately.

'A-ha. Quite so. Good fellow. Good fellow. Lucky you got my message, Branas. To think you wanted to talk to them. *No, no*, that's what I said. *Put your faith in our good Rôman soldiers.* And by God, I was right. Good for you, Branas. A man who can admit he's wrong is my kind of man.'

Men of rank, many of whom had not even taken part in the battle, began to shout praise to the glory of the emperor, calling the battle a triumph such as had not been seen for a generation.

'The City is saved!'

'God has given us a great new leader!'

But there was another rumble amongst the ranks, quiet but insistent. The soldiers were shouting one word, one word only.

'Branas! Branas!'

The autumn of 1186

Agnes was passing through the hall where Isaakios's marriage to a Magyar princess was soon to be celebrated. She was returning from an errand between the bride – Margit of Hungary, white-blonde hair, blue veins on pale skin, ten years and ten months old – and her dressmaker, which would normally make her twitch with suppressed rage, but she had just heard some news that made anything other than total delight totally impossible.

He's here. In the palace. He's here.

It had been a year – *a year!* – since she'd last seen Theo, and even then they'd been in church, surrounded by hundreds of others. She hadn't seen him alone since the day after Andronikos died, that morning when everything changed.

When the troops swept back into the City after defeating the Normans, she'd assumed he'd be with them. But he wasn't. It took days of casual chit-chat with demobbed officers to discover that Theo and his father had been deployed straight to the Adriatic. Bolstering our defences, said one young man. Boosting morale, said another.

Whichever euphemism they lit upon, she knew the posting was a pretext. She'd heard the talk, the whispers, same as everything else. *If it hadn't been for Branas, we'd never have whipped the Normans. Branas is the real hero. Branas. Branas. Branas.* Altogether too much talk of Branas. And so Isaakios had sent him to cool his heels as far away from the City as possible.

Agnes was torn between anger at Isaakios for being so gutless, anger at Theo for not ignoring orders and sneaking back to the City, and anger at herself for being such a hopeless, mooning, lovestruck *idiot*.

That kiss. That one kiss. She revisited it every morning, every night, and far too many times in between.

She'd had no particular hope that that morning would turn out any different from the one before. Dora was prattling on about some Latin newcomer, how he was a *very* great soldier, how he would probably be teaching that Alexios Branas a thing or two . . .

'Oh, the general's back, is he?' said Agnes, with all the indifference she could muster.

But Dora had already moved on to how *nice-looking* this Latin was, how *distinguished*, how *respectable*, when Agnes was pleased to remember that she'd promised the dressmaker a sample of some border trim that had especially taken the little empress-to-be's fancy.

Job done, Agnes took a detour to pass right by Isaakios's audience chamber, and there, lounging about with the other body-servants, was Mikhail. He gave her a friendly grin and a wink, which she returned, and she skipped off down the corridor.

They *were* there. They must be back for the wedding. She was going to see him. They'd have to be careful, of course, but the thought that the waiting was finally over made her . . .

. . . crash straight into a man who was hurrying backwards, shouting orders and not looking where he was going. Sheaves of papers flew everywhere.

'Watch out, you—' She stopped. She'd seen who it was and couldn't help gasping with delight. 'Constantinos, what in the name of all that's holy are you doing here?'

'Such a warm welcome for your old friend.'

'Friend? Really?'

'As close to a friend as you get in this place.'

'You could have fooled me. But are there two of you? I thought you'd been killed when the mob sacked the palace.'

'And you sound so very devastated at the thought.'

'You'd have deserved it, and you know it. A quick, clean death, though, nothing worse.'

She smiled, and he smiled back.

'Thank you for wishing to spare me any great suffering.'

'Come on, tell me how you escaped.'

'Well, I am a little ashamed about it, to be honest.'

'Nothing can shock me now.'

'You might be wrong.'

'Try me.'

'I took all the money I could lay my hands on, and escorted Susa and her two little boys on to a ship. Then I lay low until—'

'You did what?'

She would have assumed he was lying, except Constantinos never lied on his own account – only for other people.

'I know, I know. Tell no one, or my reputation is forever ruined. But she was such a dear, sweet girl. And her boys were so charming. Little Alexios. He used to bring me leaves and caterpillars while I was trying to work. I knew what would happen to them if I did nothing. I forgot myself. I am mortified.'

Agnes flung her arms about him and covered his face in kisses.

'In that case, I forgive you everything. That was a truly good deed. I am thankful.' She paused. 'Although I should ask you why you didn't come and save me. I could have done with some saving.'

'Oh, I knew you could look after yourself. And see, I was right. You are here – alive and well.'

'More or less. And now you are here too. What exactly are you doing here?'

'Making myself indispensable.'

Agnes gave him a little shove.

'All right, sorry. When I heard that Isaakios had decided to be *flexible*, shall we say, towards Andronikos's old associates,

I offered my services, and he was gracious enough to accept them. And so now I find myself in charge of securing the financing for the imperial weddings.'

He rustled his papers under her nose.

'Weddings? I thought there was only one.'

'In a day or so we shall all be told the good news that the emperor's sister, the incomparable Dora, will marry Conrad of Montferrat.'

'Not . . . ?'

'Poor Renier's elder brother, yes. Or one of his elder brothers – there is yet another, called Boniface, if I am not mistaken. Doubtless even larger and more martial.'

So that was who Dora had been rabbiting on about earlier.

'Does he know what he's letting himself in for?'

'I believe the bride and groom have yet to be formally introduced.'

'And won't be until the wedding day, in case he does a runner.'

Constantinos chuckled and patted her arm.

'Now, diverting though this is, you'll have to excuse me. This wedding won't pay for itself.'

'Oh, come on. I can't imagine it's that difficult a job.'

'That is where you and far too many other people are wrong. We're broke, my dear Agnes, stone broke.'

'But that's absurd. What's all that?'

She waved her hand at the dozens of servants who were laying dozens of tables with mounds of gold plate, silver spoons, gem-encrusted goblets – a treasure trove that was so commonplace she hadn't particularly bothered to look at it until then.

'Don't be deceived. A few jewels on the fingers of a woman mean nothing if her husband's coffers are bare. When Andronikos was overthrown, the people plundered the mint. And what was lost? Twelve hundred pounds of gold, three thousand of silver, twenty thousand of copper. And that's on top of what the Protosebastos got his hands on, which was a lot – he had big hands, remember. And money was leaching out even at the end of Manuelos's reign.'

'I didn't know.'

'Of course you didn't. When it comes to money, people never want to know. They think it's dull. Especially men like Isaakios, who never had to do anything so distasteful as *budget*. He is the emperor, and so, to his mind, he has unlimited means. And he will not believe me if I try to tell him any different.'

He sighed.

'He wants money for a wedding the like of which has never been seen. He wants money to shore up our foreign alliances. He wants money to lure men back from exile – compensation, he calls it. He thinks he knows the drill – splash enough gold about, put on a good enough show and everyone will be your friend. *Long live the emperor.* But those were the glory days, when money was no object. And those days are over.'

Agnes smiled.

'I can see why he doesn't want to listen to you, if that's what you've got to tell him.'

'So you see how I spend my days. How about you? Keeping busy?'

Agnes made a face.

'That bad?' he asked, not unsympathetically.

'Worse,' she said.

'Let me guess. The women all hate you because they think you're after their husbands . . .'

'. . . while their husbands are tumbling over each other – I've lost count, Constantinos, truly – to be my *protector.*'

'So that's what they call it these days. And you're not tempted to plump for the one with most teeth?'

She shook her head.

'Things haven't got that desperate. I am glad to see you, though, Constantinos, a friendly face from the bad old days.'

He gave her a look.

'Speaking of old friends, I ran into Alexios Branas and that nice son of his just before I ran into you. A shame they won't be staying for the wedding, but he's been given command of the Bulgar campaign and they're to leave immediately.'

Even her years of experience couldn't keep the disappointment off her face.

'Come on, Agnes,' said the eunuch, gently. 'You're going to have to do better than that. Good thing I told you before someone else did. Agnes?'

There was real concern in his voice, which only made it worse. Her eyes were prickling, but she wouldn't cry. She wouldn't.

Also in the autumn of 1186

'We'll be all right now your father's here.'

That – or variations on the same theme – was what Theo heard from every mouth as he wandered through the sodden Rôman camp high in the foothills of the Bulgar mountains.

With the weather so bleak, and rations so tight, it was no surprise that morale was fragile. When he and his father had first ridden in, they'd expected hot kid stew, even a bit of deer, but the cook had apologised and handed them hard tack, dried pig meat and sour wine. If that was what the commander got, Theo pitied the ranks.

His father had swallowed a few mouthfuls and ordered the captains to report to him.

'Want to listen in, Theo?'

'Maybe I'll head out and get the unofficial version.'

'Good idea. Mikhail's got a few skins stashed somewhere. Tell him I said you could have one.'

Theo grunted as a rivulet of rainwater spilled off the tent roof and ran down the back of his neck. Autumn in these mountains was no place for a human being. The endless pine forests, the muddy streams, the bowls of early snow-slush, they were already getting on his nerves. And he'd only just arrived.

Most of the troops had been up there for months, ever since two brothers, leaders of one of the Bulgar tribes, decided they didn't fancy paying the empire's taxes any more – especially the one levied to fund Isaakios's wedding.

The brothers had locked a bunch of soothsayers in a spirit

hut with an unlimited supply of unmixed wine and toadstools and left them to it. Unsurprisingly, they started to hear voices. The soothsayers – holy visionaries or a bunch of hairy, cross-eyed, frothing lunatics, depending on your point of view – said the gods wanted the Bulgar people to rise up against the Rôman emperor. And the people had obeyed.

His father had expected to be given the command, but Isaakios thought it was going to be nothing more than a there-and-back punitive mission and decided to head it himself. He'd ridden out of the City with an enormous entourage, travelled slow and easy, burned a couple of lowland villages, butchered a handful of boys and a few old men, and returned claiming a great victory.

But the unrest continued, and so Isaakios dispatched his blind old uncle, a great operator in the City but no kind of warrior, with orders to slap the insurrection down. He'd blundered badly, embarrassing himself and the empire as the Bulgars wore down his forces with ambushes and night raids.

Finally, after months of vacillation, Isaakios bowed to the inevitable and put Branas in charge – although Theo knew he had only sent him because there was nobody else to send. And even then he'd been jumpy, bleating.

Can I trust you, Branas? That is the question. Can I trust you?

Of course you can – Theo'd heard a sharp intake of breath where his father would normally have said, *Fucking trust me, basileus.*

When they left, it was still warm in the south, in the City. The fine days of late autumn when the air was soft, the light gold. Figs would be in season. He loved figs. He loved Agnes. *There.* He'd gone a whole morning, near enough, without thinking about her. That was some sort of record.

'Here, by all that's holy, isn't that young Theodore?'

He was passing a sentry post and saw a particularly grizzled gang of foot soldiers clustered round a badly smoking fire. He went to join them, hoping he'd recognise the man who'd hailed him when he got closer. They weren't a pretty sight. Their beards hung lank down their chins. Their mail shirts looked rusty, their padded jerkins mouldy. They were supping off hunks of baked squill, picking bits out of their teeth with sharpened sticks.

'Alexios!' It was usually a safe bet.

The man grinned. 'You remember me?'

'Course I do. Thracian call-up?' The man's accent was a dead giveaway.

'See, boys, I said things'd get better. His dad's one of us. They'll do right by us.'

The other men were wary at first, but Theo let them feel they were speaking to the boy their mate remembered, not some smart City officer, and that – together with a few swigs of wine all round – soon softened them up. They began to talk, first in winks and hints, and then plain and free.

'Bulgars stinking like wolf bitches on heat didn't fit with his idea of being emperor.'

'Isaakios's uncle wanted to fight pitched battles like he was Julius fucking Caesar.'

'They've had us squeaking behind this stockade like bloody chickens.'

'It's fucked up, Theo, fucked up.'

Theo grimaced. *Fucked up* was about right.

He left them with the remains of the wineskin and went to find his father. Branas was listening to a review of supplies from the senior quartermaster, and Theo waited quietly until the man had left.

'It's bad, son, but I think we can right it. We'll need to play the Bulgars at their own game. Bribe some local men to act as spies and guides – can you believe we have none? We need more mobility. We need to take the fight to them. By the time the leaves are back on the trees, we'll have them whipped.'

Theo nodded. He didn't doubt him.

'And then what, Father?'

'We fight the next war.'

Theo was silent.

'What's on your mind, boy? Spit it out.'

'Fighting for this empire, it's like stopping up a leaking roof.'

He paused.

'A leaking roof, you say?' said his father with an expression that was hard to read.

'Yes,' said Theo. 'The roof might be made of gold and we might be catching the rain in silver buckets – but it's still pissing down outside and we're still running back and forth with another man's pots.'

'Talk straight.'

'All right. While we're up to our armpits in mud, Isaakios is sat in the City, laughing at us. He's fucking laughing at you, Father. He thinks you'll do his fighting for him and ask for nothing in return. It's wrong, and we both know there's not a man in this camp who doesn't feel the same way. And the people who live between here and the City, I bet they'd agree. They know the borders are weak and they know they'll only get weaker with a useless prick like Isaakios on the throne. They want an emperor who can keep them safe.'

Now or never.

'An emperor like you, Father.'

They both whipped round as somebody entered the tent – but it was only Mikhail with the general's supper.

'Rabbit. Or near enough. Might be a big bugger of a rat. Thought you might want something hot. I'll leave you to it.' A pause. 'The boy's right, you know, boss. Just say the word . . .'

'That's enough, Mikhail.'

'Like I said, I'll be off.'

The sound of rain rose a little as the tent flap opened and shut. Theo waited as his father sat down and started to tear strips of thigh meat from the rabbit – or rat.

'There's one problem, Theo,' he said, sucking the fat off his fingers. 'I don't want it. I don't want the throne.'

'But that is why you should have it, Father. You wouldn't take it out of greed or pride. You'd be doing it because it was your duty.'

Duty. The magic word. Theo tried to look stalwart and sure. He tried not to think about Agnes. *When the wheel turns again . . .*

His father stood up and flung the bones in the fire. He dipped a cloth in a pitcher of water and rubbed the day's dirt from his face and hands.

'We'll finish what we came to do first, Theo.'

'Yes, Father.'

He's going to do it.

'No man will be able to say I left the frontier weak.'

'No, Father.'

He's going to bloody do it.

'Forget we spoke of this for now. Come spring, we'll talk again. Understand?'

'Understood, Father.'

Theo was about to take his leave – night was falling, and he needed to make sure Mikhail had fixed him a place to sleep – but his father was looking at him curiously.

'What happened to my boy who cared for nothing but three-copper whores and fist fights? The boy who had no taste for politics?'

'He grew up, Father. Like you told him to.'

Late in the spring of 1187

All through the winter, the news from the Bulgar mountains had been good, and once the snows started to thaw, it grew even better. Every day, every hour, everyone in the palace expected a messenger to arrive with word of a decisive victory.

Agnes might have picked up sooner that something was amiss if she hadn't been staring blankly out of a window, trying to ignore the voice in her head that said an arrow, a pike, a falling branch might have killed Theo weeks ago and she'd only find out today. A small postscript to the official dispatches. *Regret to inform . . . the general's son . . . sad loss . . . servant of the empire.*

'Give that here!'

'No, it's mine.'

'You just come and . . .'

She was distracted by a pack of girls – the empress and two of Euphrosunê's daughters at their head – running riot in the women's quarters. Agnes was never good at remembering ages, and Euphrosunê wasn't the kind of friend who cared whether you did or not, but Eirene and Anna must have been about fourteen and twelve. Agnes was closer in age to them than to their mother, but as she watched them clustered in an alcove, giggling with Margit, she felt the weight of every one of the years that separated them.

They were baiting Isaakios's little boy – from an earlier marriage; Margit didn't share his bed – dangling toys out of his reach and scampering away when he chased after them, tripping over his own feet and crying.

Dora was glaring at the lot of them, torn, Agnes imagined, between telling them to act with the dignity befitting their rank and worrying that they'd probably ignore her if she did. Dora's mood would be especially sour because her maid, so Agnes's own maid had been all eagerness to report, had left the quicklime on too long when she'd been stripping the hair from her legs. Agnes groaned. Why did she fill her head with such pointless, moronic tattle?

Suddenly, something about the hysterical pitch of the girls' squeals told Agnes to pay attention. They always got rowdier if there was tension in the palace; they picked up on it like little animals. She tried to block out the noise around her and listen, really listen. Yes, there were more men moving about than usual. Shouting, as well, but in the distance, too faint for her to guess what it was about.

She nudged Euphrosunê. Ever since Isaakios had married off her youngest daughter, Eudokio, to a Serb prince, her friend had been subdued. Euphrosunê was, of course, the last person to underestimate the value of an imperial niece when it came to propping up the empire's frontier, and so in public she'd been matter-of-fact about waving goodbye to her favourite daughter – blasé, even. But Agnes knew red eyes when she saw them.

'Euphrosunê, d'you think . . . ?'

'Mmm. Maybe.'

If a messenger had come, they wouldn't know a thing until Isaakios sent word. It was beneath Dora's dignity to swap favours for news. Worse, she actually looked down on the eunuchs, the bureaucrats – all the really useful people, who could tell you anything in a flash. Both Agnes and Euphrosunê might have had the answer in minutes, but first they needed to get away from the women's quarters.

It was ridiculous how much time they spent shut away, but that was how Dora fancied things ought to be. She thought it was chic and refined. *Komnenian.* As if Marguerite-Constance or Maria would ever have dreamed of cloistering themselves away like this.

The sound of hurrying footsteps came closer. A door slammed, and then they all heard Isaakios's voice, indistinct but angry.

'Husband, oh husband!'

Margit squeaked and collapsed on the floor in a faint. Anna was giggling so much that Agnes was sure the basilissa was mostly faking, but everyone flew to her all the same.

'You,' Dora called to one of the serving girls, 'run along to my chamber and fetch me my tincture box. Quick now.'

'I'll go,' said Agnes.

'Nonsense,' said Dora, fussing at Margit's clothes. 'You stay put.'

Margit opened her eyes.

'Oh, please Agnes to go. That one, she is so slow, so stupid. Always she bring wrong thing.'

'Your wish is my command, basilissa.'

Agnes didn't wait to hear Dora's reply, but darted out of the room, exchanging the smallest wink with Euphrosunê on her way. She ran down the corridors to Dora's chambers and pushed open the door. She was so busy calculating how much time she'd have to duck out and find Constantinos that at first she didn't see there was a man in the room, a man as startled as she was.

'Conrad,' she said, backing out, 'forgive me. I didn't know . . .'

'How could you?' said Conrad. 'Come in.'

'I can't . . .'

'Come in,' he repeated, taking her arm and pulling her inside.

When Dora's husband had first arrived from the west, Agnes thought a ghost had started up through the marble, so very like was he to his brother, Renier. But now she looked at him more closely, she could see that his face was put together differently. The features were cut a little finer, a little sharper. His eyes were blue, but not so sweet. They saw more than Renier's had ever done, that she was sure of.

'What are you doing in here?' she asked, when it was clear he wasn't planning to speak.

'Can a man not visit his wife's chambers?' he said, smiling the lazy smile that made the palace women blush and titter whenever he passed.

'Of course. How . . . how romantic. She'll be delighted. I'll go and tell her you're here.'

He rolled his eyes.

'I beg you, do no such thing. Show a little compassion, sebastê. Have a seat.'

Although the last words were said in a tone of unmistakable command, she ignored him and remained standing.

'Agnes,' he said, positioning himself between her and the door. 'Agnes, Agnes, Agnes.' He pronounced her name properly, the way her family had done, the *g* and the *n* soft in the roof of his mouth. 'Don't you ever get sick of these Greeks?' He had switched to Latin, and was looking her over in a way that she knew from experience was dangerous.

She said nothing.

'I imagine you're wondering what I'm doing in here if I don't want to see my wife. I'll tell you – although God knows it does me little honour. You see, she – my most beloved Dora – she does not give me much money. And a man needs money, does he not? To do those things a man needs to do.'

'You're stealing from your own wife?'

'I know. Hopeless, isn't it?'

Again that smile, playful and conspiratorial, shutting out the rest of the world. Once upon a time, it might have worked a certain magic – but not now. Now it only made her wary. He leant back against the door and she felt his eyes travel her body.

'You know how I feel, I'm sure. She does the same to you, doesn't she, Agnes? I've been watching. I've seen it. She loves to feel the pull of the leash in her hand.'

'You're imagining things, Conrad. Your wife loves and

respects you. And she treats me with all the kindness of a sister.'

He stiffened, annoyed that she wasn't playing his game.

'How about Maria? My brother's wife? Did she treat you like a sister, too?'

It was the first time she'd heard him speak openly of Renier, the boy who'd sicked up his life and probably never truly understood why.

'Yes. She was very kind to me. As was your brother. Their deaths were a great misfortune.'

'A misfortune shared by many who came too close to Andronikos. But not by you. Tell me, Agnes, why are you alive when my brother is dead?'

'I was very young and very unimportant. I prayed to God for my salvation.'

'Oh, I'm sure you did. But my brother was also very young. Maybe he did not pray enough, maybe that's it. But I think there's something else. I think you must have some secret. I would love to know what it is, Agnes. There is much I would know about you. Much I would enjoy discovering.'

He'd left his post by the door and was moving towards her. He took her arm. She gave it a little shake, but he didn't let go.

'There's no need to be like that, Agnes. We could be friends, you and I, good friends. I know you must be lonely . . .'

His hands were tight about her waist and she could feel his excitement pressing hard into her stomach. Her arms were trapped between his, but she let her hands fly up and touch his face. He smiled, complacent, triumphant, and leant down to kiss her. His eyes had glazed, and she knew he'd stopped thinking about anything other than burying his cock between her legs. She gave a little gasp, the sound of fear and pleasure mingled that she guessed he would like.

'But Conrad, we mustn't, we mustn't.' A hoarse whisper. 'She . . . your wife . . . she's coming. She sent me ahead of her

303

to prepare her chamber. I forgot. Your attentions. They are so overwhelming. I forgot. But we cannot risk it, can we?'

She glanced at the door, hoping the fear would shine real in her eyes. He let go of her, and for a moment she thought she had not been convincing enough, but to her relief, he nodded.

'You're right. I fancy you'd be worth taking time over.'

She whirled away from him.

'Oh, I am. I learnt from the best, remember that.'

He pulled her back to him and pressed his mouth hard on to hers.

'I am not a boy to toy with. Try that tone again and I'll have you now, on the floor, against the wall, like the slave I took after breakfast.'

He was pushing her backwards. His hands were chasing up inside her skirts. *No! Don't!* She wanted to scream, but she couldn't, she mustn't. If they were found together, it might be awkward for him, but it would be catastrophic for her.

'Agnes? Agnes! What are you doing?'

Dora's voice in the corridor. *Dora!*

Conrad ran to the window and tumbled over the balcony, leaving her bare moments to scoop up a handful of phials and bump into Dora on the threshold.

'Forgive me. I couldn't find—'

'You are impossible, Agnes. A simple errand like this – for our empress of all people – and you . . . But never mind that now. She's back on her feet. My brother has summoned us. I must change. Arrange my hair. My husband likes to see me at my best. Quickly now.'

'I'll send for your maidservant.'

'Oh, but you do it so nicely, Agnes,' said Dora, sitting down before a gigantic looking glass.

Without a word, Agnes picked up a little flask of oil and began to brush it through Dora's hair. Another humiliation to swallow. When she looked up to set a few strands in curls about her forehead, she saw Dora was looking hard at her.

'Tell me, Agnes, what do you know of Alexios Branas?'

Agnes could see no reason not to answer truthfully.

'I know that he is a good man. And a good general.'

'And now,' said Dora with some satisfaction, 'now they will say that he is a traitor. There. What do you make of that?'

Agnes saw her own eyes widening.

'He . . . ?'

'He is marching on the City with the western armies at his back.'

And I would wager that every city in his path has bowed down before him. Agnes buried that thought and met Dora's gaze.

'Your brother shall punish his insolence.'

'He shall, Agnes, yes, assuredly he shall.'

Agnes nodded and clipped gold on Dora's ears, clasped gold about her throat, her head a whirl of pleasure.

When the wheel turns again . . .

The summer of 1187

Theo and his father reined in their horses before the City walls.

The bishops were parading an icon along the battlements, their chanting audible above the clink of arms, the stamp of horses. It was, Theo knew, the Hodogetria, an image of the Mother of God painted from life by St Luke the Evangelist. For centuries, its power had kept the Queen of Cities safe from her enemies. Theo said a prayer, quick and fervent, begging Mary to know them for who they were – the City's truest friends.

He glanced over at his father, who was sitting – unusually stiffly – astride his best charger, the black one with a little crescent of white hairs above its brow.

'I'll tell you something, son,' said Branas in reply to Theo's look. 'I never thought I'd be standing on this side of the walls.'

'Isaakios'll give up the City once he sees we mean business. The same way he gave up Nicaea. Either that, or the City will give him up. You'll see, Father.'

Branas grunted.

'Let's hope so. Those are the only ways we're getting in.'

It was true. The soldiers behind them were proven fighters, devoted to their general, hardened by months in the wilds, fired by the prospect of a good time once they'd won. But enough to mount a siege? No. There wasn't an army in the world that could take the City head on.

Instead, his father was calculating that Isaakios wouldn't risk leaving them camped outside the City for long. It was too dangerous, too destabilising for him – politically, not militarily. The emperor would have to try to drive them off, and that was when they'd show him.

To that end, his father had ordered his forces to form ranks before the walls, with barely half their numbers visible. There was no heavy horse to be seen, and foot soldiers outnumbered the cavalry by seven to one. He wanted them to look inviting.

The singing reached a climax and the icon disappeared from view. Theo had feared they might be in for a long wait while Isaakios and his advisers quarrelled over what to do, but to his delight, the Gate of Charisius clanked open and thick lines of City troops trotted into position.

Immediately, the tension vanished from his father's face. He snapped his fingers and Mikhail passed him his helmet.

'Go,' he said to Theo. 'The right flank. You know your orders.' And he clapped the helmet down hard on his head.

Theo nodded – although this was the moment he'd been dreading. His father was laying himself wide open to the City's first attack. Worse, he was provoking it, offering himself up as a target, as bait. Theo had begged him to command from behind the lines. *Fuck that*, was his father's reply. *These men are risking their lives as a personal favour to me. They're going to watch me fight, not the other way around.* He was right, of course, but that didn't make it any easier.

As Theo cantered in a wide arc towards the higher ground where the men he commanded were stationed, he heard the City's trumpeters sound the charge. He wrenched his eyes away. His father had been in more battles than any man on that plain. He could take care of himself.

Instead, he looked west, waiting, waiting . . . *There they are.* The rearguard, the iron-clad kataphraktoi, were thundering into view. Theo gave the nod to a signals boy at his side, who broke out a plain red standard. His father's line disengaged, split and scattered.

The City men thought they had won. Theo heard cheers,

but the sound died fast when the leaders saw that a brutal counter attack was almost upon them. A few, a very few, held firm, but most panicked and turned for the gate, not wanting to get mown down a few hundred paces from the safety of their own walls.

Now it was Theo's turn.

He motioned to the men beside him, and they began their own charge, swooping across the field on a diagonal, aiming to reach the gate at the same time as the defenders. Theo urged his horse on, faster and faster. The gate was opening to let the men in. *Faster, faster.* A handful of City riders shot through. But then somebody – somebody both callous and clever – gave the order to slam the gate shut.

Theo swore and wheeled his horse around under a hail of arrows.

Hundreds of City men were now trapped on the wrong side of the walls, begging for help – a rope, a ladder, anything to escape. Theo and his soldiers darted amongst them, risking the stones from overhead, slashing, hacking, slicing – it was more like butchery than fighting – until his father called them off.

'Best to leave a few poor sods alive, eh, Theo?'

'The gate, I'm sorry . . .' Theo began, but Branas cut him off.

'Don't be.'

'But if we'd ridden faster, we might have—'

'It doesn't matter.' Branas waved his sword in the direction of the City men, who were now fleeing in all directions. 'The stories they tell will do our work for us. They'll make us out to be a band of ravening basilisks. They'll have to. How else to explain their cowardice?'

'They say it was like house dogs fleeing a wolf pack,' Euphrosunê murmured to Agnes through the side of her mouth. 'Conrad ordered the gate closed only just in time. My dear brother-in-law is done for. Mark my words.'

308

They were leaving the chapel in the grounds of the Blachernai Palace, having spent hours praying with the other women for the City's deliverance. Dora had wept quietly; Margit noisily.

'You must be overjoyed, Agnes,' Euphrosunê added. 'You'll not forget me, will you, when your beau comes riding in?'

Agnes shot her a look. *Shut up.* Euphrosunê stuck her lower lip out, a mock pout. Agnes felt for her hand and gave it a little squeeze.

'Don't tempt fate, Euphrosunê. All right?'

Her friend made a small face of apology and they walked on in silence. As they crossed the courtyard that led back into the main building, something on the high ground to the north caught Agnes's eye.

The sun was setting. Its rays, where they touched the hillside, splintered into thousands of points of fire, flashes of lightning coming to life. The other women had seen it too.

'A storm?'

'Fireflies! A plague of fireflies.'

'No, it is stars, falling to earth. A sign! A sign!'

Agnes and Euphrosunê looked at one another. They at least knew what it was. Hundreds upon hundreds of swords were shining in the last moments of sunlight. Branas was sending a message to the people of the City. He was telling them that he was coming. Agnes crossed herself and – lest God had not heard her before – silently asked for His blessing on the general and his son.

She bade Euphrosunê good night, pulled her shawl tighter about her head and hurried to her room. In the alcove next to her door, a shadow was waiting. It stirred, and she stopped. It was very quiet. Whoever it was must have heard her coming.

The shadow stood up, and with relief, she realised it was altogether too small to be Conrad. He'd been trying to run her to ground, and it was taking all her skill to dodge him while at the same time giving the impression she hungered for him.

'Hello, Constantinos,' she said. 'Do you want to come in?'

She pushed her door open and walked inside, knowing that he'd follow. Her room was small, its furnishings almost insultingly simple, but it had a balcony that faced the Golden Horn, and it looked well enough in the red glow from the candles the maids had already lit. Normally it made her feel pleased and proprietorial; it was, after all, hers.

'I wanted a word, my dear Agnes.'

'As many words as you like, my dear friend,' she said, making a show of seating herself comfortably on her divan.

'Or maybe I should start with a warning. You look altogether too cheerful.'

'Only to somebody as perceptive as you. I can't match Margit's vapours, but I'm sure I've been looking suitably distressed.'

Constantinos grunted, a small *humph*, which could have been either amusement or disagreement.

'You,' she continued, 'haven't been looking exactly heartbroken, either.'

'Ah, but I am a steely servant of the empire. I can get away with looking studiedly neutral – even when my emperor is in grave danger.'

'And is that how you feel? *Neutral?*'

He laughed his quiet laugh. 'No, Agnes, I do not feel neutral. Alexios Branas is a man of parts. Fair. Measured. Frugal. An ideal emperor. I salivate at the prospect of him on the throne. And so do many others. But . . .'

'But . . . ?'

'The City is not yet his.'

She nodded, and waited.

'It is no easy thing, taking this City. In fact, it has never been done – not, that is, from the outside. Even the greatest generals have needed a little help from their friends – their friends on the inside.' He sat down beside her and leant in close. 'Your ears have pricked up like a little rabbit's.'

'Rabbits be damned.' She pushed him away. 'I want to help. You know I do. What do you have in mind?'

He lowered his voice to a whisper, although that was only his love of theatre. They had already said far too much – but she trusted Constantinos only to speak when it was safe.

'It is Conrad who leads the City's troops, not Isaakios. And Conrad, unlike Isaakios, is a good fighter. Better than good. But if he were . . .'

'. . . to see a brighter future alongside Branas?'

'Exactly.'

'There's one problem,' she said. 'Why would he? He is kin to the emperor.'

'And he must give nightly thanks to have Isaakios for his emperor. And Dora for his wife.'

'You think he has regrets?'

'I know he does not bed her.'

Agnes gasped, delighted.

'But she tells us, well, hints to us that . . .'

'. . . he rides her five times a night, part pure-bred stallion, part rutting bull. Yes, I've heard. But it's a pack of lies. Fantasy. He has an appetite, no doubt about that, but he doesn't service it in the marital bed.'

He paused.

'Conrad isn't stupid, Agnes. He can see which way the wind is blowing. I think we could turn him.'

Another pause.

'I say we, but really I mean you. *You* could turn him.'

'Me?' She didn't know how much he knew. 'Why me?'

'Like so many gallant western knights, he has a marked distaste for men such as I. He winces when I speak. He thinks me effete, scheming . . .'

'You *are* eff—'

'Yes, yes, maybe I am. So he does not like me. You, on the other hand, he likes.'

'How do you know?'

'A little bird told me.'

'Good God, does the whole palace know?'

'No, only myself and my little bird.'

'How many little birds do you have, Constantinos?'

'Never as many as I'd like. So, will you try to persuade our brave soldier?'

'He's not going to turn his back on Isaakios just because I open my legs.'

'For shame, Agnes. When did you become so crude? I remember a nicely brought-up girl who blushed so prettily.'

'I am beyond blushes now.'

'And that is why it is you who must go to Conrad. You have a glamour. A potency.'

'That's nonsense. I am the same as I ever was.'

'I can see that. But I see clearly. Other men – men like Conrad – do not. Every man in the palace knows you don't . . .'

'Put out?'

'Your words, not mine. Very well. You do not, as you say, *put out.* A wicked past and a pure present. That makes you quite unreasonably enticing.'

Agnes pursed her lips.

'I know what you are doing, Constantinos. You and whichever faction stands behind you. I am the good wine and sweetmeats that the merchant provides when he wants you to buy something. I do not flatter myself.'

'But you will flatter him. And you will convince him. I have no doubt you can do it.'

Convince him. She'd have to get him alone, and that would mean . . . She couldn't pretend she didn't know exactly what that would mean. *I am yours. I'll always be yours.* Theo would understand, wouldn't he?

The eunuch was frowning at her.

'For God's sake, Agnes, I hope that's not the face you're going to present to Conrad. I wouldn't peg him as the sort of man who finds a troubled conscience very alluring.'

'How about this?'

She smiled her sauciest smile.

'Perfect. Perfect. You'll do it?'

She nodded.

'I'll try.'

'Good.' He actually looked relieved. 'Stop at nothing, eh, Agnes?'

'And if it doesn't work? If he tells Isaakios?'

'Then, my dear, you're on your own. But you knew that . . .' His voice trailed away as something outside caught his eye. 'Quickly now. Your sight is better than mine. Can you make out what's happening down there?'

She stood and looked down into the gathering dark.

'Ships. I see ships.'

'Merchantmen?'

'No, galleys, I think. Maybe three, maybe more. It's hard to pick them out against the other shore.' She frowned. 'It's late for boats to be manoeuvring, isn't it? What do you think they're doing?'

'Unless they're deserting, which I wouldn't rule out, I'd say Isaakios was preparing to land men behind Branas's lines. It's not a bad plan.'

'Is there anything we can do?'

'Nothing – except hope that Branas's scouts have seen them too.'

The next day

An hour at least before dawn, Theo felt his way into the largest fishing village on the stretch of coastline that ran west from the City.

He and two hundred of his father's best fighters had ridden as fast as they could through the night. Even though the imperial galleys would have to wait for the sun to clip the horizon before they ducked out from behind the Great Chain, he knew he didn't have much time. He had to persuade the fishing fleet to side with them.

He had a great deal of money with him – and the ability to promise a great deal more. But you never knew with fishermen. They loved money, everyone knew that, but they loved their independence more. They might live in the City's shadow, but they were not of it, a band apart, with their own rites and rules, and proud of it. That was why he'd left the other soldiers half a mile inland and was entering the village alone.

Although it was early, the settlement felt like it had been out of bed for hours. Children – the ones too young to be on the boats or at the stoves – ghosted about his horse's hooves, begging for a coin, a ride, leaping up to touch his sword.

He reached down and hauled a small boy, no more than four or five, up on to the saddle in front of him. The boy smirked down at his friends and tried to grab hold of the reins.

'Hands off,' said Theo. 'Now, who speaks for most men here? Who do your people listen to?'

In his experience, children always intuited such things.

Grown men might hedge or lie. The boy grinned and pointed.

'My cousins. Over there. They're with their boats. What do you want with them, mister? Mister?'

He followed the boy's finger and saw two men, one built big, one small, silhouetted against the water, folding a net with quick, precise movements into the stern of a little boat. Theo jumped down. Big animals might impress children, but no man liked to be talked to from the back of a horse. He handed the boy a small coin.

'Hop it,' he said. 'Grown-up talk.'

By that time, the men had seen him and stopped what they were doing. As he approached, picking his way over pebbles still slippery with the previous day's catch, they nodded. Not a bow. At best, a sort of wary acknowledgement.

'Greetings. Might I know your names?'

'I'm Andreas,' said the little one, 'and he's my brother, Petros.'

Brothers, fishermen, Petros and Andreas. They waited to see what effect that had on him. Either they were teasing him, or their mother really had named them for the two apostles. Either way, Theo knew better than to react.

'And my name is Theodore Branas.'

'Good for you,' grunted the big one, Petros, and turned to where a pot of pitch was balanced over a small fire.

Theo took a deep breath.

'I need your boats and your skill.'

'We bet you do,' said Andreas, who'd joined his brother slapping pitch on to the planking of an upturned boat. 'The big birds are on the move, aren't they? Going to run a ring-net about you and your dad, aren't they? Round you up and choke you off?'

Theo smiled to show he was impressed they knew so much. He *was* impressed. He only wished they were more impressed with him. He'd rehearsed a nonchalant little speech about honour and history and the difference between good men and bad, but he already realised that they'd laugh and turn their backs if he tried that on. He was reluctant just to offer them the gold, straight up. It might well do the trick, but he needed more than a *yes*. He needed a *yes please*.

They were waiting. And so, he saw, were a handful of other fishermen who had approached through the gloom.

'How much tax does a boat this size pay?' Theo asked.

'One hyperpyron every fourteen days,' said Petros.

'For the boat?'

'Boat and catch,' said Andreas.

'Well, Alexios Branas thinks you should pay one hyperpyron every new moon.'

'And what does Alexios Branas have to say about the City's fishmongers setting the prices?' asked a new man.

Theo thought for a minute. He hadn't a clue.

'He says that's how it needs to be on the big catches. Bonito and mackerel. That's for the good of the City. But you can sell the quality stuff, the sturgeon, the bass, for whatever price you can raise.'

'And sell it to whoever we want?'

Theo nodded.

'To whoever you want.'

He kept quiet while he listened to the men, about three dozen of them, debating amongst themselves. As he waited, he sized them up. Angular faces, sinewy bodies – they were tough as any of his father's veterans.

Andreas stepped forward.

'You've got a deal. On those terms, we'll keep the big birds away from your general.'

Theo grasped the hand the fisherman held out to him.

'Good. How many more men do you reckon you can summon before the galleys reach us? I have soldiers waiting not far from here – soldiers and weapons enough for you and more. I've heard you fight as well as you handle your boats.'

The fishermen looked at each other and laughed.

'The kind of fighting you're talking about?' said Petros. 'Swords and bows? Not us, mister.' But then he winked. 'Trust me, we won't need to do much fighting.'

The other men were all grinning broadly.

'That's right, mister,' Andreas continued. 'What d'you smell?'

Theo sniffed. He could smell a lot of things. Mainly fishy and rank.

'Nothing. I smell nothing.'

'Fog, mister. Soon it'll be down so thick they won't be able to see the nasty beaks on the end of their boats. Then they'll shout us for help, like they always do. And then we'll show them.'

The last of the stars had winked out. The sky was a deep grey, untouched by blue or pink, and everything was very quiet. Theo crouched in the bow of the brothers' boat, listening to the creak of the boom, the plash of the paddles, the only sounds he could hear.

He blinked.

The fishermen were right. The far shore of the straits, which he'd been able to make out as a darker grey line stretching away to the south, had vanished. The world was drawing in. Soon the northern shore disappeared as well, and finally the other boats.

Petros and Andreas shipped their paddles and the boat drifted to a standstill. He heard the *drop-drip, drip-drop* of water running off the blades into the sea. The quiet deepened until his breath, his very blood, sounded loud in his ears.

Anything he thought he could see was strange and distorted. A ship loomed to starboard, then dwindled before his eyes into the branch of a tree, spinning slowly. The fishermen hadn't been pretty on shore, but out here they looked like ghosts. A fish broke the water, bringing with it a strange smell, cold and forbidding.

'How do you know where you are?' Theo said, instantly regretting how loud his voice sounded.

Petros shrugged. 'How do you find your cock when you need a piss in the dark?'

A man's voice hallooed in the fog. Then another. Theo knew it was the lookouts on Isaakios's boats calling to one another, but it was still a shock when the prow of a war galley suddenly reared above him. With a few tweaks of their paddles, the brothers eased their boat alongside.

'Need piloting, bosun?' Andreas called up. 'Fish ain't biting, mister. Here to serve, mister.'

A man, a big black shape, leant over the guardrail. If he was surprised – or suspicious – to find them under his stern, he didn't show it. A couple of poor men after a bit of easy money, what was remarkable about that?

'Bring us into Green Creek and there's gold in it for you.'

'Let's see it, then,' said Petros.

The man cursed, but a handful of coins clattered into the bottom of the boat.

'There's more when we land.'

'Aye, aye, mister, follow us.'

Theo knew that somewhere out there in the fog, two more boats were making the same offer to the two remaining galleys.

Slowly, they closed the land, heading not, of course, to where the City ships wanted to go, but towards an altogether different place, one chosen by the fishermen. A spit of sticky mud.

'Nearly there,' Petros muttered.

The trap was opening up. For a moment, Theo was convinced the fog was lifting, but no, that was only his paranoia. He could see exactly the same amount of nothing as before.

'There,' said Andreas.

There was still nothing to see except maybe the slightest disturbance in the water beneath the boat, so Theo was totally unprepared when a moment later the galley grounded. Its bow ploughed into the bank – the bank the fishing boat, with its much shallower draught, had easily cleared – with an apologetic wheeze, nothing more dramatic than the sound of a fat man settling into a soft chair.

Theo heard the bosun roaring at the oarsmen to back up, but the west-going current was spinning them beam-on to the bank. There wasn't enough water for the port-side sweeps. The long blades groped and splashed, helpless, in the muddy shallows.

Theo was turning to grin at the two fishermen when a second galley emerged from the fog bank. The men on the first boat yelled in warning and the helmsman reacted fast, slamming the steering oar hard over. The boat's nose veered sharply away from land, away from danger, but it was too late, its momentum was too great, and with a most satisfying smash, the second boat piled into the first.

Half a dozen red spots, gigantic fireflies, loomed upstream.

Theo knew what they were, but the men on the galleys didn't and the boats listed as they hurried to the rail to peer into the murk. Some thought it was the third ship – where *was* the third ship? – and were frantically trying to tell it to keep clear. But as the spots grew bigger and bigger, their cries changed to alarm as they realised that six fireballs were drifting down on them.

The fishermen had packed a handful of coracles with pitch and kindling, upended firepots in them and set them floating towards the City boats. If Theo was lucky, if the current was kind, the coracles would set the oars ablaze and send fire jumping up the galleys' topsides.

Soldiers, tricked out in mail, hated being at sea at the best of times, and panic hit long before the fireships. Theo watched as men from the second galley started to clamber on to the first. From there, dozens of them leapt overboard, hoping, he supposed, that if the galley was beached, they could wade ashore. A few looked as though they might make it, but the spit was slender, the mud treacherous, the current over it surprisingly fast, and Theo could only pity the figures he saw lose their footing and disappear.

Meanwhile, the fog had finally started to thin.

'There's the last one,' Andreas said, pointing.

With the visibility improving, the galley had plenty of time to assess the situation. The port bank backed their blades, the starboard bank pulled triple time and the ship coasted clean round the end of the spit.

'Fuck,' said Theo and Petros at more or less the same time.

The boat was gathering way and its purpose was horribly plain. Whoever was in command had identified them as hostile and had ordered the galley to chase them down.

'Pull for that inlet,' Petros roared. 'You—' this to Theo '—take my oar.' Theo tried to pull in time with Andreas, while Petros fumbled with the halyard at the foot of the boat's little mast. Up flew a sail, brown and patchy, to catch what little onshore breeze there was.

'Can the galley follow us in there?' Theo gasped between strokes.

'You bet, mister. It's good deep water.'

'Then why are we—?'

'Shut up and row.'

Theo wasn't afraid to take good advice when he heard it, and blocked out everything but the paddle in his hand. Land closed about them. He could hear little waves running up the shore.

'You swim, mister?' said Petros, who was standing in the stern, peering into the water in front of them.

'Yes, but . . .'

'Good! Ready, steady . . . jump!'

Petros dived into the water and struck out for the shore. Andreas followed, then Theo. He felt something snatch at his feet as he kicked out behind him, but after a couple more strokes he was clambering on to a patch of shale after the brothers.

'What the hell . . . ?' he spluttered.

He looked behind him and saw for the first time who was standing at the prow of the galley, sword drawn. The emperor's brother-in-law, Conrad, his face a snarl. Their eyes met, and he knew he'd been recognised.

But then Conrad fell over. The galley had juddered to a halt. Theo turned to the brothers, wide-eyed. It looked too much like witchcraft for comfort.

They grinned.

'Nets, mister,' said Andreas.

A smile spread across Theo's face as he made out the slender lines criss-crossing the inlet. Better still, Theo heard shouts coming from further up the inlet. The troops he'd brought with him must have spotted him land and were now jogging through the undergrowth to meet him – a nice reception for Conrad if he made it ashore.

Theo was calling a greeting when something sped across the water and flashed between him and Petros. The two fishermen flung themselves straight to the ground, but Theo, despite all his years of training, made a mistake – he turned to look back at the galley.

A bolt slammed into his belly.

He staggered backwards, appalled. The last thing he saw was a sailor handing Conrad another loaded crossbow.

'Look, his eyes are open,' said his father to someone who was standing out of sight. 'Son, son, can you hear me?'

He could. But he couldn't talk. No more than he could move.

A man appeared behind his father. Mikhail. He reached out and touched the general's shoulder, gently. Theo had never seen Mikhail do anything gentle before.

'Come on, boss. We've got to go. Boy'll be safe here.'

'Damn you, Mikhail. I can't leave him like this.'

'We'll be at battle in a few hours, boss. You've got to eat, get some sleep.'

His father dragged himself to his feet and lumbered towards the door. Then he turned and came back. He kissed Theo on the forehead, on the lips. He buried his face in his hair and breathed in deeply. When he stood up, Theo realised his face was wet with his father's tears.

I'm not dying, Father, he whispered, or tried to. *Please don't worry about me, Father.*

But his father did not hear.

That evening

The imperial family were sitting down to their evening meal at Blachernai. No word had come from Conrad's sea force, but Isaakios, far from looking nervous, was gleefully recounting his tour of the stylites, the hermits who lived on the top of columns dotted about the City.

'*Most* propitious, I must say. That runtish fellow on the Porphyry Column shouted down a few words of especial solace. With the holy men on our side I have nothing – *nothing* – to fear from Alexios Branas.'

Agnes doubted that the threat to his throne had moved Isaakios to such radical piety, and was deciding that it was simply his idea of a good joke when an attendant entered and begged leave to announce that the kaisar Conrad was approaching.

She expected Isaakios to hurry out to meet him, to stand, to notice, something – but he was utterly engrossed in the antics of his dwarf troupe, who'd been trying to stand on each other's shoulders ever since he'd mentioned the hermits. They'd managed a wobbly pyramid and a dwarf-child was scrambling to the top shouting, 'Long live the basileus.' Conrad made his entrance just as the whole edifice collapsed.

He was a mess, spattered with fresh mud or dried blood, impossible to tell which. Agnes could actually hear the slop and slosh of his wet boots on the floor.

'My dear fellow,' said Isaakios, still applauding the performance. 'You look quite out of sorts. I take it your enterprise didn't come off as planned?'

'Darling, are you hurt? Darling, let me . . .'

Dora had jumped to her feet and was running over to clutch Conrad's arm. He kissed her forehead, turning her pink with pleasure, before unclenching her fingers and planting himself across the table from Isaakios.

'Basileus, we must talk.'

'Talk away, brother. I am, as they say, all ears. Here – you look like you could use a drink.'

He clicked his fingers and a servant poured a glass of wine, but Conrad pushed it impatiently aside.

'Not here, please, basileus. The ladies . . .'

'Come, come, we can trust these women with anything.'

'I do not doubt it. But I do not want to . . .'

'To . . . ?'

'Alarm them.'

'Oh, they shall not be alarmed, shall you, my beauties? They shall be the most stoical of matrons, such as would gladden the heart of Markos Tullios Kikerôn himself.'

Agnes had no idea who Markos Tullios Kikerôn was, but she did know that at that moment she'd never seen two women who looked less stoical than Dora and Margit.

'Basileus—' said Conrad.

'Call me brother, do. It sounds so much more friendly.'

'Brother—'

'Or does that sound too informal? I never can tell. And now you're cross. Forgive me, dear Conrad. I shall say no more. Speak. I am all ears.'

The only possible sign that Isaakios was the slightest bit anxious was the way his fingers rubbed incessantly at his collar – studded, so the rumour went, with jewels plucked from one of the Holy Wisdom's finest altar crosses.

'As you know, basileus . . .' but Conrad broke off as the dwarves started to settle themselves in a semicircle at his feet, their upturned faces all innocence, as though readying themselves to listen to the best bits of the tale of Odysseus. 'Basileus, I beg you, could you . . . ?'

'What's that? Oh, do my little friends bother you? They can be so tactless. Off with you, off with you.'

The dwarves filed out, casting baleful glances over their shoulders, and Conrad began again.

'As you know, basileus, I planned to outflank the traitor Branas and fall upon his army from behind, but—'

'Yes, it did rather sound like there was a *but* on its way. Sorry, go on.'

'—but he had bribed the Propontis fishing men to attack us.'

'Forgive me, did I hear you aright? My imperial navy was attacked by a gang of stinking sea-peasants? And who prevailed in this ill-matched contest?'

'The fishing men.' Embarrassment coloured Conrad's voice. 'But they had help. Theodore Branas had organised them.'

He was there. Of course he was there. Agnes looked down at her hands so that nobody could read anything in her eyes.

'*Give me the command,* you said.' Isaakios's voice had turned cold. '*I promise you victory,* you said. Well?'

Conrad bowed, stiff and angry.

'I am sorry to prove such a disappointment, basileus.'

'You must be thankful that you never met my predecessor. What d'you think Andronikos would've done to him, eh, Agnes? Baked him in a pudding, perhaps?'

Isaakios laughed. Agnes laughed. Everyone laughed.

'Enough,' said Isaakios. 'Forgiveness, we all know, is divine. And tomorrow, so the philosophers assure us, is another day. Bearing those two things in mind, do you, brother, go and prepare your men for battle. Not you, Dora,' he said as his sister gathered her skirts to follow Conrad from the room. 'You stay here. Your husband doesn't need your ministrations, tender though I'm sure they are.'

Agnes made a quick assessment – Isaakios was busy with his food; Dora was busy remonstrating with him; everyone else was busy trying not to look utterly petrified – and edged towards the door. She was about to slip past the guards when she felt a hand on her sleeve.

'I just need to . . .' She turned, an excuse ready on her lips, until she saw it was only Euphrosunê.

'Good luck.'

'You know?'

'I do. You and Constantinos aren't the only people in the palace praying for Branas to succeed. Quickly now. After him.'

Conrad was approaching the gatehouse that would take him back into the City when she caught up with him.

'Conrad! Wait!'

He stopped. The courtyard was edged by a colonnade, a torch burning in a bracket on every second pillar. She drew closer.

'I cannot bear how they treat you, those Greeks. You are better . . . so much better . . . They are worthless . . . worthless.'

She laid a hand on his arm and found the muscles knotted.

'You understand. I knew you did,' he muttered, adding a few more words in his own dialect, the bitter curses of badly bruised pride. 'It is hard. Fighting for such a man.'

'Then don't.'

'Don't?'

His face was no more than a collection of shadows, impossible to read.

'A man can choose who he fights for,' she said. 'Even as a woman chooses who she beds.'

'You make two interesting points.' He glanced towards the gatehouse, where half a dozen men stood watch, and led her into the deeper dark beneath the colonnade. 'Care to elaborate?'

'Which would you prefer to discuss first?' she asked.

A soft snort of laughter. 'The fighting's more on my mind.'

'All right. The man who delivered the City to Alexios Branas would be guaranteed a great future.'

'You speak prettily, but you speak treason.'

'So call the guards,' she whispered. She held up her hands, her wrists crossed, in front of his face. 'Have them bind me.'

He took both her hands and pulled them down to her sides.

'You come like a dove, cooing in my ear.' He kissed her neck, her shoulder. 'Coo some more, little dove. Tell me why you've been trying to fly away from me.'

'Every girl knows not to say yes the first time. Or the second.'

She could tell the answer pleased him, as if it confirmed something he'd long thought about her – or about women. She pushed him backwards into an alcove, and in deep little whispers started to tell him what she wanted to do to him. He liked what he heard; his breathing quickened. His mouth was on hers, raw, hungry. His right hand was already fumbling with the belts of his mail shirt, but the knots wouldn't give. She laughed and slowly, slowly worked them free; then she pushed him down on to the stone seat and he pulled her down after him.

Afterwards, he lay with his head in her lap, his eyes closed, while she ran her fingers through his hair. The moon, two or three days from full, had risen above the walls, casting enough light on the pale stones for her to be able to make out his face.

'How do I do it, then?'

'Do what?'

She leant down and kissed his forehead, as if she'd forgotten what they'd been talking about. A woman satisfied.

'How would I let them know? We fight tomorrow. Should I trot my horse over the field?'

'That would serve, wouldn't it?'

She traced the lines of his mouth, twisted the curls of his beard.

'What if they put an arrow in my chest first?'

'They won't.'

'How can you be sure?' He opened his eyes and tipped his head back to look straight up at her.

'Branas and his son will welcome you with open arms.'

'Branas may, but his son definitely won't.'

'Why not?'

'I put a bolt through his middle. If the wound doesn't kill him, the rot probably will.'

A coldness unfurled in her belly. Conrad was still talking. She was nodding, but maybe she was meant to be shaking her head. *Listen. Listen to him.* But she couldn't make her ears hear. A thousand bats beat their wings inside her head, whirring, blurring everything. *What's he saying?* She saw that her fingers, which had been so languid, so tender, were locked, motionless, a bird's frozen claws.

He sat up.

'Ah. There's the catch, is it? You played your part well, I'll say that. But I think some of those nice things you were saying to me just now were meant for someone else. I think they were meant for—'

'No, Conrad, no.'

'Liar.'

'You're wrong.'

'Am I? Convince me.'

He stood up, folded his arms and waited. How could she do it? How could she make this man believe she desired him when her head was full of fear for another? *Go to him. Make him believe you. Now, now.* But then she saw a curl to his lip and knew that whatever she did, however hard she tried, it was already too late.

He knows.

But that didn't mean she was beaten. She leant back, tilted her head to one side and adopted an altogether new tone, cool and aloof.

'I'm sorry if I offended you. But I can't imagine it matters much to you who a woman is thinking of when you take her.

What matters is that Isaakios is weak and Alexios Branas is not.'

But he shook his head.

'You don't understand, do you, Agnes? Weak? I know he's weak. But he's also the man who killed the bastard who murdered my brother, and I swore to serve him. We call it fealty back home. I don't know what the fuck you call it here. You probably don't know the meaning of the word.'

He was already shouting for the guards.

'Escort the sebastê Agnes to the women's quarters. Place her in the care of my wife and no one else. Set a triple guard. No one is to go in or out without my word. Understood?'

The guards nodded.

'Why don't you just tell Isaakios now?' she hissed.

He leant in close.

'Why? In case Branas wins tomorrow. Make sure the general treats me right and if – *if* – his son's still alive, I might just not tell him about our . . . what would you call it? Our encounter?'

He smiled, and she hated him.

'He will win. He *will.*'

'You'd better hope so, Agnes. You'd better bloody hope so.'

It was a hot day, and the room reeked. Nobody was allowed to leave, even to go to the latrines. Instead, a row of chamber pots stood in a closet.

A few women had tried to object, but Dora said that orders were orders, and Euphrosunê snapped that it was for their own good. They'd be much better off together if Branas won.

'If you all go wandering about all over the place, you'll get picked up by one of the general's overenthusiastic underlings. And that's never much fun for the women concerned – or so I've heard.'

Nobody complained any more after that, but there was

plenty of weeping to make up for it. They knew it was all over. Their moment in the sun.

Agnes sat in a corner, repeating the same words to herself over and over, a prayer, an incantation. *He's going to win. He's going to win. He's going to win.* It didn't matter what Conrad knew. He'd be dead by noon. And Branas would be emperor. And Theo would be alive. And . . . and . . . and . . .

Damn this room.

The air was stuffy. The women's fear was breaking through their scents and balms. Foreheads shone with sweat. Painted faces ran. Damp patches showed through silks.

A great stillness descended. Even the girls were listless. Nobody spoke. Nobody met anyone else's eye.

A stir.

Who heard it first? They were all listening. One door crashed in the distance, then another. Footsteps. Then a report, military, staccato. A flurry of knocks at their door. Dora rushed to open it, and the guard captain outside snapped to attention.

'Reverent Theodora. Esteemed—'

'What? What? For God's sake, what's happened?' said Dora, protocol abandoned.

'Victory. The emperor has beaten his enemies. The traitor Branas lies dead at the gates. Victory.'

Pandemonium. Shrieks, the happiest of tears, everyone embracing everyone else. Children jumping up and down, yelling their heads off. A few more sensible types shook their heads in disbelief before they realised that wasn't the most judicious response, and then they too were waving their hands in the air, their joy unbounded.

Agnes slid through the mayhem to Euphrosunê's side.

'You have to help me. I have to get out.'

'Now?'

'I failed with Conrad. And he *knows.*'

'About . . . ?'

'Me and Theo.'

'How did the hell did he . . . ? Never mind. We'll think of—'

But it was already too late. Margit was hugging Agnes. And where Margit went, Dora followed.

'Agnes, Euphrosunê, come, come. My brother wants to receive our congratulations. Come! Our victorious emperor awaits.'

Margit was still holding her hand, running, *skipping*. Dora hurried close behind. Ranks of Varangians lined the way. An honour guard. A prisoner's escort.

They spilled into the throne room.

'If you can't get out, you can save yourself another way,' whispered Euphrosunê. 'Beg and plead. Can you do that? Name names. Name who you like. You're a beautiful woman. Isaakios will want to spare you. You can do it. You can save yourself.'

Agnes was nodding. Yes, she could, couldn't she? She'd done worse, hadn't she? Much worse.

Raucous cheers heralded the emperor's approach. Isaakios strode into the hall, his hair standing on end, his face puce, his eyes shining. He opened his arms wide and his mouth split into a grin.

'God truly loves me,' he roared.

And there was Conrad, yelling incoherently, blood on his hands, battle lust still clouding his eyes, a sack swinging from his shield hand.

'Victory,' he bellowed.

He held the sack aloft, shook it open and something tumbled to the ground. Before Agnes could see what it was, soldiers crowded round, kicking it like a rat in a storeroom. Conrad took aim with his boot, and the thing, whatever it was, landed with a dull thump at her feet.

She looked down.

A head.

Branas's head.

She was screaming before she could stop herself, screaming

331

before she even knew it was her. She clamped a hand over her mouth and the sound ceased. But she couldn't stop her tears falling. She couldn't stop her body shaking. The women nearest her backed away, as if her loss of control might be contagious.

Into the sudden silence, a gong sounded.

'The feast! The feast is ready!'

The fighters, slapping backs, shedding armour, hurried away, the women following in their wake. Wives found husbands; daughters hugged fathers. Other women looked left and right and, not finding who they sought, became frantic, grabbing anyone they knew, begging for answers. Eunuchs were making their way into the hall, against the flow. Gently they removed the most hysterical women; firmly they ordered servants to start mopping up the blood; sorrowfully they mourned the metamorphosis of the staid chamber into a barbarian bacchanal.

Agnes tried to lose herself in the melee, but a hand landed on her shoulder. She turned and found herself face to face with Isaakios and Conrad.

'The sight of the traitor's head saddened you, my dear?'

'It shocked me. That is all. Basileus.'

'Womanish vapours, is it?'

'Yes, basileus.'

Beside him, Conrad laughed. Followed by Isaakios. Nasty laughs, and she knew at once that they had spoken. Out of the corner of her eye she saw Dora hurrying towards them. Agnes did not look at her. She did not look at Conrad. She had eyes only for Isaakios.

'Vapours. That is all?'

'Yes, basileus.'

'My brother Conrad assures me otherwise.'

She made herself kneel. She made herself press her head to the floor. She made herself kiss the mud-encrusted toes of his boots.

'He was mistaken, basileus. I rejoice in your victory over the empire's enemies.'

'I love beautiful women kissing my feet as much as the next man, but I am inclined to believe the man who saved my throne rather than . . . What are you? A traitor, it appears. Conrad says you tried to turn him. He says you were very . . . persuasive.'

Dora descended like a gull diving towards a smashed-open crab, her mouth rounded into an O of disgust and delight.

'Death, brother,' she shrieked. 'She must be put to death.'

'No!' Agnes cried.

'Oh, I don't think we need to kill you, Agnes,' said Isaakios, patting her. 'My sister's sweet nature, I am sure, will lead her to beg for clemency once she gets over her shock.'

Dora simpered. 'But of course, brother.'

'For myself, I have no desire to – ah – emulate my unworthy predecessor. Chop, chop. Slash, slash. No. We'll have none of that. So you lost your heart, eh? Greater power at work? Eros, potent force, so on and so forth? I am moved. I shall be lenient. Not death, no, but the convent, yes?'

Agnes closed her eyes to stop her head spinning. *A life immured.* She'd escaped that fate once before. *Dear God, let me escape it again.* And as if in answer to her prayer, she saw something take shape in Isaakios's eyes.

'But perhaps I have a better idea,' he said. 'Give it a kick, there's a good girl. Show me what you think of traitors.'

Had she heard him right? She had. He winked at the head at their feet.

'That's right, Agnes. Don't mind your pretty slippers. Just give it a nice good kick. One little kick for me, and then we can all go and enjoy ourselves.'

Could she do it? Of course she could do it. He was dead. The thing at her feet, that wasn't him. It would be easy.

To one side, almost out of sight, she felt rather than heard an impatient movement. It was Euphrosunê. *Do it.* That was what she'd be thinking. *Do it.* Behind Isaakios, Conrad grinned at her and shrugged. *Do it.* Isaakios smiled encouragingly. *Do it.*

'No,' she said. 'I won't.'

A flicker ran across his face. She'd surprised him. A new feeling buoyed her spirits. Pride. It was a good moment, but it didn't last long. The jocular Isaakios had gone. In his place was an emperor defied.

'Take her away,' he snapped to his guards.

Two of them seized her arms and she started to struggle.

'Oh dear, oh dear, oh dear,' Isaakios said. 'Why not go with your dignity intact? After all, it's all you have left.'

Afterwards

Theo woke, and knew not where he was. He started to lift his head, but that made the pain come and his eyesight splinter, so he flopped back and stared at the ceiling of the . . . what was it? Not a house, no, nor a tent. A hut, a mud-and-wood shack, but different from the one he remembered, the one where his father had knelt by the side of his bed and prayed as if one of them were dying.

Father. The word escaped his mouth as a gasp.

He heard soft footsteps and saw a woman peering down at him. She vanished, and was replaced by two more faces, men he knew, men he remembered fighting alongside. But what their names were and why they had fought, that he could not remember.

'You're awake,' said one.

He tried to muster a *yes*, but all he managed to do was nod and blink and groan.

'Lie still,' said the other. 'You're weak. Anna, bring him some water.'

Anna. Empress Anna. My Agnes. My . . .

But the man only meant the woman with the brown plaits and the pale moon face.

'Our sister, she's been looking after you. We'd given up on you. Not her, though. She doesn't like to see things die. She used to cry over dead fish, and still would if our father hadn't beaten it out of her.'

The woman touched his forehead.

'Do you think you could drink a little broth?'

Without waiting for a reply, she slipped a hand under his head and tilted his mouth towards a wooden bowl. He managed two, three swallows and felt something warm, something very like life, seeping through his limbs.

'Rest now,' she said. 'God has spared you.'

The next time he woke, he found that despite a dizziness dancing like needles inside his skull, he could push himself up. He patted his body and found his belly swathed in bandaging. Suddenly, he remembered a bolt, Conrad's bolt. He'd watched it disappear, a moment out of time, and then the world had fled.

He fingered the edge of the dressing, both wondering and fearing what lay beneath, working it down to reveal a warped hollow, pink-rimmed, the skin twisted in strange whorls like the bark of a tree.

'You've been very lucky.' The woman had entered the hut, carrying a basket.

'And you've been very skilful.' His voice worked. It croaked, but it was there. 'My father will reward you handsomely.'

Her basket missed the edge of the table and rolled on to the floor.

'I'll get my brothers, sebastos,' she said, making for the door.

'Why?' he said, kicking his legs free of the blankets and trying to swing his feet on to the floor.

'Don't move,' she said, starting towards him. 'You mustn't . . .'

But he was no longer trying to move. His eyes were fixed on the basket – or rather, its contents, which were now on the floor. Three pomegranates. They were scrawny, mottled, sorry things – but they were fresh. He could see where the stalks had been broken. The battle had been in late summer. Nobody could make a pomegranate ripen before the feast day of the Theotokos – at the start of October.

'How long . . . ?' he whispered.

'A moon's turn,' she replied. 'A little more. A long time.'

'My father . . . ?'

She shook her head.

'How?'

'A battle before the City walls. After you were wounded. They say Conrad cut him down.'

'It's not true.' He was shouting, and she was trying to tell him not to. 'Why are you lying?' A black shadow raced up in front of his eyes and the dirt floor lurched. The woman – Anna – started towards him and eased him back on to the bed. He turned his head away from her and stared at the wall.

He lay still as the room darkened, listening to her coming and going. She placed a bowl by his side. He ignored it, as he tried to ignore her brothers – he remembered their names now: Petros and Andreas – when they squatted next to him.

'You're not the only one who's suffered, mister. Your father's dead, that's true enough. But you want to know what happened after?'

While Petros was talking, Andreas gripped Theo's shoulders and rolled him over to face them.

'Conrad didn't like losing to us, so he came back and torched our villages. Some of us put to sea in time. The rest, well, if they didn't burn alive, Conrad's men hacked them to pieces.'

Andreas took over.

'See this place?' He jabbed a thumb upwards at the shack. 'We built it again. From the ground. You lost your father? Well, my uncle lost three sons. The youngest a boy of eight. So—' his voice hardened '—pray be so kind, sebastos, as not to lie there feeling so fucking sorry for yourself.'

'You could have left me to burn . . .' Theo felt ashamed. 'I don't know how I can repay you.'

'Some gold wouldn't go amiss,' said Andreas with a sudden grin.

'Aye, gold and Conrad's head.'

'We can kick it along the shore like he did to your—'

'Andreas—' his sister tried to hush him '—don't.'

337

'Don't what?' Theo demanded.

Andreas looked abashed.

'What?' Theo repeated.

His brother shrugged. 'It's ugly, but he may as well hear it from us as anyone. There's not a man in the City as doesn't know.'

And Theo listened, hearing and not hearing, while Petros told him what had happened. How everyone – from the highest-born aristo to the lowliest kitchen boy – had laughed and clapped and cheered.

Agnes was so hungry that it was hard to think of anything else. The relentless, nagging, gnawing pain was meant to bring her closer to God, but her head was too full of food to think much about Him. Instead, she thought about the next meal, even though each one – and there was but one a day – was as disappointing as the last.

Water, soft beans, greenstuff, cabbage. No salt. No spice. No meat. No milk. That was all they seemed to eat – if they ate at all. Every other day brought an excuse to fast. The others were delighted. They took tiny sips of water with rapture in their eyes, bliss on their lips, while Agnes dreamt of partridge baked in spikenard and cinnamon and watched her breasts fade away.

The nuns were not cruel to her – as companions, they were in many ways preferable to Dora and Margit – but they were nothing if not single-minded. They loved God and God loved the emperor and the emperor had told them to watch over a sinful woman. *Keep her close. Keep her obedient.* And they were pleased to do as the emperor bid.

The abbess, Helenê, was a tall woman, thin to the point of emaciation. The novices loved to speculate about her past, some claiming that she was Manuelos's love-child, others just as sure that she'd been found swaddled in an apron on the steps of the Holy Wisdom. She had a crisp voice, a cool manner, and although she did nothing to comfort Agnes when the boatmen pushed her, almost hysterical, on to the island, neither did she hector or gloat.

'Submit to God's will,' was all she said. 'You will find peace.'

But Agnes knew something Helenê didn't. She didn't need to find peace, because Theo was going to come and save her. She had to be patient, to play along for a month or two, and then she was going to be free.

Theo entered the City and made for home.

Anna had only reluctantly agreed that he was fit enough to leave, and he'd sensed she didn't want him to go, but it was clearer still that her brothers were keen to be rid of him. They gave him a parcel of dried fish, and he swore he'd return with gold.

With his father dead, Theo knew there was every chance Isaakios had confiscated the house and exiled his mother, so he approached warily, at dusk, and was not surprised to find the windows dark and the gates barred.

Nevertheless, he crept round the back to where a few rough patches in the brickwork offered good handholds and levered himself on top of the wall. His mother's cherry trees grew close enough for a lucky jump to land him on one of the larger branches. He'd crept home this way dozens of times as a boy, but it was harder with an aching middle and wasted limbs, and he was relieved to make it to the ground unscathed.

The door into the kitchen was open.

At that hour, woodsmoke, food smells and the calls of the cooks should have filled the evening air, but all was still. He peered inside. A small fire flickered in the hearth, which in the past had housed a blaze big enough to feed fifty men, and in front of it sat a woman on a chair, dozing.

At the sound of his feet on the stone floor, she started awake and slapped a hand over her mouth to stifle a scream.

'Master Theo!'

Agathê ran to embrace him, stopping a couple of paces short when she remembered he was a man grown, not the little boy she'd helped bring into the world.

'We thought you were dead. I thought your ghost had come to me in my dreams.'

He laughed.

'I know I look bad, but I'm real all right – and you, you're here. I can't tell you – I'm so happy to find you. Let's go and tell my mother. No, better, you go first. I don't want to terrify her as well.'

And then Agathê did embrace him. She wrapped her arms full about him and held on tight. By the time she spoke, he already knew what she was going to say.

'My mistress . . . your mother is dead. I'm sorry. I'm so sorry.'

'They killed her. How could they kill her?'

'No, they didn't. Not that.'

'Then how?'

Agathê shook her head. 'I cannot . . .'

'Speak.'

She took his hand to give herself strength – maybe to give him strength, he didn't know.

'After the battle, after your father . . . she was summoned to the palace. She went, and there in that hall where they were all feasting, stupid with wine, Conrad showed her, he made her look at . . .'

'My father's head.'

Agathê nodded.

'She didn't cry, not her. She came back home and told me what had happened, what that man had done, and asked me to leave her alone awhile – and God forgive me, I did. I sat down here and wept all the tears I thought she couldn't weep. It was only towards the middle night that I thought to take her a little wine, some food.'

Tears were rolling down her cheeks.

'I . . . I found her in the corner of her chamber. She'd opened her veins. She'd placed a bowl underneath – to catch the blood. But there was too much. She was soaked in it . . .'

She stopped and stared at Theo, aghast.

'I shouldn't be telling you this.'

'No, you should. A man should know how his mother died.' His throat was pinched tight. 'I'll kill him. I'll kill him.'

Theo hadn't come.

Agnes began to fear that something had happened to him. Not that he was dead. Never that. But maybe he was trapped . . . helpless . . . in need. Whatever the reason, it was obvious he couldn't get to her, so instead she would have to go to him. It was simple. She would escape.

She'd noticed that on washing days, the fishermen from the neighbouring islands let their boats drift close to shore to tease the girls and make them scream and scatter. She volunteered for laundry duty, to approving nods and knowing smiles from the abbess and her acolytes.

They think I'm becoming one of them.

She was laying bed linen to dry on some boulders on the southern shore of the island, weighing down the corners with rocks, and waiting for her chance. Her hands were raw from scrubbing, her back ached from bending over the tub, and everything itched.

But none of that mattered, because the fishing boats were idling closer and closer. If the fish were biting, the fishermen didn't bother the girls, but the day was obviously slow. They came within a dozen boat lengths of the shore and one of them, young enough to have no beard and handsome enough for some of the novices to be peeking at him, stood up in the prow and started crooning a comically mournful love song.

The girls squealed and darted for the trees, and Agnes, without giving herself time to think, flung herself into the water. It was deeper than she'd expected – already up to her chest – but she started wading towards the men.

'Save me! I beg you! Save me!'

When they got over their astonishment, the men started to cheer her on, whooping, whistling and – crucially – paddling their boat towards her. *It's going to work. It's going to work.* Behind her, she could hear the other girls shrieking for help, but she didn't turn round. She was floundering, the water was nearly up to her neck, her robes were tangling her feet, yet the nearest boat was only three paces away . . .

But then the expression on the men's faces changed, and from the shore behind her she heard the unmistakable voice of the abbess telling the fishermen about the exquisite punishments God had in store for them if they did not put out to sea *that instant*. They looked at each other. This game wasn't worth God's wrath. Already they were turning their boat, gathering way. She plunged onwards.

'Come back! Come back!'

She opened her mouth to call again, but as she stepped, the ground disappeared and water flooded into her mouth. Her feet couldn't find the bottom. She spluttered and panicked. Her legs kicked, her arms flailed as she tried to keep her head above water, but her dress was sucking her under.

She took a gulp of air before the sea closed over her head and she sank, sank . . . There, there was the bottom. She pushed as hard as she could and bobbed up again. More air. She thrashed her arms, but it was no good. She was sinking, sinking. Her strength was draining. Stupid clothes. Stupid plan. Stupid, stupid . . .

And then somebody was trying to get a grip under her shoulders.

'Still, be still.'

She fought, but the woman was determined. She had an arm round Agnes and was hauling her back on to the rocks. Agnes coughed, choking, sobbing, struggling to be free. She got the water out of her eyes and looked up to find the abbess pulling her habit back on over her dripping underclothes. Dozens of other nuns were watching, open-mouthed.

'And what do you think you're staring at? Get back to work.'

Helenê turned to Agnes, who was still sitting on the ground, curled into a ball of cold misery.

'Is drowning so preferable to life here with us?'

Agnes didn't answer. Her teeth were chattering too furiously to speak, even if she'd had anything to say.

'God has given you a wonderful chance, Agnes. In time you will learn to thank Him for bringing you to this island.'

'N-never.' Agnes forced the word out. 'Never.'

The abbess smiled.

'Never is a very long time – longer than ten years, longer than twenty, longer than a lifetime. Do not say never when you do not understand what the word means.'

She leant down and pulled Agnes to her feet.

'But I will do what I can to help you.'

The abbess locked her in a small solitary cell, letting her out once a day for prayers.

Theo gravitated towards the cramped quarters by the docks, like so many others whose homes were lost or far away. If he'd expected anyone to ask questions, he was mistaken. With his pinched cheeks, patched clothes and limping walk, he was one of them.

Unlike the others, though, he had money. His mother's strongbox was still in its hiding place in the storeroom, although the scent of mastic and aniseed, her favourites, that lingered in the musty air had been indescribably painful.

He had money, and he had a plan. It was simple, like all the best plans. *Kill Conrad. Get Agnes.* It had to be in that order, because once he'd got her out of the palace, they'd have to leave the City. He could live incognito in half a cupboard above a phouskarion, a cheap drinking shop that reeked of sweat, sour wine and sex – but she couldn't.

But how to get to Conrad?

He was sitting on a rotting stool in the phouskaria, ploughing through a plate of fried fish-and-pepper, licking the hot fat off his fingers, trying simultaneously to come up with the answer and block out the greasy patron's conversation with the whoremaster next door.

Three times he'd glimpsed him – on horseback, shielded from the crowds by ranks of guards, a demigod trotting past. What made it worse was knowing that Agnes would be sitting in one of the covered sedans that followed in the men's wake. Once he'd even thought he'd seen the contours of her face as the drapes fluttered briefly aside, but he couldn't be sure.

It'd be easy to get her away. A message. A rendezvous. Two horses saddled, the walls receding behind them, the open road to the west. No. He mustn't think about that. Not yet. He had a job to do first.

On the streets, Conrad was untouchable, but how was Theo, a man with a price on his head, ever going to get inside the palace? Offer himself for hire as a servant? Enlist in the guards? It would never work. Too many people knew him. Pay someone else to kill Conrad? But who could he trust? And besides, he wanted to do it himself.

He finished his fish and was about to call for some more of the revolting wine when his ears started to listen to what the whoremaster was saying.

'Oh, he's one of our best customers. Likes the western type. Pink and fair.'

'Homesick?' said the barman.

'You bet.'

'His brother was the same, didn't you say?'

A chuckle.

'Yes, terrified his wife would find out. This one's being more careful, though. We used to bring them up to the palace, but he doesn't want that no more.'

Theo had heard enough to give him hope. He lay in wait for one, two nights, and on the third, an evening so hot and close and heavy that it seemed the sky could not hold one more drop of rain, he saw him.

Conrad.

A dozen guards accompanied him, but when Conrad entered the brothel, they loitered outside. Nor were they interested in Theo as he hobbled round the back of the house, mumbling to himself in singsong Greek, his sword hidden beneath his cloak.

The tenements were built so close that Theo could wedge himself between the outer walls, clamber up and drop through a second-storey window. He found himself at one end of a narrow corridor, the ceiling too low for him to be able to stand straight. Doors led off to the left and right, and at the far end he could make out an old woman dozing over her spindle, a single candle guttering on a table in front of her.

Now all he had to do was keep out of sight and pray that Conrad didn't fuck in silence.

He wasn't disappointed.

Two girls entered one of the rooms, and before long he heard giggling and guffawing, followed by a blast of bellowing and finally a few triumphant shouts. After a polite pause, the girls stumbled out, grinning, but their faces changed once the door closed behind them. One stopped to shake the old woman awake.

'He wants wine. And bread and a goose egg, he says. And to be left to sleep for an hour. Then he wants two more girls before sun-up.'

The woman told them to tidy themselves – they each had another customer waiting.

When a serving boy stumbled up with the food, the woman was already snoring again, so it wasn't hard for Theo to clap a hand over his mouth and drag him into an empty room. The boy's eyes widened in panic as Theo held a dagger to his throat, but all Theo did was put a finger to his lips and press two coins into his hand. The boy made no sound as Theo bound and gagged him.

He tapped on the door to Conrad's room, waited for a grunt, opened it and walked inside. Conrad was sprawled naked on the bed, sheets draped across his chest, blankets rucked about his feet, eyes closed, one hand idly scratching at the hair around his cock – which was still half up.

'Leave it there and get out.'

Theo walked towards the bed, set the tray down and gently placed the tip of his sword against Conrad's neck. At first the man smiled.

'Back for more, sweetheart?'

'That's right. I want everything you've got.'

Conrad's eyes snapped open, his elbows dug into the bed, ready to push himself up, but Theo let the point sink into his skin. Blood blossomed on his neck and Conrad lay still.

'Who are you?'

'The son of a man you killed.'

'I've killed many.'

'None like my father,' Theo said, and shrugged his hood back.

'Theodore Branas. I hoped I'd killed you too.'

Theo pushed the sword in a little further and Conrad winced and pressed backwards into the pillows.

'All right. I get it. He's dead, and you're angry. But it was a fair fight. We met in battle and I won because I'm half his age and a fucking good fighter. Cutting my throat isn't going to make you feel any better.'

'Yes it will. A lot better.'

'This is a coward's trick. But I shouldn't expect anything else from the son of a filthy Greek traitor.'

The words caught Theo like a blow and his concentration wavered. It was what Conrad was waiting for. He rolled halfway off the bed, but Theo recovered in time to flick his dagger out from his belt and into Conrad's left shoulder. The big man crumpled on the bed.

'Wait,' Conrad gasped. 'Isn't there something you've forgotten to ask me?'

'What could I possibly want from you?' said Theo, drawing his sword back for the kill.

'Where's Agnes? Ask me that.'

Theo froze.

'I don't need to ask you that. She's in the palace.'

'You're wrong, my friend. She's not in the palace. She's not even in the City. Nobody knows where she is. Nobody except the emperor and me. And he's not going to tell you, is he?'

'All right, where is she?'

'Why do you want to know?' said Conrad.

'I . . . That does not concern you.' Even as he said it, he knew he sounded prim and foolish. Knew what was more that even though he was the one with the sword in his hand, he was being played like a fish.

Conrad smiled.

'Ah. So I was right.'

'About what?'

He was wriggling, squirming, a stupid fish on a hook.

'About something she said to me. Something about you.'

'Don't lie. She never spoke to you.'

'Didn't she? She lived in the palace. You didn't. You've no idea who she spoke to.'

Theo flinched. He was right. He didn't. He didn't know anything. Conrad sat up, and for some reason Theo forgot to jab his sword to make him lie back down again.

'She told me there was a man who bothered her. A man who followed her about like a puppy. She never said who it was, but we used to laugh about him together. *My faithful little puppy.*'

'You're lying.'

347

'Am I?' His eyes sparkled. 'Poor Agnes. My wife found out about us and Isaakios sent her packing. She's in a convent. Kill me and you'll never know where. Let me go and I could tell you. Or perhaps I might visit her myself. She'd like that. I'll tell her that her faithful puppy came whining—'

Theo's anger boiled over. He roared and lunged with his sword, but it was a wild stroke that skewered the mattress a heartbeat after Conrad tumbled clear. By the time Theo had freed his sword and spun round for another stroke, Conrad was at the door.

'Guards!' he yelled, shoving the door with his back without taking his eyes off Theo.

'You're lying.' Theo took a couple of steps towards him. 'Tell me you're lying.'

'And pretend I've not tasted her sweet little . . .' Whatever he saw on Theo's face made him shout with laughter. 'You've not even had her, have you? Not once. Fucking priceless. You want my advice? Leave her to it. She's not worth it. She's a hungry, ambitious, wild little—'

Theo lunged again, but Conrad disappeared backwards through the door and was replaced by half a dozen Varangians. Theo swore, but at least he was no longer paralysed. It was easier to fight men you did not hate.

So long as he kept them at the door, they could only fight one to one. And the corridor was tight – too tight for them to swing their axes. His sword darting back and forth was a better weapon. Pity he'd left his dagger in Conrad's shoulder.

Hooves, snorts – he heard at least two riders thunder away down the street. They'd bring more men. They'd surround the house. They'd have him. For a moment, he didn't care. He could go down fighting. That was what should have happened. He should have been with his father before the City gates and died right there by his side. A good death, doing what was right, believing that the woman he loved loved him.

No.

If he died, Conrad lived. And Conrad had to pay.

There was a window behind him. He had no idea what lay beneath it, but he was only one floor up, so he decided to risk it. He felled the guard at the doorway, and before the next one could take the dead man's place, he ran full tilt at the shutters. They shattered, and he burst out into the night.

When the abbess released Agnes from her cell, autumn was giving way to winter. She gave her a hoe and told her to turn the melon patch before the frosts came. It was a lonely spot at the edge of the kitchen gardens, near where the island fell away sheer into the sea.

Agnes dug all morning and was glad of the work. It meant she didn't have to think. The bell calling them to the midday prayers came quickly and she leant briefly on the hoe, wiping her forehead with her sleeve.

A ship had sailed round the point and was dropping anchor off the island, probably planning to wait for a fair wind. Agnes looked at the water, the cold waves lapping, and knew that to jump would be death.

She was about to follow the others to the chapel when something made her look back.

A splash of red, a man in the rigging.

Theo?

She told herself she was imagining things, her mind playing tricks. It couldn't be him. She went and prayed and ate, and when she returned for the afternoon shift, the boat was gone.

Lying on her pallet that night, looking at the moon, listening to the sounds of the other women sleeping around her, she knew it was a sign.

He's dead. Dead.

She pulled her thin blanket further up under her chin and shivered. As she shut her eyes, two tears rolled away down her cheeks.

The winter of 1194

Snow lay thin on the ground, little more than a frost in truth. On the road it had already, even at that early hour, been trodden into the mud and the rest would vanish as soon as the sun cleared the City walls. The sky was a delicate blue, promising a perfect midwinter day, something to treasure amongst the months of fog and freezing rain.

Even though his boots were holed and his clothes far too thin for a City winter, Theo might have been able to savour it. He did still find himself enjoying simple things – warm bread, say, or an unexpected kindness. But his father had died within a hundred paces of where he stood. Somewhere near here, seven years ago, Conrad had cut Alexios Branas down and sawn his head from his body.

And now Theo had heard that Conrad was dead, butchered by Assassins in Tyre, the victim of some impenetrable Latin quarrel. Despite himself, he laughed. What else could he do?

Seven years he had waited to hear that news. Seven wasted years.

After Theo had missed his chance in the brothel by the docks, Conrad became even more elusive, rarely setting foot outside the palace walls. Scarcely a month later, word spread through the City that he had skipped town, leaving behind a hysterical wife and a troubled brother-in-law.

The scurrilous claimed he was tired out servicing Dora's insatiable demands. The generous suggested that he'd had word of the western kings' determination to wrest the Holy

Land back from Saladin and was honour bound to join them. Theo even heard a few men guess that Conrad feared vengeance from friends of Alexios Branas.

It made no difference to Theo why he'd left. All he knew was that if Conrad had gone, he would follow. It mattered little whether he took his vengeance on the City streets or in some desert in the south.

The days, months and years that followed folded into one – the noxious inns, the mangy camels, the lice and fleas, the stink of the Frankish troops, the dusty rivers, the baked walls of war-struck towns. He'd as soon remember none of it. He wished he'd come home sooner. But whenever he'd thought of taking ship for the City, he'd pictured himself reflected in Conrad's eyes and heard himself saying, *that's for my father, that's for Alexios Branas,* as he opened up his guts.

Twice he'd got close. Twice he'd thought Conrad was his.

The first time was at the siege of Acre, but he caught a wasting plague and lost months and all his money in the care of the Knights of St John. The second was after Acre was won, but a bull-headed Flemish sergeant picked a fight with him. The man died, and Theo walked away with what he thought was only a scratch on his hand, but it turned bad and he'd raved for weeks in a tent full of other dying men. He lived, but lost more than time – the tips of two fingers on his left hand rotted away.

When he was strong enough to stand, the men who'd cared for him suggested he take a walk down to the mill-pool to bathe.

He'd stood over the still waters and seen himself. Truly seen himself. He looked malnourished, shifty, rackety, almost rat-like. He looked like a man who would be easy to rob if you thought there was half a chance he'd anything valuable on him. He looked like that because that was who he had become. A chancer who'd steal to stay alive. A mercenary who'd fight and not care why so long as he was paid enough to keep moving.

Suddenly, Theo had known that he no longer wanted to be that man. No vengeance was worth it. He would go home to the City. He did not know what he might find there, but he knew it was the only place where he could hope to salvage some last scraps of honour.

And so now he knelt and prayed on the cold ground that seven years ago had been a battlefield. It was the closest his father had to a tomb.

He sprang up and turned round, certain he was being watched – if there was one thing he had acquired, it was a sense of self-preservation.

He was right. He counted a score of armed men on horseback, not City guards, certainly not Varangians, but not bandits either. He lifted one hand in a weary sort of greeting, and didn't even bother to draw his sword. With odds of twenty to one, he wasn't going to beat them, nor outrun them on foot. Besides, if they'd wanted to kill him, they'd have probably done it already.

Agnes was turning the melon patch.

She'd left it a bit late that year and the ground was already hard. She hacked and jabbed at it as best she could, but she had to admit she wasn't making a very good job of it. She stopped to take a drink of water before returning to the fray.

How many times had she done this? Six, maybe? Was this really the seventh?

She winced as she remembered the first year, when she had still been so unbearably sad. The next couple of years she'd squandered in a rage, blaming everything she could think of – reserving her scorn for herself until last. That hadn't been fun. By the fourth year, she'd probably accepted that this island was going to be her lot. She could remember the fifth year clearly. She'd spent the day in a sort of daze of bewildered nostalgia. Had that really been *her* life? It seemed impossible.

Last year she'd started thinking that maybe the abbess was

right after all. Her life had probably turned out for the best. Every seed she planted, every pot she scrubbed, every country girl she taught to read the Bible made her fear God less, made her less afraid of dying, and as a consequence she slept extremely well.

'Agnes!'

She looked up, and to her surprise saw the abbess striding towards her, swaddled against the chill.

'I've come to say goodbye,' she said.

'Oh,' said Agnes. 'I'm sorry.' And she *was* sorry. 'Where are you going?'

'I'm not going anywhere. But you are. There's somebody waiting for you down at the boat dock.'

'Who?'

But the abbess shook her head. That question belonged to the outside world, not to hers. She nodded towards the melon patch.

'Would you mind asking somebody to finish off here before you go?'

'It's all right,' said Agnes. 'I'll do it.'

The abbess smiled and touched her cheek. Her fingers were surprisingly warm. 'God go with you, my child.'

When she was done, Agnes washed the earth from her hands and from her feet, said a few disorientating goodbyes, and followed the rutted track to the landing stage. She knew how she ought to be feeling. Exultant. Vindicated. *Free.* Instead, she felt bewildered and bereft, like a child who's been told its mother is too busy to see it before bed.

Her pace slowed further as she approached the shore. She could make out the boat – not grand, not the opposite of grand – that was waiting for her. Waves gulped and slapped. The captain caught sight of her and leant down to tell whoever was sitting in the shelter at the stern.

A strange woman emerged. No, not strange. She only looked strange because she was plump and made up and wearing the finest of clothes. Agnes drew closer and saw a pair of pale brown eyes she had once known well.

'Sorry I took so long,' said the thin mouth. 'I have a little proposition for you.' She patted the seat beside her. 'Hop in. We can talk on the way.'

Late in the afternoon, the men reined in before a small summer palace, not far from the water's edge. It was shuttered, a place for idle warmth, not winter. The shadow of the high walls had kept the snow on the ground here, and Theo saw two sets of footprints – slender boots, women's footprints – leading from the gates, through a courtyard and into a room off a colonnade.

He glanced at the man beside him, wondering whether he was going to get an explanation now.

'Who's in there, then?'

'Search me. We just were told to bring you here. In you go, mate.'

Theo pushed the door open. Although a fire sputtered in the grate, the room was still cold. The logs weren't as dry as they should be, and the air was smoky, musty. A few pieces of furniture, handsomely carved, stood in a haphazard circle, as though they'd only just been dragged out of storage.

One woman only could he see, heavily veiled in clothes so neutral it was hard to tell whether she was young or old, rich or poor. She stood.

'Greetings, Theodore Branas. Welcome home. It's been a long time.'

'I know you, don't I?'

'You do.'

She drew aside her veil and the sharp eyes of the emperor's sister-in-law were upon him.

'Euphrosunê Angelina,' he said. And then, 'How the hell did you find me?'

'The emperor's security detail was on to you, Theodore. They'd noticed a man taking too keen an interest in Isaakios whenever he appeared in public. Careless. You've only been back, what, a month?'

'Two.'

'Two, then. You're lucky that the fellow who recognised you is in my pay, not Isaakios's. I've had him follow you. He said you're a bit down on your luck.'

Theo frowned.

'Tell me something I don't know – like what you want with me.'

'I don't want you dead, if that's what you're wondering. I want nothing you won't be glad to give.'

'You know nothing about what I want.'

'Don't I? Do you want Isaakios to remain emperor?'

He looked at her. Why lie?

'No. No, I don't.'

'And neither do I,' she replied. 'Dead or exiled or imprisoned, it makes little difference to me. But believe me, I mean to have him off the throne before the year is out.'

'You are very sure of yourself.'

'I have reason to be. This has been long enough in the planning.'

There was a quiet conviction about her manner that he couldn't help liking. No flash or bluster. Methodical.

'Why?' he asked.

'You need to ask?'

'I've been away a long time.'

'You have. People will be surprised to find you alive. What have you been—?'

But Theo shook his head. 'We were talking about Isaakios.'

'Very well. Isaakios, then. He is not a bad man – or not as bad as some – but he is a terrible ruler. Catastrophic. We are losing the western empire. Some say it is already lost. A poor soldier – and a worse diplomat. His dealings with Barbarossa brought nothing but shame on the empire. It cannot continue.'

There was a knock at the door and a servant entered carrying a tray, cups and a jug of something spiced and warming. There was fresh bread too, and meat. Theo tried to keep the hunger from his eyes, but he was unused to food like this, made at leisure by well-fed servants. Euphrosunê nodded at the table.

'Eat. Please, you are after all my guest.'

Theo compromised and poured himself a cup to drink. He would not be able to speak the truth with her food in his stomach.

'And who is to replace him?'

She gave him an even smile.

'Why, my husband, of course.'

'*Of course*. It's always the same story, isn't it? It's always for the good of the empire. Why can't you be honest? Why can't you say you want power and be done with it?'

If he'd hoped to provoke her, he was disappointed.

'Power is a manifold thing, Theo. Who can ever truly say where it lies? I am not so vain nor so foolish as to imagine my husband will make a perfect emperor. But he will be better than Isaakios. He has the right name, the right manner, the right bearing. Let him sit upon the throne. And let the best men of the empire – united in their purpose – run things as they need to be run.'

'With you pulling the strings.'

'My friends do not like to think they have strings. Still less that a woman might be capable of pulling them.'

'And who are these friends?'

'George Palaiologos, John Petraliphas, Constantinos Raoul, Manuelos Kantakouzenos. And they in turn speak for many others.'

Theo nodded. 'I'm impressed.'

'Exactly. The chief families are all agreed. No loose ends. No resentment. No mess.'

'What about the Doukai?'

'We have them too. Your old friend Murzuphlus is one of my staurchest allies.'

'He's not my friend. He's a slippery bastard who should have come out of the City and fought for my father.'

'He didn't take arms against him, did he?'

'That's almost worse.'

'He's prudent, Theo. Prudence can be a great virtue.'

She waved a hand, dismissing Murzuphlus for the time being.

'So, what do you say? Will you join us?'

She raised one eyebrow, sure of herself.

'Why do you want me?'

'You want me to talk sweeter? I'm surprised, Theo. I didn't think that was the Branas style.'

'Why do you want me?' he repeated.

'Three reasons. First, I want nobody on the outside. Second, your name works in Thrace. Third, it works with the army. And if our plan is to work, we need the army.'

My name. You mean my father's name.

He shook his head. 'I'm not interested.'

'No?' Only the briefest thinning of her lips betrayed her irritation.

'No. This is not why I returned to the City. You say the empire is dead? Well, I say you're jackals tearing at the carcass.'

'And your father – was he one of your jackals?'

As soon as the words were out of her mouth, he could see that she regretted them.

'I'm sorry,' she said. 'Your father . . .'

'. . . is dead. Dead. I'd leave it at that if I were you.'

'But I can't, can I, Theo? He is dead and it was Isaakios who ordered him killed. If you don't want to join me for my reasons, do you at least not want revenge? I came here as your friend—'

'We have never been friends.'

'Can we at least agree I am your enemy's enemy? I am offering you revenge. Take it.'

357

'Not on your terms. The price is too high. Never again will I be another man's creature. Nor a woman's either.' He stood up. 'Enough. There are only so many ways I can say no. I beg leave to depart – unless of course I now have to listen to all the terrible things you'll do to me if I don't fall in line.'

He smiled, briefly, and found that she was smiling back at him.

'Oh, you'll hear no threats from me. I want willing friends.'

'Then let us say farewell.'

'I haven't quite finished. I have one more argument. I hope you will find it compelling.'

Theo was about to tell her to save her breath, but instead of speaking, she left the room. He heard hushed voices from the other side of the door. It creaked open.

Agnes.

He wanted to shake her and tell her that in seven years he'd never stopped hating her, never forgiven her, never forgotten how she had betrayed him.

Agnes.

He wanted to gather her in his arms and tell her that in seven years he'd never stopped loving her.

Theo.

She'd dreamt a thousand times of opening a door and finding him on the other side.

Theo.

But in her dreams he never had a face set and mean and unkind. He never threw himself on to a chair and laughed.

'What in God's name is so funny?'

Those were never the first words she'd imagined she'd speak.

'Nothing. Everything. Euphrosunê thinks you'll win me round. *You.* Go on, then. Let's hear it. Let's hear why I should play along with—'

'Stop! Stop it!' She groaned, running her hands through her hair. 'What's wrong with you?'

When Euphrosunê had said that Theo was alive, she'd refused to believe her. It was a mistake, some horrible joke. Even as she peered through the mildewed drapes, saw him cross the courtyard, still she'd doubted. And then, from one breath to the next, doubt fled and joy seized her. It *was* him. Changed, as she was changed, but alive. Only Euphrosunê's hand tight on her arm had stopped her running to him.

Not yet, Agnes. Remember what we said? Not yet.

But as she waited while they talked, that first wave of elation had retreated, revealing darker feelings. First hurt, then anger.

You're supposed to be dead. That's what she wanted to say to him now. *If you're not dead, where have you been?*

But that wasn't what she was meant to be doing. She was meant to be winning him round. That was the deal she'd struck. That was the price of her freedom. *Sweet Theo, do as Euphrosunê bids. Sweet Theo, you and you alone can save me.* But how could she talk like that to this cruel, cold stranger?

'*What's wrong with me?*' He leant back, making a big show of folding his arms, a miserable smile playing on his lips. 'You need me to tell you?'

'Yes, Theo, I do. I don't understand. How many years? Seven. Seven years. I have been . . . and yet you look as though . . .' Tears were gathering behind her eyes. 'Tell me, tell me why I have been alone in a convent. Why, Theo, why?'

'You can spend another seven there for all I care.'

'That's . . . Theo, have you gone mad? I loved you, and—'

'*Loved me.* You betrayed me.' He no longer sounded forced and distant. 'You betrayed me – with *him*. With the man who killed my father.' He was back on his feet. 'How could you, Agnes?' Shouting. 'How could you?'

A chill swept over her.

'I did it for you, Theo. For you and your—'

'So you admit it?' he said, his voice cracking with incredulity. 'You stand there and admit that you . . . and he . . .'

He began to cry – great gulping sobs. She started towards

him, on instinct. She had to comfort him, she had to explain, but he pushed her away, hard, hard enough for her to fall to the floor. And he was running, rushing for the door, and she had to stop him, or he would disappear and her life would end a second time.

'Yes, yes, I admit it,' she shouted, almost screamed, after him. 'And why shouldn't I? What I did, I did only for you.' He stopped. She'd made him stop. 'I went to Conrad and tried to persuade him to fight for your father. Where was the betrayal?'

'Where was the . . . ?' He whirled round, white and shaking. 'You and he, you . . .'

'Once, Theo! Once!' She scrambled to her feet. 'I thought it was a risk worth taking. What if it had worked? A night's work for all our futures?'

He was staring at her.

'But it wasn't a night's work, was it?'

'What do you mean? Of course it—'

'He told me that—'

'He . . . ?'

'Conrad. Conrad told me.'

'What . . .' she could hardly get the words out, 'what did Conrad tell you?'

'He told me you were lovers.'

'When did he tell you this?'

'When I tried to kill him.'

'You . . . you believed what a man told you with a sword at his throat?'

But she no longer knew how to rage and storm. Instead, she sat down and her head fell into her hands. She felt small and very, very sad.

'I understand everything now,' she said, her voice muffled. 'You believed him, and that is why you did not come.'

She looked up and realised she could hardly see him, she was crying so hard.

'It took me long enough to accept you were dead, Theo, but I did. I accepted it. But never, never once did I imagine you had forsaken me.'

She tried to wipe the tears away, but it was no use. They kept on coming.

'I've been sitting on that island, loving you, and you've been wherever the hell you've been, hating me. What a waste. What a stupid, stupid waste.'

'Agnes . . .'

A different voice, a different Theo. *Her* Theo.

'I didn't hate you. I . . . I loved you still. I hated myself. It was . . . it was my fault my father rebelled. I encouraged him. I thought if he was emperor then you and I could be happy. But I was wrong. It wasn't what he wanted. Not truly. And so he lost. Conrad struck the blow, but it was I who killed him.'

She watched his face, appalled at the pain she saw there.

'But I couldn't admit it. How could I? How could I admit that I'd killed my own father? So I lost myself in some fool's mission of revenge.'

He sat beside her, and spoke without quite looking at her.

'I'm sorry. I'm so, so sorry.'

She took his hand and held it between her own. She felt the warmth of his body close to hers.

'So am I,' she said. 'So am I.'

8 April 1195

From his hiding place, Theo saw a little group emerge from the trees by the banks of the river. *Damn.* Isaakios's son, another Alexios, the child of his first wife, was with him.

The boy looked excited to be the emperor's son, excited to be out of the City, excited to be wearing long robes and riding a man's horse. He kept touching his hand to his sword. That must be new, too. Theo tried to remember being that old – or rather that young. He'd thought his father was invincible. Did Alexios think the same about Isaakios? Probably. Boys always thought that, whatever their fathers were really like.

Theo watched Alexios – Isaakios's brother, not his boy – reach down and fiddle with his stirrup. A groom, bought off with a lifetime's supply of gold, trotted up, dropped from his horse and picked up the horse's off fore hoof. He shook his head and tutted. *Don't overdo it, for God's sake.* Alexios shrugged apologetically, clapped his brother on the shoulder and turned back to the camp.

Theo didn't have a brother – not one who'd lived beyond the cradle – so he couldn't imagine what that touch felt like. His mother had given birth to a baby boy when he was, what, seven or eight? His father had named him Manuelos. Theo remembered holding him on his lap to please them. He'd leant down and kissed the baby's brow and it had squirmed and kicked. *He likes you,* his mother said. Two weeks later a fever carried him off. What if that baby had grown to manhood? What if he had grown to hate Theo enough that one day he too might have touched his arm and ridden away, leaving other men to destroy him?

Alexios disappeared through the trees. The emperor and his boy remained on the bank with half a dozen guards. Not Varangians, Theo noted with relief. The emperor liked to leave them in the City, a guarantee that all would be well while he was gone.

The boy was pointing across the river Maritza, probably begging to be allowed to cross to where the hunting grounds lay. His father was laughing, shaking his head, telling him to be patient.

'Your uncle won't be long.' Isaakios's voice was loud enough to carry. 'He needs a new mount, and then you'll have your hunt, my boy.'

Isaakios looked happy. Was he happy?

Enjoy this moment, emperor, if you are.

The mighty roar of thousands of voices burst above the trees, fast and frantic as birds beaten from their roosts.

Alexios looked up at his father, delight and expectation on his face. He'd be guessing the hunt was a ruse. He'd be picturing a tournament, a day of games, something designed especially to please him, the son and heir. The boy turned, beaming, to the guards, waiting for them to grin and tell him all about the treat he had in store.

It was a delicate moment; the guards had not been bribed. Euphrosunê had argued that so many men could not be trusted to keep a secret. It wouldn't be disastrous if they stuck by the emperor, but it would make Theo's job harder. He needn't have worried. Before even the first wave of cheering had died down, they had turned their backs and were riding fast for the camp.

They knew what was happening, and so, Theo could see, did Isaakios.

He'd grabbed the boy's shoulders and was shouting, trying to make him ride away, trying to make him run for it. But the boy wasn't listening. He was shaking his head, bewildered.

That was when Theo rode out of the undergrowth.

'Come with me, Isaakios,' he called, 'and your son will not be harmed.'

Isaakios paused long enough for Theo to know that he recognised him, then he wheeled his horse and spurred it at the river. It snorted with surprise, but obeyed, scrabbling down the bank to a muddy patch of foreshore, where it sank up to its hocks. Isaakios's legs beat against the horse's flanks, and it edged forward into the current, a good mount, well trained.

Theo turned to the boy.

'Go back to the camp. Now. Go. You will be safe. Upon my honour, you will be safe.'

Then he plunged towards the river in pursuit. His horse was less biddable, and it baulked at the water. He had to jump off and coax it forward, swinging back into the saddle only when the water was up to his chest. Isaakios was already up the bank on the far side, about to disappear under the trees.

Theo's horse struggled against the current, and they emerged from the river fifty paces downstream, but it was plain to see where Isaakios had entered the woods, and, when Theo stilled his horse a moment, easy to hear him.

He gave chase. He could see Isaakios looking over his shoulder, again and again, his horse pulling against him, galloping out of control, so that Theo began to fear that his own horse might not be able to keep up.

But as they passed into a little clearing, where Isaakios ought to have been able to double the distance between them, Theo saw his left foot fly loose from the stirrup. With every stride, he was keeling further over to the right. He was trying to cling on to the horse's neck, its mane, but it was shaking its head, angry, and Isaakios lost his grip and tumbled to the dirt. The horse nearly came down on top of him – that would have been the end – but the animal righted itself and disappeared between the trees.

Theo reined in and jumped down.

Isaakios was lying on his back, his eyes closed, wheezing, making no attempt to sit up, let alone stand and fight.

'It's over?'

Theo nodded.

'It's over.'

Isaakios opened his eyes.

'Who, might I ask?'

'Your brother.'

For a moment Theo saw real pain on Isaakios's face – before he laughed his silly laugh.

'Oh, but it isn't really him, is it? It's his wife. That woman with the horse face and the snake eyes.'

'Does that make it easier for you? Blaming her?'

'Yes, as a matter of fact it does.' Isaakios levered himself on to his knees. 'If somebody you love ever plots against your life, believe me, you'll try to find excuses too.'

'You're very calm.'

'It's an act, Theo. All an act. I'm quaking. Look.' He held up a quivering hand. 'Get on with it, then. I don't want to embarrass myself. Kiss your boots and beg. Or piss myself. And believe me, I will if this goes on much longer.'

'You are not to die.'

'No? Am I to trust to a brother's pity?'

There was a bright sort of hope in his voice.

'Up to a point. Your life will be spared, but you are to lose your eyes.'

Isaakios crumpled.

'Not that. Please not that. Please. I would rather not live. Please not that. Give me a clean death. Clean and fair.'

He was scrabbling at Theo's feet.

'Clean? Fair?' Theo shook him off. 'Is that what my father got? You kicked his head about the fucking palace.'

'I . . . I was drunk. I couldn't believe I'd survived. I was showing off. I'm sorry, I'm sorry.' He started to splutter and blubber, then with a great gasp fell silent. 'You see. There I go – embarrassing myself.'

Theo stared down at the man at his feet. Hatred finally found him. Isaakios was at his mercy. He didn't have to wait for the others. He could do whatever he wanted, right there, that instant.

'What's wrong, Theo?' Isaakios was looking up at him.

'Nothing.'

'Are you . . . are you going to kill me?'

Theo drew his blade and stared at the point, wondering whether to drive it in. Where would be best? Heart? Stomach? Face? Did he want to kill him quickly or make him suffer? He had slain more men than he could ever hope to count, but never before had he killed anyone in cold blood.

Something moved in Isaakios's eyes, and at the same time Theo heard the snap of a twig behind him. He turned around in time to see a small figure dart into the clearing, trying to hold a sword that was plainly too heavy for him above his head with both hands.

The son.

Theo sidestepped easily and Alexios stumbled as he tried to swerve. A quick blow on the boy's upper arm with the hilt of his own sword knocked his weapon from his hands. But the boy still fell upon him, biting and scratching. It was painfully easy for Theo to knock him to the ground, but he was up on his feet again, charging, head down, trying to butt him in the stomach like a ram.

Theo seized the boy by the wrists.

'Stop – or I'll have to make you stop.'

'Don't, don't, you can't . . .'

He writhed and wriggled, his legs kicking out.

'Alexios, stop,' Isaakios shouted.

The boy fell limp. Theo let him go and he ran over to his father.

'Get up, Father. Fight him, Father. What are you doing?

Why are you sitting there? Come on. Look, my sword. Pick up my sword.'

He was shaking Isaakios, tears coursing down his cheeks, like a tiny child who couldn't understand why his father wouldn't play with him. The emperor patted him on the shoulder, awkwardly.

'There, there, son. It'll be all right.'

'Get up. Get up,' the boy screamed, and started to pound Isaakios on the chest. 'I hate you. I hate you.'

Hooves thundered down the forest track and half a dozen soldiers crashed into the clearing. The boy abandoned his father and bolted for the trees, but Theo had him by the collar before he'd gone far.

'Everything in order, sir?' asked the commander.

Theo nodded.

'I'll put Isaakios on my horse and bring him back via the ford. I want you to take this boy and ride for the City now. You're to deliver him to Euphrosunê. Tell nobody who he is. You understand? He is not to be harmed.'

He fumbled in his saddle bags and pulled out a small purse.

'Here's for the journey. There's more if you do as I say.'

The man still hesitated.

'But sir . . . ?'

'Now,' said Theo. 'I do not want to ask again.'

He was left alone with Isaakios.

'Thank you.'

'Don't thank me. I don't want your thanks.'

'Nevertheless, you've made sure that he won't see what they do to me. I owe you thanks for that at least.'

'I said I don't want them.'

Isaakios stood up and made for Theo's horse.

'Stop—'

'Don't worry. This is not a desperate bid for freedom. I just want a drink before you march me back to the camp. Allow me that at least.'

He unslung a wineskin from the saddle, upended it and gulped, his throat working hard, the drink spilling out of his lips.

'They'll do it in front of the whole army, won't they? Make a big show of it. Place bets on how much noise I make?' He drank again.

Theo nodded. 'Probably.'

'Please . . .'

'I can't stop it happening.'

'No. I don't mean that.' He took another long draught. 'Let me finish this. Then you do it. Quickly. Here. Alone.'

'Why? Why should I do that for you?'

'I don't know why. But I know that you pity me. I can see it in your eyes.'

'I despise you. You do not deserve pity.'

Isaakios laughed.

'Oh, but I do. I brought about the death of your father, the best man of his generation, a man who might have saved the empire – the empire that I'm losing to a bunch of bloody savages. I can't even remember which tribe is attacking which city. And now my own brother has usurped my throne and ordered me blinded. And you say I don't deserve pity.'

Another gulp.

'In truth, I shall be glad to put it all behind me.'

'What do you mean?'

'If the price of not having to run this blighted empire any longer is two eyes, then I am willing to pay it.'

'You're drunk.'

'Not drunk enough. Not yet. Men know nothing, Theo. They want power. They want to rule. And they have no idea what it costs. The fear. I have not slept for years. I go to sleep praying I shall wake up and be nobody. *Amusing Isaakios Angelos*. Nobody admired that man. But they liked him well enough. They did not hate him. They did not want to hurt him.'

'Enough.'

'Go on, Theo. You're a good man. Do it.'

His words were starting to slur, his head to loll. He took one last drink from the skin, then his grip slackened and he dropped it. A trickle of wine disappeared into the earth.

Theo heard the shouts of soldiers encouraging their horses into the river. They were coming. He'd played his part. He didn't have to do anything more. He could hand Isaakios over to one of the sergeants. They'd sober him up and the next day they'd do it. It would be bright daylight and Isaakios would have a dry mouth and a pounding head and everyone would watch.

What would his father have done?

Not bloody stood around wondering what another man might do.

Theo knelt down, still unsure. As he hesitated, Isaakios's eyes rolled open. He saw his own face looking back at him, shimmering on the surface of the other man's eyes. Theo raised a hand. Two hands. He placed one on either side of Isaakios's head. The eyes swam shut and Theo's face disappeared.

He looked down at his thumbs. It was easy, he knew, to pluck the eyes out of a sheep's head, but only if it was well boiled. Without looking away from Isaakios's face, the mottled skin, the purpled nose, the pouched cheeks, Theo fumbled his dagger from its sheath.

Hooves sounded on the track.

I've played my part. I don't have to do anything more.

He pushed one eyelid up. A quick turn of the knife. The other eyelid. Another turn. It was easier and harder than he'd expected. And it was done. He did not know whether it made him a better man or a worse one. But it was done.

Soon afterwards

'But Alexios is his brother. How could he . . . ? I don't understand. His . . . his . . . eyes?'

Isaakios's Magyar wife was staring up at her, wringing her hands, her watery blue eyes full of questions.

'I thought something was wrong, but I couldn't tell what. People weren't looking at me. I kept hearing footsteps, but nobody ever came.'

For a moment, Agnes wished Euphrosunê had asked someone else to tell Margit the news.

'It is hard,' she murmured. 'But it happens. Do not fear. You will be quite safe. Nobody means you any harm.'

She was trying to be kind, but the girl batted her hand away and began to wail.

'Y-you don't know what's it's like. Y-you can't possibly . . . It's not fair . . . It's not . . .'

There was more, a lot more, but most of it was buried under frantic, hiccuping sobs.

That's life, Agnes was tempted to say. *You had a good run, but it's over now.* But she didn't. Instead she made soothing, hushing noises and waited.

'Come,' she said as Margit's grief subsided. 'We must find Dora, and then the guards will escort you to your new lodgings.'

'You mean to prison.'

'No,' said Agnes. 'Not prison. Prison is a very different place. You shall even be permitted to visit your husband, to offer him solace.'

Maybe that *was* a little bit cruel of her. She couldn't imagine that being married to Isaakios was particularly appealing now that he was no longer emperor.

'My life is over. *Over.*'

The tears were starting up again.

'Your life is not over, Margit. Look at me. I was you once. I married an emperor. He fell; I married another. He died; I lived. I had no family, nobody to protect me, but I survived. And you shall too. You are not yet twenty. Trust me, many very wonderful things may yet happen to you.'

It worked. The tears gave way to sniffles, and Margit followed her meekly enough. It had been a pretty speech – although it was only half true. Of course, Margit might never take another free breath of air so long as she lived.

Dora wanted no such solace – and Agnes was less inclined to offer any.

'You? What are you doing here?'

'You'll have to ask your brother that.'

'My . . . my brother?'

'Your other brother. Alexios.'

'Alexios? He couldn't. He wouldn't . . .'

'But he has. The throne is his. And you, Dora, he has ordered from his palace.'

Dora fell silent, and Agnes could see that she was frightened. It was strange to inspire fear. Some men liked that power above all things, but she found it unsettled her.

'We women are born to suffer, are we not, Agnes? Buffeted by the affairs of men. Margit and I shall bear our lot as bravely as you did.' Dora's voice was sweet, but her eyes spat and scratched, a small creature cornered. 'You will pray for us, Agnes, will you not, as we once prayed for you?'

Agnes said nothing. This wasn't a game she wanted to play. Instead, she summoned the guards and led the two women down the corridors until they stood on the threshold of the palace. It was there that Dora's composure deserted her.

'Look as serene as you like, Agnes,' she hissed. 'It won't last.'

Agnes could only laugh.

'Dear Dora. I know that better than anyone.'

Agnes watched the guards hand them into a carriage, then – her first task in the service of the new empress complete – made her way to her own chambers. She stretched out on the bed and reflected that it was extremely refreshing *finally* to be on the right side of a coup.

Later that night, Theo walked in, still dressed in travel gear, and she saw immediately that a black mood was upon him. There was no triumph on his face, no joy. She jumped up and took his hands.

'What's wrong?'

He did not look at her, not immediately. She waited, stroking his cheek. Still he was silent.

'What is it, Theo? Everything is as we planned. We are together. We are free.' She touched his arm. 'Shouldn't we be the happiest we've ever been? And yet you, my love, you are scowling.'

'I'm sorry.' And he wrapped his arms around her so tight that she knew she had nothing to fear – not from him. 'I'm sorry,' he said again. 'I am glad. More than glad. But I'm also worried. About the future.'

'We are each other's future.'

He was silent.

'Aren't we, Theo?'

'We are.'

'Then please—' she kissed him '—can we not enjoy this one moment?'

He returned her kiss and she drew him towards the bed. He went with her. They tumbled down, faces close, hands in each other's hair, breathing hard.

'Agnes . . .'

He was sitting up.

'What is it?'

'I did it. You know I did it. I . . . his eyes.'

She nodded – and tried to keep the horror off her face.

'Do you understand why?' he asked.

'Yes. It had to be done.'

'No, no.' He was shaking his head furiously. 'That's not it. That's not what I want you to think.'

'Then tell me.'

'You won't understand.'

'I can try. I can always try.'

'I thought I was sparing him something worse. But maybe I wanted to do it.'

'You're not that man. You never were that man. I wouldn't love that man.'

'No?'

He looked up sharply.

'No.'

She was smoothing his hair, stroking his hand.

'There's another thing,' he said. 'The empire. I hadn't realised how bad things were in the west. Seventeen rebellions Isaakios faced. *Seventeen.*'

'But he was weak, wasn't he? It'll be different now. Everyone is united behind Alexios. The aristos, the bureaucrats, the army – they all chose him.'

That was what she wanted to be true.

'Maybe,' said Theo. 'But what do we know about him?'

'He's nice, and—'

That made him laugh.

'Nice!'

'I hadn't finished. I was going to say—'

'What? That he has a nice face, nice manners? You're right, but I'd wager you'd struggle to find anyone, man or woman, who could say anything more about him. God knows, I bore no love for Isaakios, but he was real. There was something to hate, something to get hold of. But I fear we've made a man emperor because we all find him utterly unobjectionable.'

'Better that than mad, better than crazed, greedy . . .'

'Is it? I hope so. I've tried talking to him. But it's like talking to your own reflection in a pool. He's a shadow of a man.'

Agnes didn't want to be having this conversation. She wanted to pretend, even if only for one night, that there were no emperors, no frontiers, no past, no future. Only him. Only her.

'Alexios is surrounded by good men, Theo. His wife, too. Euphrosunê is—'

'The most vauntingly ambitious woman I've ever met.'

'But what is wrong with that, if her ambitions tally with ours?'

Silence. She'd said the wrong thing.

'What's wrong with that, Theo?'

'Agnes, tell me, what are your ambitions now?'

'Is that what you're worried about? There's no need. I swear I shall not fall asleep this night and dream of you swathed in purple.'

His face softened. She'd said the right thing.

'What shall you dream of?' he said.

She pulled him close and spoke with her lips almost touching his.

'Before you arrived, I was lying at peace with no fear for the future. It was a new feeling. I shall dream of feeling like that tomorrow, and the next day, and every day of all the long years that I intend to spend by your side. That is what I shall dream of.'

'Then this is the end?'

'Yes, Theo, this is the end.'

The Fifth Emperor

Alexios is so far lost in the pain that he doesn't notice that the people gathered before him have changed. His servants have gone and his council has entered. His council and his wife.

To him, they do not quite look like real people, more like shades, shapeshifters, things from between worlds. That is because his eyesight is slowly failing him. But he does not tell the shades that; he does not tell them anything. He does not even tell them about the pain. That is his secret. His and the pain's.

Their mouths are moving fast. Urgent words fill the room. They are all worried about something and they are trying to make him worried too. But nothing worries him, not now. The pain protects him from everything. And the poppy protects him from the pain.

They are saying that the boy has escaped. Which boy? Ah, that boy. His nephew, Alexios, his namesake. No, the other way around. I am his namesake. Which is it? No matter.

The boy. He has escaped? To the west. The west. What of it? Isaakios's son. The setting sun. A red ball. Orbs. Eyes. Gone. His boy. The west.

The pain is coming and he welcomes it. When he has the pain, he can do nothing else. It is his revenge on those who made him emperor. The pain stops him listening to them, stops him doing what they want. When the pain is with him, he cannot hear his wife.

She can't get him. She can't.

The summer of 1203

On a blessed morning, the kind when only lovers and invalids stay in bed after sun-up, the City was massing as though for a great holiday. Everyone was fighting for a patch of ground on one of the hilltops, clambering on to the roofs of houses or pleading with guardsmen to let them up on to the sea defences.

Everyone wanted a view of the water.

Agnes had a prime position – naturally. She was sitting high on a portion of the Great Palace walls, hastily furnished with chairs and shade. She would not miss a thing. Soon, soon, the men of the Cross, the almighty Latin fleet, would sail up the Bosporus in front of her.

But right now, several women and a few men were trying to catch her eye. Probably desperate to tell her about a *dear little silk merchant* or a *divine new poet* they'd discovered. If it wasn't that, they'd be asking her whether she mightn't see her way to taking an interest in their niece, *such a sweet girl, but a little shy, I know a few moments with you, sebastê, would really bring her on.*

That was who she was – and if a few people tried to whisper about her living unmarried with Theodore Branas, Euphrosunê or her daughters soon put a stop to that. A woman of influence – she might not be empress, but she was the next best thing, the empress's best friend, her closest confidante. A woman of standing, as rich as any of them, thanks to a generous annuity from the state. A woman of fashion, past the perfect pitch of youth – *long past*, she corrected herself – but still a damn sight better-looking than most of them.

It had all turned out so well, hadn't it? Well, hadn't it?

It won't last. I know that better than anyone.

She'd thought she knew everything a woman could know about danger and despair. But she hadn't known that it was possible to be happier than she ever could have imagined – to wake every morning with a perfect golden feeling bursting in her chest – only for that happiness to disappear drop by drop, like water seeping out of an unseen crack in a cup.

Happiness felt strange at first. She'd held Theo's hand very tightly as they walked through the gates of his old family house, remembering how she had first come there, driven by a dead man's shade. To then find herself discussing jam-making with Agathê, one of many old Branas servants who'd returned, was . . . odd. But perhaps no odder than waking up and discovering Theo lying next to her morning after wonderful morning. Odd and wonderful. It *was* wonderful. To hide from the world with the man she loved, the man who loved her.

But then, out of the blue – to them, at least – the emperor accused his wife of adultery and banished her to a convent. Agnes and Theo had been leading too quiet a life to be involved, but it caused their first argument.

Theo thought there might be some truth to the charges. Agnes didn't. She tried to persuade him she was right. He said he didn't care either way so long as he was left in peace. She said that was all very well but Euphrosunê was her friend and she was going to visit her. Theo said she owed Euphrosunê nothing and told her not to go. She said he had no right to tell her what to do, and packed a bag – only to arrive the same day as a letter recalling Euphrosunê to the City as if nothing had happened.

Theo and Agnes made up, easily, passionately. But the golden days – when it seemed that nothing and nobody could ever come between them – were over.

The emperor gave Theo command of some campaign – which one, she couldn't now remember. There'd been so many since. She didn't want him to go. She was convinced he was going to die. She couldn't stop crying. At first he was sympathetic, reassuring, but finally at dawn on the day he was due to leave, he lost his temper. *Don't you understand? This is what I do. I can't around sit in the City curling my fucking beard.* She'd found that hard to forgive.

Theo didn't die, but the campaign didn't go the Rômans' way. He returned, despondent, rejecting her attempts to comfort him. She asked him what had happened, what had gone wrong, but that made him irritable – as if it were all her fault.

When the fighting season next came round, she announced that while he was away, she was moving back into the palace. Euphrosunê had need of her. Theo begged her not to, which she thought was ridiculous. He said he was losing her – she thought that was ridiculous too. *What else am I supposed to do while you're gone?*

Worse followed.

Late one night, two years previously, Theo's old friend Murzuphlus came to their house and asked him to join a plot against the emperor, led by a man called John the Fat, of all things. Theo was furious, told him he was mad, said he'd have none of it. Murzuphlus left, promising that he'd forget the idea. Agnes wanted to warn Euphrosunê anyway, but Theo said he wouldn't betray his friend.

It's all right, Agnes. I cooled him down. He's probably only upset that they won't let him marry that daughter of theirs. It'll blow over.

Agnes thought he was wrong and told him so. And he *was* wrong, wasn't he? The coup went ahead and Theo had to help put it down. John's body, headless, was staked out for the birds at Blachernai – a throwback to uglier times. *You could have stopped this* – those were the words she hurled at him when he came home. *I haven't slept for three days. I've had to throw Murzuphlus in jail. And this is how you welcome me?*

'Agnes, darling, Agnes?' A piercing voice interrupted her reverie. 'Look, look, *there* they are. Don't they look just like disgusting little centipedes, scurrying over the water?'

She laughed and patted the arm of the pretty woman beside her.

'Very like, Anna.'

'They're pests. Little pests, and Father will wipe them out. Splat.'

Anna, the middle of Euphrosunê's three daughters, married to an ambitious man called Theodore Laskaris, still acted like a pert fifteen-year-old even though she'd never see thirty again.

'They're heading right towards us. They're coming really close,' said Eirene, the eldest, stately, pale and nervous. Her husband had just dropped dead of some fever and she was embracing the role of widow.

The three girls treated Agnes like a special and slightly dangerous aunt, and in return Agnes teased them and amused them and tried to ignore how jaded they made her feel. That was on a good day. Sometimes she felt she was playing nursemaid to three sheltered ninnies.

Well, to two. The youngest, Eudokia, was different. She'd had to grow up fast when Isaakios married her off to an unpleasant Serb. Her husband had treated her appallingly and eventually, when he wanted to pick a fight with the empire, sent her back to the City in her underclothes. Agnes was the only person Eudokia had talked to about the whole episode, and in return, she had told her a little, a very little, about her own girlhood. The truth, that was. Not the version she amused people with at parties. Eudokia had also confided in Agnes when she fell for Murzuphlus – but now he, of course, was in jail.

'Are you sure we're quite safe up here?' Eirene appealed to Agnes.

'They can sail as close as they like,' said Agnes. 'It does us no harm. They are down there on the sea, you see, and we are up here on the walls. There's nothing to fear.'

She pointed to one of the larger ships.

'See that one, the one with the blue and white banners? That belongs to my little nephew, Louis of Blois. He used to cry when I pinched him, and once—' she lowered her voice to a whisper '—he peed his underthings at church.'

They laughed, delighted. That was the sort of thing Agnes *always* said.

'Do you really know them?' asked Eudokia.

Agnes was silent for a moment, looking out at the great fleet that was riding a fair wind up the Propontis, hundreds of white sails bathed in light, hundreds of long sweeps dancing in and out of the water.

Louis's were not the only colours she knew. She had learnt them all before she was ten years old, poring over lists until her eyes hurt because she liked the way everyone clapped and exclaimed over her when she recognised some knight from the colours he wore.

'Yes.' She nodded. 'I know them. All of them.'

'Agnes, why have they come?' asked Anna. 'Nobody says why they are here. Are they going to attack us?'

'No, pet, no. They have sworn to their Pope that they will destroy the sons of Saladin . . .'

'The evil man who took the Holy City?'

'Yes, the man who took Jerusalem.'

'So the Franks got in their ships . . .'

'No – those are not their ships. Those ships belong the men of Venice. The men of Venice are bearing the Franks to Alexandria.'

'I thought they were going to the Holy Land?'

'Eventually they will, but first they must defeat the sultan in Egypt.'

'I don't care about Egypt. Why are they *here*?' Anna wailed.

'I don't like it. Father should order our armies to fire upon them.'

'They have not yet declared themselves to be enemies,' said Agnes gently. 'You have to wait until your enemies declare themselves before you are allowed to fire on them.'

'Then that is what we shall do,' said Eirene emphatically. 'We'll fire on them and end this impertinence.'

'No we won't,' said a man's voice behind them.

Agnes and the girls turned round. Theo was coming up the steps. He bowed to each of them in turn, the serious bow of a serious man, no concession to the vanity of the three princesses, who might feel they deserved a more courtly greeting. Not for the first time Agnes wondered what had happened to Theo, the laughing boy. Men and women called him Branas now.

'We won't fire on them,' he said. 'We'll prevaricate and equivocate, we'll hedge and haggle, and pray to God that they leave us in peace.'

'Don't talk like that, Theo, it—' Agnes began, but a squeal from Anna interrupted her.

'Look, look.' She was pointing down at the lead galley, which was now within bowshot of the Great Palace. 'They're waving. They can't want to fight if they're waving, can they?'

She was right. On the prow stood a young man, beardless, still a little gawky, in high-day Rôman dress – or a scratch approximation of it – flanked by an old man and a bristling warrior.

'So the rumours are true. They do have him,' said Theo, almost to himself.

'Have who?' Anna demanded.

'Your cousin, princess. Isaakios's boy.'

'Little Alexios, the one you used to tease so cruelly,' Agnes supplied. 'But how can you be sure, Theo? It's years since he was seen in the City. It's probably just another pretender. There are always pretenders.'

But Theo shook his head.

'It's him.'

Agnes was about to ask him to at least have the grace to look at her when he was speaking to her when the voice of a herald boomed up from the ship below.

'Good people of the City!'

'Speak up, we can't hear you,' the people of City, good and bad, yelled back.

'Here is your rightful lord.'

'Where? Where?' the people hooted.

'We have not come to harm you, but to aid and protect you.'

'Fuck off,' the mob cried with glee.

'The man you now obey as your lord rules over you in defiance of God . . .'

The rest of whatever the herald had to say was drowned out by a barrage of barracking.

'Oh, but what was that Latin saying? Everyone's shouting so much, I can't make it out,' Eirene complained.

Theo folded his arms over his chest.

'They're saying your father did wrong to wrest the throne from his brother. They're saying they have Isaakios's son with them. And they are saying we shall all suffer greatly if we do not acknowledge him as our emperor.'

'But that's ridiculous! That boy there? He doesn't look like an emperor,' said Anna.

The people of the City evidently agreed with her. Their jeers were turning to laughter as they began to understand what the man down on the boat was suggesting.

'Look . . .' Eudokia pointed. 'The other two men are angry with our poor cousin. I do believe they're scolding him. Who are they?'

'The greybeard is Enrico Dandolo, doge of Venice,' said Theo. 'You can see the pennon of the Lion of St Mark at the masthead. I'm not sure about the other . . .'

'It's Renier and Conrad's other brother,' murmured Agnes.

'Who?' asked Anna.

'Sorry. Two men from long ago. You see the other banner – the red and white? Those are the colours of Montferrat.'

'Well, whoever they are,' said Eudokia, 'they're furious with him.'

'You're right,' said Theo – and Eudokia beamed. Theo rarely said anyone was right about anything. 'I wonder what he told them. Maybe he swore we'd all be throwing flowers down from the walls.'

Theo waited until the ships had paid off across the current, making for an anchorage on the far shore of the Bosporus, before he left the walls.

Agnes was obviously angry with him, but then she always seemed to be angry with him these days. He wished he understood why, but he hated the gulf between them so much that it was easier just to keep away. She was always busy, anyway, surrounded by other people, laughing with those girls – or closeted with the empress. He hated sitting alone in his parents' house – they who had always seemed so happy – wondering what had gone wrong. But what else could he do?

He grimaced, and hurried to the chamber, where the emperor's men would be gathering. When he entered, Euphrosunê was nowhere to be seen, but Theo knew she'd be watching from behind some curtain, through some chink in the wall. Even if she wasn't, it was best to imagine she was. Several men had found that out to their cost.

'What now?' boomed Constantinos Raoul. 'Shall we marshal our forces?'

It was always hard to tell whether Raoul really was as big and stupid as he sounded.

'May I make another suggestion?' intervened Theodore Laskaris, a sensible fellow, for all that he was married to that irritating woman Anna. 'Let us send to our visitors first. Let us ask them why they are here.'

'We know why they're here,' Raoul said with a fist thump to a table. 'The same reason Latin scum always come here. To weasel what they can out of the empire. I say we crush them.'

His family had migrated from Italy not so very long ago, which partly explained why he was always the first to denounce *Latin scum.*

'But we need to hear their explanation,' returned Laskaris. 'Then we can modulate our behaviour accordingly.'

'*Modulate?*' Raoul growled, incredulous. 'Is that soldier talk?'

'We're not on a battlefield, friend, not yet, so no – it's not.'

Theo listened as the arguments raged about him.

'Offer them provisions.'

'Let them starve.'

'They'll sack the countryside.'

'Let them try it.'

'We are safe in the City.'

'Don't antagonise them.'

'Don't let them get away with it.'

Theo sighed, wishing he were still eighteen and could feel angry and military. He glanced at the emperor, who was nodding and turning his head to each man as he spoke, a fair-minded ruler listening to the counsel of his best men, though Theo knew he could sing the bawdiest brothel song he'd ever heard and Alexios would continue to smile.

'Peace, gentlemen, peace.'

Euphrosunê had entered the room. The men bowed very low and made way for her as she came to sit by the emperor's side. Her authority was a habit now. That spell in a convent aside, her power had grown like a weed, becoming established without anyone being able to say how it had happened.

Alexios nodded and said, 'Just so.'

She ignored him.

'Gentlemen, let us not be hasty. I have a message here that I propose we send this evening.'

She smoothed out a piece of paper and began to read.

'My lords, the Emperor Alexios has sent me to say that next to kings – remind them what a ragtag bunch they are – you are the noblest men alive. Why and for what purpose have you entered this land over which he rules? You are Christians as he is – we must be sure to get that in early – and he knows very well you have left your own country to deliver the Holy Land, the Holy Cross and the Holy Sepulchre. If you are poor – if? Of course they are! – and in want of supplies, he will share provisions with you on the condition that you withdraw. If you refuse to leave, he would be reluctant to do you harm, and yet it is in his power to do so.* There. I think that makes the matter quite plain. Comments? Questions?'

Theo stepped forward.

'I have a question, basilissa.'

'What is it, Branas?'

'You say it is in the emperor's power to do them harm. But that is not true. You know it. I know it. Do you not fear they know it as well?'

That provoked an uproar. They told him he was a coward, a traitor, a lackwit, a provocateur, a defeatist, but Theo let it wash over him. He knew he was right.

'Gentlemen, gentlemen, enough,' called Euphrosunê. 'Pay him no heed. They cannot harm us while we stand firm and resolute behind our walls. That is the truth of it – whatever Theodore Branas might have to say. Let me tell you what their game is. They are hoping that some man here is nurturing a petty grievance against my husband. They are hoping that man will turn traitor against our City. But they will hope in vain, will they not?'

Theo listened impatiently to the inevitable protestations of loyalty.

'Send your message, by all means,' he said when they were done. 'No man in this room wants to hand the City to the Franks. But tell me, what will you do when they reply that they want their Alexios on the throne instead of ours?'

The empress's laugh jangled.

'Oh, but that is only their starting position. We shall bargain them down. I think they will find they are no match for us around the negotiating table. Mark my words, we shall be wishing them good luck and Godspeed before the month is out.'

'God grant that it be so,' said Theo. 'But while you treat with them, may I at least have your permission to bolster the City's defences?'

He tried to find the emperor's eye as he spoke, but Alexios took no more notice of him than he did of the fly that was creeping along the back of his hand. The only reply came from the empress.

'You have grown nervous as an old woman, Branas. Go home to Agnes. She at least knows better than to be afraid of a rabble from the west.'

Agnes sat in the shade of the little orchard. Theo would be talking state for hours into the night, probably badgering Euphrosunê about the state of the City's army, earning himself no friends. The empress had even hinted that were it not for the love she bore Agnes, she would struggle to tolerate him.

Once Agnes had tried to warn him, tried to tell him to be a bit more positive, *more constructive*, was how she put it, but his face had closed and he'd walked out of the house. He was always doing that. Not, she thought, to go to other women. Only to drink with old soldiers. Maybe that was what he was doing now. Drinking – leaving her alone with Agathê.

'What cheek,' Agathê was saying. 'Do they not know the Virgin protects us? They can sail hither and thither, beat their shields and blow their horns, but in the end the City shall watch them go, as it has watched so many others before them.'

She talked on – occasionally reaching over to top up Agnes's cup of lemon-water – until the back gate creaked open. Both women looked up as Theo stumbled in.

'I'll brew you something cooling, Master Theodore,' Agathê said, and vanished into the kitchens.

Agnes stood to follow her; he looked belligerent – and drunk. But he grasped her arm and sat her back down in her chair.

'Please, sebastê, pray bear me company. It is such a pleasure to find you here.'

'Why should I not be here? This is my home, is it not?'

He nodded, as if to say that much at least was true.

'How are you, Theo? Were you not excessively diverted by today's events?' She wrapped her shawl about her. 'I don't know what my kinsmen think they're playing at.'

'You should be pleased at any rate, Agnes.'

She saw that he still had a wineskin with him, and watched him take a large swig.

'Pleased?' she said.

'Half your family has rolled up. Send a message or two, and your passage away from here is secured.'

'How can you say such a—'

'How can I not? In truth, Agnes, how can I not?'

They stared at one another.

'So you admit you'd be glad to be rid of me?' she said, her voice pinched and rising.

'What keeps us together, Agnes? We have no ties in law or religion. We have no child—'

She bolted into the house, up to her room, slamming the door behind her. *We have no child.* She was crying. *We have no child.* And she'd sworn she'd never cry about that, ever, ever again.

Once upon a time, she hadn't thought too hard about why she never bore a child to either of her husbands. Once upon a time, she'd prayed to be spared all that. Yet with Theo she'd somehow imagined a son would be lying in the crib – the crib she'd caught Agathê dusting when she first moved in – nine months after they first shared a bed.

When it didn't happen, she confided in Agathê, who

recommended herbs, saints, positions, potions, and prayers, a panoply of solutions that strained the limits of godliness – but didn't work.

Agathê didn't like to admit she'd run out of ideas, so instead she pursed her lips and said that Master Theodore was too much away fighting. She said Agnes had borne a great deal and babies did not always come easily to women who had suffered. She said Agnes was too thin.

'Maybe I have sinned too much?' Agnes once asked her.

That made the servant explode with laughter.

'If that were the case, then the City's whores, forgive me, would sleep a sight easier. No, mistress, all the sin in the world never yet stopped a woman getting with child.'

'Perhaps I am too old?'

'Nonsense. Remember Abraham's wife. Remember Elizabeth – she was *much* older than you when she had John the Baptist.'

But with Theo, Agnes never mentioned it. If they'd talked of it sooner, they could perhaps have consoled one another. But once their childlessness had been unspoken for two, four, eight years, it became a cold lump at the heart of their . . . their what?

That was part of the problem. Because they couldn't marry, she had wanted to give Theo something she had never given her real husbands. A child to wash away the past. Once he held their child in his arms, she was sure the promises they had whispered to each other in the dark, between the sheets, would feel as true as if their union had been blessed by the patriarch and cheered by the crowds up and down the Mesê. But the child never came, and they began to make love less often – and with less pleasure.

Or, rather, the child did come, but it never grew. A dozen times, maybe more, the same strange feeling came to her. She started to ache deep inside, but she did not bleed, and hope danced inside her. She imagined telling Theo. She imagined telling the women at court, who she knew looked at her and wondered. But after a day or at most a moon's turn, she would bleed, sometimes for days, sometimes very painfully. Always and always.

It hurt less each time.

That was a lie. It hurt every time. Not a sharp shock like too-hot water, but a slow, bottomless, lingering pain that crept into every corner of her life.

Click.

The door opened and Theo walked in.

'What's wrong?'

He'd stood outside her door for a long time before opening it. He could hear her crying. But he didn't want to go in, see her tears, ask her what was wrong and hear *nothing, nothing.*

'Nothing. Nothing.'

She put her hands up as if to push him from her. He tipped his head back and groaned.

'Very well. I'll see you tomorrow. Or the day after. Or one day soon.'

'Where are you going?'

'The City's defences—'

'Oh, shut up about the City's defences! I'm tired of hearing it. Nobody wants to hear it, Theo. Nobody. It's boring.'

'Really? Two hundred ships packed with armed men are boring?' He was leaning over her on the bed, shouting. He didn't mean to shout. He never meant to shout. 'And what the fuck would you call exciting, Agnes?'

She shrugged, and shifted backwards on the bed.

'I see a few boats on the other side of the Bosporus. I see our walls and our armies. That doesn't excite me.'

'Look again. The City is on the sea, but every seaman is Italian-born. Our armies? They're bought men. Our walls? They look big, but it's our gold that's kept us safe, and we don't have much left. Once, we could offer up one of our princesses when money was short, but now . . .'

Agnes yawned. *Yawned*. He knew she was doing it on purpose. He knew she was trying to provoke him. But knowing didn't help. He grabbed her arm and shook it in a stupid, helpless, childish rage.

'Get off me,' she snapped. 'You're drunk. You're drunk and tiresome and I want you out of my room.'

Very early the next morning

Somebody was hammering at her door. Somebody was shouting her name. *Theo.* It was Theo coming to see her.

'Go away,' she shouted, but the hammering continued.

She rolled out of bed and wrenched the door open. He stood on the threshold, dressed for the world outside, sword buckled.

'What?' she asked. 'What?'

'They've set sail across the Bosporus.'

'So?'

'They're trying to take Galata. *Galata.*'

'But why? It's only . . .' She stopped. *It's only a little merchant settlement. Only a little merchant settlement that houses one end of the Great Chain across the harbour mouth.* 'They're trying to cut the Chain,' she gasped.

'Exactly. I have to go. The Galata garrison is tiny. Barely a hundred men are stationed there.'

'Only a hundred. Why?'

'It's too fucking late to ask why.'

'There's no need—'

'Isn't there? Agnes, there's every need. If they win Galata and take the Kastellion Tower, they control the harbour.'

'But that's not the same as taking the City, is it?'

'Isn't it? The sea walls by the harbour are nothing compared with the land walls. They've caught us with our cocks out, pissing into the wind. So arrogant . . . so blind . . .'

He was too angry for his words to come out properly.

'Theo, wait, tell me—'

'I don't have time. The City doesn't have time.'

And he rushed away down the corridor, flinging on his cloak, calling for his horse.

'All right,' she yelled after him. 'You were right. Say *I told you so*. Go on, say it.'

He stopped and stared at her.

'I don't give a damn about being right. It's the City that matters.'

That touched something in her. Something that made her throat tighten with a new anger, an anger greater than his.

'Why? Why must it matter so much? Why must it matter more than me? What has the City ever done for you? For us? It's full of madmen – greedy, mad, hungry men who do nothing but lie and cheat and steal. It stinks. It—'

'You seem well able to tolerate it, Agnes.'

'What do you mean?'

'What do I mean? You . . . how can you say all this? You who are always at the palace. Always by Euphrosunê's side. Making up to her. Making up to her girls.'

'What else am I supposed to do? I have nothing else to . . . nobody else . . .' She stopped herself before the thought of their unborn children, their unlived lives overwhelmed her. 'You're never here. You're always fighting.'

'If I've been fighting, it's only because *you*—'

'*Me?* I'm to blame?'

'Let me finish! *I want to live at peace, with no fear for the morrow.* That's what you said. I've been trying to keep you safe. But every time I come back, it's as if you're not here. Where are you? If I can't fight for you, I don't know what I'm fighting for. And if men don't know what they're fighting for, they lose.'

And for a moment he did look lost. The stern-faced man she had become accustomed to vanished, and the boy from long ago, his cheeks unlined, his eyes bright, was pleading with her. He started towards her, to kiss her, embrace her, to say something, she knew not what – but before he could reach

395

her side, men started to call his name from beyond the gate, and the look left his eyes and he turned from her.

'You see,' she said. 'None of what you said is true. You fight because it's easier than being here. Because you love it. Because it's the only thing you understand.'

He had reached the threshold. One of the servants had his horse by the reins, another was hauling the gates open. Other men were streaming down the road, torches aflame, a fearful hubbub in the middle of the night.

'Agnes,' he called. 'You must understand. Please. I have to—'

'Go and fight.' She was shouting. 'Go and be a hero. Go and die for all I care. But don't expect the City to be grateful when your blood seeps into her stones. Don't expect the City to mourn you. And don't expect me to either.'

Theo fought his way on to the last boat crossing the Golden Horn, one of the two dozen rotting hulks that comprised the City's navy. He'd be lucky, he thought, if it didn't disintegrate beneath his feet.

To his right, through the pre-dawn light, he could see the Franks grunting across the Bosporus. The galleys, towing heavy transports behind them, had left the far shore under cover of darkness, but they'd misjudged the silent westward sweep of the waters and had missed the mouth of the Golden Horn. Now, with no wind to help them, the oarsmen were sweating the boats back upstream.

Theo's boat touched and he raced through Galata, past the Kastellion Tower, down on to the waterfront, where the Franks would land.

He didn't expect to find a disciplined defence – and nor did he. There was no order, no strategy, only men plucked from their beds, men half armed, half dressed, men looking for their commanders, commanders hunting their men. At best, they might prove a human barricade, but how much use would they be without missiles, without horses – and without a leader?

But then, through the pandemonium, Theo saw the emperor, decked out in full fighting gear, flanked by his axemen. He blinked. Alexios had proved himself no more a soldier than his brother, yet there he was, shouting encouragement to the troops.

'We shall not give them the shore. We shall drive them into the sea! They shall swim home like frightened fish!'

His cry was taken up, first by his guards, then by the soldiers jostling up and down the shore. Good words – good, strong Rôman words – but Theo feared words would be little use on their own.

Out on the water, the Venetian crews were working their ships as calmly as if they were docking silks and spices back home in their lagoon. The galleys put in a final burst of speed, dropped the tow ropes, and sped out of the way – leaving the helmsmen on the transports to spin their vessels while there was still enough way under their keels. So it was that their fat-beamed sterns crunched first on the stones.

Unseen crewmen flung open giant doors and ran out sturdy gangplanks. And out came horse after horse after horse, cooped, maddened animals, stampeding, and atop each, a knight in full battle armour, lance lowered.

The men on the shore were ready to fight – but none of them were prepared for the death charge of the western knights. With their own kataphraktoi at hand, with time for the foot soldiers to form a shield wall, they might have stood a chance, but faced with uncut stallions, barely under control, the Rôman ranks cracked and broke.

'Form up! Hold firm!' Theo shouted to the men at his side.

But they were not soldiers he had ever fought with. He did not know them and they did not know him. He could not give them the courage they needed to stand and fight – and most likely die.

Theo felt hot, wet horse breath on his face, a boot in his chest, then he was on the floor, eyes squeezed shut, his hands over his head, one of the numberless, nameless men the first Frankish charge had ploughed into the dirt. He forced air back into his lungs. He forced himself back on to his feet. The emperor had disappeared. And the Franks, the ships disgorging more every moment, were about to spur their horses into a second charge.

'Retreat! Retreat!'

The cry went up around him, and every man who could turned and ran.

'We cannot hold them here!'

'Back to the City!'

'Back inside the walls!'

'The walls! The walls!'

Theo was swept backwards, powerless as foam on the tide.

There, to his left, rose the Kastellion Tower. It was no castle, nothing like it, only a stone building that housed the Great Chain. But it was tall, well built – worth defending. Maybe a few determined men could hold it long enough for the emperor to rally his forces, to summon the cavalry. To do something. Anything.

'The tower! To me! The tower, the tower!' he yelled.

He did not expect many to follow him – fifty, maybe a hundred men at best. But when, panting, chest heaving, he arrived at the foot of the tower and turned, he found barely two dozen fighters behind him. The remainder of the City's soldiers stumbled past, deaf to his pleas.

Many of those who had stopped were Varangians. At least they'd know how to fight. But why did the City have to rely on them? What about the boys who had come to manhood inside the frontiers of the empire? *Stop thinking. Thinking won't help now.* But he couldn't help it. Not one man of blood or wealth had answered his call.

He was standing with such men as he had inside a small keep, little more than a courtyard, stacked with food and fuel. Behind him, a door opened on to the steps that ran up inside the tower, and high above his head jutted a parapet on which stood the vast drum that held one end of the Great Chain.

'You three, block up the gates,' he began. 'You there, haul anything that would kill a man if it landed on his head on to the walls. Light fires up there, if you can. The rest of you, hunt for arrows, crossbows. There must be an armoury. Quick. Quick.'

Theo himself darted up the steps – he'd have a good view from the parapet. The Rômans were fleeing up the eastern side of the Golden Horn, probably hoping to cross at the bridge where the inlet narrowed to the north of Blachernai. A few lucky ones might have made it on to the boats, but most of them looked empty. The captains must have cast off for the safety of the harbour once they realised the Franks were prevailing.

He could see several detachments of Franks pursuing the City soldiers, but most of them had drawn up in good order while their ships dropped anchor close inshore. As he watched, they started to fan out through Galata, the biggest unit by far heading straight for the tower.

Theo looked down. The courtyard walls were high enough to allow his men to thwart any attempt on the gates – for a while at least. A pity they had no pitch, no tar, and were outnumbered by more than he cared to count.

The Franks were coming, circling the tower, burly foot-fighters jogging into position under the command of half a dozen men on horseback. And, much worse, he could see a gang of crewmen dragging what looked like a pair of scaling ladders, hastily knocked together from bits of rigging, and a blunt section of mast – he could see the raw wood where the axe had bit – that would serve as a ram. At least he saw no proper siege engines – a few well-judged shots from a petrary would have brought the walls down in no time.

One man rode forward.

'Yield!' he cried in Frankish-accented Latin. 'You are surrounded. You have no hope. We shall ransom you fairly. Yield!'

'Never!' replied Theo first in Latin, then in Greek for the benefit of his men below.

He saw the mounted men confer for a few minutes. They must know they had to flush the Rômans out fast, before help arrived from the City. An arrow whistled past his ear, and he stopped thinking.

The attack had begun.

Agnes left home soon after Theo, ordering the housemen to take her to the Great Palace in the sedan. Men and women, soldiers and servants, eunuchs and kitchen maids – there wasn't a single human being who wasn't haring back and forth in panic. She dodged through the corridors, in and out of buildings, asking every person she met,

'The empress, where is the empress?'

After taking many wrong turns and entering many empty rooms, she came upon Euphrosunê, all but unattended, returning across the gardens. The hem of her cloak was damp with dew, and Agnes could see she was wearing slippers and a nightgown underneath, instead of her usual stark finery.

She kissed Agnes. 'You are good to have come to me.'

'Of course I came. What . . . ?'

Euphrosunê shook her head. 'Dishonour. Disgrace. I cannot yet be sure of the details, but I fear the worst. I fear they have taken the Galata.'

'But how? Why was it not—'

'I did not know you for an authority on civil defence.' Agnes put up her hands as if to ward off an attack, but Euphrosunê was already apologising. 'Sorry, pay me no heed. I misjudged them. It was my mistake.'

'And, surely, your husband's?'

Euphrosunê looked at her sharply, as if to see whether there was humour in her words or not.

'My husband—'

'Is coming,' said Agnes, who had just caught sight of the emperor weaving towards them. 'Shall I . . . ?' She gestured vaguely, wondering whether she should leave. Euphrosunê shook her head.

'No need,' she said, and turned to Alexios.

He was bare-headed, the morning light showing the pale pink of his scalp through his thin brown hair. His arms and calves were brown with dust, but his clothes were pristine where his armour had been. He stopped in front of them, kneading his forehead with his knuckles. He looked like nothing so much as a boy fighting tears, a boy who would crumple and cry if you scolded him – or worse, offered sympathy.

This was the man who was meant to be closest to God. The isapostolos: the apostles' equal. Agnes shivered. *God help us.*

'I told you not to go,' said Euphrosunê. 'I said you couldn't. I knew you would fail.'

Cold words, nasty words, meant for Alexios alone. He shrank.

'What happened?' she demanded.

'They brought their horses across. I had not expected that.' His eyes had been fixed on the ground, but then he looked up, pleading with her. 'What could I do against so many mounted men?'

'You could have been a man. You could have fought. That was what you wanted to do, wasn't it, husband? I told you to stay here. I told you to give the command to a real man, a real fighter. But you defied me. What did you say? *I won't hang on your skirts, Euphrosunê. I shall go and save Galata, Euphrosunê.* A fine job you made of it. You oversaw a rout. My congratulations.'

Alexios's face flickered. He'd remembered something.

'Not a rout. No, not a rout. A man . . .' he looked at Agnes and nodded, as if her being there proved something. 'Theodore

Branas said he would hold the Chain Tower. That is good, is it not?'

A shadow of a smile passed across his face, even as Agnes's heart contracted with alarm.

'He's still there?'

Why was she surprised? Of course he was there. Proving to everyone that he was right and they were wrong by dying . . . *No, please God, not dying.*

'He's a brave man,' Euphrosunê said.

He's a dead man, that's what she means. Dead and foolish, and once he was mine.

Agnes's feet twitched beneath her. She must be able to do something. She reeled and might have fallen had Euphrosunê not put a hand at her back and murmured,

'Do not weaken now, Agnes. Not today.'

Agnes nodded, and turned to the emperor.

'Forgive me, but can you not send a force to relieve him? To hold the tower?'

'Yes,' he said, and looked at Euphrosunê. 'Yes,' he repeated, 'that is what I shall do. Certainly, that is what shall I do.' And he hurried away, glancing back over his shoulder, once, twice, and then disappeared as half a dozen servants closed about him.

The gates were down. The courtyard was full of dead men, Franks and Rômans. The only defenders still living had retreated inside the tower and barred the door. Theo dared not hope it would hold for long, but they had a small, a very small breathing space.

He had sent two of the surviving men up on to the parapet, one meagre quiver between them, with orders to shoot down the Franks who were battering the tower door.

'What can you see?' he yelled up.

No answer. They must have been shot from the ground. He looked at the other men.

'Anyone care for a turn with a bow?'

They looked at one another, but did not speak – nor did he blame them. There was little shelter up there, only a low wall, scant cover, and dozens of crossbowmen below with all the time in the world to reload and take aim.

'I'll go,' Theo said. 'Have heart. They must send reinforcements soon. If we can hold another hour, they'll be here.'

The other men nodded, too exhausted to speak.

He sidled out on to the parapet and saw, as he had expected, two men slumped on the floor, one dead, one beyond hope. Theo stopped the second man's mouth and nose until his eyes rolled up and back – then he scooped up his bow.

He loosed three arrows at the Franks clustered round the base of the tower, felling one man before they saw him. A hail of bolts shot towards him and he flattened himself on the ground, or rather on the still-warm corpse at his feet. He crawled a little to his left, leapt up and loosed again – no time to aim – and again hugged the ground as they fired back.

He heard the door shatter below him, and the sound of heavy fighting boomed up the stairwell, the crash of metal on metal, metal on stone. He dropped the bow, grabbed his sword, and ran down the steps in time to see the last Rôman fall. He took his place in the narrow stairwell and began to fight backwards – always backwards – up the steps.

He lost count of the number of men he killed. As each fell, the men below hauled the dead man away and another stepped forward. At first they were too heavily armed to manoeuvre in such close quarters, and it was easy to unbalance them with a good sword-thrust or a boot in the chest, to make them slip on the blood of the last man he had slain. But they were replaced by lighter-armed men, better fencers, and he was forced upwards, one step at a time.

I will not yield a step without killing three men. But three soon became two, then one, until all he could do was tell himself over and over not to give up, not to give up.

So intent was he on every lunge and block, no finesse, no

style, shove, parry, stab, gut, that he nearly stepped past the doorway to the parapet. He felt a sudden breeze on the back of his neck and stumbled out into the open air, knowing that a bolt or an arrow from the ground could end it right then. But there was nothing he could do about that, so he raised his sword and set his face at the doorway. A knight came through, and instead of attacking Theo, he roared down at the men below,

'Leave him. He's ours.'

Theo found a pair of very blue eyes looking at him.

'Will you yield now?'

Theo took the chance to mop the sweat out of his eyes and drew in two, three deep, sweet lungfuls of air. Involuntarily, he glanced over his shoulder, across the harbour, along the shore, and the man before him laughed.

'Do you still expect them to come? Your compatriots have long since abandoned you. Come. No need to lay down your life. Yield.'

Theo shook his head. 'Never.'

'Then I must kill you. And I warn you, I am entirely fresh.'

Tentatively at first, then with increasing conviction, they began to fight. The knight was a fair swordsman, light and nimble, but Theo was fighting for his life – while his opponent thought he only had to finish a man on his last legs. One word, and the bowmen could do the job for him, but the Frank didn't want Theo dead – he wanted to beat him. He wanted to win.

And Theo was happy to let him try.

The Frank was driving him steadily backwards around the circle of the parapet, around the drum. Theo felt the Chain chill against the back of his neck and ducked to pass beneath it. They fought on, the Chain between them, until the knight thrust his sword a little too high and caught the tip in one of the metal links. He faltered, not for long, but long enough for Theo to close the gap between them, drive his boot into his knee, his fist under his chin, and stand over him, the man's life in his hands.

'Do you yield?' Theo croaked.

Already he could feel the prick of half a dozen enemy blades at his back.

'Do you yield?'

The man looked up at him. For a moment, Theo thought he'd refuse and he'd have to kill to him – although he would survive the man he'd beaten by no more than a heartbeat. But the Frank smiled, if a smile with neither humour nor warmth could be called that, and said,

'Assuredly.'

Theo stepped backwards and found his sword seized, his arms gripped tight, ropes already snaking around his wrists. There must have been four men holding him at least, but he was glad they were there. He could hardly stand, let alone fight. They were about to bundle him down the stairwell when the knight called,

'Stop.'

He had picked himself up off the floor and was holding his arm tight where Theo's sword must have pierced a join in his armour.

'What's your name?' he asked, removing his helm.

'Branas. Theodore Branas.'

The man's eyes narrowed.

'Branas. We have heard . . . rumours. Tell me, you are the – what shall we call it? – the *protector* of the widow Agnes, am I right?'

'I have that honour.' Theo's answer was stiff as dead men's limbs. 'Who are you, sir?'

'I am Louis of Blois – her nephew. You fight well. I was preparing to ransom you, but maybe I should rather hang you by your boots for the dishonour you do her – living unwed. Not that I blame you. She always was—'

It was perhaps meant lightly, but Theo found a last store

of strength and launched himself free of the men holding him. They pulled him back, all too easily, and one kneed him in the stomach and another punched him in the back of the head. He went down, a thousand stars bursting in the sudden blackness before his eyes.

'Well? Has the emperor's relief force departed?'

'No, no, he . . .' The messenger's face was pink with running and unspoken knowledge, pinker still when Euphrosunê seized him by the shoulders and snapped,

'What? What have you come to tell me? Speak!'

The man, who Agnes thought had looked almost cocky when he first appeared, mislaid his courage and started to wave his hands in odd directions, stumbling over a jumble of words that made no sense. A sharp jab in the chest silenced him.

'Breathe, there, that's right. Better? Now, tell me slowly, what has happened?'

The man swallowed and glanced at Agnes, grateful that there was somebody else in the room.

'The . . . the emperor has gone.'

'Gone? I should hope so. What was all that fuss about, heh?'

She flicked her hand to dismiss him and would have turned her back on him, but the messenger, abandoning long centuries of protocol, tugged at her sleeve to stay her. Euphrosunê stared at his hand.

'You'd better have a good explanation ready if you want to keep that.'

'I do . . . that is, the emperor has left the City – not to fight. He took ship at the Bukoleon. He sailed west. He has gone. He . . .'

The man tailed off and edged away from the empress, who was white and wheezing, the fingers of her right hand fluttering in front of her. Agnes took her hand and gripped it tight in her own.

'Courage,' she said. 'We shall need all our courage now.'

Still Euphrosunê could not speak.

'Wait,' Agnes commanded the man, who had almost managed to creep away. 'Do you know more? Where has he gone. Who with?'

The man glanced at Euphrosunê, then at Agnes, scared not so much of them, she realised, but of what might happen to a man seen with them now. He could scent trouble and plainly wanted to be as far from them as possible. She left Euphrosunê's side and stood close by the messenger.

'Please, tell me what you know.' She smiled, and he smiled back, and when he spoke, it was almost conspiratorially.

'The emperor ordered the company commanders to assemble by the Petrion Gate and wait for him before advancing. When he did not come, they sent runners to find him. I was one of the runners. Somebody told me they'd seen the emperor hurrying towards the harbour with a few servants and his daughter.'

'His daughter? Which one?'

'I did not see her face, but I think it was the eldest.'

Agnes nodded. Eirene, that would make sense.

'You saw them board a boat with your own eyes?'

'I did. Should I have stopped them? I did not know how to. I did not know who to—'

'It's all right,' said Agnes, although it wasn't. 'You did the right thing,' she added, although he hadn't.

'Now . . .' She glanced over her shoulder at Euphrosunê, who was looking down from the wall, strangely oblivious. 'Now,' she repeated, 'the empress wishes you to . . .' She left a small pause so the empress could say what she wished, but when Euphrosunê did not turn around, let alone speak, she decided there was only one thing to say.

'Return to the gate. Tell the commanders not to delay a moment longer. Tell them the empress wishes them to advance on Galata. Tell them—'

'Agnes, wait.'

But Agnes did not want to wait. She wanted soldiers to go, now, that moment, to help Theo.

'Euphrosunê, surely that is the right, the only—'

'It's too late. Look . . .'

Agnes followed where her finger was pointing. What was she meant to be looking at? A line of ships was sailing across the water. Her eyes widened.

'The rest of the fleet is making for the Golden Horn.'

'Which means . . .'

'Which means they have the tower. Which means the Great Chain is down.'

Which means Theo is dead. But I won't, I can't think about that now.

They were both running outside, through the peaceful courtyards, out and up on to the wall. They were not alone. Word was racing through the palace.

'The emperor's gone.'

'The chain's down.'

'They're coming.'

'They're coming.'

Agnes and Euphrosunê stood between guards and cookboys, maids and money-men, watching the fleet advance. Everyone forgot who was who and only stared at the impossible thing that was unfolding before them.

'What can we do?' asked Agnes.

'Nothing. We have no ships. The harbour is theirs,' Euphrosunê said, her voice somehow sad and completely calm. 'I know what you're thinking. There's no need to say it.'

'You do?'

Agnes hoped she didn't. She was wondering how the greatest empire the world had ever known had such miserable harbour defences, how Euphrosunê – who she had always thought was an able woman, whatever anyone else said – had known this and done nothing.

'All the danger seemed to come by land,' Euphrosunê said,

and Agnes realised she was imploring her to understand. 'The tribes, the Serbs, the Bulgars. They were no threat by sea. None. The only men who came here by water wanted to trade – not to fight. Or so I thought.'

Shouts broke out below them.

'Euphrosunê! Euphrosunê!'

No title. No honorific. No courtesies.

Agnes looked down. Below her, approaching the walls – at a run, if youth and health permitted – were dozens of people, court people, whom fear and panic had turned into a dangerous swarm. The real enemy, the enemy on the water, had outmanoeuvred them, and they were looking to console themselves the only way they knew. They were looking for somebody to blame – somebody to punish.

Euphrosunê had enjoyed too much power for too long, and it would be easy to find people who hated her. They probably hated her more than they hated the Franks. With the Franks, nothing was personal – not yet. The Franks had broken no careers, emptied no pockets, blocked no marriages.

'Her too, her too.'

Agnes felt men take both her arms and march her down the steps after Euphrosunê. She'd been her friend, and that was more than enough to make them hate her too. Nobody was hurting them, though, not yet. But as men, all of whom she knew by name, none of whom looked her in the eye, hustled them back to the palace, she smelt the sour sweat of panic in the air, and knew it would take very little for life to become death, a quick bloody end that would leave those who did it breathless and ashamed.

Where were they going? Not to the prisons. That was something. The noise of many voices was building in front of them, many voices arguing. She was pushed into the Hall of the Golden Couches, where fifty, maybe a hundred people were locked in debate.

It was impossible to make out who was arguing in favour

of what, let alone who was winning. Everyone was calling for a new emperor, but she heard as many names bounce off the walls as there were churches in the City. And when one name was taken up and shouted loudest, it would turn out the man was at the other end of the empire, or if he was in the room, he would shake his head, put up his arms, back away, say he was unworthy.

'In trouble, Agnes?' murmured a voice behind her.

She turned. Constantinos was leaning against the back wall, watching. The men guarding her bristled, but he laughed and said,

'Don't worry, gentlemen. I'm not planning to whisk away your charge from under your noses. I only want to talk to her.'

Money changed hands. The guards relaxed and let him approach.

'And there I was thinking you were going to save me.'

'You didn't really think that.'

'No, of course I didn't.'

'Don't worry though, my dear, I should imagine the Franks will do that for you.'

'Do what?'

'Save you. It's only a matter of time before somebody walks out of this room and opens one of the gates in return for a place by the side of the boy Alexios.'

'And that doesn't bother you?'

'Of course it does. But I have to admit that I am at a loss as to what to do other than go and practise my Latin.'

'How can you say such a thing? Think. *Think.* We cannot, we must not let them in.'

'But the momentum is all theirs. Our forces are scattered. Everyone is demoralised. As for the Franks, they've sworn to put the rightful ruler on the throne. And they are mad for honour; mad for oaths. They will stop at nothing until it is done.'

The rightful ruler.

'Constantinos . . .' Agnes began, and stopped herself. It was a ridiculous idea, and yet it would buy them time. And time was what they needed.

'What, my dear?'

'Could we not call their bluff?'

'What do you mean?'

'I mean, there's one name nobody's said yet.'

For a moment his face was motionless, thinking, but she knew it would not be long before he understood. She was right. A light she could swear was delight glinted in his eyes. He took her hand and kissed it reverently.

'You think they'll go for it?' she asked, gesturing towards the men arguing all about them.

'Yes, I rather think they will. Excuse me . . .'

But she put out a hand to draw him back.

'After you've made them agree, might you point out to a few useful people that if they find themselves negotiating with the Franks, it would help not to have caused me any undue distress? Best not to lock up the Frankish king's sister?'

He smiled.

'I think I would feel comfortable making that point on your behalf.' He touched her briefly on the shoulder. 'Well played.'

Agnes watched Constantinos weave through the room, whispering a word here, a word there. It was like watching a confused sea resolve itself into stately billows, the winds eased, the rocks sank out of sight, the cliffs retreated.

This was how decisions were made, she thought. Not by godlike figures perched up high, wise and capable and knowing, but by frightened men and women trying to salvage anything they could from the wreckage.

But the Franks wouldn't think that. The Franks would think it was a classic piece of Greek trickery, and she allowed herself to feel proud. That was how empires lasted, wasn't it? They were built by soldiers and fighting – but it was through cunning that they endured.

The next day

Theo couldn't remember being wounded, but when he woke – or came to; sleep was not the same as lying numb and lifeless – he found that his arms prickled with the sting of countless cuts and his right thigh burned where a deep gash had been roughly bound. An immense thirst had sealed his mouth and throat, stopping him thinking about anything other than *water, water.*

He lifted an arm to dip a pitcher into what he prayed was a water bucket, and moaned aloud. A dead weight had stolen into his whole body, as if he were moulded from wood and stone, not flesh. He propped himself up, his back against a wall, his head ringing so loudly that he could not tell where dizziness ended and pain began.

After the Franks had laid him in this cell – a little storeroom, probably, with one barred window – he'd returned to consciousness long enough to see the Chain floating away and the boats, so many boats, streaming into the harbour. Then his eyes closed again and he was suffocating under the weight of thousands of sails, heavy and wet with brine. The ships' prows were pointing at his throat, but he couldn't run. Every time a ship was about to skewer him, it veered aside, to be replaced by another and another.

He shivered, whether from cold or weakness he did not know, and strained his ears. It was quiet. Not absolute silence; there were soldier sounds on all sides. Shouts and horses – the normal noises of a camp. But there was no urgency, no sense of a battle close at hand nor preparations for an attack.

Somebody removed the bar of the door and it creaked open.

Theo hoped it was a jailer bringing him some of the breakfast he could smell wafting up the stairwell, but instead, to his surprise, the Frank – Louis, the one he'd bested on the parapet – walked in. The next surprise was that he was holding a bundle of fresh clothes – and Theo's sword.

'Come on, Branas. You're going home.'

'You've not ransomed me already?'

Louis shook his head. He looked angry.

'No. No.'

'Then what . . . ?'

'Your emperor fled in the night. Turned tail. So whoever was left in command thought they'd amuse themselves with a little trick. They've sent – as innocent as day – to say that Isaakios is back on the throne and is longing to be reunited with his son.'

'Isaakios?' Theo thought he could not have heard right. 'Isaakios Angelos?' he repeated.

Louis looked at him, sharp. 'You do not rejoice?'

I took his eyes and his throne both one day. Of course I do not rejoice.

'If God has willed it thus, let it be so,' was all he said.

'Have it your own way. I have come to say that we are sending four envoys to treat with this emperor. You may return with them. A gesture of our goodwill.'

Theo stumbled to his feet, praying that his legs would not shame him, and followed Louis out into the courtyard. There he caught sight of the boy Alexios, the boy who had returned from the west with a foreign army at his back.

He had a lot of his father in his face, the same bloom to the cheeks, the same full lips, the same small eyes, but whereas Isaakios had a sort of imperviousness, a blithe public confidence – which God knew his qualities did not warrant – this boy looked ill at ease with his borrowed armour, his borrowed strength. Theo saw that he was quarrelling with an old man, a Venetian, bent and bowed, leaning on a stick.

'It's my right. You can't stop me. You can't.' He was whining, pleading, and Theo longed to silence him. 'My father, my people, they are waiting for me. They will honour my words.'

He began to swear all manner of sacred oaths, but they had no effect on the old man. He shook his head, tutting, and patted Alexios on the shoulder.

'My dear boy,' he began, in a voice that fluted, 'your faith in paternal love does you credit. But forgive an old man's suspicions. I have treated with the Rôman race these long, long years and if I know aught, it is that they know how to drive a bargain. They have opened negotiations, that is all. You are not yet crowned.'

'But they cannot crown my father alone. They cannot.' He all but stamped his foot. 'He is old and stupid and blind . . .'

The man coughed, and Alexios stuttered to a halt.

'I mean . . . I should . . . you cannot forbid me to board a boat to my own City. You cannot. You . . . you . . . you will not.'

His face grew redder still, but the old man turned his back on him. It was only then that Theo saw that his eyes were white blanks, a milky emptiness. So this was the doge of Venice, Enrico Dandolo. Every man knew that he had lost his sight when the Rôman mob had stormed the Venetian quarter back in Manuelos's time; but every man also knew that he loved the City's wealth more than he hated what it had done to him.

Dandolo took the arm of a young aide and walked slowly to where two Venetians and two Franks were mounted and ready, the seamen's horses mere ponies beside the Franks' massive chargers. Theo could not catch what he said. His voice never rose above a murmur, but there was no doubt he was giving his countrymen very clear instructions, no doubt that the men respected him and would obey.

A squire brought a horse for Theo, and he did not refuse when the man cupped his hands to boost him into the saddle. Only then did Alexios catch sight of him.

'You . . .' the boy gasped, and drew his sword.

Theo kneed his horse into a fast trot to follow the four envoys. He glanced behind him to see Alexios trying to argue with Louis, but the Frank had a good grip on his arm and was shaking his head. *Luckily for me*, thought Theo. But he found he was ashamed the boy had given up so easily.

Theo and the envoys rode along the Galata shore, the City unrolling to their left on the other side of the Golden Horn. He tried to talk to them – the two Franks, Mathieu something and Geoffroi something, and the two Venetians, whose names he had not caught at all – but they ignored him, as politely as possible. He also noticed that although each pair of men exchanged a few muttered words, they did not talk to each other.

He began to guess at the divisions and difficulties that might lie at the heart of this campaign. It was tempting to lump them all together as Latins, westerners, not-Rômans, but he knew the Venetians and the Franks were as different as the moon and the sun. The Venetians had the boats and were interested in money and trade; the Franks had the arms and sought something less tangible – the glow of pride, not the glint of gold.

The Venetians had probably seen the City before, but the two Franks rarely took their eyes off the walls, off the great cathedral domes looming behind them. Theo remembered riding into Paris when he was a boy. *That pitiful town is the largest city they've ever known. What do they make of our City?* He did not need them to answer that. *They fear it. They covet it. And they hate us for possessing it.*

Despite everything, Theo could only smile when they rode up to Blachernai. He knew the City must be reeling from the previous day's rout, the flight of the old emperor, and whatever demented scheming had placed Isaakios on the throne, but the envoys would have struggled to guess that anything was amiss when they beheld the aristos assembled in the palace.

415

However much it might frustrate him, the City was doing what it did best – it was putting on a great show.

Every woman, every man, too, was bathed, curled and polished, the women painted and beautiful, the men fragrant and grand as they stroked their beards. Theo saw men he knew but a day since had fled caterwauling before the Frankish charge, but this morning they looked like guests at the country wedding of a favourite niece – calm, benign, even a little superior. It was as if nobody had thought of swords or battle or defeat in a generation.

It was only when he looked at their red eyes, at the way they blinked and shifted from foot to foot, that he knew how few of them had slept that night.

But he doubted the envoys would notice. They had looked pretty fine amidst the rest of the westerners, robed in their ceremonial best, but here, alone among the flower of the City, the brave Frankish knights and the powerful sea-lords stank of sweat and horse and the stewed onion and blood sausage they had breakfasted on that morning.

The crowds parted before them, and there – there was Isaakios on his throne. So it was true. Up until that moment, Theo had not really believed it.

A wrap of purple silk masked his eyes and cast much of his face into shadow, so it was hard to form a sense of him. His face, where it was visible, was pale and puffy, set against wet blood-red lips, which were working slowly. His neck had sunk into his shoulders and his hands were shaking, very slightly, fluttering up and away before coming back to rest on the arms of his chair.

Theo felt a surge of anger. It was a mockery. Men might grow sick or old or mad or all three while they sat upon the throne, but to raise a man like Isaakios so high, that was against God, against everything.

His eyes raked the room. Who had been behind this? All the old council were still there. He could see Constantinos a few steps behind the throne. Only Euphrosunê was absent. And where was—

A gasp and a hand grabbed him out of the crowd.

'Theo, I thought, dear God, I thought . . .' and there she was. Agnes. Burying her head against him. He pressed her to him. *She does love me. She does. I swear she does.* A feeling of triumph, relief, something, raced through his limbs, easing the pain. She had not held him like that for a long time. Only for a moment, though. They both remembered where they were and drew themselves upright.

'I thought you were lost,' she whispered. 'I saw the Chain fall. I thought you were . . .'

He shook his head. 'No. I live.' He smiled, squeezed her hand, and lowered his voice further. 'But Agnes, what madness happened last night? This idiocy, it's a travesty . . .'

Something flickered in her eyes.

'I . . . I don't think it's madness,' she replied. 'Think, Theo, who else? The Franks can't attack the City now. They can't. Not when the man they say should be emperor *is* emperor. They can't. Don't you see? It would be against the Pope, God, the Faith. They will have to go now. They'll have to.'

He was about to argue when Isaakios's voice sounded above the throng. Once it had boomed, full of wine and belly-deep cheer; now it quavered, weak and querulous.

'Gentlemen, and ladies too, I hear your sweet voices, come, speak. I feel like I am playing that game, you know the one? One child covers his eyes and gropes in the dark trying to seize his playmates.' He giggled and waggled his fingers in front of him. 'Shall we start the game? Whom do I hunt? I am ready.'

A few men snickered, and Theo grimaced. The man's humour had soured, but it was still there, still unseemly, still ready to turn great men into clowns, clowns into great men. If Isaakios could not see the effect he was having on the room, he could taste it, smell it. He smiled.

'The emperor bids the noble envoys approach,' the translator supplied.

The two Franks and the two Venetians exchanged wary glances and walked between the ranks of City people.

'Are they on their knees?' Isaakios called. 'Do their foreheads touch the floor?' He turned to one side and whispered to nobody and everybody, 'Being emperor is precious hard when you cannot see.'

The translator made a sign and the men, uneasy, did the proper obeisance.

'Is my boy here?' Isaakios clapped his hands together. 'I long to feel his strong arms about my neck to hear his sweet voice. Such a brave boy to deliver his dear papa. Where is my boy?'

'The emperor enquires after his son.'

One of the envoys, Geoffroi, Theo thought, stepped forward and coughed, a little pompous, a little uncertain.

'Imperial majesty, our greetings. We have done you and your son a very great service, and have thereby rightfully fulfilled our part in our sworn covenant. We cannot consent to his coming to your side until he can in turn guarantee his part.'

The translator did his best – although the words came out even more twisted in Greek than they had in Latin.

'What's this? What's this?' Isaakios twitched his head from side to side. 'Covenant? Does anyone here know anything about any covenant? Nobody told me about a covenant.'

A murmur rippled through the room, and Geoffroi looked about him as if hoping for the charade to stop, for the real emperor to appear.

'Perhaps we might speak apart?' he asked.

'What's that he says? He wants to speak in private? No, no. Do not leave me alone with them. I know why they are here. For the same reason the old barbarian Barbarossa came here. To steal. To steal.'

418

The envoy reddened a little when the translator said his request had been denied – omitting the rest – but he continued boldly enough.

'Your imperial majesty would know of the covenant your son made with us. I shall name the particulars. If we returned him to his rightful place on the throne of the empire, he swore to reward our armies with two hundred thousand silver marks and to furnish them with a year's supply of provisions. He swore he would send ten thousand of your finest knights in your own ships to fight in Egypt and henceforth maintain a further five hundred knights in the Holy Land. Finally, he pledged to return the eastern church to the jurisdiction of Rome. That is all. That is what he swore, so help me God.'

A few in the hall knew enough scraps of Latin to understand at least part of what he was saying, and a roar was building steadily even while the translator was doing his work.

'Does he jest?' Isaakios called. 'Are we to service your wives as well?'

The translator opened his mouth and shut it again. Isaakios continued.

'Yesterday I was a blind man in a tower. I had sea breezes and food, good food. The days passed. Last night the men who stole my throne appeared at my bedside and told me they needed me back on it. I rejoiced then; I do not rejoice now. My son has hawked my throne to a gang of wandering swordsmen. If he wants to join me up here, he is welcome. For the rest I say only this. I love you not. Be gone.'

After a small pause, the translator said,

'The emperor is grateful for your efforts, and would be happy for his son to assume the purple. But as to your other requests, he regretfully says they cannot be granted.'

The envoys looked at one another. They did not like it, but they had obviously prepared for this moment.

'We hold the harbour. We shall take action to claim what is ours,' said Geoffroi.

'Threats! And you say you came here to help me. You bewilder me. Am I not right to be bewildered?'

And he looked about him, an old man seeking reassurance, although it was hard to see where the line lay between truth and play-acting.

Geoffroi forged ahead. 'We will attack. We are not afraid to fight.'

Theo could not restrain himself.

'And neither are we. You have the harbour, yes, we'll grant you that. But the harbour is not the City, and no army can take the City.'

'As your father found to his cost, eh, Theo?' Isaakios murmured. 'It is you, isn't it? No, no, don't mind me. Speak on. Speak on. Time for reunions and so forth later.'

Theo swallowed and did as he was bid.

'You have no reason to be here. None. No Christian cause. Why are you here? Why? What did you say the day you sailed here? *Here is your rightful lord.* Well, we say our rightful lord is already here. What do you say?'

It was one of the Venetians who answered. He had long silken moustaches and a rich silken voice. He spoke good Greek, tainted only slightly with the words and phrases of the dockside.

'My Frankish friends are righteous, brave and noble. When they say they are not afraid to fight, they do not lie. I am sure these two alone would fling themselves at your walls armed with nothing but their teeth.'

He earned a little chuckle for that, especially as it was plain the other two had no idea what he was saying.

'No,' he said, 'they are not afraid to fight, but let me say this by way of warning: we men of the lagoon are not afraid to wait. We are owed money, and we feel no shame in saying we intend to claim it. Your walls are high and thick – but there are other ways. Our doge wishes you to understand that we will blockade your port, wreck your trade and ruin the

City. And what will your restive western provinces do, he wonders, when they realise all your strength is required here?'

He smiled as he saw that he had the room's full attention.

'Surely, so great a city as your own will not struggle to find a little, a very little money. Our cause is, after all, a just one. The cause of Christ. What would the world make of a city that is too poor to contribute?'

The room was silent as everyone absorbed his meaning.

'A blackmailer,' said Isaakios, 'but an honest one.' He turned and beckoned over his shoulder. Constantinos stepped forward and leant down to listen. 'Come, tell me, do we have two hundred thousand silver marks?'

Everyone knew – everyone save the four envoys – the answer to that was simple.

No.

'I cannot say that I have it here up my sleeve, basileus,' the eunuch replied, 'but it is not so fearsome a sum. It can be procured. Our western friends will have to be patient, that is all.'

The Sixth Emperor

The first Rôman emperor to bear the name Alexios lies in state, dead these hundred years or more, his bones revered by all.

The second sinks infinitesimally slowly into the mud at the bottom of the Golden Horn, a bowstring around his neck.

The third quakes in the back room of a fleapit inn halfway between the City and safety.

The fourth is wondering why nobody is cheering as he rides up to the Blachernai Palace. Maybe they do not recognise him. He must tell the guards that in future a herald is to ride before him to proclaim the emperor is nigh.

Alexios enters the palace – his palace – and allows the aristos to congratulate him on his safe return. Their warmth is palpable, their words are gracious. They at least know an emperor when they see one.

He approaches his father, who is wearing womanish robes and too much jewellery. All he can think is that he bets his father never sat a horse half so well as Boniface.

Alexios submits to his father's embrace, his fingernails – very long, very yellow – digging into the skin beneath his tunic, his voice piping in his ear.

'We'll crown you, my boy. Oh yes, we'll crown you. And perhaps then you will be so good as to tell me how you plan to pay the price you set upon your throne.'

'I thought you'd be pleased. You ought to be pleased.'

'Pleased?'

His father's voice disappears under a barrage of coughing and wheezing, but he waves one hand in front of him as if to say he is not yet done.

'You, boy, are a fucking idiot. A buffoon. A poltroon. A . . .'

He slumps in his chair, a line of spittle weaving down his chin. Alexios is at a loss. He turns and appeals to the room.

'These attacks come over him. Sometimes he is lucid. Sometimes not.'

The speaker is a man with deep red hair and broad shoulders. He does not look violent, dressed in long robes and gold. But Alexios knows he is. He knows he is Theodore Branas.

'W-what are you doing here?'

'Looking out for the City. What about you?'

Alexios does not know what to say. He is half this man's age. Half his size. He tries again.

'Why has my father not—'

'Locked me up? Killed me? Just look at him.'

Alexios is about to issue his first order to the Varangians, but judging by the way they are eyeing him, he has a nasty feeling they remember him as the boy the palace girls used to tease, and his nerve falters. He looks back at Theodore Branas, his four-square stance, his easy confidence, and decides to postpone ordering his arrest.

That night he returns to the Latin camp – as the old doge bade him – and drinks wine and rails about the Rômans.

'They're all still there. My uncle's men. They're at my father's side. I'll lock them up. I'll blind them. I'll destroy them. Those men. I'll—'

'You shall do nothing of the sort, dear boy.' Dandolo places a hand on his arm. 'And put that wine down. You have had enough.'

'You shouldn't call me that,' he says, keeping an obstinate grip on his cup. 'Not now I am emperor.'

The doge smiles his dry smile, removes the cup with remarkable dexterity for a man who cannot see, and says that at his age he cannot be expected to remember everyone's names.

'Until we have our money, dear boy, you will not upset this apple cart with talk of revenge. Do you understand? You have your crown. Do not carp about the details. Our money, dear boy, our money . . .'

Alexios realises he finds the doge more frightening than all the Frankish knights put together. If you crossed Boniface, he would only kill you. The doge would probably pursue you all the way to hell.

Early in the autumn of 1203

Agnes and Eudokia were stacking a pair of trays with food and drink while Agathê looked on, telling them from time to time that they were doing it all wrong.

'You're sure you don't mind waiting on Theo's friends, Eudokia?' asked Agnes. 'You don't have to, you know.'

'Of course I don't mind,' she replied. 'I'm just grateful you took me in. Otherwise I'd be stuck with my sister.'

She put a histrionic hand to her forehead, and Agnes laughed. Anna had always been a little bit precious, but ever since their father had vanished – *without even telling me* – and their mother had been locked up – *poor Mama, dear Mama* – she'd been intolerably tearful. Agnes and Eudokia tried to point out that Euphrosunê wasn't chained in a sewer, but confined to three irreproachably comfortable rooms in the Great Palace which Anna visited *every day*, but she wasn't having any of it. It was all a disaster, and the person who was suffering most was her.

But even if things weren't exactly disastrous, it was undoubtedly a strange, topsy-turvy time.

The people of the City, far from shunning the Latins as would-be invaders, were delighted to have so many overawed foreigners wandering the streets, practically tripping over themselves to fall for even the most hackneyed scams.

Agnes lost count of the number of Franks she saw, naked as newborn pups without their armour, clutching armfuls of memorabilia, trailing after guides down some back alleyway – *Holy Wisdom, she this way, your worships.* She knew a gang of pickpockets would be lying in wait to thieve the junk back off them – as well as anything else they had in their pockets – only to reunite with the guides and split the proceeds before waiting for the next boatload of starry-eyed sergeants to cross the Golden Horn on leave.

But although the City streets were merrily fleecing the Latin rank and file, it was a different story inside the Great Palace. The emperors had the bureaucrats working all hours to stockpile enough gold to keep the Latin leadership sweet, ordering it to be shipped over the Golden Horn – often under cover of night – to where Venetian account-men waited with tablets to note the size and shape of every last goblet that passed through their hands.

Agnes and Eudokia carried their trays into the back room, where Theo and a dozen other men were locked in talk.

That was another thing that was upside down. For a man who'd been so angry about the Franks' arrival, Theo had done rather well out of it. Overnight, he'd stopped being a grumpy loner and turned into a sort of hero. Men who'd avoided the old, blunt, graceless Theodore Branas now gravitated towards him, congregating at his house to discuss the farce that was the Isaakios–Alexios regime.

They had to be stealthy. If the new emperors were more confident, they'd already have locked up half the men in the room, and everyone feared they might yet do that – or worse – if only they could prove that dissidents were gathering in large numbers. Some men arrived disguised as tradesmen and left under cover of dark. Others were even reluctant for the servants to see their faces – which was why Agnes and Eudokia were handing out cups.

Faces Agnes was used to seeing in the blaze of grand palace receiving rooms looked smudged and rough-edged in the dim light that glanced through the shutters. Their voices had shrunk, too; no booming oratory, no gales of laughter. The conversation was taut, focused.

'They all seem to be getting on, at least,' whispered Eudokia as she passed Agnes at the far end of the room.

Agnes made a non-committal noise.

Euphrosunê had kept the aristos together, kicking and screaming, for eight years – not that they would ever admit it, let alone thank her for it – but that had all changed with the return of Isaakios. So although the men were supposedly gathered as friends, Agnes thought they looked more like wrestlers sizing each other up before a big competition, eyeing weaknesses, assessing strengths.

'Look,' said Eudokia as they met up again by the door. 'They've hardly touched the sweetmeats.'

She was right. Most of the men were gnawing on strips of dried beef. *They're aping Theo*, she thought with a bubble of amusement. His spartan habits, his soldier stance, the little ridges of his frown – he suited a City infiltrated by enemies.

'What are you two whispering about?' called Theo.

'Nothing, nothing,' said Agnes with a smile.

She stood by his chair, dropped a kiss on his head and he squeezed her hand. That was something else that was different. She and Theo were happy again.

'What news?' she asked him, dimly aware of raised voices coming from the courtyard.

'Laskaris was telling us that our emperors sent their bailiffs to the Church of the Holy Apostles this morning. The wagons are probably halfway to the docks already. Icons, church plate, holy vessels. It's a bloody dis—'

The voices were growing louder. She nudged Theo, who signed to the others to be quiet.

'He's not at home, I tell you.' That was Agathê, sounding strained.

'Then I shall sit myself down right here and take advantage of your hospitality until he returns.'

She knew that voice – and so did Theo. He jumped to his feet, unbarred the door and flung it open. There, on the threshold, stood Murzuphlus, his skin prison-pallid, his body soft and bloated by long confinement. He was mobbed.

'How the devil are you?'

'When did they let you out?'

They were silenced by a crash of breaking earthenware. Everyone turned. Eudokia was standing in the middle of the room, a dozen cups shattered at her feet, the tray clattering on the floor. She was paler even than Murzuphlus, pink-eared and trembling.

'Alexios . . .' she whispered, the only person in the City ever to call him by his right name. 'You're free.'

She threw herself into his arms.

'Yes, I'm free.' That was to her, his eyes tender. 'I am free.' That was to the men in the room. 'No thanks to any of you, my erstwhile friends.' He held up one hand to stop their protests. 'No, no, I'm not here to pick a fight. It was my own fault. I should never have believed a man called John the Fat was going to be emperor.'

Most of the men laughed at that – not Theo, though.

'You're bloody lucky to be alive at all,' said Raoul.

'Correct,' said Murzuphlus. 'And I know who I have to thank.' He kissed Eudokia. 'Your influence with your mother saved me, did it not?'

'She used to really like you.'

'But not enough to let you marry me.'

'No. And then you—'

'And then I tried to depose your father.'

'She went off you a bit after that.'

They were grinning at each other; it was infectious. Everyone was enjoying their reunion. Only Theo was unsmiling.

'Murzuphlus?' he said. 'What exactly are you doing here?'

'Well, Branas, if we are to cut straight to business . . .'

'We are.'

'. . . then I shall tell you. My star has waxed at court.

Because I once tried to toss his brother off the throne, Isaakios has conveniently forgotten I once did the same to him.' He shook his head. 'By God, he's unhinged. Sometimes he thinks Andronikos is still alive. Sometimes he thinks it's his old friend Barbarossa at the gates. When he curses *Alexios*, I never know whether he's talking about his brother or his son and, to be honest, I doubt he does either.'

He was chuckling, probably about to regale them with more palace gossip, when Theo cut across him.

'Tell us why you're here.'

'Give me some credit.'

'I give you none. The last time we spoke—'

'Let me see, was that when you put your sword to my throat and handed me over to the Varangians?'

'No. I wasn't much in the mood for talking then. I mean when you swore blind to me that you'd given up any idea of fucking up the peace of the empire to put John's fat arse on the throne just so you could—'

'Stop!' Agnes planted herself between them. 'In fact, don't even start. You're meant to be friends. *Be* friends, for the love of God. Murzuphlus is obviously here for the same reason as the rest of them. Because he hates—'

'They're coming, sebastê!' Agathê was having to shout to make herself heard. 'They're coming! Hide, everyone, hide!'

'Who? Who's coming?'

'*Franks.* Our watch boy on the Mesê's seen them. *Franks.* Any number of them. Asking for the dwelling of Branas. They'll be here any moment.'

Everyone stared at Murzuphlus.

'You . . .' Theo had him by the throat. 'What the hell have you done?'

'Get off me, Branas. I wouldn't . . . I swear . . . This is but chance.'

'Chance be damned. You've led them straight—'

Laskaris tore them apart.

'Quiet, be quiet.'

Agnes threw him a grateful look and turned to the servant.

'Agathê, please compose yourself. Go out into the courtyard – nice and calm now – greet them and ask what they want.'

Nobody spoke after Agathê left. Theo walked, soft-foot, to where the men's weapons lay piled, and handed out swords. After a moment's hesitation, Agnes saw him toss a blade to Murzuphlus.

Agathê returned.

'Mistress, there's only two of them that want to come in. There are others, lots of them, but they're waiting outside. Their interpreter says they beg leave to visit with the sister of their king. Agnes, it's you they want to see.'

Murzuphlus gave a low laugh.

'A social call. Brilliant. Who knew the Franks had it in them? Can I hand round the cakes?'

Everyone was relaxing – although still taking care to be quiet. Agnes was not amused. She'd been hoping that they'd forgotten all about her.

She nodded.

'Show them into the orchard, Agathê. Tell them I am here alone and cannot receive them inside.'

'You don't have to—' began Theo.

'I do. I must. They might come again. And that is too dangerous for you – for all of us.'

Theo nodded and kissed her cheek.

'Good luck.'

She gave him a grim smile. 'You should be wishing them luck. After I'm done with them, they won't show their faces again here in a hurry.'

'Agnes, wait a moment . . .'

Murzuphlus was trying to stop her, but she didn't want to listen to any more of his jokes. She swept out of the room before he could finish, flipped her veil down and strode to the orchard, where the Franks were waiting – Louis, and a man who could only be Boniface, the third son of Montferrat, Renier and Conrad's other brother.

They looked at their interpreter. The interpreter looked at Agnes, expecting her to speak. She looked at them.

'Is this the lady Agnes?' asked Louis.

The interpreter repeated the question in Greek.

Agnes nodded.

The interpreter nodded to Louis, who bounded towards her. He might even have embraced her, but she took several steps backwards and folded her arms. He stopped, looking foolish.

'Is it you, Agnes?' he said, uncertain. He turned back to their interpreter. 'Ask her again. Is it Agnes?'

Again he asked; again Agnes nodded.

'Tell her who I am,' urged Louis. 'Tell her I am her nephew, Louis. Ask her whether she remembers me. Ask her how she does.'

She waited while the interpreter finished and then answered in Greek.

'Tell him I know exactly who he is. Tell him he ought to be ashamed of himself.'

Louis's face fell as the interpreter murmured his translation. She was going to enjoy this.

'Tell him that he is here against God, against religion, against the express wishes of his Pope. Tell him that if he had one jot of honour he would never have come to the City. And now he *is* here – to his eternal shame – now he has robbed our churches, drunk our wine, fucked our whores . . .' the interpreter changed that to *lain with* but she saw him flinch all the same '. . . now he brings his friend to gawp at his own mother's sister. Begone! Begone, before I set my dogs on you!'

She turned on her heel and returned to the room to find Theo and his friends weak with laughter. They heard the gate clang as the Franks hurried away.

'You heard?' she asked.

'Did we hear?' said Laskaris. '*Begone?* Priceless, Agnes, priceless.'

'Although,' grinned Theo, 'technically we don't have any dogs.'

Suddenly Agnes was aware that she didn't feel well. She carried on smiling, but that meeting, the tension in the City, something was making her sick and light-headed. *I'm going to be queen of the world.* Out of nowhere, those words rang in her head. A little girl, dancing and whirling. She felt dizzy remembering her.

'Um . . . gentlemen . . .' said Murzuphlus, as the laughter died down. 'Much as we all enjoyed that, I'm afraid we – or rather, Agnes – may have made a small tactical error. We need to know how things stand inside the Frankish camp. A source would have been extremely useful.'

They all turned to her. She put a hand out to lean against the table. Of course. Why hadn't she thought of it before? What could be simpler? Everyone was still looking at her.

'Agnes, are you all right?' said Theo.

'Yes.' She swallowed, and breathed in and out a few times. 'Yes, I'm fine. I understand. You're all thinking I should, spy on them. Why not? I can be a spy.'

'I beg your pardon, Agnes,' said Laskaris, 'but after that – ah – that display, aren't they going to be a little chary?'

'Bloody terrified, more like,' said Raoul.

Agnes thought for a moment, then shook her head.

'Not necessarily. Perhaps I can even make it work to my advantage. I'll tell them my servants are paid to watch me. I'll tell them I feared my cruel master would punish me if I met with them with kindness.'

'Your cruel master?' Theo looked partly amused, partly offended.

The others laughed.

'I'll spin them a good story and they'll believe it because

it's what they want to hear. How low I fell. How my only hope was to cleave to Theodore Branas. How I bear him no love and he bears me no honour, but I have no choice, tossed as I am on the rocks of fate. How does that sound?'

'Convincing,' said Laskaris.

'Very convincing,' said Murzuphlus.

'Too bloody convincing,' muttered Theo.

'Then we're agreed?' said Agnes.

A week later

Two hours before dawn, robed as inconspicuously as possible, Agnes was waiting on her knees in the Hagia Eirene, one of the smaller churches in the old Latin quarter, close to the Golden Horn. It was a run-down area of rickety wharfs and abandoned tenements. A dead dog had been rotting in the street outside. The memory almost made her retch. Maybe she was hungry. She wished she could have a sip of water.

She stared at the marble blocks of the church walls. They were shot through with different patterns, like the hides of various creatures stitched together. No, she mustn't think about dead animals. Maybe they were like the outline of distant hills, layers of rock and snow, of haze and cloud. She looked away. The undulating patterns were making her queasy again. Or maybe it was the thick scent of the candles that was so oppressive.

She heard footsteps and bowed her head still lower.

'Madam.'

Louis's voice was stiff and wary. She tipped her veil back and took his hands.

'Forgive me, oh, but can you forgive me?'

'For what do you owe me forgiveness?'

He withdrew his hands and she saw his expression harden. She realised at once that she had misjudged him. He was no longer a boy to be tormented as she pleased. She dropped her gaze.

'I'm sorry. That's all. I was frightened.'

A pause.

'Because that man . . . ?'

'Yes. He was listening. I had to be short with you. I'm sorry.'

'You are with him against your will?'

Even though she knew Theo would understand, she did not want to deny him.

'Do you doubt it?' she said. 'I have suffered. I cannot tell you how much. And now you are here – my own flesh and blood. All I ask is that when you leave, you take me with you. Can you do that? Will you help me, Louis?'

'Aunt Agnes . . .' Louis began, and she smiled. He caught the smile and returned it. 'Aunt Agnes, I feel as keenly as you do all that you have endured at the hands of the Greeks. The dishonour, the humiliation . . . no, I will not speak of it. We shall bear you hence. Of course we shall. I swear it.'

'How long must I wait?' she asked.

'That depends.' He hesitated and glanced at the doors. 'We are not overheard?'

She shook her head. 'I took every precaution.'

'Good.' He leaned in closer. 'The situation is delicate. Alexios is a good boy. Well, he tries to be. He fears the Greeks will kill him the day we sail, so he is offering us more money – a great deal more money – if we stay. He has said he will pay the Venetians for another year's service. *Another year.*' He pressed her hand as if to make sure she understood. 'With that sort of money, we cannot fail. We can free Jerusalem and our names will forever be spoken with honour.'

His eyes were shining with something sweet and simple – zeal; something she hadn't seen in a long time. Then he frowned.

'But there is a problem. The men. They do not understand why we are here. They want to fight Saracens, but they see churches and crosses. The situation is . . .'

'Delicate?'

'You understand. There is some division.'

'Oh, there is division in the City, too.'

He glanced towards her.

'Could you tell me what the mood is towards us in the City? Does your . . . does Theodore Branas speak of it?'

She paused as if in thought, although she had her answer ready.

'He and many like him believe you want to take the City. They believe everything else is posturing and lies.'

'And what do you believe, Agnes?'

'That he is wrong. I told him the Pope would never sanction an attack on fellow Christians. I told him he does not understand you. I said you only came to do your duty – to restore a young prince to the throne. Is that not so?' She smiled at him. 'It is easy to ignore wrongdoing, but you brought justice. I admire you for it.'

Louis shifted and looked away.

'Yes, justice. Yes, that is all. Farewell. I shall write to your brother the king and tell him that we have found you.'

'No!' Her voice sounded too loud in the church. Her brother. Philip. Her virtuous, self-righteous, sanctimonious brother. 'Please, tell him nothing. You have taken pity on me. But I fear he will not be so merciful.'

'No man should judge you. Not after all you have borne.'

'My brother will not see it that way. He always said I wanted to ride too high. He always said I would get burnt. He'll tell his daughters to be good or they'll end up like me. A man's mistress, childless, friendless, alone.'

And suddenly she was no longer pretending. She was crying for real. She buried her face in her hands.

'You can stop now. He's gone.'

She stared up at Theo, who had appeared by her side.

'I am a failure. I am. I am. I cannot bear it. He will go back to his friends and laugh and say I am old and ugly and barren . . .' The sobs overwhelmed her again. 'I am a concubine. A courtesan. A soldier's whore.'

'That's not true. What's wrong with you? None of that's true.'

'It is. You don't understand. You couldn't understand. How could you?'

Theo seized her by the shoulders and shook her until the tears changed from self-pity to anger. She threw him off, ready to shout at him. But he was shouting at her.

'Stop it. Stop wallowing. Stop thinking you alone have suffered. Of course I understand. I understand too well.'

When he saw that she was not trying to shout over him, his voice quietened a little.

'I have no family. They are dead. All dead. All gone. My boyhood friends and I have changed sides so many times we none of us can look each other in the eye. I have become what your Louis says we are. Disloyal, sly, devious, treacherous. I have become the kind of man my father and I used to despise.'

'That's not true.'

'It is, Agnes. It is. At your wedding – your first wedding – I stood beside my father and we laughed at the Angelos brothers, at Isaakios and Alexios. I remember it so clearly. I was happy because I was a Branas like my father and we were good men. And I knew those other men, men like Isaakios, were smaller and weaker – worse than us.'

'They *are* worse, so much—'

But he cut her off.

'No. All that was my arrogance. My conceit. I thought I could wade through it all and still come out a decent man. But what have I done? I've sat back and watched one fool after another clamber on to the throne. How did that happen? Tell me – how did that happen?'

'I don't know. But at least you've always tried to do what was right. Not like me,' she added bitterly. 'I've only ever done what was necessary.'

'Sometimes they're the same thing,' he said, pulling her fiercely to him. 'You never give in. That's right. You never give up. That's right, too.'

The same day

Theo sent Agnes home in the company of six of his men, and set off to find Murzuphlus, Laskaris and the others to tell them what she had learnt.

As he skirted round the approaches to the docks, he came upon a gang of Frankish soldiers, not grand knights, but men from the ranks who were allowed to cross into the City according to a strict rota. They were drunk, singing snatches of songs in soaked voices, jumping on each other's backs, play-fighting and catcalling. They'd been whoring. Several were too addled and clumsy to have done up their breeches. There were two, maybe three dozen of them – and any City folk out on the streets were melting away as they approached.

Theo followed them as they stumbled down the hill towards the sea walls. He was angry. He told himself he wanted to make sure nobody was hurt. Maybe he was actually looking for an excuse to hurt them.

Ahead of them stood the tiny mosque of Mitaton. They might have passed it by, but one man stopped to piss against its walls. A shutter snapped open and an angry voice shouted down at him in Arabic-accented Greek. The Frankish soldier, who doubtless did not understand, turned around, lowered his breeches and opened his bowels. The others laughed and cheered, their red faces flickering in the torchlight, oaths clotting their mouths. One or two at the fringes of the group called him away, pointing to the dockside, where the barges were waiting to carry them back to their camp, but they were a minority.

Theo fingered his sword – and ordered himself not to do anything foolish.

A glimmer of dawn was beginning to show on the horizon, and from above he heard an old man's voice begin the call to prayer. Normally he would have paid it no mind. There were a handful of mosques in the City to service the merchants and travellers who prayed to Allah, and the Rômans did not mind them much. There were not too many of them, and they weren't obviously richer than anyone else.

But the Franks did not feel the same way.

The call to prayer acted like a hunting horn on a pack of hounds. They cocked their ears and called their fellows back from the boats. They shouted up at the man singing his Arabic words – it was easy to drown out his voice, old and shaky as it was – then ran round the side of the mosque and started to batter the doors. Somebody must have barred them in haste, for they did not give, not immediately.

The Franks were calling for blood – revenge for Jerusalem – stirring each other up. After all, they had come all this way to fight Saracens, and they had found some who would be easy to beat.

Theo knew it was time to draw his sword.

'Get back to your camp,' he yelled in Latin. 'Stop this now. I command you in the name of the emperor.'

They turned.

'And who the fuck are you?' slurred a big fellow. 'Who the fuck is he, boys?'

A few men edged away, but most stood their ground. They could see that Theo was alone.

'Saracen lover.' The big man hawked and spat. 'What do we do to Saracen lovers?'

He was weaving left and right, tottering towards Theo. He'd be easy to handle on his own, but his mates were lumbering after him. Theo knew he could kill three or four before he'd be in any danger, and hopefully the rest of them would run for it. No man wanted a good night out to end in death.

Before the first man was on him, Theo realised he would not have to fight alone. City men who had heard the shouting and were coming out of their houses to see what was going on. They weren't soldiers, far from it, but there were a dozen, two dozen, fifty at least, carrying smithy tools, kitchen knives, and their numbers were growing.

'You want a hand there, sir?' asked a lean Rôman. 'We got your back.'

'Thanks,' said Theo. 'Let's give them a fright. Send them back with their tails between their legs.'

'Screw that. Let's chop their tails off.'

The other men liked that, and the Franks started to look scared. More men were coming up from the barges. Theo peered through the half-light. They were City ferrymen, carrying poles, angry after too many nights swallowing insults as they shipped drunk soldiers home.

It was hard to say what happened next. One moment, there was a stand-off with men shouting insults in bastard versions of each other's languages. The next, Theo was fighting for his life in the middle of a sprawling brawl.

The Rôman mob may not have been trained, but they were sober, angry and there were a lot of them. Soon they had backed the Franks into a narrow alley of shacks and storehouses, and Theo was sure he was about to witness a massacre.

But the Franks stopped trying to fight back and began to grab at handcarts, timbers, roofing, anything that lay to hand, anything they could fling in the path of the mob. Theo saw two soldiers upending jars of cooking oil over their barricade – they must have broken into a little shop – and half a dozen fires blazed up between them.

The Rômans cursed and tried to beat the flames down, but they skipped up on to the roofs on either side and jumped over to the next alley. The fire was pale against the dawn light, but the heat pulsing above his head, the roar in his ears told Theo the blaze had already spiralled out of control.

The Franks had vanished, whether to safety or not it was impossible to say. But nobody was thinking about that enemy any more.

'Fire! Fire! Fire!'

On all sides people were spilling out of their houses, screaming, eyes streaming, nearly naked or bundled in sheets, clutching a baby, coins, a sack of meal, a grandmother. For a moment, they stared, and then they ran. And Theo ran with them.

Some things men couldn't fight.

Four days later, Agnes – unwashed, sooty, tired, relieved – sat in their new house. It was north of the church where she had met Louis, a smart merchant's house. Whoever it had belonged to had cleared out shortly after the fire – not because of the flames, they hadn't reached this far north, but because he'd feared retribution. It was no longer safe to be a Latin in the City. Not after what their fire had done.

That first day, Agnes and Theo stood on the roof of their house and watched the City burn at their feet. The flames climbed into the heavens. Embers the size of boulders took flight on the updraught and danced like demons above the roofs before falling to earth to devour districts that might otherwise have survived unscathed. Houses, streets, colonnades, entire quarters of the City perished.

As dusk began to fall, they ordered their servants to load the household's most valuable belongings on to three carts and rode north-west to higher ground. Their leaving was strangely calm. If it hadn't been for the light in the sky, the smell of a thousand cook-fires and the packed streets, they could have been going on a spring visit to Thrace.

Behind them the fire zigzagged, capricious, sweeping over

the Forum of Constantinos, splitting into tributaries, pillaging the Mesê, scorching the hippodrome, and only finally losing its appetite three streets away from the Holy Wisdom itself. *God's mercy.* If the City had lost its church, it would have lost its soul.

Theo and Agnes were only two amongst the tens of thousands, rich and poor, who the fire made homeless. They, like so many others, came wandering back into the centre and gazed, stunned, at the blackened, smouldering wasteland.

Once it was clear they wouldn't be able to find where their house had once stood, let alone live there, Theo moved fast, riding ahead to the abandoned Latin districts and requisitioning a place for them to live. He saw Agnes settled, and he made straight for Blachernai to find out what the two emperors had to say about what their Frankish friends had done to the Queen of Cities.

Agnes wandered in and out of the strange, empty rooms. She tried to think practically – *this will serve as our bedroom; Eudokia and Murzuphlus can lodge here if they wish; Agathê will say the kitchens are too small* – but she was too distracted. Eventually, she just sat down in the hallway, while servants arrived with what possessions they'd salvaged – and anything they could scavenge.

A knock.

The doorman drew his sword and asked who it was. They no longer had the security of an outer courtyard, and a lot of other people were starting to have the same idea about commandeering empty – or not-so-empty – houses.

But it was only Theo. Dirty, exhausted – but with joy burning unmistakably in his eyes. She jumped up and ran to him.

'So . . . ?' she said, already smiling.

'Some of the heat got into Alexios's belly, Agnes. He summoned their leaders to Blachernai yesterday and he told them to go.'

'He what?'

'He's ordered the Franks from our lands.' Theo picked her up and whirled her round. 'That useless boy found a drop of Rôman courage at last.'

'Why are you being so gracious, Theo? He was probably terrified the City would tear him limb from limb if he let them stay.'

Theo grinned and put her down. 'You're right. But he's broken with them and that's all that matters. I wish to God I'd seen their faces. Even the doge lost his famous cool, by all accounts. *Miserable youth*—' Agnes giggled at Theo's impression '—*we dragged you from the mire and to the mire we shall return you.*'

'Not a nice way to talk to an emperor. But what now, Theo?'

He shrugged.

'Either they fear the walls and God's wrath and they go.'

'Or?'

'Or they attack, and if they do, by God, I am ready to fight.'

January 1204

The Franks did not attack, nor did they leave. As the autumn rains gave way to freezing fogs, Agnes could only imagine the arguments that must be plaguing their ranks. But the year failed and still they did nothing – until the winter storms closed the seaway and they no longer had any choice but to remain.

From the scraps of intelligence that made their way over the Golden Horn, from camp to City, it appeared they were starting to hunger. What had been an impressive army was now nothing but thousands of mouths to feed, and the prices set by anyone willing to sell to them were sky high.

But if the men of the Cross were in trouble, so too was the City.

Isaakios was now more mad than not. Agnes often found herself keeping him entertained while Theo and the others tried to persuade his son that as emperor he should ride out against the Franks' foraging parties. She was sure Isaakios had no idea who she was as he babbled gleefully, telling her – *for your ears only, my dear* – that he was a snake, a snake that would shed its skin and rule over the entire world.

Meanwhile, she could hear Alexios umming and aahing, reluctant to commit himself to harrying the Franks. Maybe he felt guilty about his old friends – or maybe he was just scared of Louis's swordpoint. Not Louis, she reminded herself. She'd tried to get word to him soon after the fire, tried to arrange another meeting, but she'd heard he was out of action, prostrate with the quartan fever. Poor Louis.

While Isaakios raved and Alexios stalled, the mood on the streets grew blacker by the day. Not because food was short – the road west was still open, and Alexios did at least understand the need to provide handouts – but because the Franks were *still there*. Only the day before, a mob had smashed up a bronze statue of Athenê, centuries old. Apparently they'd thought she was beckoning to their enemies.

We'd better watch out, Theo had muttered before he left to spend another cold, muddy, probably fruitless day hunting down scavenging Franks. *It won't be long before they start blaming something other than statues.*

And Agnes knew it wasn't just the people Theo was worried about. The aristos, too, were getting jumpy. She'd even heard him and Murzuphlus speculating about who might be the first to break ranks.

Agnes and Eudokia passed a dull day alone in front of their small fire, trying to keep warm, trying to think of cheerful things to talk about, trying not to worry when darkness fell and there was still no sign of either Theo or Murzuphlus.

'I'm going to bed,' said Eudokia after they'd been sitting in tense silence for what felt like hours. 'Then we'll wake up and they'll be home. You'll see.'

'All right,' said Agnes, although she doubted there was any chance she would sleep.

She must have drifted off, however, because some time in the middle of the night she opened her eyes and heard,

'What the fuck were you playing at?'

That was Theo, sounding angry enough to make her spring straight out of bed. She wrapped herself against the chill. She could hear another voice – pacifying, maybe – but quieter, much quieter.

'I don't give a fuck.' Theo again. 'You made me look like a fucking coward.'

She was at the top of the stairs. She could see the tops of two men's heads in the hallway.

'*A coward*. And we all know what a big word that is for you, Theo.' She recognised Murzuphlus's voice, saw his coarse black hair, hanging limp with rain or sweat. 'But I wouldn't go so far as that. Not a coward. A mother hen, maybe.'

'Stop, Alexios.' Eudokia had appeared beside her. She was barefoot, shivering. 'We are guests here. Why are you talking to him like that? Whatever happened?'

Agnes followed her carefully downstairs. A sleepy Agathê was trying to take their cloaks, scowling at the pools of filth spreading around their discarded boots and greaves.

'Theo, what happened?' Agnes asked.

He took a cloth from Agathê and rubbed a layer of grime from his face.

'Ask him,' he said, flinging the cloth at Murzuphlus.

'Murzuphlus?'

'If you insist, Branas. Allow me to relate, Agnes,' he said, twisting the cloth between his hands, 'how I led a bold attack against a unit of the enemy who had dared approach within bowshot of our walls.'

'Like fuck you did. You bit off a party of Franks that was bigger than you could chew and they ran you down and you had to hide behind the walls. But when you saw there was an audience, you charged your men out of the gates like a fucking imbecile and you'd all be dead if I hadn't covered your imbecilic arse.'

'Theo, please.' Agnes put a hand out.

'No, Agnes, no. Don't tell me to calm down. He's a liability. He's a fucking showman who knows everything about looking good and fuck all about fighting.'

She could see that Murzuphlus's customary insouciance was under strain.

'*Fuck all*, was it? I led a tactical retreat into the City, and when I judged the moment right, I counterattacked. How many Frankish dead, Branas? Dozens. And food for a thousand men recovered – food stolen from good Rôman citizens. I doubt they're calling that *fuck all* on the streets. I imagine they're calling it . . . oh, maybe a daring sortie by a brave man. Just what the people needed. A bit of good news.'

'Is that what your cronies are putting about? *A daring sortie?*'

A great deal of shouting had started up outside, and Agnes could hear their doorman trying to tell whoever it was that it was late and they'd be welcome after sun-up. Eventually the man slipped inside, barring the door behind him with difficulty.

'Gentlemen to see you, sebastos. Saying it's urgent.'

'Who is it?' asked Theo.

'Beg pardon,' said the doorman. 'Not you. The other sebastos.'

'Well,' said Murzuphlus, shooting an unfathomable look at Theo. 'Well, well. Show them in.'

Inviting people into another man's house. That was an insult. Maybe it was a mistake – it was late; he'd been fighting – but somehow Agnes doubted it. But before she could see how Theo would react, Laskaris burst in.

'They said you were here, Murzuphlus. The City talks of nothing but your triumph. They say you alone felled three-score knights. They say you've got blood up to your armpits.'

Laskaris might look a little sceptical, but the dozen, no, two dozen men who followed him looked anything but. She'd seen it before. The way men suddenly chose to surround another man and act as if he had all the answers.

More shouts from the streets. She couldn't make out what they were saying, but Laskaris knew.

'Word's spreading. The people are moving to the Holy Wisdom. You know what they're saying? *Murzuphlus, Murzuphlus for emperor.*'

Murzuphlus shrugged his shoulders, a smile almost of resignation on his face.

'Well, gentlemen?' he said. 'The will of the people and all that? A new broom to keep them sweet. I say we end it. Tonight. Who's with me?'

Everyone was, as Agnes knew they would be. Maybe Laskaris wavered an instant – he'd probably had designs of his own – but he was not a man to try to turn the tide. Not like Theo, her Theo.

'I'm not, Murzuphlus. I'm not with—'

'I think we could all have guessed that,' said Murzuphlus, and the other men laughed as readily as if he were already crowned. 'Are you going to shout at me, Theo? Because, you know, I think I've had enough of that for one night.'

'No,' Theo replied, and Agnes ached to hear how his voice shook. 'But I beg you to listen to me. We do not need a new emperor.'

'Why not? You have no love for the boy Alexios. You know he will not lead us to victory. You know—'

'I only know that we don't need a fourth emperor in six months,' Theo continued, dogged. 'Do away with Alexios, and all you do is give the Franks a reason to stay and fight.'

'Oh, you don't care about that, Theo. We all know how much you love *fighting*. Your problem is that you don't think the new emperor should be me. I find that rather hurtful, if I'm honest. Am I so much worse than Isaakios? Than his spineless son?'

'No! That's not the—'

'Then what in hell's name *is* the point, Theo? Do you think it should be you? Want me to run out into the streets and shout your name as loudly as they're shouting mine?'

'It's not about names. It's about . . .' Agnes watched Theo bring himself back under control. 'Since when did you want this, Murzuphlus? Since when?'

Murzuphlus came close, so close that only she and Theo would be able to hear what he said.

'Since I realised I could have it. There comes a time, Theo, when you think *why not me*? It's a long game, after all. The longest there is. But I always knew you didn't have the heart for it, nor the stomach. And neither did your father.'

Murzuphlus stopped, fear on his face. Agnes held Theo's right hand tight in her own.

'Don't, Theo,' she said. 'Just don't. It won't do any good.'

'It's all right,' Theo said. 'I won't rise to that. Very well, Murzuphlus, I can't stop you—' his eyes lit up '—not unless I run you through.'

Murzuphlus flinched and stumbled backwards. Theo laughed.

'*Really?* You think I'd cut you down, here, before these women? Maybe you are the right man for the job after all.' He started up the stairs, but turned around halfway. 'All of you, get the hell out of my house.'

As Agnes followed Theo, she glanced back and saw Eudokia trying to bid Murzuphlus farewell, but the other men were crowding round him, urging him onwards, and they'd raced out into the night before she could reach him, leaving her alone in the hallway, a young woman with tears streaming down her face.

Agnes found Theo stretched out on their bed, looking surprisingly cheerful.

'Should I have done it?' he said, making room for her next to him. 'Should I have killed him?'

'*No!* Of course not. You'd all have butchered each other and I'd be mopping up blood rather than getting into bed with you.' She pulled the blankets up around them. 'Are you really all right?'

He rolled on to his side and kissed her instead of replying immediately. They lay in silence for a while.

'My seventh,' she said suddenly.

'What's that?'

'My seventh emperor. Funny. I once thought Alexios and I would rule until we were old and grey. I thought I'd see my first son take the throne, and then I would die. What did you think?'

Theo smiled.

'My thoughts were never that orderly. But I can tell you

one thing. I never thought that I would love one woman, forsaking all others. Nor did I think I'd be content to lie in bed with her while other men played politics in the dark.'

Now, now is the right time.

She turned so she was lying with her back to him and reached for his arms so they rested on her belly.

'What?' he asked.

'Nothing,' she said. 'Don't move. Just wait.'

She willed it to happen.

A kick. A kick and a roll. Unmistakable.

'What the . . . ?'

She turned round to face him.

'I am carrying a child. Our child, Theo. It has quickened. It is growing. Agathê says maybe four months more.'

He was staring at her.

'Why . . . why did you not tell me before?'

'I wanted to be sure.'

He was shaking his head, bewildered.

'But this changes—'

'Nothing, Theo, it changes nothing. It only means that when you fight the Franks, you have two reasons not to die. You hear me – two. Me and this child.'

'But you cannot stay here.'

'Where am I to go, Theo?'

'Anywhere. To our lands beyond the City. I have friends there. You could—'

She shook her head.

'I won't. You know I won't. Those lands are not safe, anyway. Nowhere is safe. So I will stay where I belong, which is here, with you.'

'In a borrowed bed in a borrowed house.'

'In my borrowed City. At home.'

The Seventh Emperor

Emperor Alexios Doukas, known to friends and foes alike as Murzuphlus, is standing on the sea walls a little south of the Petrion Gate.

Two things are irritating him.

One is how badly he slept the previous night – and the one before and the one before that and in fact every night since he stopped being Murzuphlus and became a merciless usurper. He is troubled by dreams – he who always slept so easily. Or, rather, one dream. Alexios's mouth, jabbering bits of the Bible. That's all. But it stops him sleeping, although God knows a man about to fight for his empire needs his sleep.

At least Isaakios died of his own accord. Keeled over. That was a stroke of luck.

The other thing that's irritating him is how cheerful Theodore Branas is. They are meant to be inspecting the walls together, but all Theo can do is burble about Agnes, Agnes's beauty, their baby, their baby's likely beauty. And all this before the child is even born.

He tries telling Theo he's become very dull, but his friend – and, strangely, they do still seem to be friends – only grins, lowers his voice and asks him whether it's perhaps a bit dull sitting on a throne still warm with the backsides of three other men. Once upon a time, Murzuphlus had a comeback for everything. Now he resorts to pursing his lips in imperial displeasure and Theo looks mock-chastened and – still, still – offensively cheerful.

'Any day now,' Theo says.

Emperor Alexios Doukas looks across to where the Venetians are working on their ships. At the first report of activity, there was general rejoicing. Spring was coming. The Franks were readying to leave. He even allowed himself a small frisson of triumph – the City would be his without so much as a fight – but then spies came back with the truth.

They are preparing to attack.

9 April 1204

'Branas, where's Branas? I must find the sebastos Branas.'

Dodging along the City side of the great sea walls, Theo spied one of his household messenger boys. Soldiers were trying to swipe him out the way as he jumped over rock piles, stacks of crossbows, slabs of masonry, barrels of pitch, the City's defensive arsenal. Unremarkable, nimble, with a piercing voice. He must remember to tell Agathê she'd picked a good one.

'Here, I'm up here.'

The boy stopped and stared up at him. Theo nodded to his second-in-command, a professional soldier from one of the City guard regiments named Gregory.

'I'm going down to see what the lad wants.'

The boy bowed. 'So it please you, sir, the ladies have sent, sir, to say it'll soon be time, sir, to say you're to come, sir, at once, sir, before it's time, sir . . .'

'Stop, stop. Agnes wishes to see me? No – don't speak. A nod will do.'

The boy nodded, and Theo cursed under his breath. A soldier shouldn't leave his post to see a woman before a birthing.

'Wait here,' he told the boy, and jogged back up the steps.

'Hold the fort for me, all right?' he muttered to Gregory. 'Urgent summons to the emperor.'

Approaching the house, Theo fought down a slew of childhood memories. His mother withdrawing. Him being told to keep out of the way. His father either at the other end of the empire or stamping around the courtyard. Cries that

457

couldn't possibly come from his mother. Bloodied sheets soaking. One lifeless body, and another, and another. And then a little boy, Manuelos. His mother pale and abed for weeks. The whispered knowledge that there could be no more children. And then the little boy dead as well, leaving Theo behind, the only child, the only son.

He knew it all and tried not to think about it. Instead, he thought about a son, a practice sword in his hand. He thought about a daughter, riding on his shoulders in the orchard. And then he remembered the orchard had burnt to the ground and the only sword he owned was the one on his hip.

He found Agnes standing in the middle of their bedroom, the air heavy with the scent of oil of violets. He hadn't smelt that since his mother's last labour. She was wearing a long red-brown tunic, no sleeves, her hair bundled up in a white turban. She was swaying slightly, but when he came in, she looked up at him and smiled.

'The pains have come. But they are not too bad. Agathê laughs at me if I so much as wince – she says there is a lot worse to come.'

'But you are ready?'

'Is any woman?'

Her mouth opened slightly and her eyes fixed on the wall behind him, so intently that he almost turned round to see what she was staring at. She breathed a little harder until whatever it was passed, then she touched his arm, reassuring him.

'See. Nothing.'

He tried not to look uncomfortable. It was easier on the walls, waiting for an enemy he could see.

'It's all right,' she said, gently. 'I know you cannot stay long. I should not have called you here, but I needed to see you. Once. Before they . . . They're going to attack soon, aren't they?'

He took her in his arms – as best he could.

'Yes, soon. Today, everything points to today.'

'Today? I'm sorry, I shouldn't have . . .'

'No, I'm glad you sent for me. I wanted to see you, too, before . . . I wanted to wish you—'

She shook her head.

'No, Theo, don't let either of us say any of those things. They sound too final. They sound . . .'

She squirmed free of his embrace, and again a great distance opened up between them as she concentrated on the thing inside her. This time her silence was broken by a very quiet moan, a hum so low it was hard to be sure it came from her. Her eyes were closed. He touched her arm. She nodded without opening her eyes and gave him a little push.

Go, go.

'Agnes?'

Her eyes opened. She smiled at him. 'Theo. Stop looking at me like that. Please. I'll be all right. You'll see. I haven't lived through . . . through all that I've lived through for childbearing to finish me. I won't let it, I tell you. I won't.'

It was only then that he realised how scared she was.

Theo kissed her palms, her fingers, her eyes, her cheeks. He grasped her hands. 'Tonight. I'll see you and our child tonight.' He was shocked at how raw his voice sounded, how close to tears. 'Tonight,' he repeated.

'Tonight,' she said. 'We'll be waiting for you. We will.' A few tears spilled down her face. Her grip on his hands tightened. He watched her force a smile on to her face.

'Go,' she said. 'Go, Theo, go.'

One final kiss, and he was cantering back through the bright spring sunshine, praying for Agnes, praying for their baby, fearing all the while that his prayers would count for very little when the City itself was in danger.

He cleared the final streets and leapt off his pony. The steps up to the walls were crowded with men who shouldn't be there – reserves, auxiliaries, signallers, all craning, tugging the arms of those in front, shouting for news, discipline momentarily abandoned.

'Get back. Get back!' he roared.

The men scattered to their posts and Theo hurried up, in no doubt what he would find when he reached the top.

'What word from the emperor, sebastos?' Gregory shouted as Theo joined him.

'The emp—? Final orders. All in hand,' he replied.

A stillness descended on the walls while below, on the water, the pounding of drums grew louder and louder. Nine months of waiting was over. No more speeches, no more lies. The real fight was about to begin.

The galleys, heavily laden with men and gear, were aiming for the tiny strip of land between the foot of the walls and the water. A foothold. A toehold. But to beach their ships, let alone scale the walls, the Franks would have to run the gauntlet of the City's defensive arsenal. Already to Theo's left and right eager commanders had launched their first barrage, but the missiles were falling short. Theo had done enough ranging shots over the past week to know exactly when to give the order to—

'Fire!'

A neat ripple of action and his petrary crews catapulted their rocks upwards, arcing almost in perfect unison, until the missiles reached their zenith and began to plummet towards the enemy.

The galleys had giant nets strung in their rigging, but they could absorb only a fraction of his battery's killing power. Theo saw many, many men blotted out as rocks ploughed into the decks, killing some instantly, jerking others overboard to die slower deaths beneath the waves.

But the Venetians were quick to regroup. The line might be ragged – one ship at least had taken a hit on its steering post – but they were still coming on. Theo watched soldiers tear off their armour and toss dead oarsmen aside.

A nod to Gregory.

'Two dozen paces closer should do it.'

He kept his eyes on the boats. He didn't need to look at his men – he knew they would already have reloaded, reset the counterweights and would now be adjusting their aim. It wasn't as easy as picking off targets with a bow and arrow, but a petrary only had to be lucky some of the time for the damage to be crippling.

The horse transports – harder to manoeuvre than the oarships, but many times their size – were lying off, acting as launch platforms for the westerners' arsenal. But Theo guessed they wouldn't be carrying enough ammunition out on to the waters to pose a real threat, and their aim was diabolical, too erratic to provide cover for the galleys.

'Incoming,' bawled a burly soldier to his left.

Theo tensed, fighting the instinct to flatten himself behind the parapet, as half a dozen bolts streaked through the air. Most crunched into the stones below him, chipping the stonework, nothing more. One skimmed over his head. He twisted round and saw it hammer into the ground behind the walls, startling a water donkey.

Around him, soldiers were stumbling – a little sheepishly – back to their feet. Theo caught an admiring glance from Gregory. He was a youngish man. He'd probably pegged Theo as a soft aristo who'd panic. Theo gave him a grin. *Nice.*

Three more times the defenders' rocks rose, fell and blasted the galleys. Of the twelve ships that were Theo's concern, two were limping back to the enemy shore, three were holed, in chaos, but seven had breached the range of his petraries. Behind them, the horse transports had stopped firing – too much risk of skewering their own men.

He ordered his men to switch tactics, from long to short range. Archers and crossbowmen formed ranks between the petraries and began to fire smooth salvoes across the water. From that distance, they'd struggle to pierce good chainmail, but the hiss and blur of arrows would be terrifying.

Close, they were very close.

A large galley grounded hard and Theo saw a soldier – tricked out in full armour – leap over the side, misjudging the depth. He sank, imprisoned in metal, unseen by his comrades. Others were more careful, testing the way with spear butts, running out planks, hurling gear ashore to lighten the galleys enough for the oarsmen to grunt them to safety.

At his feet, Franks spilled from their boats, passing their tools – ladders, pickaxes, giant skin-and-wood shells – man to man in lines like labourers on a building site. He could see their expressions, almost hear their arguments. They were near panic. And why not? They stood on a sliver of ground, water at their backs, dwarfed by the walls above them, a double line of deep ditches barring their way. The braver ones did not look up or back, not once, but shouldered ladders, grabbed pickaxes and pressed ahead.

The walls were stacked with blocks of masonry, the scorched rubble of hundreds of fine houses blasted by the fire. As the Franks massed around a postern gate, axes flying, Theo's men tumbled the stones over the lip of the wall.

The crunch and crumple of stone on metal. Men pinned. Men screaming. Men dying and men dead. Theo saw it all.

A ladder reared up, spindly, almost funny, like the first two legs of a spider climbing over the rim of a plate. Theo glanced down and saw one man push another aside, desperate to be the first to climb. At his signal, a sweating City soldier lugged over a bucket of sand, heated murderously hot, and tipped it on to the upturned faces of the attackers. One flattened himself against the ladder, clinging on as the sand skittered down his back. The other caught it in his eyes and reeled backwards, screeching, scrabbling, not dead, not yet, but he'd bear those burn marks for ever.

'Is this the best they can do?' roared the sand-man happily in Theo's ear as he upended another tub for good measure. 'Is this what we were so fucking worried about. This?'

Theo was about to grin and reply, something rude and

exultant, when he saw that a few of the big-bellied horse transports, which he'd last seen floundering in the light airs, had gathered enough way to advance on the walls. He frowned. Each one was steering straight for one of the towers that studded the walls.

Theo ordered the petrary crews to reload. These towers, which had two wooden storeys jury-rigged above the stones and mortar – were the key to the walls. And the walls were the key to the City.

'Double round,' he yelled, pointing at the ship closest to them. 'Fire!'

The stones parted its port-hand shrouds and fractured the aft mast, but it had enough momentum to beach. Above the screams, the roars, the noise of war, Theo heard the prow, reinforced with metal, butting against the stones.

Gregory was at his side.

'What's their game?'

Theo didn't answer – only pointed up into the ship's rigging. A ladder, laid flat, stretched between foremast and forestay, extending out beyond the bow, forming a sort of walkway, no more substantial than something a pair of boys might rig between two trees.

'What,' said his second-in-command, 'the fuck is that?'

'Flying gangplank,' said Theo.

'They're not coming across it?'

'Looks like.'

'Ballsy fuckers.' Gregory licked his lips, whether in fear or relish Theo had no time to guess.

They both stared, mesmerised for a moment, as a seaman, nimble, barefoot, almost simian, his toes somehow gripping the swaying planks beneath his feet, swung a grappling hook back and forth, back and forth. He let it fly and the hook dug into the wood of the tower's platform and stuck fast. The Venetian pulled in hard, while a crewmate readied another line, another hook.

Theo ran for the tower, scrambled up the makeshift ladders and emerged at the top – ducking smartly before another hook clawed his skull. With his knife, he hacked the rope free, but one, two, three more hooks landed while dozens of men raced up the ship's stays, ready to swarm on to the tower.

He risked a glance along the walls.

On the waterfront, the Franks were retreating. Ladders lay in ruins. The few men who'd been minded to mine the walls were burning to death under their coracle. The ground assault was a failure, but up in the air . . .

Four boats, Theo saw, had closed four other towers. To his left he could make out Varangians, axes flashing, attackers tumbling to the ground, but those to his right were struggling. A wily captain had hoisted half a dozen crossbowmen in a rough cage to nearly the height of the tower, and they were firing determined rounds at the defenders.

Back to the Franks in front of him. One was almost in range – summoning the will to leap – and Theo was ready for him. He'd gut him before both his feet hit the planks of the tower platform.

But the man did not jump. He wobbled, dropped to his knees and clung on to the walkway. The ropes securing the ship to the tower tightened, strained, and Theo heard the bow grind against the stones as the ship bore off to starboard. The man he'd been about to kill was no longer facing him. He was swinging out of reach as the boat turned beam-on to the walls.

For a moment, Theo was thrown. What were they up to? Then he saw that the sun, which had earlier had the sky all to itself, was now racing in and out of streaks of cloud. The wind was squalling from the south.

With the wind filling in hard from that direction, the Venetians would have struggled to hold their ships against the towers even if the Rômans had been eager to take their lines. But with every man on the walls, hell-bent on a fight, there was no way any captain could stop his ship paying off, at the mercy of the wind.

As the boat in front of Theo turned, its bowsprit swept away a solitary assault ladder, tipping the attackers to the ground, leaving some dead, some dying, and the rest crawling broken-limbed back to the water. The galleys, too, joined the transports in ignominious flight across the Golden Horn, and the City's batteries fired in their wake, the stones sending jets of water dancing into the air.

The defenders, shocked by the suddenness of victory, red-faced from fighting – and the abrupt end to fear – gazed at the beautiful sight in silence. But not for long. Soon laughter was gusting along the walls, laughter, jubilant hoots, wild jeers.

A few of the younger soldiers flipped round and dropped their breeches and waved white buttocks at the attackers. And why not? They stood proud atop their walls while below the last of their enemies cringed and cowered, flopping into the water, screaming for the boats to come back.

Theo embraced every man he could lay his hands on. None dead; only a couple of burnt hands. He couldn't stop laughing. How had they ever feared this? Of course the City would not fall. God-loved, God-protected, it could not fail.

Accompanied by trumpets and timbrels, the great victory cry of the City flew up into the sky, even as it darkened with rain clouds.

'Jesus Christ conquers! Jesus Christ conquers!'

Theo left the walls and ran up to the command post at the Monastery of Christ the All-Seeing, where he found Murzuphlus on his knees offering prayers of thanksgiving. The emperor looked at Theo; Theo looked at the emperor. Then the emperor put his dignity aside and hugged Theo tight.

'I won't make you say it,' said Murzuphlus. 'But you can if you like.'

Theo laughed.

'All right, I will. Well done, Emperor Alexios Doukas. Well prepared. Well executed. *Well done.*'

'You're a generous man, Theo.'

'Today we can all afford to be generous.'

Other leaders were arriving – Theodore Laskaris and Constantinos Raoul, with a bandaged arm.

'Bad luck,' said Theo.

'Blasted crossbow,' Raoul muttered.

Slipped, mouthed Laskaris.

Wine appeared in silver flasks and Theo drank it down in a happy daze, watching the sun setting, listening to the flap of canvas, the men rejoicing below, the bells ringing across the City.

An adjutant fought his way in.

'Branas? Branas? There's a messenger here for you.'

'Send him in,' said Theo, feeling his chest tighten. He told himself that today was a good day, a lucky day. The Holy Mother of God had not forsaken them. She would not let Agnes, his Agnes, come to harm.

'Ah,' said Murzuphlus. 'So Agnes has been delivered?' He slapped Theo on the back. 'Tell you what – if it's a boy, you should name him after your victorious emperor.'

The same messenger, small amongst so many men, edged into the tent. At the sight of his anxious face, the men closest to Theo had the grace to fall silent. Further away, the merrymaking, the guffaws, greetings and shouts, continued unchecked.

'Speak, lad,' said Theo.

The boy looked up at him.

'Agathê, she says, she says the baby has not turned. She says—'

'What? What does that mean?' Theo demanded.

The boy looked like he would cry.

'I don't know, sir. She only said to say that. I didn't like to ask more, sir. She said to find you, tell you, *the baby's not turned.*'

Theo silenced him. He couldn't speak. He couldn't ask about

these matters here, the wine of victory already staining men's lips. Other men, older men, men who had already fathered babies – lost them too – did not meet his eye.

It was Raoul who spoke up, bluff and embarrassed.

'Had some experience. With my wife. Um . . . late wife. Babies come head first into the world. This one's head is still hard and fast under its mother's ribs.'

'And that's . . . ?'

'Um, I'm no expert, but . . .'

Theo turned to Murzuphlus. 'I must . . .'

A nod.

'Go.'

12 April 1204

The pain. Make it stop.

'You have to be strong, Agnes. You need the pain. You have to be strong.'

Strong. Yes, Agathê. I can be strong. I cannot speak, but I can be strong.

At some point – that morning? the day before? the day before that? – Theo had come to the house. Or that was what Agathê had told her. She had not seen him. Agathê had forbidden it. He came with news, Agathê said, good news. He said the enemy were beaten back. The Rômans had won. Or at least they were winning. Something. She couldn't remember.

That was when she could still breathe and think.

Now she doubted he had come at all. Maybe she only hoped he had come. Maybe she only hoped they were winning. Maybe he was dead and the City was gone and she would be alone in one room for ever and ever with the pain.

The pain. Make it stop. Be strong. The pain. Make it stop. Be strong.

The pain make it stop be strong the pain make it stop be strong. Pain strong pain strong pain.

Once, twice, half a dozen times, messengers came summoning Theo – haughty from Murzuphlus, nervous from his troops. *So please the sebastos Branas.* He told them all to get lost. Or that was what he told the steward to tell them.

But finally, at dawn on Monday, a messenger came that he could not ignore.

'The Franks have sailed. A second attack! The Franks are coming back. The sebastos Branas is to report to the walls.'

He rode out into the morning, his limbs leaden, his head fizzing and his eyes gritty from lack of sleep. He mounted the walls. A nod to Gregory. A nod to his men.

The mood up there was unhealthy. The Rôman soldiers had celebrated their victory in an orgy of illicit drinking. They thought they had won. The returning ships inspired exhaustion and despair – not the red, raw anger that the City needed. Theo saw it all around him. Worse, he saw it in himself.

'They've learnt their lesson,' grunted Gregory.

Theo nodded. No galleys, no intention of trying to land at the foot of the walls. Only their big ships were crossing the Golden Horn, the giant transports, roped together in pairs, twenty pairs, forty ships.

'All right, boys. Ready to give the Latin bastards another good hiding?'

He raised his voice enough for an uneven sort of cheer to bump along the walls nearby.

Stones flew up.

Here we go again.

They took a length of chain, wrapped it around her stomach and pulled it tight, the links searing into her spine, everything in flames.

Theo tried to concentrate. He tried to make his world shrink to the two ships that were bearing down on the tower he was sworn to defend. He should only be able to see the steel in the hands of the men in the rigging. He should only be able to hear the ragged breathing of the men beside him.

But voices whispered that nothing mattered. That she'd be dead anyway and his child too and then what would be the good in winning? Cities had to exist for somebody – otherwise they were nothing but brick and stone.

A foolhardy bird which had been nesting in the tower

469

exploded into the sky, and something cold gripped him. For an instant, he thought it was a portent, some sign that Agnes had died and gone from him. But it wasn't death.

It was the north wind beginning to blow.

The wind filled the ships' sails. Moments before, they had been lumbering oxen, hobbled and clumsy – but the wind brought them alive. Their sails ballooned and the banners, brighter than ever against the darkening sky, jumped into the air, streaming towards him.

The men about him looked nervous.

'It doesn't matter, boys,' he called. 'A puff of wind is neither here nor there.'

But then, fifty paces to his left, the first pair of ships rammed into a tower with a rending crash that sounded like both would surely break apart. A madman – a Frank in full armour – staggered across the walkway and tumbled into the midst of the defenders. He couldn't get up. How could he possibly get up?

'Kill him, kill him, kill him!' Theo roared, although he knew the men on the other tower couldn't hear him.

The Frank surged to his feet and laid about him with a massive broadsword. He shouldn't have had room to wield it. It should have caught on something. But somehow, backstabbing, thrusting, sideswiping, cutting, hacking, he was driving the defenders back.

And then Theo had to stop watching. The ships were upon him.

They fired a sheet of metal until it was hotter than a hundred suns, clamped it on to her back and welded it to her skin.

A man flung himself on top of Theo and knocked him backwards. His lungs emptied, his breath would not come, but the man had lost his sword as he leapt. He was writhing on top of Theo, clawing at his throat. Theo drove his knife under

470

the man's helmet, felt the blood spurt and the man shake and slacken. He rolled the Frank off and jabbed his sword high above his head to gut another man mid-dive.

Theo clambered to his feet, and almost immediately lost his balance. Somebody had cut away his knees. The earth was shaking. But no, it was only the ships and the tower locked in a violent dance. The ship an insistent lover; the tower trying to flee its embrace – but it had nowhere to run, so it writhed and twisted. The wind gusted hard and the ships surged.

Something clawed his face. Blood, blood. His face was opening up. A slash. A cut. He turned to fight, automatically, doggedly. But it was only a rope kicking out at him. Ropes, spars, stray bits of their diabolical boarding platforms, all were thrashing, flogging, lashing out as if they too had sworn an oath to take the City. This was a battle on neither land nor sea, neither siege nor plain war. It was chaos, a monstrous frenzy, a storm of wood and hemp and swords.

He cursed, then heard cheers – cheers from his own side. What was happening? A lull in the breeze. The ships that had been hard against the next tower had fallen back. Were they retreating?

He should never have doubted, he should never have . . .

But then he saw a man with a big bundle of white under his arm scramble up the outer rim of the tower. He reached the top and hunted for a post, a staff, and propped it vertical in the roof slats. He tethered his bundle and the banner of one of the western bishops unfurled.

'Down him. Now!' Theo bellowed at the archers firing from the walls.

The Frank, his moment of glory brief, froze, mid-yell of exultation, as half a dozen shafts buried themselves in his body. Slowly, he crumpled, slipped and flopped over the edge of the tower into the sea below.

But it was too late. The first Frankish flag flew proud on the walls of Constantinople.

They snatched at her womb with hooks and claws, squeezing it, twisting it, groping for her baby.

At the sight of the banner, a roar of triumph sounded from the ships, from every western mouth along the line of battle. Thousands of pairs of eyes feasted on the square of cloth punching the grey sky, proof that the walls were not invulnerable.

Could the City see it? Would the City know that the Franks had done what the emperor had sworn they would never do.

Another banner took flight. They had two towers – and, worse, the section of the walls between them.

Theo shouted at his men to attack the tower closest to them. Nobody looked keen – the wall was not broad, and the Franks they would face were now armed with the Rômans' supply of rocks and bolts – so he went first. God only knew where his shield was. He held a mangled bit of planking in front of him and raced along the wall.

Down on the water, he saw a galley accelerate from nowhere at attack speed, aiming for the wall between the Franks' two towers, the pacemaker's drum pounding so fast that each blow blurred into the next. The ship reeled into the shore, wrecking the bow, upending the rowers, splintering their oars.

A gang of knights, well armed, tumbled over the bow and made straight for the wall – now undefended. What were they planning? They had no ladders, only tools. There – that was what they were making for. A postern gate. They knew where they were going. They must have spied it during their first failed attack.

The Franks fell on it like wild dogs, picks, crowbars, axes, swords, all flailing madly. Two men pummelled it, then retreated, reeling with exertion, while two more stepped up to take over. Others, the tallest, held huge shields above the heads of those at the gate – not that they had much to fear. It was their men who held the wall above them.

The gate held, but for how long?

Theo tried to turn round. He had to tell the Rômans on the ground to reinforce the gate, to pile rubble, bodies, anything in front of it. But the men behind him thought he was retreating. Some were glad to get out of danger, others were angry, still wanting to go forward. Too much noise to make them understand; not enough space to dodge past. Theo found himself fighting his own men, wrestling, shouting,

'Let me through, let me through.'

The noise escalated behind him.

Theo turned and saw that a Frank, a big man made bigger by full armour, had broken through the gate and was standing inside the walls, inside the City, waving his sword above his head and roaring, a man alone against a whole army. Everyone on the walls stopped and stared down at him.

A detachment of Rôman men-at-arms, on foot, lightly armed, maybe two dozen of them, were stationed directly in front of the knight. Theo – and every other man on the walls – waited for them to charge him down.

But they hesitated.

Maybe they'd been drinking, maybe they hadn't been paid, maybe their commander was taking a piss; whatever the reason – and who would ever admit to being one of them? – they did not act. They did not sprint across the tiny gap that separated them from the lone Frank and bring him down.

And as they hesitated, more men poured through the gate, still no more than a dozen, but they were fanning out, hammering their swords on their shields. Then, as a body, they charged.

And the soldiers standing before them, proud Rômans, the heirs of Julius and Augustus, of Constantinos and Justinian, soldiers who were supposed to fight in the name of something that had endured beyond the length of man's understanding, those soldiers turned their backs and ran before a handful of knights from the west.

Be strong, Agnes, fight, Agnes.

Beneath him, Theo saw the Franks turn to their left and charge towards the Petrion Gate. Open that and a whole army could get in. Open that gate and . . .

Down! He had to get down. He hacked a tension rope clear of one of the petraries, made it fast about the machine and backed over the edge, descending hand over hand, bracing his feet against the wall.

The pack of Franks was nearly upon him. He dropped the last ten feet, landed in a roll and came up, sword on guard.

But they didn't want to fight, not yet. A couple of men blocked his attempts to engage, while the rest dodged round him, moving astonishingly fast under their helmets and mail. Theo gave chase. Brought one down. Another.

But now half a hundred of them had reached the Petrion Gate and were tearing it open. He couldn't kill them all – but it would be easy to stop them from above. He looked up. *Fuck.* The defenders had abandoned the walls. *Fuck.* It didn't matter. An attack from the rear could still scatter them. Where was Murzuphlus? He must be able to see what was happening. Where was the emperor and his Varangians?

And then he heard silver music.

A charge sounding from the Monastery of Christ the All-Seeing. A charge! The emperor was coming. He had horses and the blood of centuries in his veins. He'd butcher the Franks where they stood. They could mend the gates. Re-arm the walls. It was a breach, a tiny breach. The emperor was coming!

The cavalry, Murzuphlus at its head, cleared the final buildings and thundered on to the sea road. A battle cry welled in Theo's throat, but it turned into a sob, a howl, a roar of rage.

The Rôman horsemen did not attack. They veered right and galloped to the south, along the open road towards the fire plain and the Great Palace.

Theo, on his knees, watched the emperor's standard disappear from view.

The Franks' jeers were swallowed by a great crash as the Petrion Gate gave way. Through the jagged opening, Theo spied dozens of galleys landing on the shore beyond. Hundreds of soldiers, leading their horses, were splashing ashore.

Rage turned to fear. Soon, the waterfront would be overrun with Franks. And nothing – *nothing* – would stand between them and Agnes. He had to get her out of there – fast.

I can't I can't I can't.

As he sprinted towards their house, Theo told himself he was nothing like Murzuphlus.

If I was emperor, I wouldn't run. I would do what I had to do. But I'm not the fucking emperor, so I can go to her. I can. I can. I must.

When he arrived, the last servants were running out. The guards. Where the fuck were the guards? He'd paid them enough to stay. But the door was unmanned. He ran inside shouting, shouting.

'Theo . . .' Agathê darted out of Agnes's room.

'The Franks . . .'

'I know. One of the boys was up on the roof. We heard.'

'I've come. You're too close. They're streets away. We must move her. Now. They won't . . .'

Why wasn't the stupid woman fetching Agnes? Why was she shaking her head. What was she saying? He began to push past her.

'Stop, Theo, listen, Theo. You can't move her. You can't.'

'But the Franks could be here.' He heard panic in his voice and hated himself. But before he could draw breath and explain it all calmly, Agathê was speaking.

'If you move her, she is dead. Dead. And Theo, prepare yourself, please, I cannot say otherwise, she may . . . even if

475

she stays. A first baby. This late in life. It is not easy. She is fighting. She is. But she is tired. I fear the baby is tiring too. I fear—'

'Theo!'

Agnes's voice, weak.

'Theo!'

And again, stronger.

'She knows I am here?'

'No. Yes. Maybe. She's delirious. She's been calling your name since noon.'

Her calling. Him not coming. A chill. He pushed into the chamber.

'Theo, it's you. Have we won?'

She was kneeling astride a chair, her arms wrapped around a wooden pillar at the side of the room. But otherwise, she looked so normal. Wan. But normal. What had he expected?

'No, no. We have not. Not won.' He was at her side. 'They are here. Inside the walls.'

'Then why are you here? Why . . .'

Then he lost her. Something, beast, demon, he knew not what, seized Agnes, his Agnes, and she raged and stamped and howled and punched the wall. Then it left and she slumped to her knees, her head against the pillar. He knelt behind her.

'Agnes . . .'

'Go. Go,' she muttered. 'You can't help me. Only God can help me.'

'But . . .'

'Go. Help the City. Go and fight. Nothing you can do. Nothing. Only I can. I alone. Go, go, go—'

And then it, the thing, returned. He stared. Slack-mouthed. Stunned. He'd seen men in pain. But he'd seen the blood. The guts. The pike. The bolt. How could so much pain be invisible?

When it was over, he tried one more time. He had to make her understand. But she shrieked at him. Wailed and yelled.

Agathê pulled him up, driving him towards the door with all her strength.

'Do as she bids you, Master Theo. Do her that honour at least.'

'I want to say goodbye.' A child himself.

'You think she is dying? If you go in there with *goodbye, I love you* on your face, you will kill her faster than this baby will. She needs to know you *believe*, or she will stop fighting. Understand, Theo? Understand?'

He went back in. She was rocking, on her hands and knees. Again he knelt beside her.

'Agnes, bring our child into the world and make for the Great Palace.' He knew it was not real. He knew it was impossible. But he did as Agathê had told him and said it anyway. 'Come to the Bukoleon. I'll wait for you there. You'll meet me there. Say yes? Say yes?'

'Yes,' she said. 'Yes. I will.'

Yes. I will. Yes.

They retreated, for a moment they retreated.

Yes. I will. Yes.

She repeated it. Louder. Loud and louder. The words became a scream and the scream became a golden noise, louder than pain, brighter than fear, a beautiful surge of sound.

He left the house. He ran south towards the palace. He did not know how he ran. How he moved, how he saw. Clouds clearing. Stars pricking. Night deepening around him. People fleeing to the western gates. No sign of any soldiers. Neither Rômans nor Franks.

A pause. A breath. The soldiers of the Cross, he allowed himself to realise, were not snapping at his heels.

Maybe the City will not fall this night.

He scrambled up a section of the walls and saw that the attackers had lit fires on the high ground where the emperor's command post had been. They must be digging in for the night. With the Blachernai garrison to the north of them and darkening streets to the west and south – full, for all they knew, of crack troops – the Franks would not dare advance until the sun returned.

Agnes would be safe until dawn.

Theo dropped to the ground and ran on, a soldier once more. As his legs lapped up the distance and his breathing found its rhythm, he told himself to hope. They only held a finger of land inside the walls. It wasn't the end. The City could rally. The City could win.

He had to slow his pace as he passed through the burnt-out plain the great fire had left behind, now a sprawling slum in the middle of the City. The spring rains had stirred the ash and mud into a thick black soup, a living latrine where once some of the grandest had lived. There were no roads here, only the embers of cook-fires warned him where people slept.

As he left the fire damage behind, he expected to see torches burning around the perimeter of the Great Palace, soldiers regrouping in good order, the Varangians mustering in full strength, staff officers formulating a plan, the emperor bolstering morale.

Instead, darkness and the sound of his feet on the paving stones.

He groped his way through the faint moonlight to the main gate and was reassured to find two Varangians at least on guard. At their challenge, he gave his name and they saluted him.

'Where's the emperor?' Theo demanded.

'He go to the City,' said one the guards.

Before Theo could ask what that meant, he saw a familiar face emerge from the shadow.

'Constantinos.'

'Theodore.'

'Where is he?'

'Our beloved emperor? I believe he's attempting to rouse the people to come to the defence of the City.'

'He . . . what? Why does he need the people? What of our troops?'

'Good question. Unfortunately, we do not seem to have any left. Saving our loyal Varangians, our armies have melted away.'

'That's impossible.'

'If you say so.'

'I left Agnes to come here and—'

'You left her? Where? At your house? What of her baby?'

Theo had time to register alarm in the eunuch's eyes – and to be surprised by it.

'Yes, she's there, but the baby's not—'

He broke off as he saw a line of torches coming towards them. He tensed. Could he have been mistaken? Could the Franks have advanced this far? But no, it wasn't the enemy. There were too few men, walking too openly.

'Murzuphlus!' Theo recognised the man in front.

'Ah, Branas,' said the emperor, his voice vague and distracted. 'Is that you?' He was walking fast. He didn't stop.

'What's happening?' Theo fell into step behind him. 'What of the people? How many Varangians are under arms here? Are the lines of communication open to Blachernai? I was thinking, if we counterattacked now, while we still have the advantage, we could—'

Murzuphlus stopped so suddenly that Theo nearly crashed into him.

'We do *not* have the advantage, Theo. I would rather say we were at a particular disadvantage.'

'What are you talking about? Of course we—'

But Murzuphlus was off again, moving swiftly deeper into the palace, his guards closing ranks. Theo chased after him. He saw Murzuphlus muttering instructions to the men about him. He assumed they were military and left him to it. Until he saw him fling his mail shirt to the floor.

He blocked the emperor's path.

'What the fuck are you doing?' he said, and shoved him in the chest for good measure.

Two pikes were levelled at him, but Murzuphlus shook his head at the guards who lowered them.

'It's over, Theo. Over.'

'What are you talking about?'

'The Franks do not know it yet, but when day breaks, they will learn that the City is theirs. My armies have deserted me.'

'But what of the people? Constantinos said you had gone to rouse them.'

'They were . . . unroused.'

'But how can that be?'

'I do not know. It is galling.'

'Galling? *Galling?* It's a—'

'Damn you, Theo, do you think this is easy for me? I do not want to go, but—'

'*Go?* You are planning—'

A new voice cut him off. A woman's voice.

'It's his only choice, Branas.'

He saw Euphrosunê and Eudokia hurrying towards them. Murzuphlus embraced them and all three rushed onwards. Theo knew where they were bound now. The docks.

'You're welcome to join us, Theo,' called Murzuphlus over his shoulder. 'You and Agnes. Where is she, by the way?'

A casual question, but it made him mad. Had he left her side for *this* – for a man who could think of nothing but putting a dozen sea miles between himself and danger? Theo lost control. He grabbed Murzuphlus by the scruff of his neck and pulled him in close.

'I'll kill you before you get on that fucking boat. It's not over.'

'Don't be an idiot, Theo,' said the emperor, withering. 'It's been over a long time. The empire curled up and died while we weren't looking. Maybe it was Andronikos's fault. Or Isaakios's. God knows, maybe we should blame Manuelos . . .'

'Don't talk to me about dead emperors. You − you are emperor now, and by God, it is your duty to behave like one.'

But Murzuphlus only laughed.

'Behave like an emperor? Fine words, my friend. But what do they mean? Do you want me blind, mad?'

'You're wasting your time, Alexios,' called Euphrosunê. 'Hurry, for God's sake, we must hurry.'

'Let me go, Theo,' said Murzuphlus.

'No.'

He only had time to see Murzuphlus jerk his head before two, three, who knew how many guards emerged from the dark, grabbed his arms and hauled him off. One of them punched him in the stomach, and when he tried to get up, they all kicked him in the head, over and over again.

Something changed.

The hopeless pain that had pounded, unrelenting, blow after blow, the pain that made her feel alone and forsaken by all men, all women, that had gone and in its place was something persistent, something with meaning, something she could use.

Agathê, too, had new hope on her face.

'The baby. It's coming, Agnes, it's coming.'

And then she started towards the window. Agathê, who had not left her side these long hours.

'What, what it is?'

'Nothing, nothing. Push, Agnes. Bring your baby, Agnes.'

But it was not nothing. On the woman's face was fear, poorly masked.

'Tell me—'

Agnes could not finish. The wave was breaking. Her insides were breaking. Bursting. Surely . . . No, nothing. No baby.

'Agathê,' she pleaded, panting. 'Tell me.'

A moment's indecision.

'All right. Fire. I see a fire. Look for yourself.'

She flung open the shutters and Agnes saw a bright light at the window – not the pale promise of dawn, but the red-orange rage of war.

'You see? You understand. Now. It has to be now, Agnes. Or we shall both, we shall all . . .'

There. It was coming. Another wave tore through her. Everything disappeared into blackness and nothingness. Nothing in the world mattered but—

Agathê yelled. Agnes looked down and saw black hair and something blue-grey and slippery between her legs, and then there was a baby – her baby – lying limp in Agathê's arms.

'Dead,' Agnes wailed. A pain she had not known she could feel. A cry that came from a deep place she wished she had never found. She would live the last three days again and again for eternity rather than this.

'No, no . . .' Agathê was frowning, rubbing it, pummelling it. Agnes wanted to make her stop, but she didn't know how. The baby did, though. It spluttered and howled and Agathê's frown vanished. Sudden tears coursed down the old woman's cheeks.

'Your daughter, Agnes, you have a daughter.'

And she kissed Agnes hard, placed the baby in her arms and for a long, long moment the two women marvelled at each other and at the child.

'The fire—' said Agnes with a start.

'Don't think about that. It's two houses away. Damn the Franks.'

'I can move.'

'I know you can. You can and you will. But not yet. Not before the afterbirth comes.'

'I'd forgotten . . . You go, Agathê. Go now while you can.'

'Nonsense. It'll come. It'll come. Now where is . . . ?'

She found a knife and cut the cord that still joined them. Agnes nodded. She was exhausted and sore, so sore, but her head was clear.

'She's tiny.'

'And thank the good Lord she is. Or you'd both have died hours ago.'

She could hear the fire now. A roaring like the breath of great lions. Hell must sound like that when it opened beneath you. Tongues of flame, licking, lapping, longing for you.

'Agathê—'

'I know. I know. But we can't move until . . . There. It's come. It's come.'

Agnes stared in shock as Agathê bundled the thing away and rammed wads of ripped sheets between her legs.

'There. That'll do. Stand. Can you stand?'

She forced herself on to her feet. It was getting hotter and hotter. Smoke was seeping in through the roof. She glanced towards the window. Closer, it was coming closer. She clutched the baby tight.

'Go, go, go.'

The two women stumbled down the stairs and into the hallway. There was the door. Through that door lay the street and safety. Agnes did not know how she ran, but she did. They reached the door. The bar was across it. Agathê was worrying at it, working it free. There was a sound overhead like workmen or giant insects, a fearful kind of drumming.

And then the roof burst over their heads.

13 April 1204

Dead. I am dead. I am dead and in hell.

The fire was all around her. The heat. Smoke. She couldn't see. She couldn't breathe. This was the first day of eternity. Or maybe she'd been there for ever. Her knees were buckling. Her heart was giving way.

But then she looked down and saw the baby curled in a ball at her chest, her arms locked about it. If they were together, they were alive. Alive, but boxed inside the burning house.

She began to crawl. If it was the wrong way, it was the wrong way. One hand groped in front of her, the other gripped the baby. Sweat poured off her face, pooling, dripping. Dimly, she saw a body, Agathê's body, a burning beam where her face should be. Horror threatened to overwhelm her, but she beat it back.

She heard sounds – sounds that weren't the crackle and spit of burning wood. They were shouts. And then she could see more than roaring red. She could see the cold grey black of an April dawn, and she knew where she was.

The doorposts were burning, the door was in flames, ragged, skeletal, but still there. She had to go through the door. It would burn down soon enough – but she couldn't wait. The fire was welling behind her.

She saw people on the other side of the door, screaming at her. She couldn't hear the words. Or maybe there were no words.

She tore off her clothes and wound the baby in everything she had, everything including the blood-, sweat- and birth-soaked shift she had put on three, four, however many days ago.

Before she could think what she was doing – if she waited she would not dare – she threw the baby through the flames and watched her shift unravel like a streaming tail.

It caught fire, a tiny comet.

But a man had seen. A man leapt forwards and the baby, her baby, landed in his arms. She watched him tear it free. The noise of the fire behind her was too loud. Her eyes were blurred. She could not hear. She could not see. It was dead. Her baby was dead.

Then it arched backwards and Agnes saw its tiny mouth gape open, black and angry. It was alive. And now she had to live too.

She jumped. And screamed as the flames bit into her.

Theo woke. Distant screams piercing his skull. Who . . . ? He wrenched his eyes open. A huge flock of gulls screeching, circling under a pale pink sky. Dawn. It was dawn. Agnes—

His grogginess vanished. He sprang to his feet and immediately sank back to his knees. Pain, too much pain. He touched his face. It was wet, pulpy. There was blood on his hands. He readied himself and tottered to his feet, feeling the stab of a cracked rib. He made himself ignore it.

He took a step and stumbled. There, at his feet, lay his sword. Wincing, he leant down and picked it up, and using it as a prop, he hobbled out of the palace, retracing the path he had travelled the night before.

Somebody was rolling Agnes over and over, smothering her, pounding her back. Somebody was hurrying her away from the fire into empty streets, wrapping her in a cloak, telling her she was safe, that it was all right, that she was alive. Somebody . . .

'Constantinos? How . . . ?'

The eunuch stopped.

'Everyone at the palace was arguing about whether to run or fight, but seeing as I had no intention of doing either, I thought I might be more useful here.'

He handed her the baby.

'And I see I was right.'

Agnes looked down. The baby's eyes were swollen shut like a fighter's. Its nose was squashed. *Its.* She shouldn't say that any more. It was a she. *Her eyes. Her nose.* Her tiny fists were balled. Even in sleep, she looked ready to defend herself. *Good.*

She searched for words. None came. She pulled the eunuch to her and kissed his cheek.

He nodded. 'You're welcome. Come. We must hurry. The fire's still burning.'

'I can't. I can't hurry anywhere. I am . . .'

Sudden weakness assailed her. *I am broken, Constantinos, broken.* But before she could say the words, he placed a hand on each of her shoulders.

'I know what you are. And so I still say we must hurry.'

'But where?' A memory came back from her delirium. 'Constantinos, have you seen Theo? He came to me. I think he did. I said I'd find him . . .'

She broke off, listening. Constantinos was too. From the south came the sound of many, many people on the move.

'Our soldiers?' she began.

But Constantinos was shaking his head. 'Not soldiers, I think, no.'

The noise grew louder, and then they saw them, following the road that lay between the sea walls and the City, hundreds of men and women, some beautifully dressed, others in soot- and dirt-stained robes, many she recognised. No armour. No weapons. They were processing north, led by the highest clergy, many bearing icons and crosses, others holding baskets of dried flowers. The ones who didn't look half-dead with exhaustion or terror or both were chanting prayers. It looked like a festival, a saint's-day procession.

'I believe we are looking at a delegation preparing to welcome – to propitiate, I should say – our new rulers.'

'We're not . . . we can't be surrendering? I don't understand. When . . . *how* did we lose?'

The baby squirmed in her sleep. Agnes looked down and saw her lips pursing, a frown wrinkling her brow. Her eyes rolled open and her mouth gaped. Agnes rocked her as she'd seen Susa rock her babies, willing her not to wake. She looked up and caught the tail of a smile in Constantinos's eyes.

'*How* is too long a conversation to have now. But surrendering we definitely are. The Queen of Cities is bending her knee.'

He did something that surprised her. He turned his head away and spat.

'We had better stick close to them,' he continued. 'Safety in numbers. Many men – and not only Franks – will seek to take advantage of the chaos. We'll follow them. But first . . .' He pulled off his overshirt. 'Put this on. And let me swaddle this little creature.'

He held out his arms for the baby, and she gave her to him. He set to work with strips of material torn from his cloak.

'When she's grown, you can tell her that on her first day on earth, she witnessed the end of an empire. The last day of the last Rômans. The end of the world. There – she looks more comfortable now.'

'How do you know how to . . . ?'

'Once upon a time, Agnes, I was the eldest of many little brothers and sisters. Once upon a time.'

Their eyes met.

'Once upon a time,' she repeated, with a very small smile, and they fell into step behind the procession.

Theo stared at the ruined house – the blackened timbers jutting out of the wreckage, the smouldering orange rubble, the swirls

487

of smoke – but he didn't really see it. He only saw her face at a window, screaming for him.

Theo! Theo!

'Agnes!' he yelled. 'Agnes!'

He wandered through the ashes, looking, not looking, hoping, not hoping. Then, there, at the tip of his sword, a charred corpse. He reeled backwards, retching, over and over.

The tinkle of bells, a pitiless sound. He turned and saw a procession winding up the hill – visible now that the houses were burnt flat – to greet the men who had killed her. He started towards them.

No. Not that way.

He wanted to fight, but he wanted to fight the leaders, the men who'd made it all happen. He would lie in wait at the Great Palace. They would come there and he would kill them – and then he too could die.

The sooner he was dead, the better.

Agnes and Constantinos had reached the foot of the hill. The leaders of the procession were nearly at the top, and a dozen Frankish knights, their helmets veiling their faces, were riding to meet them. Agnes looked at the ground sloping up before her.

'Constantinos, I don't think I can . . .'

'It's all right. I won't flog you all the way to the top. We've come far enough. Here, lean on me.'

Agnes listened to the Rôman voices carrying on the air, the Frankish responses, but they were too far away for her to make out what they were saying. Her attention drifted to the wings of the army, drawn up behind the leaders. They were armed, shifting about. A few shouts rang out, loud enough for her to understand the Frankish words no one else in the crowd would know.

'Cowards.'

'Blood.'

'The City's ours.'

This courtly capitulation was not what the rank and file wanted.

A Frankish squire kicked a stone, a little piece of bravado. It bounced down the hillside and ricocheted into an elderly matron. She cried out and shook her fist at the young man responsible.

Agnes glanced at Constantinos.

'I don't like it,' she said, quiet.

He nodded. Slowly – imperceptibly, she hoped – they dropped backwards through the people who were thronging behind them.

'Don't run yet,' he hissed.

'Don't be ridiculous. I can't run.'

'You might have to.'

They were a few paces clear, preparing to hurry their step and put as much ground as possible between them and the Franks, when a volley of shouts made her look back. First one soldier, then two, then the whole left wing broke and charged the unarmed crowd. Within a heartbeat, the right flank followed.

'The palace, Agnes.' Constantinos was pulling on her arm. 'We must get back to the palace. Their leaders will want to secure it, and they will not see you harmed. Quick. Don't look back. Don't look.'

Agnes hugged the baby with one hand, clutched her stomach with the other and stumbled, ran, lurched, ran, while Constantinos urged her on and on. They reached the end of the devastation left by the previous night's fire and plunged into one of the hundreds of winding alleyways that led south.

Behind them rose the screams of hundreds of people being butchered, and then another sound filled her ears, closer, infinitely more terrifying – the thunder of hooves. She glanced back even as she tried to run. Two knights were charging them down, swinging their swords, great scything circles of steel.

There was no time to hide, no time to think. Agnes dropped to her knees and pressed her face into the dirt, her body hunched over the child in her arms. She waited for the hooves to stop, waited for a blade to slice into her back, but nothing happened. The hooves disappeared.

She staggered to her feet.

'Thank God. They must have been after richer prey. Constantinos? Constantinos?'

He was still lying on the ground.

'They've gone,' she told him, although she already knew there was nobody left to listen.

A pool of blood was spreading from under his head. A sword had caught him clean across his face. *Clean*. Why did she think that? There was nothing clean about it.

She turned her back and staggered onwards. The sun was getting hotter. It was turning into a beautiful day. Occasionally, disappearing round a corner, a flash at a crossroads, she saw horsemen racing ahead. She shrank into the shadows of a doorway, an arcade, and carried on. People who'd survived the first onslaught overtook her, calling out the horrors they'd witnessed, babbling, crazed. They crowded the doors of every church she passed, seeking sanctuary. She almost joined them, but she knew God alone would not keep her safe.

Abruptly, the streets ended and she stood on the edge of the first fire-plain. Her legs buckled. All that open space. It looked too far. And there was a horrible new cry, so close.

It was the baby. Her dark eyes were wide open. She was starting to writhe against her swaddling bands. And the noise she was making, it was loud, much too loud. Why was she . . . ? Of course. She was hungry. Babies were always hungry.

She stumbled towards one of the many makeshift shelters that littered the plain and collapsed in the shade beneath it. She ripped Constantinos's shirt aside and without thinking too hard thrust the baby towards her breast. For a moment, she thought it wouldn't work, but then the squealing and nuzzling became eating.

She shut her eyes and pictured the Porphyry Chamber, the magnificent room where empresses gave birth to emperors. She imagined lying on perfumed sheets, surrounded by wet-nurses, handmaids, the very best physicians in the empire. She told herself that it would have hurt all the same.

Her baby was asleep again, her mouth twitching slightly. She didn't have any eyelashes. Agnes tore her gaze away. She mustn't look now. She would wait until they were safe. Then she would look. Not now.

Carefully, carefully she placed the baby on the floor and examined herself. She was bleeding, between her legs, where the baby had come. But although she knew that women often bled to death after birth, she did not think she was dying. She felt alive.

Come to the Bukoleon.

Yes, I will, yes.

She fixed her eyes on the dome of the Holy Wisdom. In its shadow lay the Great Palace. And inside the palace lay the Bukoleon. That was where she was going.

Theo banged into the abandoned guard mess-room, hunting for a pike or two, something with better reach than his sword.

A scream, a massive scream. Margit, Isaakios's young widow, and dozens of other women were cowering in a cupboard. He ignored them and ran towards the main gate to wait.

Agnes saw one man standing on guard outside the palace. She hoped he would recognise her and let her pass. Why was he staring at her like that? Why was he running towards her like a madman?

Theo.

'Theo!'

He stopped two paces short of her, shaking his head, stunned and staring.

'Alive,' he said. 'How . . . ?'

'I do not know.' She smiled. 'Not everyone can die. Some people always have to live. Although I do not know why we three were chosen.'

'We three . . . You cannot . . . you mean . . . ?'

'Yes. She lives, too.'

She opened her cloak and showed him – but he did not look down. He did not look at his child. He only looked at her.

'I thought you had died. I thought the fire had killed you.'

'It nearly did. She took a long time to come.' She didn't know how to say it all. 'And then there was the fire. And then I got out. And then the Franks began this . . . this ruin.'

'Your face,' he whispered, and reached out to touch it.

'It's burnt. I know. My body, too. But it will heal. And see – the fire took most of my hair.' She pushed back her shawl and touched her scalp. It felt prickly and alien. 'But it will grow back.'

She kissed the cut over his brow where his eye was bleeding and closed.

'We'll neither of us be quite whole again.'

Footsteps clattered behind them. And there, panting, red-faced, stood Boniface of Montferrat, come to claim the palace, and half a dozen men.

'Drop your sword.'

Theo's grip did not slacken.

The Franks raised their blades.

'Drop your sword,' Boniface repeated.

'Theo . . .' Agnes murmured.

'I cannot, Agnes. Do not make me.'

'Do not make me watch you die.'

'I cannot live if we have lost to them.'

The Franks were edging towards him. She didn't have much time.

'We've not lost. Don't you understand? We've won. We're standing here, together, alive. That's winning. Don't you see, Theo? That's victory.'

Still he did not move, and the Franks came closer.

'Stay,' she called in the finest Latin she could command, 'I bid you stay.'

Her voice – imperious, certain of being obeyed – was strange to her own ears, but it was enough. The men hesitated. She turned back to Theo.

'We made this child, you and I, and by God, she will grow up with a mother and a father. I will not tell her that her father threw his life away for a rotten city, a city that was lost before ever she was born. Instead, I will tell her how you chose her, how you chose me. Live, Theo. It's braver by far to live.'

She touched his hand where it held the sword, and she felt it shaking. Then she heard the sound of steel ringing on marble and his hand, warm and real, was around hers.

'You win,' he said. 'I can fight anyone but you.'

He looked down at his daughter and smiled even as Boniface approached.

'Hello . . . but what is her name?'

Agnes smiled back at him and spoke an ancient word, a noble word, a Greek name shared by empresses, saints and fisherwomen, the only name that could describe the miracle between them.

'Zôê.'

Life.

Historical Note

Agnes and Theo were real – but they lived in the margins of history rather than on its title pages.

In the sources, we meet Agnes at both her weddings and during the fall of Andronikos, after which she fades from view only to reappear in the Frankish chronicles of the Fourth Crusade, reported to be living with one Theodore Branas. Crusaders did visit her, she was rude to them - and they did chance upon her during the sack of the City.

Theo's life is sketchier. He's named as a key player in the plot to unseat Isaakios and we find him taking part (not entirely successfully) in various campaigns under the Angeloi. We don't know what his role was during the Fourth Crusade, but he and Agnes did throw in their lot with the Franks once it was over.

Agnes was relatively easy to site in history, at least during the First, Second and Third Emperors. Theo might have been harder if his father's life hadn't been relatively well documented. You read about Alexios Branas fighting the Magyars, supporting Andronikos and beating the Normans and the Bulgars, before rebelling against Isaakios and being killed by Conrad. The sources go on to speculate that one possible reason why Conrad quit the City was because he feared the vengeance of Branas's relatives.

If history handed me the general arc of *The Empress*, it was also very generous when it came to the gory particulars.

Marguerite-Constance did have an affair with her nephew, and she, Maria, Renier and Alexios all died gruesome deaths.

Isaakios's mother on the battering ram; the public stoning; Stephanos's brutality and Seth's prophecy; the Norman barbarism at Thessalonikê; Andronikos's death at the hands of the people; the fishing fleet taking on the galleys; the game of football with Alexios Branas's head; the blinding of Isaakios (although not necessarily by Theo) – all true.

There are two other areas which might feel fictionalised, but in fact aren't. Firstly, the influence of the key female players: Marguerite-Constance, Maria and Euphrosunê did all aspire to, and indeed did, wield significant political power. Secondly, Andronikos: I have, if anything, undersold him. Despite his well-documented descent into vicious mania, the sources remain giddy about his looks, his talent and his charisma.

There are, however, a few areas where I'd advise caution – where I chose the needs of my story over historical truth.

Agnes was probably younger than thirteen when the book opens, but I didn't want her so young that you'd be revolted by the thought of her in bed with Andronikos. And Theo probably made his peace with Isaakios rather than remaining in exile until the coup, but the Theo I'd written would never have done that so I kept him out in the cold.

The encounter between Conrad and Agnes and its consequences are made up - although I like to tell myself that there's nothing actually stopping it being true. Just none of the chroniclers thought to note it all down for posterity . . .

The broad shape of the Fourth Crusade is accurate – the grand arrival of the fleet; the destruction of the Great Chain; the surreal episode where Isaakios is placed back on the throne; the quarrels about money; the Latin attack on the mosque; the fire that all but obliterated the City; the surprise elevation of Murzuphlus; the decisive battle on the sea walls; the needless loss of the City - but I have given you a heavily condensed version of events from the imagined viewpoint of Agnes and Theo.

As for Agnes and Theo's daughter, history records her

existence, but gives her no name and no birthdate. No prizes for guessing why I chose the day I did. And Zoê? Well, it's the name that crops up most after Maria, Anna and Theodora – and we've seen with our many, *many* Alexioses that the Rômans weren't over-imaginative when it came to first names.

Finally, here is a quick run-down of what happens to everyone who hasn't already come to a sticky end.

Murzuphlus and Alexios Angelos (senior) met on the run. Alexios allowed Murzuphlus to marry Eudokia – only to blind him shortly afterwards. Murzuphlus subsequently fell into Latin hands and was thrown from the Column of Theodosius for the murder Alexios Angelos (junior). Alexios Angelos and Euphrosunê survived nearly another decade, partly in exile, partly in captivity, and both appear to have managed to die of natural causes.

Margit, Isaakios's little Magyar wife, married Boniface, the third of the Montferrat brothers. He became ruler of Thessalonikê, but a couple of years later he was ambushed by Bulgars and had his head cut off. Louis was also killed while fighting the empire's old enemies.

Susa and her little boys – as you'll already know if you've read The Girl King - made it back safe to Tbilisi. Alexios and Davit, with a little help from their aunt Tamar, established a Byzantine successor state in Trebizond.

Theodore Laskaris probably did best of all. He founded what became known as the Nicaean Empire, which recaptured the City in 1261 – until the Ottomans ended the Rôman Empire for good in 1453.

And Agnes and Theo? They lived happily ever after.